THE HIGHLANDER'S KISS

Something primitive erupted deep inside Conor under Laurel's glittering gaze. His hand brushed her cheek as he pushed her wet locks behind her shoulders. His other hand stroked her arm as he looked all the while into her eyes. Without a word, he leaned down and brushed his mouth lightly across hers, urging her to comply.

Her lips were soft and warm. He slanted his mouth against hers, and she kissed back, increasing the pressure. Her fingers splayed across his back, and he carefully pulled her up against his chest. The effect of her roving hands on his body caused the constant ache in his loins to grow painful with need.

He deepened the kiss and played with her lower lip, encouraging her to open her mouth to him. When she finally did, he dove in, absorbing her into himself while his hands slid slowly up her spine. She tasted so good. Just like her scent, her kisses were fresh, new, and innocent . . .

BOOK YOUR PLACE ON OUR WEBSITE AND MAKE THE READING CONNECTION!

We've created a customized website just for our very special readers, where you can get the inside scoop on everything that's going on with Zebra, Pinnacle and Kensington books.

When you come online, you'll have the exciting opportunity to:

- View covers of upcoming books

- Read sample chapters

- Learn about our future publishing schedule (listed by publication month *and author*)

- Find out when your favorite authors will be visiting a city near you

- Search for and order backlist books from our online catalog

- Check out author bios and background information

- Send e-mail to your favorite authors

- Meet the Kensington staff online

- Join us in weekly chats with authors, readers and other guests

- Get writing guidelines

- AND MUCH MORE!

**Visit our website at
http://www.kensingtonbooks.com**

The Highlander's Bride

Michele Sinclair

ZEBRA BOOKS
Kensington Publishing Corp.
www.kensingtonbooks.com

ZEBRA BOOKS are published by

Kensington Publishing Corp.
850 Third Avenue
New York, NY 10022

All Kensington titles, imprints, and distributed lines are available at special quantity discounts for bulk purchases for sales promotion, premiums, fund-raising, educational, or institutional use.

Special book excerpts or customized printings can also be created to fit specific needs. For details, write or phone the office of the Kensington Special Sales Manager: Attn. Special Sales Department. Kensington Publishing Corp., 850 Third Avenue, New York, NY 10022. Phone: 1-800-221-2647.

Zebra and the Z logo Reg. U.S. Pat. & TM Off.

ISBN-13: 978-1-4201-0013-6
ISBN-10: 1-4201-0013-0

First Printing: June 2007
10 9 8 7 6 5 4 3 2 1

Printed in the United States of America

Chapter One

Scotland, 1307

"Are you ever going to get married?" It was a tiresome question that had been asked too many times these past few weeks. Since his younger brother decided to wed, everyone assumed he should now want to as well. "Your turn, Conor!" was heard everywhere he turned.

Those who knew him, knew better than to ask, but those who didn't eventually uttered the cursed question: "So, when are you going to get married?" By the time they had finally left the wedding to return home, he had probably angered more than a few with his replies of "When I damn well want to—never."

"What say you, Conor—are you ever going to select a wife?" came a grating voice mimicking one of the many Scottish mothers he had encountered this past week. Quiet laughter buzzed from a group of men, all blue eyed and dark haired.

"He's going to clobber you one of these days, Craig."

"I hope he aims for Craig's mouth," chimed in one of the younger riders, enjoying that someone else was the object of his older brother's ridicule.

Conor ignored the banter of his younger brothers and led the small group to a nearby river to refresh their mounts. This obligatory trip was finally coming to an end. In a few days, he would soon be on McTiernay land again and resume his duties as laird of his clan. "See to the horses. We'll camp at the valley ahead."

The men nodded and began to take care of their mounts. Tonight's destination was several miles to the north and it would be nightfall before they made camp. While the valley Conor had chosen had not even a stream to alleviate the parched throat of man or horse, the small group of highlanders all understood his decision. None of them wanted to sleep too close to Douglass soil.

While only a small portion of Douglass territory bordered the allied land upon which Conor and his men currently rode, it was in a strategic location. Sheltered on two sides by large cliffs, only two sections needed to be fortified and protected. It was an excellent place to build a fortress, and that is exactly what the Douglass ancestors had done.

Conor thought on his brother's question as they continued towards the valley. He was a large man, even by highlander standards. His dark brown hair was usually tied back in a manner atypical of Scottish soldiers. For years, women and their mothers had pursued him relentlessly, employing various tactics to persuade him into a commitment. The idea of becoming the wife of a powerful laird was too compelling, especially when that laird was young and exceedingly attractive.

Over the years, the artificiality of soft words whispered by pretty women had changed him. He was no longer considered the desirable highlander of his youth, but a cold, hard man without warmth to share with any woman. So while still a striking man, it had been some time since he had caught a lady's eye, whether she might be sincere or not.

It mattered little, though, for Conor had no desire to marry. Most marriages were little more than contracts. They were only a means to ensure alliances, carry on family bloodlines, share work burdens, or to meet physical needs. His talent with the sword and the unswerving loyalty of his men gained him alliances enough. His many brothers would ensure the McTiernay name would continue for generations, and he had found that his physical needs could be met any time without the prerequisite of a marriage contract.

He could recall only one marriage—his parents'—that had been something more. His parents had forged a union built on support, desire, and the assurance that—no matter what the circumstances—they would always believe and trust in each other. As a naive young man, he desired to find someone and create a similar life and bond.

After barely escaping one conniving woman, Conor began to look for pretense in women pursuing the idea of becoming Lady McTiernay. He was never disappointed. While most of his admirers were polite, not one had desired him for himself. When confronted about their title-searching designs, a few panicked and others cried. Some had called him cold, declaring him to be the only highland laird alive without a heart. After a series of disappointments and stomach-churning experiences, he decided the joy and bond his parents shared was a unique gift that would never be his.

As the group reached the valley and began to make camp, Conor refocused his attention from the past to the present and began to relax. The air was getting colder now and he was glad to be going home. There were many things to do before winter came upon his clan and, in a just a few weeks, his mountains would be covered with snow.

Conor casually observed his younger brothers building a big fire located in the center of the gathering. They were a small group, five of his six brothers and four of his elite guard. Rarely did Conor allow all of his family to journey beyond McTiernay borders, but weddings required family attendance. Conor had reluctantly agreed to allow even his youngest brothers to come since the journey was mostly upon lands of allies or neutral clans.

"I bet Colin is having a good night, being his wedding

night and all," Craig cackled loudly. His fraternal twin Crevan grinned, nodded, and leaned over to get a piece of meat. The seventeen-year-old twins were similar in physical appearance, each tall men with deep brown locks and bright blue eyes. Their personalities, however, were as different as night and day.

"Colin is lucky. Deirdre is sure pretty," commented Clyde, the youngest McTiernay just approaching twelve years of age. His brothers constantly teased him about his name, saying that it was too bad their mother had run out of all the good names that begun with *C* by the time he came along. When Clyde was very young and susceptible to such jibes, Conor reminded him that they were the only two men to inherit the McTiernay silver eyes; the others had the bright blue eyes of their mother.

"Think you will ever get that lucky with the name Clyde?" returned Conan, the second youngest, who at fourteen, relished any chance to join the antics of his elder brothers.

Clyde retaliated by kicking dirt onto his brother's plaid. Conan, seeking revenge with just a bit too much force, sprayed dirt not only onto Clyde, but onto Conor as well. After a long day's ride, the deed seemed ample reason for the other brothers to exact retribution. It would have turned into a full brotherly brawl if Cole, the eldest after Conor and Colin, hadn't intervened. It was now Cole's responsibility to keep his younger brothers from too much mishap since Colin had married. As laird, Conor was too busy to be troubled with such details.

"Enough," stated Cole in his most firm voice, trying to imitate Conor on the training field.

Conor moved to sit down away from the commotion and leaned back against one of the elm trees surrounding the small clearing. He was relieved when Cole took their younger brothers in hand before they tore up the camp they had just built. Cole was already a big lad at twenty-one, but he would have to work on his carriage to make his commands convincing. Conor stood up, dusted himself off, and walked over to have a word with his guardsmen about the night's watch.

Though on allied land, they were still uncomfortably close to the Douglass border. Conor's allies were Douglass's enemies. While Conor would love a good reason to meet the cruel and dishonest laird on the battlefield, he had no desire to do so while his young brothers were vulnerable and days away from the McTiernay border.

Conor met with each of his four guardsmen securing the campsite. A couple more days' ride north and the full night watches could ease. He gave his orders and returned to the campsite just in time to hear Craig relate his latest bit of ridiculous wench gossip.

"You won't believe what Hilda told me," Craig threw out, trying to bait the others. As the most boisterous in the group, Craig was an outgoing young man and always full of energy.

"Who's Hilda?" asked the youngest, Clyde.

"Ahh, she's some lass he met up with for the night," answered Conan, trying to sound knowledgeable about such things.

"Anyway," stressed Craig, trying to regain everyone's attention, "Hilda told me that MacInnes's granddaughter was coming to live with him." He looked at the group with a mischievous twinkle.

"And why should that b-be interesting?" Crevan was the opposite of his twin brother. While Craig was frequently showing off and a gregarious comedian, Crevan was introspective, even-tempered, and agreeable. However, it would be an enemy's last error in judgment to mistake Crevan's composed nature and slight stammer as weakness. He had been training for a couple of years and exhibited the McTiernay trait for strategy, cunning and ruthlessness in battle.

"Because she isn't Scottish—she's English," grinned Craig.

"Oh, ho now. I thought you s-s-said that she was

MacInnes's g-granddaughter. MacInnes is as Scottish as they come."

"That's because MacInnes is a highlander and was Grandfather's best friend. Conor says that MacInnes still practices many of the highlander traditions."

"S-So she isn't English, then, and your b-bit of gossip remains boring."

"Ahh, but Hilda said that she's been living in England for many years and that her bonnie mama—MacInnes's daughter—died when she was a child. Without her mother to guide her, it's doubtful that any of the Scot in her remains. Everyone is wondering how long she will last before she goes running home to England crying. It's well known how severe MacInnes is to live with."

"The English should remain in England," said a cold voice. Cole despised the bordering country and all those who came from there.

"Cole, can the English actually ruin the land by walking on it?" asked Clyde, who had often overheard McTiernay warriors say that the English spoil anything they touch.

Before Cole could ridicule the question, Conan, the fourteen-year-old, chimed in. "Why would an English lady come to live in Scotland with her grandfather?"

"Dunno, maybe she hated England," answered Craig with a mouth full of cold mutton.

"English are too stupid to know they should hate their homeland," scoffed Cole as he turned to rest on his plaid. "She probably just wants to benefit from being a powerful laird's only relative."

"But you said that she was supposed to be pretty," Conan directed the semi-question to Craig. Conan was gifted with a keen intelligence and was constantly in search of new manuscripts to read and understand. But when it came to relationships—especially those with the opposite sex—he was completely lost.

"First of all, a pretty girl can still be dull-witted and extremely irritating, Conan. You just remember that," Craig replied, using a patronizing voice he knew would irritate his younger brother.

"I know that," Conan retorted heatedly. "That's the reason I'm going to be like Conor and never marry. We don't want a stupid, annoying woman, even if she is pretty." Conan looked over at Conor for affirmation, but was disappointed. Conor's eyes were closed and his expression was inscrutable.

"Second of all, I didn't say *she* was pretty," stated Craig. "I just said that her *mother*, MacInnes's daughter, was noted to be a bonnie lady and was wanted by many men."

"So why is MacInnes's granddaughter English if her mother could have married a Scot?" Clyde asked innocently.

"Because," remarked Cole as if the answer was obvious. "She ran off and married an English baron. Proves you can be pretty and stupid just like I said. But more than likely MacInnes's granddaughter takes after her English father and hurts the eyes."

"That must have made Laird MacInnes sad," murmured Clyde.

As usual, Conor did not participate when his brothers conversed amongst themselves. He intentionally separated himself from them, and they knew better than to try to pull him in. It was hard straddling the roles of laird and eldest brother. He loved his family, but it was difficult to know how and when to just be their brother and not their laird. Consequently, soon after he became laird, Conor had encouraged Colin to act as the older brother, allowing him to focus on the clan and its needs.

Today, Colin had married Deirdre, Laird Dunstan's eldest daughter. Upon their return, Cole would leave to join the guard of Laird Schellden, an ally holding lands adjacent to McTiernay's western boundary. Colin and Cole were the first to leave, but eventually all of his brothers would set out and make their way.

This realization bothered him, but he could not understand why. He wanted his brothers to forge lives for themselves, either with him or wherever their destinies took them. But for some reason, it made him feel isolated knowing his future did not include them. The only way he knew to cushion the pain of their leaving was to distance himself now. His life was the clan, and the clan would always need him.

Conor was musing on all that needed to be done upon his return when Finn, the commander of his elite guard, approached from his watch in the woods.

Finn came towards Conor unsmiling and prepared for battle. "Hamish heard movement in the trees and is investigating now."

Just then, they heard Seamus release a muted bellow from the woods. They drew their weapons as they advanced to confront the attackers. As they neared the edge of the woods, Loman and Hamish dragged an incredibly disheveled woman into the clearing.

Loman advanced towards Conor with a strong grip on the woman's arm. She was no longer struggling, but Loman had seen firsthand how cunning she could be. Conor saw Loman's grip and wondered at the cause for it. She was a scrawny lass, so it was hard to imagine that she could defend herself against any man. Conor found himself surprisingly intrigued.

"She knocked Seamus pretty good in the head. We captured her trying to run away from her crime," Loman said.

When Laurel heard the word "crime," she was surprised and then outraged. The giant they called Seamus had tried to seize her. She had every right to defend herself against such a colossal man. She turned her gaze to their leader, who seemed to be the biggest of them all.

Conor did not miss the change of emotion flash across her face. She was extremely frightened, but trying very hard not to show it. He saw her look of surprise when Loman mentioned her crime and was fascinated when the shock turned into sheer fury. However, Conor was not ready for his reaction to the defiant female when she turned her attention towards him.

Her tousled appearance and torn clothing faded for a moment, and he could only see her eyes. They were the color of the North Sea after a storm—a dark blue-gray with flecks of green. They stared at each other for several moments before he regained his wits.

"Who are you?" he demanded without inflection, somehow giving the question even more power.

She was tall for a woman, but held herself regally despite the grip Loman continued to exert. Her dress was torn at the shoulder so part of her sleeve hung down to her elbow. Her eyes sparkled intensely and she protruded her chin confidently. Still she couldn't hide a faint tremor as Conor moved closer. He doubted most men would have seen or recognized her small shudder for what it was. He was surprised by and wary of the immediate pull he had towards her.

Laurel was desperate. She realized that the advancing man was her captor, but she instinctively knew this huge Scotsman would somehow also be her savior.

She rose her chin even higher. "My name is Laurel. Laurel Rose Cordell."

Conor nodded at Loman to release the proud mystery. Loman immediately let Laurel go and stepped back. Conor watched her absentmindedly massage the spot where his guardsman had seized her. Dirt and twigs from bushes were ensnarled in the long golden waves of her hair. She had high cheekbones and ideal full lips that were meant for kissing. Suddenly, he realized that he was drawn to her in a very physical way despite her chaotic appearance. It had been a long time since he had a woman. Trying to regain control of his unexpected sexual need, Conor concentrated on her qualities that would calm his desire.

She was English. She was filthy and a complete mess. But somehow, she smelled of flowers, lilacs to be precise.

His mother had loved the blossom and kept them throughout the keep when they were in bloom.

He was drowning in her scent and the color of her eyes, which had never budged from his, when he noticed the small pearl-handled dirk in her hand. She didn't even seem to realize that she was holding it. This was obviously a very confused woman if she thought she could harm any one of them with her toy dagger. He reached out to take it away before she got herself hurt.

Laurel instinctively flinched as he moved forward. She wanted to run but had already experienced the foolishness of that idea. Then the giant leader reached out and with a gentle force took the dirk from her hand.

Laurel had not intended to recoil in such a cowardly manner, but she felt overawed by one so big. The man was enormous, and she knew herself to be tall for a female. All of his features were strong. And while his large muscles made him appear to be menacing, Laurel felt somewhat comforted by them. He looked like he could fight a whole army by himself if he was so inclined.

He was now so close to her Laurel could see a small scar running along the ridge of his right eyebrow, severing it in half. But other than that single small flaw, his face was masculine perfection, unlike his arms, which were riddled with scars. It was clear this man had seen and knew how to survive battles.

The warrior had thick, dark-brown hair and mesmerizing silver eyes, unlike any shade Laurel had ever seen. They reminded her of crystal glass reflecting firelight, warm yet also cold, studying each of her movements, even the most minuscule.

Despite his enormous size and the coolness in his eyes, Laurel knew she was safe with him. He would help and protect her. He had to.

In the faint moonlight, Conor watched the Englishwoman stare at him as she calculated her next move. Her dress had been torn in more than one place, revealing a white, lacy, very feminine chemise. She was definitely a high-bred lady. No one he knew wore undergarments like those. Her hair looked to be a pale gold color, but it was difficult to tell with all the grime matted within it. Even her face was covered with smudges of what could have been dirt or blood.

As Hamish approached her with a wet rag so she could wipe off her face, Laurel instinctively shrank away.

"My men did not do this." Conor made the statement as a fact, not liking the idea that she was fearful of them.

She confirmed his statement with a simple "No." He nodded and turned to retrieve the wet cloth from Hamish. This time when he reached out to give it to her, she did not recoil.

As Laurel began wiping her face free of the dirt and grime, she revealed a portion of her beauty. Her features were that of Scottish nobility—soft, feminine, but full of strength. Her nose lifted slightly, and her fair skin was very pale. Her lips were full and round, made for a man to leisurely explore. Conor again felt the urge to kiss her hard and deliberately, deeply and passionately, and every other way a man can drink from a woman's lips.

As Laurel finished cleaning her face and hands, she heard a rustle in the woods and complete terror consumed her until she saw Seamus appear at the wooded edge. Instantly, she remembered that she was charged with wrongly attacking the emerging giant.

Laurel looked up defiantly at Conor. "I did not commit a crime." She didn't expound on her defense. Instead, she glared at Conor as if defying him to reject the truth.

Conor had seen the quick changes from panic to relief as she had seen Seamus emerge. The lass was definitely running away from something, someone.

"You are safe. No one will harm you here," Conor clarified, trying to ease her fear. "Are you running from your husband?" He dreaded asking the question, but he had to know the answer.

Laurel remembered how close she had been to being just that—married. She shook her head vehemently. "I am not married," she practically shouted. For a moment, the attractive giant seemed relieved by her answer, but that didn't make any sense at all.

Suddenly, it was becoming too much. Laurel just wanted to sit down and think about what to do. Too much evil had been witnessed and endured the past two days. She was so very tired, and it hurt just to breathe.

Think, Laurel, think, she thought to herself. She still wasn't safe regardless of what the large highlander said. She needed to find some quick means to get as far away from here as possible. She looked up and saw a quiet strength in his silver eyes. Here was someone who would honor his word—if Laurel could only get him to promise to bring her with him, wherever he was going.

"Please take me with you," she softly pleaded. "Please help me—just for a little while. Once I am far enough away . . ." and just then, her strength gave out. She reached out and grabbed Conor's arm just as she crumpled to the ground.

Conor and his guard were momentarily stunned. She had given no indication that she was on the verge of collapse. Finn reached down to pick her up. But Conor abruptly stopped him, reaching down himself to take her into his arms. A fierce desire to protect her came over him as he lifted the frail, limp form. He whispered into her ear as he walked toward the campsite, "No harm will come to you, lass. I give you my word of honor." Then he put her down on his plaid and covered her to protect her from the night's chill, smiling as he laid the small dirk next to her hand.

Chapter Two

Just before dawn, Laurel stirred from her sleep and sat up, once again feeling pain course through her body. Last night's recollection was distant, half dream, half nightmare. Looking around, she was momentarily alarmed waking up in the middle of a camp full of Scottish, bare-legged giants. Then she remembered. Her side was aching, and it still hurt to breathe, but her head was not pounding as it had been.

Laurel stood up, closed her eyes, and recalled the rugged man with lustrous gray eyes that seemed to peer into her soul. She carefully reached down and picked up the dark woolen blanket of greens and blues she had slept on. She lightly fingered the soft, well-used cloth accented with bright colors of gold, red, and burgundy and wrapped herself in its warmth. It smelled of horse flesh and of the man who had promised to keep her safe from harm. It was odd, but the blanket and its smell comforted her as she walked into the woods for some privacy.

Conor saw her rise. He had been watching her sleep for most of the night. She had moved very little while she slept, as if any change in position caused pain. It was hard to see what she looked like in her current condition, but he could not deny that something about her captivated him.

He watched her grab his plaid, drape it around her,

and go into the woods barely lit by the sun's dawning rays. She walked gracefully, with dignity and full of calm. Not at all as if she had narrowly escaped some harrowing experience.

Conor shook his head for the hundredth time, trying to get control of his wayward thoughts. He had never seen a woman in such a state of physical chaos. But even so, he wanted her on levels he couldn't explain to anyone—especially himself.

Conor stood up abruptly. He needed to concentrate on the day's ride and returning home. Once there, he would find a safe place for her, and then resume his daily routine. He went to gather his guards so they could break camp.

By the time Laurel returned, the rest of the group was up and preparing to leave. The youngest of the enormous Scots was the first to see her standing on the edge of the clearing watching them. The others, seeing Clyde's unexpected halt in activity, looked to see what had affected their younger brother so.

It was a tall, slender female with long gold hair and incredible blue-green eyes. Her arm was badly bruised, her dress was torn, and she was wrapped in a McTiernay plaid.

Laurel was also transfixed by the sight of the five Scots. They were all highlanders. Their strong rugged features, dress, and weaponry were unmistakable. Some of them were still quite young, but in a few years they would grow to be giants as well. Each had coppery-brown hair ranging from a light auburn to a rich dark shade of brown like their leader's. All of them had bright blue eyes that sparkled, with the exception of the youngest, whose unusual liquid gray eyes reminded her of the giant who had promised his protection.

Laurel looked around for their leader or any of the other men she had encountered last night, but none were in sight. A moment of panic invaded her. She needed to leave immediately. Surely, by now someone had seen what she had done and was looking for her.

One of the men approached. "Lass? Are you all right, lass? You look a mess, begging your pardon." As he spoke, the others began to surround her, each compelled to help.

Laurel quickly realized they meant no harm and were only curious. "Umm, you are right. I am a mess. I believe it was a brother of yours who helped me last night." She paused as she saw the four younger men grin. The oldest of the five, on the other hand, was scowling. She decided to ignore him and directed her attention to those more agreeable. "Do any of you gentlemen know where I could wash my face?"

All of them started shaking their heads. The youngest one with the gray eyes clarified, "There is only one place near here, miss, but it is a very small creek, and it is back towards Douglass land." He pointed down to the area she escaped from last night.

Laurel blanched noticeably.

"But there is one up north a ways, miss. We're going there today," mentioned one of the twins.

"You could come with us," offered another.

Laurel beamed at their youthful enthusiasm. Her smile caused an instant positive reaction in the group. Even Cole—who hated everything English—suddenly wanted to help this maiden who had been attacked so viciously.

Conor returned to see his brothers ogling Laurel as if she were an angel just arrived from the heavens. It was evident that her bewitching effect was not only limited to him. His guards, Loman and Hamish, had been discussing her when he arrived that morning, and now his brothers were practically gaping at her. Even he had been staring at her all night.

In the dim firelight, her hair had appeared a burnished yellow, but now, in the morning sunlight, the pale, golden halo could render a man senseless. Her face was heart shaped, with large eyes, high cheekbones, a pert little nose and full, rose-colored lips. It mattered not that her hair was matted and unclean. Men forgot who they were, their skills, and their duty when they saw visions such as this one.

He scowled at his brothers, narrowing his gaze. Laurel turned to see what had caused the men to jump in response. Then she saw him. Last night, he had given his word that no harm would come to her. Or was his pledge of protection just a dream?

"Did you mean it?" she whispered as he came near.

Damn, she had the most hypnotic eyes. Now that she wasn't angry, they were a much lighter color of blue mixed with an unusual shade of green. Framed by long dark eyelashes and a perfectly shaped eyebrow a few shades darker than her pale hair, they were a little large for her face. Her right cheek was slightly swollen and the bruise on her arm was deepening in color and size. Seeing the evidence of her injuries in daylight, Conor quelled the anger stirring in him and reached out to take the plaid she was handing him.

The gasp from his brothers was audible. Whoever had beaten her had done so mercilessly. The reason behind her restless sleep was abundantly clear. They all began asking questions at once.

"What happened to you, lass?"

"Who did this to you?"

"Here, lass, sit down."

"What's your name, lass?"

"Aye, where is your home, pretty lady?"

"Tell me who did this, and I will seek your revenge," one of the twins vowed.

"My brother will save you. He's a laird," she heard the youngest one promise.

Conor motioned for silence with a flicker of his eyes.

"Who did this?" Conor's tone was laden with controlled fury. The four guards had returned from their night's post and joined the group, wondering what had caught their laird's anger. Then they saw Laurel.

"Who hurt me does not matter. What's important is

that I don't give them another opportunity. Please, can I come with you?" she asked anxiously.

The question made no sense. He had promised her protection, and that made the answer obvious. "You will come with us," Conor clarified, his voice conveying no emotion. On the other hand, his gaze held hers, and she saw a dangerous storm brewing within the liquid gray pools.

His answer was comforting, but only if they left in time. She would see no more good men go to their deaths because of her. "Soon? Can we leave right away?"

It was obvious she thought that whoever did this was looking for her. His eyes slightly narrowed at her request. "Aye lass, we'll be leaving. But before we reach the end of our travels, I will be knowing who did this," he stated, pointing to her face and arms. He motioned for the group to decamp. "We leave immediately."

Everyone began to mount. As Laurel wondered who she would ride with, Hamish approached. "My lady." The guard gestured toward his horse. Laurel began walking to his tan-colored horse, wondering why she was disappointed that the dark leader had not offered.

The highland chief was much more fierce-looking in the morning light. His body was taught and rigid, and the complete control he had over his every move was frighteningly powerful. His dark wavy hair whipped about his face and his ice-gray eyes no longer bore any of the warmth and concern that flickered there in last night's moonlight. Yet, he was the one to whom she was drawn. With him, she felt safe and protected. Him, she trusted.

Conor had already mounted his stallion and had intended to put some distance between him and the bewitching maiden by having her ride with one of his men. But when he saw Hamish approach her and her simple acceptance, something inside him went cold. Without conscious thought, he nudged his horse into movement and, with one quick sweep of his arms, settled her across his lap. Hamish looked questioningly at his laird, and then turned to mount his horse. He was not pleased with his laird's decision, but his loyalty to the McTiernay chieftain would never waver.

"May I ask your name?" Laurel inquired over her shoulder as she twisted to ride astride.

He leaned down so that his lips only just caressed her ear. "Conor. You will call me Conor." He spoke so softly that it sent shivers throughout her body.

They rode hard that morning, stopping briefly only once to eat some food and rest their horses. Laurel ate very little and said less as they rode. Conor knew she was in great pain, as she tried not to wince each time his horse took unexpected turns through the rocky passes. But she never complained.

At first, Laurel had been reassured when Conor picked her up to ride with him. But her physical reaction to him was so intense, so unexpected, that when he whispered his name in her ear, she wanted to retreat into the unappealing arms of another.

Throughout the morning, she tried to ride with her back rigid, so as to not make familiar contact with the highlander. But by the afternoon, she had no more strength and began to relax against his chest. He was so strong and smelled so good. His scent reminded Laurel of her grandfather—earthy, warm and comforting.

Conor was relieved when she finally gave in to her fatigue. It had pained him to see her discomfort compounded by her refusal to lean on him for support. But once she did, the torture he had been experiencing was even worse.

All morning he had been dealing with the scent of lilacs, trying to ignore her soft skin when it came into contact with his. Now, with her leaning against him, he was living in agony that only would have been surpassed by seeing her in some other man's arms.

About an hour before sunset, Conor motioned to Finn

to make camp up ahead. He veered to his left, leaving the others, and rode towards a thicket shielding a small rocky river. He dismounted and lowered her slowly to the ground, handing her a small pouch.

He knew it was folly to continue holding her, but he seemed to have no power over his actions. She looked up at him expectantly but did not attempt to escape his embrace.

"There is a stream just ahead for you to bathe in. It should not be too cold this far south," he nodded towards a path through the bushes. "I must see to my men and will return shortly." He let her go and turned towards his horse. Just before he left, he added, "You are safe here," and rode out of sight, leaving Laurel to her privacy.

Conor returned to the unmade campsite and found his brothers gathered, speaking animatedly about something, or someone. He handed his mount to Cole and went to establish a perimeter watch with Hamish.

"What do you intend, laird?" Hamish ventured, wondering what his laird's plan was with the English lady named Laurel. Hamish was a stout man, muscular with shoulder-length auburn hair. His dark green eyes flashed with whatever strong emotion he was feeling. Currently, it was a mixture of protection and possession.

Conor saw the fierce need in his guard. "My word."

Only slightly appeased, Hamish needed to know the extent of his laird's promise. "Your word? Did you promise her safety? Or to return her home?" When Conor did not respond, Hamish uncharacteristically pressed, "Surely, you did not promise to return her to England, laird."

This line of questioning was unusual for his normally quiet, reserved guard. The fact that it was centered on Laurel made Conor uneasy. "Enough, Hamish. We are returning to McTiernay land. I will take care of the Englishwoman."

Hamish did not care for his laird's tone. It felt harsh and without warmth. But then, what did he expect?

Conor had made it long known how he felt about the fairer sex. Hamish decided then that if she could not return to her people, he would ask for her hand.

Conor's brief discussion with Hamish left him irritated and cross. He knew Hamish was attracted to Laurel as were most of his brothers and his guard, maybe more so. Damn, he wished he knew what it was about her that made men desire her so quickly, so definitively.

Conor told Hamish to finish checking the perimeter. He would meet up with him and Seamus near the rocky pass once he finished one more task. He told himself that he was just going to make sure that the Englishwoman was safe.

As Conor approached the clearing, he could see Laurel sitting serenely in the river, facing away from him with her shoulders just cresting the water. She had washed her hair and it now glistened in the sun's setting light. It was the color of spun gold with pale highlights that seemed to shimmer with its own light.

He was about to reveal himself when she stood up. Upon her back were several ghastly welts where she had been kicked repeatedly. As she turned towards shore, Conor could see bruises on her arms in the shape of large hands that had once gripped her tightly. He still could not see the front of her body, but he was sure the same brutal markings would be there as well. She had never said a word. He could not help but respect the English maiden's strength. She was beautiful and courageous and, as he watched the water drip off her naked form, she was more desirable than any woman he had ever seen.

Not today—but soon—he would kill the Douglass beast for laying a hand on her. He would have his answers about what happened before they arrived home. Whoever he was, he had touched Laird McTiernay's woman. And for that, he must die.

Conor paused at that thought. Laird McTiernay's

woman. Was that who she was to him? Or was she a temporary fascination that would soon fade?

The ache in his loins grew as he watched her dress, unable to turn away. The unmarked portion of her skin, now clear of the dirt and blood, was exquisite. It had been kissed by the afternoon sun, making it appear warm and sensuous. He shook his head, ran his fingers roughly through his hair, and tried to gather his thoughts. He was filled with waves of emotions—lust, possessiveness, need, and an overwhelming urge to keep her safe.

When he finally moved into the clearing, Laurel had donned her delicate thin chemise and was trying to pull on her bliaut. Both were still fairly damp from her attempt at washing them. She should have been embarrassed or at least uncomfortable by his appearance and her state of undress. Instead, she only felt relief.

She looked at him beseechingly. "Could you please help?"

He gripped the damp garment and took it completely off of her. "I need to examine your ribs." Her teal-colored eyes darted around the small clearing as if she expected others to approach.

"No one will see you. The others know that I am seeing to your safety," Conor stated.

She snatched her bliaut from his hands and covered her chest. "My ribs are fine, really."

Conor was not deterred. "Your breaths have been shallow all day, and you winced every time my horse had to turn."

Her eyes widened. "I'm just bruised. I assure you I am fine. I will not be any trouble," Laurel said, backing away.

Conor was getting annoyed. "Stop cowering. I will not harm you."

Laurel shot him a look of contempt. "I am no coward, sir, and I will tell you now that I *have never* cowered." Heated emotion flooded her eyes, turning them the color of a North Sea storm again. "I just do not wish you to feel my—my ribs," she finished in a bit of a fluster.

"Fine, my English mystery, you are no coward. But I *will* be looking at your ribs." He reached out and held her gently, but firmly, giving her no choice but to submit to his examination. He started gently pressing on her ribs one by one.

"Breathe, lass."

Laurel was trying to, but, with his hands touching her so tenderly, it was impossible. She had never been around a man quite like this Conor. He was huge, but kind. A warrior, but a protector. When he was near her, like this, she never wanted him to leave. Oh, what was wrong with her? The sheer closeness of his body with hers made her feel incredibly alive and aware that she was a woman with physical needs and desires.

She gasped and then moaned. She tried not to, but he kept probing. "Enough," she softly cried, "please, no more." She collapsed against him.

He held her gently, stroking her hair. "It's all right, lass. It's all right." He waited until she had stopped trembling. He lifted her chin. And what happened next he would blame on those sea-colored eyes.

As he softly brushed his lips against hers, Conor felt a sharp tug in the vicinity of his groin. Her lips were full and yielding underneath his. He continued his miniature foray into heaven and felt her quiver against his chest.

Instinctively he reached up and cupped her head so he could increase the intensity. As he slanted his mouth against hers, his tongue coaxed her lips open and deepened the kiss with tender possessiveness. She responded so innocently, so naturally, it unnerved him at his core. Never had a woman affected him this profoundly, this quickly. He gradually broke off the kiss and stepped away for a minute trying to catch his breath.

Laurel didn't know what to think. The kiss had ended much as it had begun, like part of a dream. This man completely unsettled her like no one had ever done before. Last night he was supportive, this morning cold and aloof, and now, with a simple kiss, he had stirred up feelings and physical reactions she had not known she possessed. The only thing she was sure of was that he had saved her life.

Conor took several deep breaths before speaking. "You have two cracked ribs that must be bound before you finish dressing. The binding should help ease the pain when riding. We have several more days journey ahead." He controlled his breathing and steadied his voice, but he had no means to quench his throbbing need for her. The kiss was supposed to have ended this strange attraction. Instead, it was like fuel to a fire.

She nodded, knowing that he was correct. She watched him tear a strip of cloth from the bottom of his leine to bind her ribs. Every touch seemed to remind her of the physical need he had awakened deep within her. It was only after they returned to camp and were within hearing of the group did she feel calm enough to talk.

"Are we safe here?" she asked no one in particular.

"Aye, milady. We are on allied land now," Loman replied readily. Loman was typically good-humored and eager to please. Yet on the battlefield, he was a terrifying sight to the enemy. He had lighter features, was extremely lean and muscular, and—grinning as he was now—he seemed harmless. But Laurel remembered his demeanor the night he had found her struggling with Seamus, and knew he was not in the least harmless.

She faced the guardsman and smiled. "Please call me Laurel."

Loman glanced at Conor, whose glower clearly made it known that no one was to be given the right to use her given name. That right was reserved for him, and him alone. "No, milady, it would not be proper."

"But surely you do not intend to keep calling me 'my lady'?"

Loman gulped. "Aye, milady. Until my laird tells me otherwise." Loman quickly retreated under Conor's withering gaze. Regardless of previous words, his laird was making it plain this Englishwoman was unavailable. Loman wondered how Hamish would react to his laird's decision.

Laurel walked over to the campfire and accepted the offering of the youngest brother's plaid. "Only if you will sit by me," she made him promise.

Using her fingers, she began to untangle the mats in her wet hair and let it dry in the heat of the flame. The brothers all stared as if they had never seen a woman with blonde hair before. As she continued to work the knots, Laurel decided to divert their attention and get to know her champions better.

"You are highlanders," she stated, as if she already knew it to be a fact. She received nodded heads for a response. She leaned over and whispered into the youth's ear, "What is your name, highlander?"

The boy beamed. "Clyde. These are my brothers—Cole, Craig and Crevan, they're twins, then Conan and myself. Conor is our laird. The only one not here is Colin."

"Colin? Why isn't he here?"

"He just got married."

"Oh," she replied. "And with what highland clan am I privileged to share this fire?"

"We are McTiernays," said Conan, who sat on her other side, with pride. She wondered if the McTiernays were a large or powerful clan. If so, whom did she just allow to kiss her? And why did he? She forced herself to concentrate and pursue a different topic.

"Do you know where we are heading?"

"*We* are heading home," replied the one Clyde had indicated as Cole. He looked to be the oldest of the brothers, besides Conor.

"Where is home, Cole?" she tested to see how he reacted to her familiarity.

"Far from England," he replied directly. It was obvious that, while he didn't want to see her hurt, he was still not liking the idea of Laurel joining them on their travels. She rose cautiously and walked over to stand next to him. She did not look at him directly but stared straight ahead, mimicking Cole's cool stance.

"If you think it best I leave, Cole, I will."

Her directness startled him. She smelled of flowers, and he could not deny her loveliness. She was by far the most bonnie lass he had ever seen. And the most abused. Despite his hatred for all things English, even he could not deny her help and leave her without protection.

"No, milady. I would not wish anyone to live with a Douglass."

"Douglass? Why would I ever return there?" she asked loudly enough for the others to overhear.

"Is that not where you're from, milady? We saw you pale at the mention of their name this morning, and we were camping fairly close to their border," Craig interjected.

Laurel returned to Clyde's side and sat down again. "No, I am not from anywhere near those hateful people."

Laurel tried to discourage conversation about her origins by pretending to concentrate on her hair. She had managed to free most of the major tangles. Spying a loose piece of lace on her torn sleeve, she pulled it completely free and attempted to tie her hair back. Yet, every time she reached to bind it, she retracted in pain.

Conor saw Hamish, who had been hovering nearby, go to help her. Swiftly, Conor interrupted his guard, took the lace ribbon from Laurel's hands, and hastily tied back her hair.

Though he tried to be quick, the feel of her soft locks and their clean smell of flowers were unnerving to his senses. Even with her hair pulled high on her head, the waves of curls still reached her lower back. He would be tormented for the rest of his days because he had touched such maddening beauty.

Conor then moved to the outskirts of the campsite as if to check the perimeter. He needed to regain control of his rising desire to know what it would be like to feel her beneath him, moaning his name.

Hamish followed. "I need to know your intentions, laird."

Conor nodded. He recognized his guard's desire for Laurel. He also realized that, while he may be fighting his own need for her, he could not endure knowing Laurel was with another man.

"She's mine."

Hamish digested this. He was unsure of how to proceed. Conor was his laird and had his loyalty in all things. But Hamish also wanted to make sure that his laird was serious about Laurel and, if not, he wanted it to be known that he was.

"Does she know this?"

"It does not matter."

"Do you know what happened? What if she is married?"

"She is not." Conor's voice was hard and inflexible.

Hamish was not satisfied. "What of her family? Will they be looking for her? What will you tell them?"

"What would *you* tell them, Hamish?" Conor countered, stopping to look his guardsman in the eye. Hamish did not flinch under the direct questioning glare.

"I would tell them that she would never be hurt again. That I would protect and support her as long as there was breath in my body."

Conor turned back to the path and continued walking. "I would tell them the same." With that, Conor left Hamish and returned to the group.

Laurel was running. She was gasping for air and, with each breath, a knife-like pain sliced through her side. She pushed herself harder, faster. Something evil, dark with black eyes, was in pursuit and if it caught her, everyone she loved would die. Somehow she knew the terrifying presence would never stop hunting her. Just as she was about to collapse from exhaustion, someone, large and faceless, lifted her and carried her high above the trees towards majestic blue-gray mountains capped with snow. There, she was safe from the hatred below. Peace settled around her like a dense fog on a cool morning and sleep was finally possible.

Conor, a light sleeper, was awakened early in the night by Laurel's agitated slumber. She was dreaming and unmistakably terrified. He realized, seeing her panicked expression, that her shield of pride she wore when awake had been masking much of her true fear. He reached down to gently wake her, but it seemed to inflame her dream state even more. Only when he sat down and gathered her into his arms did she finally seem to calm.

Laurel awoke in the middle of the night feeling safe and warm. She thought that sleep must be clouding her mind, for she seemed to be resting her head on Conor's shoulder and one of her legs was cast over his. The intimate and inappropriate position of their bodies was undeniable.

Laurel didn't move. Oh, she knew that she should, but never had she felt more extraordinarily comfortable in her life. She closed her eyes. In his arms, she found a safe haven that would be gone by morning. Conor was always the first to rise so no one would know, she told herself. So instead of moving away as a proper English lady should, Laurel remained where she was, savoring every moment of being close to Conor until she fell back into a peaceful sleep.

Conor awoke when she did. Her soft, warm breaths had turned shallow for a couple of minutes, and he wondered if she would distance herself from him. When she did not, he wanted to believe that she enjoyed and craved their embrace as much he did. More likely she was just cold, and he provided the physical warmth she needed.

He tried not to think about how wonderful it was having her by his side. He dismissed the smell of lilacs and the way it felt when she sighed her light feathery kisses of air across his chest, and concentrated on returning to sleep. He forced himself not to stroke the silky golden locks of hair that randomly found their way into his hands. Sleep finally came again, but not quickly.

* * *

The next morning, when it was time to mount their horses and leave, both Hamish and Loman volunteered to have Laurel ride with them. However, each of the brothers argued that she should ride with a McTiernay. Laurel, not wanting to antagonize any man or show preference, stood in the middle of the broken campsite searching for a diplomatic solution. Conor experienced mixed feelings of relief and strain when he settled the dispute by having her ride with him.

Their soul-shaking kiss followed by their sharing a plaid throughout most of the night had done nothing to quell his growing desire to possess her. Her calm demeanor and quiet courage only fueled his growing fire of need. Touching her all day was going to be hell, but one he strangely welcomed enduring.

He rode up to Laurel, reached down and said, "You ride with me." She smiled at him, and as she expected, her highlander scowled back in return. She was getting to understand this gentle giant better.

Laurel was feeling better today. Conor had been correct about binding her ribs. The added support was making it a much easier ride than on the previous day. She was taking in the beautiful countryside and saw the green, tree-filled mountains they were approaching.

"Are those the highland mountains?" she asked, pointing to where they were headed.

He chuckled in response, and she could feel his laughter vibrate throughout his body. "No, lass. Those are but wee hills separating the border Scots from the central Scots."

Laurel looked at the huge rocks jutting into the sky. Wee hills?

"The highlands are the most grand lands of Scotland. They tower over the rest. Only the strongest can survive there."

Laurel could hear the pride in his voice when he spoke of his northern high country.

"Tomorrow, we will be well into the valley of the central Scots. In the morning, as we crest the hills, you may be able to see several lochs to the west." Laurel smiled, remembering that was how her grandfather had referred to lakes or bodies of water.

"The valley stretches from the southwest to the northeast along the mountain line, cutting across the center of Scotland to separate her highlands from her border regions."

"How long will we be in the valley?" she inquired.

"We shall be out of the valley by day after tomorrow. Watch the terrain. It will change as we get closer."

Laurel had already noticed that the red sandstone and limestone that were characteristic of her homeland and the border lands were changing. As they rode on, the red sandstone remained, but it was now sprinkled with an unusual dense, dark-gray, fine-grained rock that was peppered with holes. She remembered her grandfather explaining its features were caused by the cooling of melted rock. Even now, it was difficult for Laurel to conceive rock so hot that it melted and then changed form after it cooled.

After their noon break, they proceeded north entering Clyde valley, which cut across the southern middle of Scotland. It was a beautiful combination of riverine and gorgeous ash and elm woodlands that were extensively covered with lush ground flora. Laurel had never seen the like.

She could feel Conor relax some and knew they must be in friendly territory once again. It was amazing how he was able to tell just by his surroundings exactly where he was in relation to his friends and enemies. After riding with him all day yesterday and now today, she could sense when they were on friendly land and able to speak.

"Clyde said that all the McTiernays were traveling home with the exception of Colin. Who is he? Will he be returning soon?"

"Colin is the second McTiernay and, in answer to your

other question, no, he will be staying with his new wife's family, helping out with their guard and eventually becoming their laird."

"Isn't it unusual for a husband to assume the role of laird in a clan?"

"Sometimes. But, in this case, Deirdre Dunstan was the eldest of Dunstan's children—all girls."

"Similar to the McTiernays—all boys," Laurel said and smiled, looking ahead.

"Similar, but no. Without boys to become laird, someone must fight for the title. In Dunstan's case, his clan is small but strong. If Colin becomes laird, the alliance among our clans will be near unbreakable."

"Because you are brothers," she tried to understand.

"Because Colin is strong, skilled, capable and most important, trustworthy."

"Ah, he will be loyal."

"He is my brother." Laurel silently shook her head, amused at his circular logic.

They rode a little further, and Laurel gathered her nerve to ask a personal question.

"Why haven't you married?"

Conor unconsciously raised his shoulders in a shrug. "I have no reason to search for a good match."

"A good match?" Laurel asked, confused.

"I have no need to marry. I have alliances with the clans I want to be united with. My brothers will continue the McTiernay line and as for physical . . . well, that requires no contract of commitment."

They rode on, each absorbed in private thoughts. Laurel had enjoyed the conversation with him up until hearing his opinion on the three reasons why men marry women. He thought a man and a woman only married due to some external need. What about love, affection, and friendship?

Conor sensed her stiffen in reaction to what he had said, but she did not contradict him. Maybe she understood and agreed with him. But, then again, a lady usually wanted babies, a family and companionship. And these things were not possible without marriage. He was not sure how he felt about such things himself, now that he had met her. The concept of marriage was still not pleasant, but the idea of having a family with Laurel sounded surprisingly appealing.

Chapter Three

That night, Conor made camp in a very small clearing that was not located near a water source. Laurel was surprised by his decision, knowing they had recently passed several larger areas with streams nearby. She thought about asking why he chose this place to make camp, but sensed that she would not get an answer.

Later, after they shared their meal, the brothers began their nightly jovial conversation, littered with familial rivalry and torment. Laurel listened to their camaraderie and was saddened that she and her brother Ainsley had never been close or shared this type of sibling bond.

Besides her mother, she could only recall true affection for one other person—her grandfather. The big Scotsman had told her stories, taught her how to ride horseback, and had proclaimed her the loveliest Scottish lass who had ever been. She knew he had been biased, but it was one of her most cherished memories.

It was strange that she could not remember her father with as much affection. While her mother was alive, he was attentive and warm. But she always knew that her father had wanted another son and not a daughter. She could not erase his words of disappointment that her mother had not born him another heir. Ainsley was his firstborn, a son produced from his first wife who had died shortly after his birth. It had been an arranged marriage, her mother had told her. But she and Laurel's father had married for love despite all the obstacles between them—mainly Laurel's grandfather, who was against his daughter's marriage to an Englishman.

Laurel understood her grandfather's confusion. After spending time in both Scotland and England, it was hard to understand why her mother chose to live in a cold, harsh world far from the laughter and singing that filled her grandfather's home. When her mother died, her father remarried again, but never sired another heir. He began running his life the way he ran his home—coldly, rigidly and emotionally detached from anyone who would show him warmth. He was never harsh or severe to his children, just distant.

For several years after her mother's death, he allowed Laurel to continue visiting her grandfather during the warmer months of the year. But, as she got older, permission to meet with her Scottish relatives diminished until it was no more. Twice, she was to be married to a neighboring baron and, twice, the baron died before the wedding took place. The first died in battle, the second from old age.

It wasn't until her father's death that Laurel felt the weight of her bleak future lessen. Her brother was disinclined to give her a dowry and find her a husband. He consistently let her know that she was either too tall, too slender or too clever with her tongue to interest any man. But when Ainsley secured his own marriage to a neighboring woman who would give him access to power, money, and connections, his sister became a liability.

Recognizing her opportunity, Laurel approached Ainsley carefully with the idea that he discard his familial responsibilities without repercussions. Only after several months of cunning work did he agree to let Laurel go to her grandfather's. He made only one stipulation—she had to promise never to return again. His words still rang in her ears.

"Fine—be a filthy Scot. But neither I, nor any of my family, will ever welcome or acknowledge you again. Once my men have successfully escorted you to your precious Scotland, my duty towards you will be forever ended."

She had quickly agreed. The moment Laurel crossed into Scotland, she had mentally and emotionally shed all things English and fully embraced her Scottish heart.

She blinked a couple of times, aware that she had been preoccupied for some time. The brothers' conversation had ended and everyone had prepared for sleep except her. Laurel looked around for Conor, but only his younger brothers were in sight. She saw that someone had found Conor's plaid and arranged it for her to lie down.

Several hours later Laurel was dreaming of being chased, and again she was saved just as she was giving up. She awoke and realized Conor was caressing her hair and soothing her with soft, reassuring words. As he lured her back to sleep, Laurel wished he would always be there to save her from her nightmares in both sleep and reality.

Laurel woke a second time in the middle of the night, but this time not because of a dream. Conor was gone. She knew he must have just left her side as the plaid was still warm. She glanced around and saw Conor and three guardsmen gathering their horses to leave. They were speaking Gaelic to a fourth man—Loman. They were going to bring back something from a nearby cabin. Loman was to have the camp broken and everyone ready to ride by dawn. They would leave immediately upon their return.

Laurel quickly laid back down, feigning sleep. She did not want them to realize she had overheard—and understood—their Gaelic conversation.

Conor and his men were going raiding. While he did not consider raiding truly dangerous, it had not been a planned activity for their trip home. Conor would have preferred to not to have his youngest brothers so close to potential danger. But they would be safe enough, he mused, and Laurel needed her own horse. *He* needed Laurel to have her own horse.

When she fell asleep against him while riding this afternoon, Conor found it difficult to focus on potential dangers. Her scent made it near impossible to concentrate, and each time she shifted to rest more comfortably against him made his mind contemplate ways he would like to touch and distract her. She seemed to fit him better than his armor. It was as if she were made only for him and would fit just him.

He dismissed the idea of having her ride with someone else. At first, he told himself that his brothers were already lovesick over the woman, and that he didn't want to distract his guardsmen, either. But, that evening, when he held Laurel in his arms, comforting her in her sleep through one of her many nightmares, he realized that he didn't want anyone touching her or holding her like he had. She was his to protect and to hold and he was not going to relinquish that right to anyone, not even to Finn—his happily married commander who apparently was the only man alive immune to Laurel's charms.

Hence, they were going raiding. Just a small raid. A fast moonlight ride, a quick plunder, then one horse would vanish and they would disappear back to the north.

Earlier, Conor had spotted a small farmhouse with several stout horses, isolated from its neighbors. Tomorrow, that farmer would be short one gray horse. He had been waiting for just such an opportunity. Dwellings near towns had added obstacles to be surmounted. Towns were more secure and tended to be well defended with local watches, and the livestock was often brought in at night.

However, this farmhouse was not near a town, and the Stirling clan was still recovering from their recent losses at the Battle of Falkirk and Robert the Bruce's last successful siege against Edward I to regain these lands. It was highly unlikely anyone would avenge the pinching of a single horse.

Conor plotted his time and their route, and prepared his assault.

Late the next morning, Laurel was still somewhat shocked to be riding her own horse. It was a beautiful gray stallion that was sure-footed despite being unshod. Conor assured her that it would be strong, swift, and only need limited grooming. Although the highlanders cared for their animals, Laurel had noticed that grooming was not something that any of them particularly enjoyed.

She decided to name her horse Borrail. Borrail was one of her grandfather's guards who had been charged to watch over her when she was young. He, like her new horse, fit the name, which in Gaelic meant swaggering, boastful, haughty and proud. Ironically, though, when translated into English, Borrail was pronounced Borrel, which meant a man was plain, rude and a boor. Laurel had often wondered as a child why so many Gaelic words had opposite meanings in English.

Finn, after speaking with Conor, fell back to ride next to her.

"Conor said that you might be interested in our progress and our lands."

Laurel visibly brightened. "Oh, yes. The variation of your land is fascinating and beautiful."

Finn noted her sincere appreciation. "Ah, lass. You have not seen beauty until you see the highlands. And then, the most majestic sights of all are the McTiernay mountains."

Laurel smiled and replied, "Conor feels the same." As he nodded in acknowledgement, she asked, "Finn, where are we now?"

"We are now approaching Scotland's 'waist' where our country is the narrowest." Laurel looked around, but could see no narrowing. The "waist" must not be that tapered for neither coastline was in sight.

"We will be entering Forth Valley soon, which acts as a gateway to the highlands. The Stirlings are our allies. They fought alongside us with Wallace and our king, Robert the Bruce. Only a few years ago did Robert lay siege to their castle and regain it from the English."

Apprehension stirred within Laurel. "Will we be visiting Stirling Castle?" She had hoped not. Finn said they were Conor's allies, but someone might spread word back to the Douglasses if they saw her traveling with them. Besides, how would she explain her appearance?

"No. I tell you so that if you see their soldiers, you will not be afraid. They know Conor and respect him. They will let us pass."

Laurel wondered about Stirling Castle. It was an old fort dating back before Alexander I. The battles waged between the English and the Scots, especially those of William Wallace, were well known. She wished to see it— if only from a distance.

Soon they crested what seemed to be a small, insignificant peak, but then the mighty River Forth the men had described during the morning meal came fully into view. This powerful river was the source of the swift cool streams she had bathed in just that morning. Once winter came, the streams the large river fed would be dangerous to pass until the water receded after the spring thaw. To the northwest, she saw a beautiful stretched piece of land. Not hills, but waves of smooth grass-covered country full of natural beauty and partially hidden bodies of water.

"Finn, what's that area called?"

"The Trossachs, milady. Aye, 'tis pretty. But if you are waiting for true beauty, wait until we reach the McTiernay mountains nestled in the highlands. Rolling lands rivaling the Trossachs await us there nestled by powerful enduring peaks capped with snow. Aye, pure majesty hits the eye from the seat of the McTiernays." Finn nudged his horse then moved forward to join Conor.

Laurel watched the two well-built men discuss something and wondered about Conor and the McTiernays. They seemed to be such a proud, close clan. The respect and admiration they had for their laird—both guardsmen and brothers alike—was almost tangible. She suspected that all Conor's men responded to him similarly.

The way they spoke of their highlands, specifically McTiernay lands, made Laurel think she would like to live there until winter had passed. Would it be possible? Would she, an Englishwoman, be accepted? Cole was beginning to warm to her, but he had been forced to accept her company.

During their noon meal, Conor called a longer halt to give their mounts a rest. They had ridden the horses fairly hard for most of the morning. He also wanted to check on Laurel, her ribs, and how she was faring riding alone.

"Laurel, walk with me." Conor commanded. His tone did not indicate that she had any option but to follow. He started walking away from the group towards some rocks surrounded by brush and elm trees.

"Yes, laird," she retorted, responding cynically to his authoritative tone of voice.

He abruptly stopped and turned around. For some reason, he did not like Laurel calling him laird. Granted, that was how all the women of his clan referred to him. But when it came to Laurel, he wanted her to use his proper name. He didn't want to be just laird to her. The idea that she saw him only as her protector and temporary leader unsettled him. Agitating him further was the concept of being disturbed by what a woman—especially an Englishwoman—called him.

"You will call me Conor," he instructed, looking straight into her eyes. Would he ever get used to their ever-changing brilliance? One minute they were dark as a sea storm, and then the next moment they were as they were now, crystal clear, luminous, like the sun sparkling on a Scottish loch. The lass was bewitching his very soul.

"But Finn said that everyone refers to you as laird or Laird McTiernay, never as Conor."

Conor's jaw tightened. "Laurel, understand this. You will not call me laird. I am not your laird. To you, I am Conor." He turned and started walking briskly towards his original goal.

Laurel was unsure whether this was a good thing or not. Not her laird? Was he not her protector? The hero who saved her each night in her dreams? She decided to look at his demand more positively. His brothers sometimes called him Conor. Maybe he only allowed those close to him to use his given name. No, Finn was definitely close to his chieftain. Mayhap, it was because she was a woman.

She frowned at the thought. It was unsettling to think of the many women in his clan calling him Conor. It seemed . . . intimate. "Does anyone else besides your brothers call you Conor?" she asked his back as he continued to lead her deeper into the woods.

"Of course."

Her heart dropped suddenly and quickly. "Umm, do any females call you Conor?"

"You do."

"Yes, yes. But besides me," Laurel said, frustration mounting.

"Besides you what?"

Laurel pursed her lips together. "You are by far, the most aggravating, infuriating, *large* man. You think because of your size you can tell people what to do and they will do it. Well, I have news for you, *laird,* I will never be one of those people. You may be a giant, but I am not afraid of you." She stopped and glared at him. When he didn't respond and continued his march forward, she prompted, "So . . . ?" Still no answer.

"Conor, are you trying to be obtuse? Are you trying to make me angry?" Laurel practically shouted at him. When he did not answer, she went over to a rock and refused to budge, letting her aggravation become even more evident. When he stopped and looked back at her, she gave him her most challenging smile.

In truth, Conor was not only interested in her train of thought, but the spirit she was exhibiting. He had only seen this bit of fire to her personality when they first captured her and she fought to free herself.

He suspected that this trait had been suppressed the past few days. She had been tired and in pain for most of the trip. That combination would typically make a person complain, whine, and, if they had it in themselves, allow their tempers to rise and take over. Conor was quite sure that Laurel had a temper, and a fiery one at that. Her ability to restrain it thus far in these harsh traveling conditions gave him a strange feeling of pride.

"Laurel, if you want to ask something, do so, straight forward." He deliberately paused. "Or are you a coward?" he gently teased, goading her further. But once he saw the result, he realized that he had just put himself in serious danger. Laurel was beautiful and tempting in any state. But angry? He had never seen the like. Even the highlands could not compare.

Suddenly, she was standing right in front of him, gold hair waving in the breeze, the sun capturing its strawberry highlights. Her hands were on her hips accentuating her heaving bosom as she took deep breaths trying to calm her anger. But the soothing effects did not reach her eyes, which sparkled with fury. Gone was the innocent English maiden. In front of him was a gorgeous vision of regal defiance. If he didn't leave immediately, he was in danger of grabbing her and giving her one more reason to be mad at him.

Laurel struggled for composure. "No one, not a laird nor a baron—not even you, *Laird McTiernay*—can ever call me a coward." She meant what she said. The seriousness radiating from her was palpable. For some reason, the concept of her being called or considered a coward was completely unacceptable to her.

He smiled and ran his fingers through his hair. "Aye,

my love. You are no coward. Indeed, you have shown more courage and strength of spirit than men have shown in similar circumstances."

Laurel looked down to the ground absorbing his words. Relief poured through her veins. Of course he didn't think her a coward. Conor would not allow a coward to travel with him, or would he?

"But, love . . ." The pitch of his voice forced Laurel to look up, her eyes widening. ". . . I *will* call you whatever I choose." Conor then resumed his march, walking ahead towards some unknown destination.

She watched him, still refusing to move. "Conor," she began, having regained her calm composure, "you underestimate me greatly." Her words were spoken slowly and deliberately, laced with indirect warnings. She stood there for several more seconds before following him.

They were starting to do some light climbing now. Not anything too difficult, although the pain in her ribs was rising due to her heavier breathing. As he climbed ahead of her in silence, she again appraised his well-formed physique.

He really was quite a large man. Yet, when he stood close to her, she didn't feel overwhelmed. Instead, she was reassured by his solid presence. He was gentle, yet firm. Controlling, yet giving. He was a man she could love quite easily.

His legs were bare and extremely distracting. They were powerfully strong, as were his arms and every other part of his body. Even his buttocks looked firm and hard under the thick pleated plaid skirt. She could see the strength in his shoulders and arms through his white linen shirt and had the crazy notion of taking her hand and caressing his back. No, the reality was she wanted to touch him anywhere—everywhere.

She imagined twining her fingers in his dark wavy hair and wondered how it would feel. Was it as thick and soft as it looked? It was such a perfect shade of dark brown and well suited to his skin tone, which was still slightly bronzed from the summer sun. His hair and skin coloring made his silver eyes even more mesmerizing. He was so intensely, overwhelmingly male. How was it that this gorgeous man was unmarried? Then she remembered. He didn't want marriage, or any type of commitment.

She had thought his viewpoint on matrimony would stop her from desiring his company as they rode, or from enjoying his voice when they conversed. But she was wrong. Laurel had never been around anyone who made her feel so alive just by being near.

She felt torn between wanting to spend time with him and wanting to keep her distance. Every moment she spent in his company just made her desire him even more. But it was all pointless; she knew there was no future for them. Why would there be? Two days protection and a kiss were far from a commitment of the heart. And that was exactly what she would have before she vowed herself to any man. She had experienced emotional isolation throughout most of her childhood. She would be foolish to do so as an adult.

Knowing the forgone conclusion of their separation, she wanted him to kiss her just one more time. Just one more time to savor the feel of his lips against hers, forever capture his scent, and remember his touch. Each night, she fell asleep knowing that he would join her sometime while she slept, for he always seemed to be there when the dreams came. Oh Lord, maybe she already was in love with him.

Laurel took a firm grip on her resolve. She had to stop fantasizing about him. He may be attracted to her, but he didn't want her—at least not as a wife. And while she admitted to herself that she definitely wanted him in ways she never had dreamed of, he was not her destiny.

She just needed a place to recover and some time to figure out a way to warn her grandfather of Laird Douglass's threat. With Keith Douglass dead and her disappearance, Laird Douglass was no doubt preparing war against her grandfather's clan—the MacInneses. She didn't know why God had sent the handsome highlander to aid her, but he was her only hope for survival. Her clan's future rested on the ability of this highland chieftain to keep her safe.

But until she could develop a plan to advise her grandfather about Douglass, she would allow herself the unwise joys of being with, talking with, and watching her miraculous dark-haired champion.

Conor could feel her looking at him, assessing him. He could feel her eyes boring through his skin, peeling away the layers to his soul. What she was thinking? Did she find him unappealing? She said she was not married, but there could still be someone important to her, someone she was intended for. Was he being compared to another man? Someone she preferred, whom she wished she was with? His fears were beginning to take hold when she called out.

"Conor, slow down!" Conor had suddenly picked up the pace, and Laurel was finding it difficult to keep up. Where were they headed anyhow? They had long since passed many places that might have provided privacy for a discussion.

"Just a bit farther. I wanted to show you something." Conor wasn't exactly sure why he wanted Laurel to see this particular vista. He had found it years ago, when he was a guardsman to his grandfather's best friend, Laird MacInnes. It was special, and somehow he instinctively knew that Laurel would appreciate it once she was there.

"Could you . . . just slow down . . . a bit?" Her breathing was labored, and the pain in her side was throbbing.

Conor looked back and felt instant guilt. Her ribs! And all of this climbing—what was he thinking! Since she entered his life two days ago, he had not been acting himself. He had deliberately provoked her anger earlier when in truth, he just wanted to be the one who made her smile. Instead of bringing her to a place of joy and pleasure, he had caused her pain. He wouldn't blame

Laurel for lashing out at him and demanding to go back. He turned around and began to return to the camp.

"Conor, what in the name of all that is holy are you doing?" She looked at him with a perplexed expression. "Do not tell me that we climbed all this way and are now turning around because I need to slow the pace. I want to see what you were going to show me. You said it wasn't far," and then a thought occurred to her, "or are you lost, Conor? Is that it? You don't know where we are?"

The combination of her question and her indignation were just too much, and he laughed aloud. She actually thought he could be lost!

He beamed her a look of delight. "No, love, I am not lost. Nor will I ever be with you." Conor didn't realize how telling those words were until he uttered them aloud. She looked at him with such longing, as if she felt as he did.

"It is just beyond those trees. But I know you are hurting so we will turn around."

Laurel straightened her shoulders. "Nonsense. To the trees it is. I just didn't want to run there, Conor. While you may not be lost, I would be if I lost sight of you."

"I would find you," Conor said in a gentle but reassuring way. "I will always protect you, Laurel." He completed the thought with a mental promise: *You are mine.* Conor felt his whole body tighten with desire.

Just then Laurel walked past him and ducked carefully under a brush to see what was beyond. The beauty that extended before her was stunning. She had thought her lands in Northumberland were beautiful, especially the North Sea coastline, but they could not compare to this.

From this vantage point, her view of Scotland was unhampered. She could see for miles. Out beyond were fingers of land, each jutting out to the sea in its own way. Some covered by trees, some with cliffs that seemed to go on forever. There were dozens of lochs nestled between. Some of the trees seem to touch the sky, and the rock formations were unlike any other. Wisps of clouds settled here and there, giving the whole scene an otherworldly look.

Conor watched Laurel absorb the beauty of his lands. Her eyes drank in everything. Her smile spread over her whole face, and her entire body seemed to relax. Conor had known by Laurel's previous interest in the land and beauty around her that she would understand his love for this place.

"It is beautiful, Conor. I have never seen the like. Is it always like this?"

"Aye, at least every time I have been here." Conor was not watching the beauty around him, but the vision in front of him. She was slim and delicate, and her golden waves of hair were pulled back by a tiny bit of lace. Her eyes were the color of the lochs she was viewing. It was amazing how often her eyes changed depending upon her mood. He wondered what they would look like all full of passion. Then he wondered if someone else already knew.

Laurel was completely unaware of Conor's brazen gaze. "There is a magical quality to it. It's like this place is frozen in time. And that you and I, here together, are separated from all the evils of the world," she mused aloud.

Conor dropped his arm to her shoulders. They stood for a long while watching the sun begin to set over the distant mountains. No words were said—no words were needed.

Despite his desire to do otherwise, Conor interrupted the peaceful silence. "We need to leave now, Laurel. It will be dark soon."

Laurel took one last look around and nodded. In just the short time they spent there, she had found peace. It was as if her problems were now manageable. She now believed that she would be able to find and notify her grandfather without letting Douglass know.

"Thank you, Conor, for taking me here," she whispered

as he took hold her hand to guide her as they descended. "It was just what I needed."

When they had returned to the edge of woods right before the clearing, she could hear the clashing of swords and several men fighting.

"What is happening?" Laurel murmured, then cried, "Conor! They are fighting! Someone has attacked the campsite. We must help them!" Visions of Ainsley's men being slaughtered a few days ago suddenly filled her mind.

"Help them? They are just having a wee scrap to freshen their skills a bit. It is harmless."

She whirled to face Conor. "Harmless?" Laurel's chin came up angrily, her sea green eyes sparkling with rage. "Men fighting with swords is fun and harmless?"

When he just stared blankly at her, she raised her voice and said, "Fine. Someone has to stop them and I guess that leaves me."

She collided with Conor when he stepped into her path.

"And what, love, do you think you are going to do?"

Laurel closed her eyes in brief, heated frustration. "Conor, you are being exasperating again. Having to repeat myself for you is most annoying," she said, her voice dangerously sweet.

He continued to stand in her way. It was obvious that he was not going to budge or let her pass. So, she tried again.

"I was just going to ask them to stop. And if that didn't work, I would use stronger encouragement," she answered, now through gritted teeth.

Laurel was beginning to show her temper, and his rumbles of laughter were making it rise all the more. She reached into her dress and pulled out the pearl dagger she had taken when she had fled the Douglass castle.

When Conor saw the small knife she held in her hand,

he could hold onto his laughter no more. His amusement at her toy was so loud that it interrupted the sword
practice his brothers were having with his guard.

By the time his brothers had come to investigate
Conor's merry roar, their laird was grinning wildly. This
sight in itself was enough to astonish every last one of
them. For it was a rare thing for Laird McTiernay to
smile, let alone laugh—and loudly. Added to their shock
was the change in Laurel. She looked furious.

Her eyes were blazing and, if hostile glares could cause
bodily injury, Conor would be permanently disfigured.
The lass really did please him, Conor thought. He
couldn't wait until he got her home.

But just as the idea of home and Laurel in his castle
and bed were taking shape, Laurel snapped. Before he
knew to react, she had changed the grip on her dirk and
taken the knife from his belt. She swiveled so fast that
later, all present would say she was just a blur when she
aimed and threw.

First, Laurel launched her dagger. Sure and swift, it hit
one of the guard's leather sporrans hanging in the trees.
With the other arm, she threw Conor's knife. The accuracy was a little off due to the unexpected weight of the
hilt, but it still hit the intended log of wood next to
Conor's plaid on the ground at least thirty feet away.

The immediate quiet that fell upon the group was palpable. Everyone just kept shifting their stares from her
to the blades she had wielded with such precision. Laurel
knew she should be ashamed of letting her temper goad
her into silencing Conor's guffaws. Still, she couldn't do
it. Moreover, she couldn't let well enough alone.

"I told you that I could take care of myself," she spoke
in a completely unrepentant voice.

"Woman, how did you do that?" asked Loman.

Instantly, Conor's anger flared. He shifted his gaze for
one moment to Loman and corrected him. "She is 'my
lady' to you, Loman," he stated in a cold tone so that
none questioned his meaning.

"Conor, do not use that voice with Loman. He was just asking me a question. There is no need to take your anger with me out on him," Laurel said, trying to redirect his anger towards its intended target.

Conor was not calmed. "I will say what I like, *when* I like, and *how* I like to him and to whomever else I choose. I am their laird," he roared back, this time with no cheer at all. He glared at Loman until he finally nodded in acknowledgment.

Laurel watched him overawe his guardsman and refused to follow Loman's example. "Well, you may be their laird, Conor McTiernay, but you sure as hell are not mine. Remember earlier? I thought you said I was not to call you *laird*. I could only call you Conor," she shouted back.

"Watch your cursing, love, or are you not a lady?" he bellowed in return, thinking that such a criticism would surely hit its mark and force her to withdraw from the argument. But his aim missed—completely. Retreat was not what she had in mind. Laurel went on the offensive.

"A *lady*? Well, I guess that is all how you define a *lady*, Conor."

She turned and looked at the brothers, who were standing with dumbfounded looks on their faces. They had never seen anyone stand up to Conor this way before. *Anyone*. Most women cowered in his presence and if he even slightly raised his voice or looked crossly at one, they slunk away, whimpering from intimidation.

What was transpiring between Laurel and Conor was nothing short of miraculous. First he laughed, next she demonstrated that she could indeed handle herself, and then they both were shouting at each other.

Laurel began pacing. "In England, a lady is any female born to a noble house. The word refers to her title of nobility or of other rank. Some people refer to the woman of the household as *lady*, meaning they are wed to men who have great houses, but are without titles. Then, again, you may be referring to women who are regarded as proper and virtuous. But all ladies should be well-mannered, considerate and with high standards of proper behavior. I sense this is the point you were making. Am I correct, Conor?"

He just stared at her. She had stopped her angry strides and stood right in front of him, daring him to counter her remarks with a wintry smile.

"Hmm? Because in case you are in doubt, I am a lady by birth, but not by action. I hunt, I ride, and I get angry. And when I am angry, I curse. My father didn't consider me a lady, and my brother sure as hell didn't. The only person in my life who believed me a true noblewoman was my grandfather. It is a great shame that he is not here tonight to witness *and support* my ladylike behavior."

Again the silence was deafening. And again she was its cause. Laurel knew she had gone too far. She had taunted Conor in front of his guard and brothers. Her father and brother were always mortified when she exhibited anything close to an emotional outburst. The tirade she just displayed would have resulted in immediate, probably indefinite confinement. What had come over her? She had always had a temper, but could control it. What was it about Conor that provoked her so? Why did she feel free to react so naturally around him?

Laurel knew that she should be ashamed at her behavior by the looks on everyone's stunned faces. She was still in shock herself when Finn slapped her on the back, smiled, and said, "You'll do, lass. Aye, you will do."

Laurel could not mask her confusion. "I will do what?"

Finn's grin grew so that it practically went ear to ear. "The highlands! We were afraid that you would wither away or shrink to nothing with the timid act you've been pulling the last couple of days. The only hope we had was seeing your courage and stamina to ride through your pain. But now, well, as I said, you'll do," Finn replied and the others around him grinned and nodded at the same time.

She stared at them dumbfounded. They were actually *happy* that she had lost her temper. The youngest two

McTiernays couldn't seem more pleased at her lack of control. Conor, however, was much harder to read.

Suddenly, a both delightful and terrifying thought occurred to Laurel. "Finn, clarify for me just one thing."

"Certainly, milady."

"Why is it so important that I will do?"

Finn looked perplexed. "Milady, a laird's lady must be strong, not just physically, but emotionally."

"Aye, Finn's right, milady," chimed in Seamus. "It would not do to have Conor constantly tending to a weak woman sensitive to the goings on around her."

Laurel was struggling to understand. "Weak woman? Laird's lady?" she repeated slowly and distinctly. They could not mean what they were implying.

"What Seamus means, is that . . . ," began Loman when Conor cut him off.

"She understands."

Laurel bristled at Conor's arrogance. "I can assure you that *she* does not." Laurel retorted.

"You do, love. You just have not accepted it."

"What you are proposing . . . Just yesterday you said that you would never . . . that you refused, didn't need to . . ." Laurel had trouble getting the words out. This couldn't be happening. She was feeling elated and torn apart at the same time.

Conor also didn't understand what was happening. His desire for her was so strong that everyone was picking up on it. Their assumption was understandable, but he recoiled from the thought of commitment and immediately went into denial.

"I am proposing nothing. Just a roof and protection."

The alarmed side of her heart sighed in relief. But the part of her that wanted him, ached for his touch, cried as she realized that he just declared that it would never happen. Pride forced her to respond.

"Good. Because when we get to your highlands, all I want is somewhere to live for just a little while, until I decide what to do next. Just for the winter. I promise that by spring I will be gone."

"But lass, you will be living with us," said Craig, "at the main castle. Conor—won't she be living with us?" he questioned, truly confused now. He had seen how his brother responded to her. She could bring him the softness and intimacy that had been lacking for so long in their laird and in their home.

Craig pressed on. "I mean she needs you, you need a wife, she's more than pretty and . . . and . . . well—Conor, she's not afraid of you." He turned and directed the question to her.

"Are you? I mean, are you afraid of Conor?"

Laurel's eyebrows furrowed at the notion. "Of course I am not afraid of Conor. What a ridiculous idea. I may be frequently aggravated where your brother is concerned, but I am not afraid of him."

This answer resulted in a bunch of grinning McTiernays. These highlanders were really a baffling bunch.

"Laurel," she turned to look at him when Conor spoke, "one more thing. You will be living in McTiernay Castle."

His clarification was heard, but not well received. Her regal but defiant stance was unbending. "I will not. It would not be proper."

"I thought you were disinterested in being a lady."

"I may not be interested in *society's* rules for proper conduct, but I still will not live under your roof."

"You will."

"No, I will not."

Conor leaned down and whispered into her ear. "Love, trust me, you will."

She twisted to reply. Pain suddenly ripped through her side, but it did not deter her from responding. "Conor, if you make me, you will rue the day," she promised in return. Just as he was lifting his head to move away, Laurel grasped his shirt and kept him near.

"Conor, I really must leave," she whispered.

Misunderstanding, Conor believed she meant to go

her own way the next day, and that he would never see her again. Suddenly, he was full of panic. Although no one would know to look at him, he was seized with fear that Laurel would leave him—that she wanted to leave him, and soon. He instantly decided never to let that happen. Regardless of her wishes, Laurel was staying with him until he decided it was over.

"Never. You will never leave," he stated with far more bite than he intended.

"I don't think you understand. I should not have been so reckless, throwing the daggers," she whispered back.

The daggers? What did the daggers have to do with her leaving? He decided that this discussion needed to continue in private. He gave everyone menacing glares for them to retreat to their previous activities. He then grabbed Laurel's arm and started hauling her towards the river.

"Conor, please," she softly cried as tears started welling in her eyes.

Immediate concern enveloped him. "Laurel? Why are you crying?"

"As I said, I shouldn't have thrown those damn daggers. But I did. My pride always was a source of problems for me," she sniffled.

"What about those daggers has you so wound up?"

"My ribs are killing me. I twisted too fast and the bindings gave. The pain is getting fairly unbearable. I didn't realize how much the bindings helped, but it hurts even to breathe now. Can you—can you help me to the river and rebind them?"

Relief and then dread filled his veins simultaneously. She wasn't leaving him at all. In fact she needed him! But his desire to touch her was barely controllable as it was. Whenever he was close to her, the elusive, womanly scent of her tugged at his insides, arousing him. If he were so near to her again, he would surely cave into his desire.

Through an extraordinary act of will, Conor suppressed his passions and led her to the river. Once he helped her unbind the twisted fittings, he waited out of sight while she bathed and prepared for the night.

He went farther down the river to bathe himself. Unfortunately, the cold water did little to calm his craving for her. Conor thought how alive he had felt the first time he had held Laurel. An overwhelming sense of rightness he had never experienced before—the need to have her—pulsed through him like fire. By the time he returned, his need for her was all-consuming. She had her all-too-feminine chemise on and was waiting for him to help with the bindings.

"Sorry," he said roughly, referring to having kept her waiting.

"Hmm? Oh, that's all right," she said, staring at his shirt that was molded to his chest. He must have bathed as well and dressed while still wet. He was so solid and strong, and his semi-wet top emphasized the natural elegance of his powerful frame. The hair on his chest was dark and tapered as she lowered her gaze. She had not realized how much the loose linen shirt hid. What had not occurred to her was that she had dressed after bathing in the same wet state, her thin, lacy chemise clinging and revealing her well-formed body.

Conor, though, was well aware of her garment and how it hugged every inch of her. He could concentrate on little else. Her breasts were ample, and he could see the rosy nipples through the thin cloth. The chemise was molded to her hips, leaving him no doubt as to her curves and beauty. The tightness in his loins multiplied.

"Conor?" Laurel inquired as she innocently handed him the bindings he had used last time. "If you could assist me just one more time. I didn't realize how much they were helping me."

He took the wrappings and began binding her ribs once again. In doing so, he inadvertently touched her breasts several times. The sensation caused a liquid warmth to pool between her legs. All of a sudden she wanted him to really touch her, not just through fabric. She wanted to feel his skin against hers.

She couldn't understand these cravings or where they were coming from. She didn't love him, did she? He was an incredibly attractive man, but he was also an aggravating, insufferable, arrogant giant who deliberately set out to goad her into anger, then enjoyed her unladylike responses. She desperately sought to control herself and her behavior.

Conor knew he was playing with fire as he bound her ribs. First, he investigated the injury to ensure that she had not made things worse by throwing the dagger. He admitted to himself that he had been duly impressed when she exhibited her skills. He had never seen a woman move more deftly and swiftly with a weapon. Her skill and accuracy evoked a pride in him that he couldn't explain. But it was there nonetheless.

Laurel not only had the traits of a real lady—beauty, charm, and grace—but she had all the requirements needed to survive in the highlands. She was smart, skilled, resourceful, courageous, and had enough stamina to outlast any female he knew, and several men.

Her damp hair smelled of highland flowers in the spring, and her skin was smooth and sensual. He hurried to complete the torturous task. As he finished, he looked up and saw gratitude in her eyes. But there was something else there. She wanted him. Aye, she was just as disturbed as he was by their proximity.

She looked at him, motionless, as if waiting for him to make the first move. Something primitive erupted deep inside Conor under her glittering gaze. His hand brushed her cheek as he pushed her wet locks behind her shoulders. His other hand stroked her arm as he looked all the while into her eyes. Without a word, he leaned down and brushed his mouth lightly across hers, urging her to comply.

Her lips were soft, warm and innocent. He slanted his mouth against hers, and she kissed back, increasing the pressure. Her fingers splayed across his back, and he carefully pulled her up against his chest. The effect of her roving hands and her breasts on his body caused the constant ache in his loins to grow painful with need.

He deepened the kiss and played with her lower lip, encouraging her mouth to open to him. When she finally did, he dove in, absorbing her into himself while his hands slid slowly up her spine. She tasted so good. Just like her scent, her kisses were fresh, new, and innocent.

Laurel didn't know that men and women ever kissed like this. When his tongue first danced with hers, she wanted to retract, but he wouldn't let her. The erotic feel of his mouth grew until she was responding in kind, kissing him over and over again. Both her hands were wrapped in his hair, keeping his head down, encouraging the embrace to continue.

Conor had no intention of leaving the sweet vulnerable warmth behind her lips. The way Laurel was responding, he knew that her desire for more was also surfacing. Slowly his hand went down her shoulder and then down her back and rested under her breasts gently on the binding he had just tied.

When she increased the intensity of the kiss, his thumbs started rubbing her nipples back and forth until they were hard underneath his caress.

Laurel was surprised at being touched so intimately and was about to pull away when he broke from her mouth and started exploring her neck. At the same time, his hands were massaging and coaxing her taut breasts, causing her to unconsciously arch her back so he would have better access.

Her response was so genuine, so unrehearsed and pure, it fueled his need. Never had he wanted a woman like he wanted Laurel. How could someone so new to the ways of love and her own passions could be so incredibly desirable?

Slowly he slipped the sleeves of her chemise down so that her breasts were freed from the linen constriction.

He looked down at her, and he saw that her passion-filled eyes were an intense blue-green. Never had he seen anything more lovely nor had he ever had the desire to make love with a woman more than he did right then.

Bending down, he took one nipple into his mouth. His tongue began to dance around the firm mound and his teeth nibbled the taut nubs. She moaned in response. Never in her life had she experienced or dreamed of anything like this. The world disappeared around her as his tongue swirled again and again, teasing each hardened nipple.

The warmth between her legs had steadily been growing and was now a blazing fire. The world around her had disappeared, and all she was aware of or cared about was Conor and what he was doing to her. She didn't know what was happening, but she wanted more, needed more.

Conor was exploding with need. Her response and her repeated moans of pleasure were causing him to forget where they were.

Suddenly, he became aware of a young male voice invading his pursuit of heaven. "Conor! Hey, Conor! Cole and Finn sent me to get you. Where are you?"

Damn. It was Craig. What did he want? Conor quickly stopped and held an unsteady Laurel in his arms. The last few moments had left them both trembling with passion. He stroked her back and tried to calm his own desires.

"Conor! I am assuming you know where Laurel is. You may want to get her and bring her back. There is some movement on the perimeter from the other side of the camp, and it doesn't look too friendly."

Conor called out to Craig before he reached them. "Fine. Return to camp and let Finn know that I will be getting Laurel and returning immediately. Do *not* do anything until I get there."

He heard Craig mumble and his retreating steps. "Laurel, love, we have to go back."

She still had a death grip on his shirt, burying her face into his chest. He could feel her nod in agreement.

She took several deep breaths and raised her head. Still reeling from unfulfilled sexual need, she had so many questions for herself as well as him. But she realized that neither of them had any answers. Not saying a word, they prepared to leave the river and return to camp.

Once they were back, Conor left with Finn and his guard to investigate the movement on the ridge. They were on the edge of highland country and close to several clan boundaries. However, tonight's disturbance was just a pack of wolves looking for their next meal. By the time Conor had returned, Laurel was asleep on his plaid.

Tonight, he wasn't going to wait until her nightmares came. He crouched down and gathered her into his arms. She instinctively turned and placed her head on his shoulder and nestled close.

The joy and peace he felt holding her in his arms was unbelievable. Earlier that evening, this captivating woman had him feeling so hard and on fire. Now, while he still wanted her with a fierce possessiveness, he didn't want to do anything to disturb this absolute feeling of contentment.

He bent his head and kissed her hair, inhaling her sweet scent. How this Englishwoman had woven a spell around him so quickly he did not know. But he knew that he was decisively caught in her enchanting web. He also knew that he was never going to let her go. His last thought before he drifted to sleep was that Laurel belonged to him.

Chapter Four

They had been traveling most of the morning when Finn pulled back to ride next to Laurel for a while. The terrain had changed, and they were now steadily climbing into higher country. Laurel was glad their horses were bred with the stamina and strength needed to continue up the mountains.

"Milady."

"Finn," she returned with a smile that would light even the darkest of nights.

Oh, this lady was going to set the clan in a whirl, he thought. "How do you fare this morn? Your breathing does not seem as labored."

She smiled in agreement. "Fine. My ribs are mending, and my breathing has much improved."

He fell behind her momentarily as the path narrowed. "I'm glad. We should be home in a day or two, depending upon the weather."

She moved Borrail closer to his mount. "Finn. Please do not let the group travel slower for my sake. I can keep up."

He saw the earnest pleading in her hazy, bluish-green eyes and decided that he could neither lie nor tell her the truth. "Aye, milady, but we can only travel at the pace of the slowest animal."

Laurel thought to ask whose animal was the slowest

and then decided that she didn't want to know if it was hers. Instead, she changed the subject.

"You mentioned that we would soon reach McTiernay land."

Aware of the tension in his laird's posture, Finn focused on the path ahead and avoided unnecessary eye contact with the bewitching woman at his side. "Aye, milady."

"Can you tell me a little more about the McTiernays?"

"Well, milady, the McTiernays are a proud, strong clan, and Conor is a wise and strong leader." Finn paused trying to determine how to talk about the respect and admiration he had for his clansmen and laird.

"The laird is following in his father's ways, leading his clan with a calm but firm hand. His skill with the sword and ability to train men have enabled him to build strong allegiances with many important clans. Recently, the McTiernays have absorbed a couple of smaller clans, so our numbers are formidable. Conor now has the job of bringing their fighting skills up to the level of their numbers."

Laurel considered what Finn had told her. "Why would Conor agree to absorb men who could not contribute to the clan as well as his other soldiers?"

"Well, milady, the laird has a reputation of leading men who are highly skilled and ruthless in battle. This gives him a position of influence and power. Some of the smaller highland bands have had no choice but to join a larger clan for support. Then there are the highly skilled warriors who have no clan to return to after fighting for William Wallace and Robert the Bruce."

Laurel nodded, knowing that Edward I had been plaguing Scotland with wars for years and was only recently driven from these lands with the exception of the three or four Scottish castles still under his control.

"Other clans," Finn continued, "are predominantly farmers or have lost most of their trained soldiers to battles. The younger men remaining have yet to be trained and are looking for leaders who can instruct and guide as well as protect. Our laird," Finn said devotedly, "is one of the few who excels at all three. This is why, milady, you are so fortunate."

As she was about to contest his last statement, he added, "But I don't think my laird realizes that it is he who may be the lucky one."

Puzzled, she responded, "Finn, I think you and the rest of this party misunderstand Conor's intentions. He finds me a mystery, something to figure out. But he does not desire me."

Finn did not react to her comment and continued looking forward, giving his laird no reason to be concerned. "Milady, that is simply not true."

"Fine, I will not insult your intelligence and say that there is not some strange attraction between us. But, Finn, it has not, nor will it ever be acted upon." The intensity of her last statement caused Finn to turn and look at her disbelievingly.

Laurel's eyes were large and round with sincerity. "I mean it. Ask your laird directly if you must. But he has told me in a most honest and candid manner that he has no intention of marrying. I do not think that his views on matrimony have changed."

Finn knew that Conor had strong views, especially on marriage, but he was sure that Laurel had shifted them. Could it be that Conor had not thought ahead to what would happen upon their return? Once news traveled that Laurel was unwed and available, many would seek her hand in marriage. Conor was deceiving himself if he thought he would allow that to happen. But maybe Conor's short-sightedness was a good thing, Finn reflected.

Finn had seen the two interacting and knew they would be happy together. Conor had never seemed so alive. He laughed and argued and was genuinely open and expressive when she was around. In her, it seemed that Conor had found what he had been searching for—someone to whom he could open his heart and soul. He may not know Laurel as well as his laird, but Finn guessed that she, too, acted more naturally around him than she ever had in the proper world in which she had been raised. If he didn't know better, he would swear she had Scottish blood coursing through her veins. It was just when she spoke with that awful English accent that the idea sounded ridiculous.

"Umm, returning to our original discussion," Laurel encouraged, "what about the McTiernay brothers? They seem to be a rather close lot. I have one brother, but he and I never were sociable."

Finn's grip on his reins tightened. "Will your brother be looking for you now that you have disappeared?"

Her somber dismissal calmed his fears for his laird. "No, Finn, I think my brother will be more relieved than anything else at my disappearance," she said sorrowfully and prodded her horse onward.

Saddened by her change in mood, Finn tried to refocus her thoughts and began describing the McTiernay brothers. "Now, each of the younger McTiernays has a reputation of being fierce warriors on the battleground. While only the three eldest have actually seen battle, the younger McTiernays are all in training and will be excellent soldiers. All of them—even Clyde—have shown a keen gift for strategy, a McTiernay trait. Unfortunately, that is the one skill most difficult to teach."

Laurel looked puzzled. "Oh, why is that?"

"Milady, one can teach any man how to swing a sword accurately and quickly with practice. But it is difficult to improve how a man thinks or the speed in which he formulates plans during battle. Concepts can be conveyed, tricks and tips can be passed on, but the ability itself has to be there."

Laurel ducked to avoid a low hanging branch. "My grandfather often said the same. He would talk of his best friend and often boast of his ability to outmaneuver any group of English soldiers—no matter what their skill—by just outthinking them."

Finn didn't say anything in response, but sat wonder-

ing at her words. Outmaneuver *English* soldiers, she had
said. Now why would her grandfather be wanting to out-
smart his own kinsmen? Unless her grandfather was not
English. He knew that Conor was waiting until they were
closer to home before asking her about what happened,
but Finn knew that he would want to know this revelation
before the questioning.

Concentrating on the terrain, Laurel was unaware of
Finn's thoughts. "How are the brothers off the battlefield? Are they always so close?"

"Aye, milady. The McTiernays are fiercely loyal and de-
voted."

"So they all live together in the castle?"

"Aye, with several others."

"The keep must be of considerable size then."

Finn cocked his head and nodded. "Aye, the castle is
very large and well fortified," Finn replied as Conor
dropped back so that he was positioned between Laurel
and his commander.

Finn had been riding next to Laurel for the past hour,
and Conor could no longer stop himself from learning
what their discussion was about.

"What about the keep?"

When Conor fell back to join them, Laurel's heart
began thumping so loud she was sure all could hear. "I
was just asking who stays there. It must be very big to
house your brothers, yourself and others."

He shrugged his shoulders. "Large enough."

Later she would blame nerves for her aimless prattle.
"I guess you need a keep of great size with your impor-
tance and considerable clan."

"Seems Finn has been speaking much." Conor glanced
at his commander with a carefully neutral look.

"If you would excuse us, Laurel, I need Finn to rejoin
the guards in their duties."

Laurel nudged Borrail, bringing her to Conor's side.
"Oh no you don't, Conor McTiernay."

"Excuse me?" Conor asked in shock.

Laurel waited until Finn was out of earshot. "Do not think to come back and accuse Finn of not doing his duties. I saw you ask him to keep me company."

He slowed his mount down, feeling his temper starting to slip. "I asked him to ensure that you were fine and able to ride. Not to have a lengthy discussion about the size of the McTiernay clan and its keep!"

Laurel's chin came up boldly. "There you go again, trying to twist things around. But not with me, you won't. I am not some shallow female only attracted in what you have. I was sincerely interested in where we were going and what it would be like."

He was completely bewildered as to how this simple conversation had flared to life. He wished he could cut this argument off with some smooth, simple explanation, but he knew that it was impossible.

Laurel was unsure why she had created such outburst over such a minor incident. But his yelling at her in front of others was inexcusable. "*You* were not willing to discuss such matters with me and sent Finn to do your dirty work. Therefore, if you want to get mad at someone, I suggest you get mad at yourself. For it was you, not I, who prevented Finn from focusing on his duties."

Conor dragged his eyes off of the maddening English firebrand to tell Finn to ride ahead when he discovered that his commander already had. Laurel and he were quite alone as the group had passed them while she criticized his behavior.

Part of him was glad at her courage; however, this desire of hers to argue with him in front others must cease immediately. It would not do to be criticized by a mere woman—especially one who sounded so *English*.

Conor closed his eyes briefly in an attempt to regain control over his temper and the situation. "I tell you this just once. Do not argue with me in front of my men." His voice was controlled, but his eyes spoke volumes.

She thought on his words and the simplicity of them. He was right. Disagreeing with him in such a way could hurt his credibility and his position as leader of the clan. No, she would not do anything to jeopardize or even diminish his standing among his people. Not when he had given her so much.

"You are right, and I will not do so again. You have my word." Laurel exhaled and focused on smoothing Borrail's mane, giving her hands something to do. She knew that no matter how hard she tried, she would not be able to keep her opinions always to herself. "Conor, may I argue with you in private?"

Conor was surprised at the question when the answer seemed so obvious. "Of course."

She sighed in relief. So, it wasn't the concept of a debate with a woman, it was just its appearance. This she could understand and accept. The thought of arguing with him in private was oddly arousing. To argue and make up as she had seen her parents do when they had not known she was near was incredibly stirring. Laurel blinked several times. These fantasies were getting stronger and more pervasive.

She was starting to fall in love with the man and did not know how to stop this mad tumble of her heart. She knew his position on marriage, and she knew hers. Right now, neither could or would commit to matrimony.

Conor watched her face and eyes as her thoughts flickered from one emotion to another. He knew the idea of being able to argue with him in private both shocked and appealed to her. But he swore for a brief moment there, she was feeling the same passion burn for him as he had been feeling for her all day. But then as quick as it appeared, it vanished into sadness and resignation.

The compelling need to kiss her, to rekindle the passion that had fleetingly invaded her eyes, was so strong that he gave in. She gave a muffled gasp of surprise as he leaned over, braced her head with one hand, and covered her mouth with his. Immediately, the kiss intensified, and she opened her lips welcoming his tongue with her own. She moaned as he ravished her with an intimate aggression that seared her senses. He gave a low, frustrated groan and attempted to pull her into his arms.

At that moment, her horse decided to shift, abruptly ending their brief but torrid kiss. Though physically separated, they gazed at each other, filled with secret wants that neither would voice aloud.

Laurel brought her fingers to her slightly swollen lips. Though the kiss had lasted just a few moments, it caused both of them to breathe irregularly. Laurel knew she could not continue to do this. She was not *falling* in love with this man, she already *was* in love with him—and somehow it happened in just a few days. But it was a love with no future.

"Conor," she said, trying unsuccessfully to steady her voice, "we cannot continue to do this. While I don't deny my attraction to you, I don't comprehend it, and I need to fight it."

Desire flooded his intense gaze. "You can fight it, love. But you won't win, trust me, for I have tried to fight my desire for you from the first moment we met."

"Well, I must fight it, and I will. You don't want marriage. I understand that. But I don't feel that way. I believe in love and in marriage. I want them both. I saw it work once a long time ago. My father and mother loved each other very much and were very happy. When my mother died and my father remarried, there was no love, no respect between him and my stepmother." She took a deep breath for strength. "So, I will not trick nor force you into a marriage you do not want, Conor. But in return, you need to stay away from me. For I cannot resist you and me both."

Conor did not respond at first. His insides clenched and a cold invaded him that spread throughout his whole body. For several moments, he stared at her, his eyes glittering with raw hurt and unmade promises. Then, he spurred his horse forward as he told her to prepare for a long afternoon ride. He wanted to get to McTiernay land by the following evening.

She felt hollow inside, realizing that she had just vanquished any hope she may have had with the only man she would ever love. The pain that filled her heart made her external wounds seem trivial in comparison. She pressed her eyes shut. She had to believe that she was right. While she wanted him, he did not love her in return. Besides, she had to leave in the spring to warn her grandfather of Laird Douglass's wrath. She hoped it wouldn't be too late.

That night Conor decided it was time to learn how Laurel had arrived, beaten and frightened, at his camp. He had delayed hearing the account until now. He'd wanted to be closer to home, wanted to be well within allied territory, but mostly he'd wanted time. Time to develop his own conclusions as to her nature. But mostly time to remain ignorant.

She said that she was not married, but he knew she was guarding some secret. He was unsure whether he wanted to know about it or not. Until yesterday, he had almost convinced himself that he did not care. But now, after her words about commitment and marriage, he needed something to bolster his resolve to keep his hands off of her. It had taken all of his will to leave when she was in such pain.

Regardless, he needed to know what had happened in order to best protect her. For it did not matter whether or not she wanted his protection, *he* was going to ensure her safety.

That night at camp, the brothers' discussion was similar to that of previous nights—light, cheerful, and animated. But Laurel paid little attention to the conversation as it continued boisterously about clans, battles, allies, and enemies. She was waiting for Conor to return from his nightly patrol. Behind her, Hamish approached and lightly touched her shoulder.

"Milady, our laird would like to speak with you."

Laurel shuddered at the unexpected touch. She mustered a smile for the group and turned to leave, grabbing the plaid as she stood. She followed Hamish in silence as he escorted her to where Conor was waiting. Perhaps it was because Hamish had been sent to get her, but somehow she knew why Conor wanted to speak to her. She knew she should be grateful Conor had waited so long to hear her story. "I suppose it is time."

"Aye, milady."

Laurel paused and looked at Hamish uncomfortably. "Would you please call me Laurel when Conor is not around?"

"No, milady."

"Can you explain why?"

Hamish crinkled his brow. "We are the laird's guard, milady. We cannot address you by your proper name without permission, and it unlikely our laird will give us that now."

Laurel was about to ask why, when she saw Conor speaking with Finn. As she approached, they separated.

"Find Loman and verify the camp perimeter," said Conor, dismissing Hamish, who nodded and left.

Finn moved off the rock he was leaning on and let Laurel take his place. She looked thankfully at him. The night air was chilly, and she was glad she had brought Conor's plaid with her.

"I expect you want to know what happened and why I asked for your assistance," she began.

Conor stood aloof, his stance open but daunting. "Aye. I want to know the whole story. But, just so we are clear, Laurel, I mostly want to know the name of the man who beat you and why." His voice was remote as well, making him seem more like an impartial judge than a supportive friend.

She took a deep breath. "Well, first let me thank you for your help," she started nervously. She was tense, and just thinking about what happened was only making things worse.

Finn, seeing her struggle and Conor's abrupt cold behavior, decided to be compassionate. "It's all right, lass. No one can hurt you now. We are far away from Douglass land and are well within allied borders. No lowlander will be venturing this far into the highlands."

Laurel smiled up at him. "My full name is Laurel Rose Cordell and, as you already assumed, I have lived in England my entire life. My brother is a baron, and his lands are near the Scotland border in the Cheviot Hills of Northumberland." She looked down. She so wanted to tell Conor the full story, but she could not put her grandfather in danger. No, it would be better if they thought her a purely English maiden abducted from her brother's land.

"I was abducted by Keith Douglass and some of his men while riding on my brother's land." She paused, hating to lie to him, but then mentally prepared herself and continued.

"I did not know who he was at first. He and his men rode in so quickly and slaughtered the escorts who were riding with me. Out of a dozen men, only two survived. The Douglass leader was cruel. He enjoyed the killing, the blood. I still don't know why he attacked, or why he took me with him."

Finn looked at Conor. Could it be the lass was unaware of her beauty? Conor shook his head at Finn, motioning him to remain quiet, and waited for her to continue.

"At first, they laughed at the nightmare they created. Two of them started goading each other as to who was to have me first. Then, their leader, a man named Keith, turned wild. He punched one and then took his sword to the other." She looked up at Conor. "He killed his own man. What kind of evil lives in a man to cause him to do such a thing?"

She looked back down at her clenched hands and continued. "I think at first I was in shock. But, after he killed his own guard, I started to fight back. Most of my injuries were incurred during the ride to his keep. I know I cut him several times with my nails across his face and neck.

The more I fought, the worse he would beat me. Still, I could not stop attacking him whenever given the chance. Eventually, he bound me and threw me over the back of his horse.

"By the time we had arrived at his home, I knew I was going to die. Then right before we got to the gates, the demon unbound me and forced me to ride with him. He told me that if I uttered a sound, made a single move, he would kill me without mercy." Laurel shuddered.

"His keep is large, but dark. Cold and cruelty fill its walls. I have never felt the like before. I thought that I had seen evil in Keith, but his father . . . I have never seen a man so full of hate. Even for his own son. It consumed him so." She sighed unsteadily and stood up, wrapping her arms around her, leaving the plaid on the rock.

"What happened next was shocking. And at that point, I was numb." She turned, looked up straight into Conor's eyes and spoke faintly. "It seemed that Keith wanted to marry me. I don't know why. He really thought I would marry him after he killed all those men and had beat me." She looked away again and stared out towards the moonlit mountains.

"His father said no. He told Keith that he could bed me, but he could not marry me. It seems that Laird Douglass had promised his son would wed another laird's daughter. He did not think his alliance would last without reliable insurance. It seems that the Douglass clan had made a lot of enemies and needed to secure allies by more than word of honor."

Especially since Douglass's honor rarely could be counted on and that fact was becoming more readily known, thought Conor.

"He suggested that his son rape me quickly," Laurel whispered. "Then his father said that he just might take me once himself."

Laurel remembered the rest of the conversation, too. But she could not risk her grandfather's life and share it with Conor. Laird Douglass told her that she should cooperate, for if she should ever return back to her grandfather's people, he would kill every last MacInnes.

Laurel, knowing nothing about her grandfather, his people, or the size of his army, could not risk not believing him. She would do anything to protect the grandfather who gave her great big bear hugs, swung her around in circles, and told her stories of Scotland and its great history.

"That is enough. You have said enough tonight," Conor said. He was barely containing his anger. Strong emotions slashed through him as her story progressed. He wanted to hear no more. He did not want to be told about what Keith did to her. The knowledge that another man had touched her, *beaten* her, was driving him to the edge. He wanted to end this now.

Laurel reached out and gripped his arm. "No, please. Let me finish. I need to tell you and then . . . then I never want to talk of it again." Laurel pleaded as tears welled in her eyes. He could see how hard this was on her and realized to make her relive it again would only prolong her agony. But while she would speak her story and forget, he would remember. And avenge her.

Laurel resumed her position against the rock. She looked at Finn. He seemed completely rattled and she felt an unconscious need to reassure him.

"Finn, I'm all right now. Remember it was you and Hamish who found me," she said, smiling at him. It rendered him completely speechless. While he was happily married and had no desire for her, Finn suddenly understood how Conor, Hamish and the others could feel so strongly attracted to her. If Conor did not claim her when they arrived on the morrow, someone would soon approach him for her hand. It would be interesting to see if his laird's stance against marriage remained strong when that happened.

Laurel began again, "Keith was enraged by his father's refusal. Actually, it was his father's suggestion that he, too, would participate that probably drove Keith over the edge—and gave me the chance to flee.

"He was now even more determined to marry me. I honestly don't think he really wanted to, he just wanted revenge against his father. Marrying an Englishwoman would be in clear defiance of his father's purpose for him. I think that is what drove him to bring me in front of the altar with a priest.

"The priest was just as shocked as I. I looked dreadful, and Keith was so serious and maniacal. The priest asked if I agreed to the vows, and while I knew what would happen, I refused. Keith swore he would kill me, but I still refused. Honestly, I did not think to live the night. But I wasn't going to die as Keith Douglass's wife."

Laurel paused for breath. She was about to tell them she was a murderess. Would they understand? She looked at Conor, but he looked devoid of emotion. She knew he had been listening, but could not ascertain what he was feeling. Did he believe her? Did he think she should have agreed? No, he would not think that. *Finish the telling,* Laurel thought. *Finish and see what he says.*

"Keith turned crazed. The priest tried to stop him, but Keith struck him and then ordered him away from Douglass lands. He dragged me by my hair back to his chambers and tried to hit me, but I avoided most of his swings. It was then that I spotted a dirk on a table near the window. I snatched it just as he grabbed me.

"Please believe I only intended to make him leave me alone, but the way I landed on the bed and the way he came after me . . . I . . . I didn't mean to kill him. I just wanted him to stop. But then he came at me, I raised my hand and the dirk plunged into his chest." She looked at Conor. Still no reaction. She moved so that she faced nobody, speaking to them and yet to no one.

"I slipped out the same way he led me to his chamber, through some vacant passageway. I followed it beyond the chapel and outside of the keep's walls and started running. It felt like I ran forever. I ran right into your

men that night. I don't know what I would have done if
you hadn't been there and helped me."

Conor's emotions were in chaos. Not revealing his raw
fury was one of the most taxing things he had ever demanded of himself. He knew that if she sensed just a frag-
ment of what he was feeling, she would not complete her
account.

Conor wanted to hold her and tell her that no one
would ever, ever harm her or those she loved. He wanted
to give her vows of protection and receive reassurance in
return. He wanted her to promise to lean on him. To
only need him, want him, Conor McTiernay.

Instead, he remained distant, watching Laurel look towards his mountains. The home of the highlanders. She
was cradling herself as if to ward off all the evil in the
world. Her tale should have relieved her, but it seemed
to have only added to her burdens.

"Laurel?" he asked gently, without anger or malice. There
was no hatred in his voice that she—an Englishwoman—
killed his own kinsman. Gone was the anger of this afternoon. Only compassion filled his voice.

She turned and he saw tears brimming in her eyes. As
she looked at him, she let a cry escape and he crushed
her into his arms. Conor held her close trying to take her
every trouble, every problem as his own.

Laurel clung to Conor as if her life depended on this
one laird's ability to understand and relieve her guilty
spirit. For just this moment, in his arms, she felt protected from the past, the present and the future. Here,
Douglass didn't exist. Conor cared for her, and her
grandfather would be safe.

Finn watched as Laurel received warmth and relief
from the laird known by most as cold and heartless. He
could see that she wanted not the laird, but the man. It
was at that moment Finn knew he would lay down his life
for her. Although Laurel did not realize it, she had
brought love back into his laird's world, and Finn would
forever be grateful.

* * *

It was fairly dark by the time they returned to the campsite. All of the McTiernay brothers were asleep on their plaids. Conor spread out his own in a vacant spot near the fire and motioned for her to use it. He then moved and relaxed back against a nearby tree. It was clear Conor was not going to sleep beside her this night.

Was it her request this afternoon for distance? Or was it her account of what happened with Keith Douglass? Either way, Conor was sending a clear message that tonight she was to sleep alone.

Laurel had bad dreams again and awoke shivering and in Conor's arms. She quickly fell back to sleep but the next time she stirred, he was gone.

Laurel awoke early, but not before Conor and his guard. They must have already left to get ready for the day's ride. It was still moderately dark outside, but she could see that the sun would be dawning soon. She rose and went to wash her face and take care of necessities.

The trees near the river were denser and much darker than she remembered from the previous night. She must have taken a wrong turn on her way to the river when she heard voices.

Finn and Conor were arguing in Gaelic, and their argument was about her. Laurel tried to control her reactions to their heated words. She had often conversed in Gaelic with her grandfather and was quite fluent in the tongue.

Finn wanted to attack Douglass land immediately. But it seemed that, although the McTiernays had no love for any Douglass, they were not currently at war. Conor was not ready to open his clan to such losses. Too many of their allies required their numbers in other matters after helping Robert the Bruce fight castle by castle in order to regain Scotland and drive the English out.

Soon though, he would take care of Douglass and his son, but in his own way and in his own time. With that,

Conor ended the conversation. Laurel waited until they left and then found her way to the river to wash up before returning back to Conor and his brothers.

Laurel was sitting on the riverbank, mentally reviewing Conor's words, when she heard someone approach. She knew it was Conor.

"How much did you hear?"

Laurel lifted one shoulder in an elegant shrug. "Enough."

So Laurel had understood what he and Finn were saying. An English lady fluent in Gaelic, Conor mused. She was a continuing and growing mystery. He had hoped that last night she would have spoken about her family and voluntarily explained her Scottish background. Her knowledge of highland customs and dress, her understanding of Gaelic, and her telling story about how her grandfather liked to outmaneuver English soldiers were all pieces to a puzzle that said Scottish blood ran through her veins.

"I won't allow you to risk your life for me, Conor."

Conor bent down and gently caught her face between his hands.

"I am my own man, Laurel, and the decisions you refer to have already been made and cannot be changed," he said quietly.

Tears started forming in her eyes. Tears for him. "But I don't want you to. Please."

"Don't worry, love." Conor gathered Laurel close, holding her protectively, letting her tears fall until they had run dry. But he did not provide anything beyond comfort. "I will be riding ahead this afternoon to meet my clansmen and handle some things that have come about since my departure. My brothers and guard will ride with you. You will not be left alone. Do you understand?"

Conor was so confusing. He was being considerate by telling her of his plans, but he was leaving her. She knew he was waiting for her to respond. "I understand, Conor."

She stood up and brushed her dusty bliaut in search of something to do. "Will I be seeing you tonight, then?"

"Perhaps," he said indifferently. "One more question and then I will go." He paused as if he didn't know how to continue. "Will your brother be searching for you?"

Laurel's brows pinched together in confusion, and she shook her head. "No. He is getting married soon and his bride wanted me out of the manor. My brother is new to his title and wealth, and therefore reluctant to put forth a dowry for a marriage contract. He is glad to be rid of me."

Conor nodded and left. Relief flooded through him. He knew how to handle Douglass, but he was unsure about how to address Laurel's family. He meant what he said when he told her that she was not leaving. He was not sure why he felt so strongly, but Conor knew his future was wrapped up with hers.

After he left, Laurel returned to refresh herself by the nearby brook. There was a standing pool of water nearby and went to wash her face. As she looked down, she saw her reflection in the standing water. She was truly a mess. No wonder Conor had felt it so easy to walk away and leave her. He was just a kind and compassionate man. It was amazing that he had felt any attraction towards her at all these past few days. Now that he was returning to his home that would most likely change, she told herself. It was important that she distance herself, emotionally, and soon.

When she arrived back at the campsite, Conor was preparing to leave. She could see now in the morning light that his eyes were slightly bloodshot, as if he had not slept all night.

"Everyone mount up. I want to be home by nightfall." With that, the men gathered their horses and quickly prepared to leave.

All morning she felt as if she had lost something very precious yesterday afternoon and had no way to get it back. Gone were the light banter, the fleeting looks, and exchange of gazes throughout the day. Conor had not looked back even one time to see how she was faring. But what did she expect after her "stay away from me" monologue? A profession of undying love and commitment?

She knew that she could not have it both ways. She had asked him to back away, and he had. Instead of being in mourning for their friendship, she should feel at ease. She didn't want any more complications, and falling in love with Conor McTiernay was just that. A major complication.

Conor could feel Laurel probing him with her eyes. What did she want from him? She wanted him to leave her alone and that was exactly what he was doing.

Her words from yesterday had played over and over again in his mind. Her mother and father, like his, had been happy and in love. Once, he, too, had been like her, desiring a relationship like that of his parents. Instead, he found false promises and desires for only wealth and power.

Here, Laurel was seeking the same thing. Except it was he who was making her abandon hope. Her story and the idea that he made her doubt her faith in love kept him awake most of the night. She wanted him and accepted him. But she wasn't willing to surrender her ideals and self-respect for the passion they shared. He was unsure whether this made him thankful or full of regret.

He signaled Finn that he was going on ahead and then pushed forward through the bushes.

Chapter Five

Late that afternoon, just before sunset, Craig settled back to ride beside her for the first time. Laurel enjoyed the gregarious twin's uplifting view of the world. And, since Conor had left as he'd promised, she could use some cheer and reassurance. It had been difficult to watch Conor leave the group and ride ahead when they crossed the McTiernay border.

As they journeyed, Laurel realized why all of them had continually mentioned the beauty of their highlands, especially McTiernay lands. They were magnificent. The McTiernay lands were nestled in the highland mountains surrounded by great cliffs, picturesque rivers, and huge invasions of sea that stretched like fingers creeping up the mountains desiring to touch their glory.

In the distance, Laurel could see the McTiernay castle on the summit of a large cliff. Situated against a large river draining into a great scenic loch, it was the most conspicuous object for miles around. Surrounding the castle were cottages of various sizes, each built of wood and stone. They looked strong, warm, and built to keep families safe during the cold winter months.

She pointed at the dwellings. "Craig, who owns these cottages?"

"Mostly farmers and their families. That one there," he

pointed to a cottage that was much closer to the castle walls, "used to belong to Old Gowan."

"Used to?"

"Aye, he died just a few months back. I honestly thought the old codger would outlive me." Craig was seventeen years of age, and the idea that anyone could outlive him from the previous generation was comical.

Laurel laughed at his ability to bring good humor even to sad events. "You must have really liked him."

His grin broadened. "He was a great soldier of my father's. While I don't remember it, Gowan was commander of the McTiernay guard for many years and was well respected by our people."

"Why did he choose to live outside of the castle walls?"

"You are right, he did choose to live in that cottage. For years, he lived with us when Mother and Father were still alive. But once they passed, he decided he would rather live in his own home than in the keep with his memories."

They were much closer to the castle now. Laurel kept expecting to see Conor ride down and greet them, but she saw no riders heading their way. The only soldiers to be seen were those entering and leaving the castle walls. The hill had flattened out now, and the land rolled with waves of green. *Finn was right,* she thought to herself, *it does remind one of the Trossachs.* It was still quite green with a short type of grass that swayed in the light breeze, but soon the cold nights would cause it to turn brown until spring.

The castle walls formed a *D* with the rear, straight wall towering over a ravine. At the ravine's base was a large river that originated high in the mountains and flowed into the great loch nestled in the valley they had passed by that morning. They truly were in the highlands now, with mountains below, above, and all around them.

The landscape on each side of the castle was similar to the rest of the countryside. Trees hugged either side of the river, but left fields of land available for farming, animals, or, as she could see in a distance, training for warriors.

Despite its size and the number of inhabitants, this area the McTiernays had forged from the mountains felt like a home. She could see it in the faces of the women and children she passed. Their lives required hard work, but they seemed happy, content, and safe. All elements she sensed were missing from her brother's estate. She hoped that his new bride would bring him the joy they had yearned for as children.

The McTiernay brothers unexpectedly closed around her on their horses. She was unsure whether it was to protect her, or to indicate that she was there by McTiernay desire.

Because of its size, the castle had seemed close for some time. But it was late afternoon when the group finally approached its outer walls. They crossed a large wooden bridge that led into a long and broad entry guarded by a well-sized barbican tower fortifying the guard gate. The guard gate was the only entry point behind the curtain walls of the castle. The entry was fortified on either side by towers providing access points to the walls.

"Cole," Laurel prompted.

He kept his eyes ahead and on those he was approaching. "Aye?"

"Why are there so many openings in the walls of entry to the castle? They don't seem to have any purpose."

"The combination of the passages from above and the sides with the open spaces between them provide an added measure of security. In times of battle, if an enemy breaks through the first gates of the bridge and breaches the entry, scalding water or stones might be cast down on them."

"Oh," she replied, looking up as they rode through. "Has there been any need to use them?"

"Not for many years. This land has been occupied by McTiernays for centuries. The original fort, which my mother named the Star Tower, was built several hundred years ago. Highly desirable, attacks were common until my great-grandfather began the building of the castle walls and erected one of the most secure, fortified structures in the highlands. This is just one of many such defenses. To my knowledge, the passages were only used once, before the barbican tower was completed."

As she passed the castle walls and entered the interior courtyard, she was again reminded how large a structure the McTiernay castle was. It was very imposing. The curtain walls seemed even larger from within, enclosing a large courtyard approximately fifty horse lengths in width. There were six round towers—two at the ends of the straight ravine wall, two at the bends and two on either side of the guard gate.

The four main towers were built on plinths, slightly widened square bases, while the gatehouse towers were situated on round battered bases instead of a plinth of continuous stone.

Surrounding the outer courtyard were ancillary buildings. The stables and armory were against the western sides of the keep, while the bake house, brew house, and other similar structures were against the eastern side. The main living quarters—lower hall, great hall, and chapel—were built along the straight wall facing north. The height of the buildings was impressive, with the tower on the western north corner reaching high towards the sky.

"Good heavens, that tower must be at least six stories!" exclaimed Laurel, looking at the structure while getting off her horse. Most towers were three stories, perhaps even four. But she had never seen a tower so large, or tall.

"Seven stories, Lady Laurel," answered Craig, giving her the title that had not been used since his mother had passed away. "My mother used to climb up to the battlement sections on clear nights to look at the night sky. She said she could reach out and touch the lights of heaven. She called it her Star Tower."

Someone came behind her and took Borrail's reins. She turned and saw a slight, older man about her height. He had very little hair and a small hump from years of bending and working with horses. Her first instinct was to caution the aged highlander about Borrail's feisty nature, but she immediately changed her mind when she saw he handled the gray stallion with a strong but gentle grip. While the man initially looked to be feeble and weak, he was clearly not. "Excuse me, what is your name?"

"Neal, milady," he said, quite startled. The woman was English by the sound of her voice and quite disheveled, but as she turned to look at him, he thought he was staring at a wounded angel. It was if she were unaware that her dress was torn and her hair was undone and tangled. "Can I help you, lass?"

The informal address caught everyone's attention. "Neal, this is Conor's woman," Cole warned him.

"Cole, that is not true," Laurel corrected and turned back to Neal. "In truth, I am but a temporary guest of your laird's. But he did give me this horse, and I would appreciate it if you could take care of him for me. I have grown quite attached to Borrail."

"Borrail?"

"Oh yes, he may not be the prettiest horse, but he is definitely proud. He has a strong heart, and never once let me fall during our journey. He carried me up these tall mountains of yours. Borrail means a lot to me."

The lady must be a little daft, thought Neal. Was not that the purpose of a horse? Who cared if a horse was pretty or not? But if the lady liked her horse, he would treat it as if it were the laird's own.

Cole handed his reins to the stable master and turned to his youngest brother. "Clyde, please take Laurel to the Star Tower and have Glynis provide her a room. Give her Mother's old sitting room."

Laurel gasped. "Your mother's? Cole, I must not. Should we not wait for Conor? I am sure he would not approve."

"He would," he said brusquely.

Laurel squared her shoulders. "Well, it does not matter. In fact, I have decided that I do not want to stay in the keep at all. How about that cottage of Old Gowan's?" She knew she was rambling, but all of a sudden she had been right to tell Conor she could not stay at the castle. A strong desire to flee seeped into her bones. How could she remain so close and yet keep distant?

"Yes, I think I will stay in the cottage. Besides, I know that Conor would not like me staying in your mother's room."

Cole bunched his eyebrows. "It was Conor who gave the order."

Just then, an older lady with a genuinely kind expression came up to her. She was fairly short and rotund, and her voice was pleasant and reassuring.

"Good day, milady. My name is Glynis. The laird asked me to come see to your needs and take you to your room."

Still somewhat in shock, Laurel did not argue when Glynis led her across the courtyard and into the keep's lower hall. It was a large room that was surprisingly bright, with large arch-shaped windows along the northern wall. Fires burning in braziers made the air warm and inviting against the cool afternoon breeze. The noise was incredible. Many of the soldiers had already gathered to eat the evening meal.

"Sorry, milady, about the mess, the noise, and the stench." Glynis waved her small, puffy hands disapprovingly at the sight. "The McTiernay clan is a fierce and strong bunch, but since Lady McTiernay passed away so many years ago, the keep has fallen into disarray. Only the laird's quarters are maintained regularly."

Laurel had already noticed the state of the keep, and its stench. The rushes were crushed and decayed. In many places, the wood floor was bare and letting in the cold.

The high table was at the far end of the room, but Conor was not present, nor were any other principal guests sitting in places of honor. But there were several soldiers sitting at tables placed along the side walls. All were so engrossed in their food and conversations, none had noticed them.

Laurel watched as servants entered and disappeared through a timber partition screening the hall from the service area. Above the screens was a minstrel's gallery. Seeing the ale and wine they were carrying, she assumed the area behind the screens was linked to the storage cellars housed below.

She and Glynis had entered the hall through a separate door and were heading towards another door, which she assumed led to the Star Tower, where the main sleeping chambers were housed. The doorway was large and mirrored the shape of hall's arched windows.

As they crossed the portico, Laurel could see a small, empty chamber to the right of the door. She guessed that, if necessary, the small sentry post would be manned to protect access to the spiral stairwell that led to the private family apartments.

She followed Glynis up the winding staircase to the upper levels. On the fourth level, Glynis stopped and went around a banister to open a door leading into a large and elegant room. It had to be Lady McTiernay's sitting room. Laurel admired its beauty. The colors were muted golds and greens that seemed to capture the diminishing light entering the room via the three smaller arched windows in the alcove. Conor's mother's taste in decor mirrored her own.

Glynis must have prepared the room before her arrival. The fireplace was already lit, providing an efficient source of heat. Even the thick and heavy stones making up the castle walls had collected the heat from the flames and were warm to the touch.

"Here you go, milady." Glynis indicated the clothes on the bed. "The laird mentioned you would be needing new things to wear." Someone had obviously been instructed to share her garments. The idea made Laurel all the more uncomfortable and intrusive.

"Glynis, who provided the clothing?"

"Oh, they were my daughter's, and she was glad to let you have them. I assure you, milady. We would do anything for our laird. I would have stripped bare for you if he had but asked."

The kind words did not bring Laurel comfort.

"But, Glynis, I do not want to take your daughter's dresses. They are beautiful and must be her best. I assure you that all I need is a bit of thread to fix my garment and a place to wash it. Until I have the means to make more, what I have will be enough."

Glynis was about to argue with Laurel when she saw the look of stubbornness in the lady's eyes. Glynis smiled inwardly. The lass was proud, stubborn, and her heart was generous to a fault. And since Laurel had spoken to her in the Gaelic tongue, Glynis began to wonder if the girl was part Scottish. She definitely had the looks of a bonnie Scot. Aye, if the rumors were true that Laird McTiernay had finally found a bride, this lass could bring this clan much joy. But was she strong enough? Would she be afraid of the laird? Would she be able to stand the cold winters?

Glynis shrugged her shoulders and relented. "I'll fetch you a needle and thread. I will also be sending up a bath and some food to eat. Most of the men have already eaten." She countered before Laurel could disagree. "Now, no arguing on this one, milady. You need a bath, and it would upset me not to help you with one."

Laurel could not refuse the kind woman this one thing. She would agree to the bath and the thread. But once clean, she would return to the empty cottage outside. She would not stay here in the great manor. And she certainly would not stay in the rooms of Conor's mother.

Upon the older woman's return with the thread, Laurel asked, "Glynis, do you know where Laird McTiernay is? I did not seem him when we entered."

"Oh no, you wouldn't, milady. The laird receives his

guests in the great hall. The lower hall is now used for the gathering and companionship of the soldiers."

Laurel tried to hide her shock. "He has guests?"

"Aye. Laird Schellden and his guard arrived this morning when he heard of the laird's impending return. I expect Laird McTiernay will be at the hall most of the night. Do you need me to get him for you?"

"Oh, no. Absolutely not. Please, do not interrupt Laird McTiernay in his duties. I have already been a bother to him enough these past few days. I was just curious."

Glynis smiled and left to fetch the bath water and the lilac soap. Oh, the lady was definitely interested in her laird. Glynis knew that many a McTiernay woman had tried to get his attention over the years, but no one interested him. But earlier that day, the laird had given her such detailed instructions to prepare for the lady's coming she would have thought the Queen of Scotland was visiting. Now, the Lady Laurel was here and though quite a mess, Glynis could see she was quite beautiful and had a giving heart. Aye, Glynis hummed to herself, if she was strong enough, Lady Laurel could be the one.

Later, after she had washed, Laurel sat in her clean chemise repairing her gown. She felt quite refreshed. Glynis was helping her brush out the tangles in her hair. It had been quite a chore to remove the filth and clean the stench that had seemed permanently stained on her skin.

"Oh, milady. You truly are the most bonnie lass my eyes have ever seen," Glynis said as she helped brush and tie back Laurel's long wavy hair.

"You are kind, but I assure you there is no reason for you to wait on me. I realize that your duties must be numerous and great here."

"Oh, no. Only the kitchen staff really have any duties here, and they rotate the responsibilities every day with other women of the clan."

"There is no established staff for the keep?" Laurel asked incredulously.

"Well, with the exception of the blacksmith, sword-smith, and the stable master, no, there is not. Some time back, the laird felt his brothers were getting complacent and demanding with the help. So, he sent the help back to their homes and lands, and with the exception of cooks, the younger McTiernays must maintain for themselves." Glynis then leaned over as if telling a great secret and whispered, "And they do a mighty poor job of it too, milady. Their rooms are unkempt. The halls are messy and filled with stench much of the time."

"But what about guests? Are they to be received in such manner?"

"Oh, in those times, the great hall is used, and guests' quarters are cleaned for the time they are here. Otherwise, there really is no housekeeping. I tell you, milady, it is a shame. The keep is need of someone." And not just the keep—the laird was in need of a lady, Glynis murmured to herself.

The hint was not lost on Laurel. "Dear Glynis, how refreshing you are. First, I insist that you call me Laurel. But second, I must clarify this misconception at once. I am not the laird's lady. He rescued me—that is all. He knows I will be leaving come spring."

"But you are staying in his mother's room," Glynis protested.

"Glynis. I understand how Conor's request gave you the wrong impression." *She called him Conor,* Glynis thought as Laurel continued. "But it was only a temporary measure so that I could rest and clean up. I will not be staying here this evening. Craig told me of an empty cottage. I will be staying there until spring when I take my leave. But I do appreciate your hospitality."

At first, Glynis thought to object, but then she decided that more would be accomplished if she let Laurel follow through with her declaration. "If you insist, Lady Laurel," she said, smiling inwardly, wondering what Laird McTiernay would do when he found her sleeping in a cottage alone outside the castle walls.

"There," Laurel stated as she finished the last stitch. "If you could just help with two more things, Glynis, I will ask no more."

Laurel looked embarrassed, but realized her requests were necessary. She could do neither without help. "First, well, I am sure you saw the state of my side. I need help binding my ribs again before I dress."

"Certainly, milady." A few minutes later, Glynis began to deftly wind the wrappings.

"Glynis, you have done this before?" It was a rhetorical statement. Laurel could see and feel that she was in experienced hands.

"Aye, Lady Laurel. Many times. Whoever bound you before also knew what they were doing." The older woman playfully paused as she began to tie off the ends of what she knew had been part of a man's leine. "I am surprised that you would allow one of the guards to help you with such a task," Glynis probed.

"Oh no, it was Conor himself who insisted. I did not want him to, but he refused to take no for an answer. I must admit though, he was right. My ribs and breathing were much improved after being bound."

"I understand. I would suggest keeping the wrappings on for a few more days or longer if your breathing is still labored." *So,* Glynis thought, *it was the laird himself who had seen to her wounds. Wait until the others hear about this.* "And what of your second request, Lady Laurel?"

"Please, just Laurel."

"But you are a lady, are you not?"

"Once perhaps, but no longer. I just want to live a normal life, contribute to this clan during the winter months, and take my leave when spring comes. To do so, I cannot live here, which brings me to my second request. Could you tell me how to get out of the castle walls and to Old Gowan's cottage?"

The request startled the older woman. It was one thing

not to prevent the laird's lady from leaving, another to aid her escape. Glynis took a deep breath and told herself it was out of love for her laird that she was going to do this. "Old Gowan's cottage? Well, yes. I suppose I could. There is only one entrance to and from the keep, and but a single guard gate. When I am done here, I am going to return to my own home. I pass Gowan's place on the way. I suggest we leave together."

"Oh, thank you." Laurel could not help it, but tears began to form. "You have been so kind. Are all highlanders like yourself?"

"Oh, milady. Are all English like yourself?"

Laurel then wiped her tears and chuckled to herself. "Let us leave, then."

"Where is she?" Conor bellowed from the great hall. He had summoned someone to fetch Laurel from her rooms. He was anxious to see if the room pleased her. Laurel was the first to be allowed to sleep there since his mother's passing. When the soldier returned to say that no one was in the room, the frustration Conor had been feeling since their separation exploded.

"I know she arrived. I saw her horse in the stables." He glared at Finn. "Search this keep until she is found. I want to know who she saw and when. And most of all, Finn, I want to know where the hell she has been."

Finn took his laird's anger in stride. He knew that it was fear driving him now. Fear that he had somehow lost her.

Conor paced the great hall wondering where Laurel could be. She wouldn't have left him. The gowns he had sent to her were still on the bed. The only evidence to show she had arrived were her horse and the used bath water still in his mother's chambers.

She had vowed she would not stay in the keep unwed. Could she really have meant it? Fear for her safety gnawed at him. His pacing increased as person after person returned with bad news.

"She was not at the river, laird. Nor has anyone been seen going or returning from there since she arrived," informed one soldier.

"Neal here, laird," the stable master gasped, winded. "I am sorry, but I only saw the lass when she arrived. I must say she is an enchanting, if not a little confused, creature. I hope that she is found without harm. It would be a shame to lose such an unusual lady."

Conor swiftly turned and said in a biting tone, "She will be found. And God help anyone who touches even a single hair on her head."

Neal would normally have been surprised at his laird's harsh response. Conor usually reserved his anger for the battlefield. But, because Neal had met the intriguing lass himself, he understood the laird's reaction.

"Neal, do you have any more to offer? Did she say where she might be?" Conor asked brusquely.

"No, laird. She gave me Borrail, and then . . ."

Conor turned and hollered. "Borrail? Who in the devil is Borrail?"

"Her horse, laird. She said that you gave him to her and bade me to take especially good care of him. Was this not true?"

Conor stifled a sigh. "Aye. Continue. And then . . ."

"Well, then, Cole came to bring her to the keep. She was very upset about something, staying in your mother's chambers I believe. Said she wouldn't do it. Then she mentioned something about Old Gowan's cottage . . ."

Conor did not listen to the rest of Neal's account. He abruptly turned and ran out the hall and across the courtyard.

"Open the gate!"

As he approached Old Gowan's cabin, he could see Laurel stoking the fire through the window. Her hair was free and she was still wearing her worn gown, but he could see the sleeve was repaired.

All the fear that he had been experiencing the past two hours converted into anger. She had refused his shelter, his offer of clothing, and his orders to stay in the keep. She would not turn him down again.

He banged on the door.

Laurel had been preparing herself for Conor's arrival. She knew that, once he discovered her defiance, he would come. She told herself that he really didn't care whether or not she stayed at the keep. It was only pride that brought him here. If she could find a way to salvage his self-respect, surely he would let her stay in the cottage.

Suddenly the door caved in and he was standing in front of her in the small main room. He was huge and radiated a primitive masculine vitality. He had bathed and changed into new clothes and his plaid was secured around his waist. His sword was missing, but his saffron shirt with long, flowing sleeves hid none of his strength. The long tunic and decorated jacket he had worn in the morning were gone.

Seeing him towering just inside the door, arrogant but powerful, was almost her undoing. She had to remain firm, she told herself. She had to stay strong. If she surrendered now, she would not be able to maintain her distance in the future. She had to get him to leave before she threw herself into his arms, damning rules of propriety and discarding all of her dreams of love and matrimony.

She cleared her throat. "Why, Conor, what brings you here so late in the evening? I was just preparing for sleep myself," she said, trying to sound nonchalant as if they were having a normal conversation.

Conor took a step closer. "Were you, Laurel? But you are so far away from your chambers," he countered, his expression ominous.

She retreated as he advanced. "You mean the chambers you had prepared for me in your keep?"

"The same."

"Well, Conor. I appreciate the offer. I really do, but I cannot accept. I will feel more comfortable here in this cottage. My staying here will help stop fueling everyone's overactive imagination that I am something other than a maiden you rescued on your return home."

"You know you are much more than that."

Laurel shivered at the dangerous softness in his voice. "I do? Conor, I am afraid that I do not. We discussed this, and you know how I feel."

"Nothing has changed, but I gave my word that I would protect you. I cannot do so with you sleeping outside of the castle walls."

She straightened her shoulders, her lips thinning with anger. "But what of your other clansmen? They are outside of the castle walls."

"They are highlanders," Conor replied as if that explained everything. He then picked her up and began carrying her back to the castle.

"Conor McTiernay! You put me down right now. You have no right! Just because you are bigger and stronger does not mean that you can just have your way."

"Looks like it does, Laurel," Conor retorted, feeling somewhat mollified by the feel of her in his arms.

When he first opened the cottage door and saw her in the firelight, he could hardly breathe. Her hair, clean and unbraided, flowed down beyond her waist in waves of curls. No longer hidden by dirt and grime, her skin was flawless.

As she half-heartedly struggled in his arms, he was reminded how soft she was. Her scent washed over him, and he felt his desire grow. He had no idea how he was going to uphold his promise to stay away from her. She had an essence about her that attracted him on all levels, not just the physical.

Once in the courtyard, he let her go and put space between them. It did not help.

"Laurel, you will stay within these castle walls."

"I will not. You can drag me here, Conor, but I will just leave again. I promise you, you will not win this war of wills. You may be a highlander, but I assure you, I can match your Scottish stubbornness!" she shouted at him, not holding any of her frustration back.

The commotion in the courtyard caught the attention of many in the keep, and they came to investigate the noise. The shock of finding their laird arguing with an arresting, unknown lady was intriguing.

"Love, if I have to drag you here one more time, it will be you, not I, regretting it."

"Oh, save your bluster for your soldiers. You would not strike a lady, child, or a horse for that matter. And don't bother denying it."

Conor closed his eyes in brief, savage annoyance. "Don't tempt me, Laurel. I meant what I said, do not leave the keep again or you will be regretting the deed."

"Are you saying I am a prisoner? I cannot ride in the meadows? I cannot bathe in the stream?"

"Not alone, no. At least not while I am away from the castle. I can only be assured of your safety if you are behind these walls."

Seeing the seriousness in his eyes, Laurel scrambled for an escape. "But your people! They are safe, are they not? Most of them live not here, but there!" She pointed outside the gate they just entered.

"You are new here, Laurel, and I cannot be assured of your safety unless you remain in here. Within these walls, someone will be on hand to help and see to your needs. You will stay here, you will sleep in my mother's chambers, and I will not be saying so again."

Laurel saw the cold anger in his eyes and knew she was defeated. She also realized that there was quite a large crowd gathering listening to them argue. She had never been so embarrassed. Her pride had been battered these past few days, and each time it had been due to an argument with this hulking man. Whether she continued her unladylike behavior or gave in to his demands, her pride was going to take another blow. It surely did not matter if she stayed here now. No one would believe she was a lady after this display.

"Fine," she murmured with undertones of frustration, "but Conor, I promised you then, and I will promise you again right now, you *will* rue this."

Conor laughed aloud. The woman did have spirit and courage. No one could deny that. And as she stood in the moonlight with her eyes dark as a North Sea storm, he could not imagine anything more lovely.

"I imagine I will, love. But it will have to be when I return. I leave on the morrow to ride with Cole and Laird Schellden."

The news startled Laurel and her anger was instantly, if only temporarily, forgotten. "Cole? Why is he going with you?"

"He is to train as one of Schellden's guardsmen." Conor was surprised at his response. He rarely explained himself to anyone. He was feeling guilty about leaving her so soon and not easing her stay at the keep. And so he found himself trying to calm Laurel and defend his immediate departure. If he hadn't been caught so off-guard, he probably would have questioned Laurel's change in attitude and the mischievous glint in her eyes.

"Conor," Laurel said in an altogether different, almost sweet tone. "The keep is not habitable in its current conditions. Do you not agree?" She did not wait for a response. "If I am to stay here, surely it would not be too much to ask if I could make this place livable. Just a few changes. I assure you—they would only improve the living conditions here." She then smiled at him beseechingly. *Let's see if grandfather was correct,* Laurel thought. *Will I catch more bees with honey?*

"Do not make any changes that cannot be undone."

"Of course, my laird. And how long will you be gone?"

"About a fortnight I expect. And, Laurel, do not call me laird."

"I wish you a good journey, Conor," she said and then followed it with a curtsy, looking completely submissive. He would realize later that her demeanor alone should have been ample warning.

Chapter Six

The next morning, Laurel was eager to begin making changes to the keep. She had one fortnight to do what should take months. If Conor thought to place her as token lady of the keep, he would soon regret that idea. She would assume the role and all the responsibilities and decisions that came with it. If Conor didn't like the changes when he returned, well, she had warned him to let her stay at the cottage. But, if she was going to be forced to live somewhere, that place was going to be livable.

"Milady?" came a quiet voice outside her door.

"Come in, please." She smiled at the young woman who walked in. She had large brown eyes that matched her dark brown hair exploding with volumes of tight curls. She seemed somewhat unsure of herself and what to do next as she repeatedly pressed her hands together.

"I . . . I came to help you this morning, milady. The laird said I was to assist you and act as your lady's maid."

"Hmm. What is your name?"

The dark-haired young woman wrenched her hands together even tighter. "Brighid, milady."

Laurel walked over and took Brighid's hands in her own in an effort to calm her. "Did Conor's mother have a lady's maid?"

"I don't recall that she did, milady. She had chamber-maids assist her for things like bathing and cleaning."

Laurel smiled and finally made eye contact with the nervous woman. She gave her hands a final squeeze and let them go.

"Well, I, too, have never had a personal maid, and I don't really relish the idea of starting the practice now. But I would love to be friends, Brighid, and to do that you must first call me Laurel."

"Aye, milady . . . Laurel." Brighid, much calmer now, began to consider the gossip about the new lady of the keep. Word had been spreading all morning about how the English guest had challenged the great Laird McTiernay and had lived to tell about it. People were saying she even persuaded him to let her make changes while he was gone. Everyone was curious to find out what she had meant.

When Laird McTiernay told Brighid that it was going to be her responsibility to tend to his guest, she nearly refused. She had never assisted a lady before, and she expected tending an English one would be especially displeasing. Then, when every conversation this morning centered on how the Englishwoman tried to defy their laird, Brighid had further assumed that the woman was both daft and ungrateful. However, the lady who stood in front of her matched none of her expectations. She was warm, kind, and gracious. Brighid was completely disarmed and suddenly found herself smiling in return.

"Wonderful!" Laurel exclaimed. "That is much better. I have so many plans and very little time to accomplish them. I am hoping to enlist help from you and, with any luck, Glynis. Can you find her for me? Do you know of any others who are looking for work in the manor?"

"Work here? In the keep? Why, aye, milady—Laurel. Many would like to work here, but the laird has forbidden it."

Laurel nodded as if she were not surprised. "Yes, but that has all changed. Laird McTiernay agreed to my request to make some changes around here, and I can think of no better time than the present to begin. It is easy to believe, as you approach this castle, that you are about to enter paradise, only to have that impression ripped away the moment you smell the stench drifting through the halls. I have no idea how anyone can live here, but I certainly cannot, not as it is."

Laurel paused a moment, then looked slightly contrite. "I apologize for my speech. My tongue sometimes doesn't know when to stop. But you have to agree cleaning the keep is a good idea. Would you help?"

Brighid's head bobbed up and down. The idea of improving the castle would be welcomed by many of the clan who had thought its current condition a shame.

Laurel smiled enthusiastically. "Wonderful! Please go find Glynis and gather anyone else you know who wants work. Any age will do as long as you or Glynis feel they are appropriate. Make sure they are hard workers and meet me in the great hall."

"Aye, milady," Brighid replied, smiling as she vanished down the stairs. She finally understood all she'd heard that morning. The laird had indeed found himself a lady for McTiernay Castle, whether or not the laird or Lady Laurel realized it yet.

Laurel went to the window and took a few deep breaths. Enlisting help was the first step down this risky path. She was committed. Now was not the time for second-guessing, it was the time to get organized, she told herself as she left her chambers a few minutes later.

When she reached the lower hall, Laurel realized that she was completely turned around. She was going to have to ask someone for directions to the great hall.

Laurel spied some soldiers conversing across the room as they sat on stools, eating leftovers from the previous night. This particular disgusting habit was going to cease today, she thought. Food should be prepared, eaten, and then disposed of. Not left lying around rotting for the next course. She wondered how these highlanders maintained their health.

"Excuse me, gentlemen?"

The men were startled. This was the one from last night, the one that had defied the laird and lived to tell about it. Seeing her now in the sunlight, they began to understand why. She was the most arresting woman they had ever seen. Her hair was like liquid gold that glistened in the light streaming from the windows.

"Can you tell me how to get to the great hall?"

They all clamored to their feet in response, each trying to get her attention. "I will show you, milady," eagerly offered one tall soldier as he was elbowed in the ribs by another.

"She looked at me, didn't you, milady? I will show you how to get there."

"No doubt taking the long way too, Arlen."

"I will be showing the lady. I am ranking soldier here," remarked a broad-shouldered man, effectively ending the verbal debate. But, by the looks in the other soldiers' eyes, Laurel guessed that they would resume their argument once she had left.

"Milady," said the large soldier, indicating to turn left as they exited the lower hall.

"Thank you for your assistance. What is your name?"

"They call me Buzz, milady."

"Buzz, well, that is an interesting name. My name is Laurel, and I would really appreciate it if you could learn to call me by my name rather than a title."

"It would not be proper to refer to the laird's woman by her name."

That comment had her sputtering. "I can assure you, Buzz, that I am not the laird's woman. Nor does he wish me to be. Therefore, continuing to call me my lady would not be appropriate. Do you understand?"

Buzz looked her directly in the eye, grinned, and responded with an intentional, "Aye, milady."

Laurel tried to grimace in return, but it was impossible

to do with him smiling at her. These highlanders were an immovable bunch once they had an idea in their head, she thought, as she followed his directions to a sizeable building on the opposite side of the north wall.

Buzz opened a large door into a grand hallway. The hall ceiling was vaulted and given an elaborate appearance by the addition of large wooden beams. Against the east far wall was a canopied fireplace. The high table was at the far end of the room, lit by a large window set in the north wall. The pointed doorway behind the high table led to wall closets, one probably housed a latrine. A timber partition, like that of the lower hall, screened the hall itself from the service area.

"Here is the great hall, milady."

"I thought it would be larger than the lower hall, but it seems somewhat smaller. Though much grander."

"Aye, it seems that way, milady, but it can sit a much larger crowd than that of the lower hall depending on how the tables in the room are arranged. Right now it is set up for the laird to dine with his elite guard. If guests are about, they will also dine in this hall. Years ago, this was the private hall where the McTiernay family gathered and had celebrations."

Laurel could see why. It was a large open room, grandly decorated, but it had a warm inviting feel as well. With the exception of new rushes and a cleaning, this room was in the least need of help.

Behind her, another fireplace was situated to allow for heating on both sides of the room when partitioned. She looked around and wondered what it would be like to entertain friends and family here.

She imagined Conor sitting on the raised dais of wood at the upped end of the hall opposite the entrance and indulged in a fleeting dream of her and Conor occupying the massive chairs, enjoying company with their friends and guests.

Reality set in again. She noticed that only a couple of

permanent tables were set up. Most must be either in the lower hall or dismantled when not in use.

"Thank you. And, Buzz," he stopped and turned back, "I may need your help with some projects in the next day or two. Whom should I ask for assistance?"

"I will send a dozen men for your service. Will that suffice, milady?"

Laurel walked over to one of the grand windows overlooking the ravine. Beyond it were mountains with white tops interspersed with green countryside and fields of trees. One could lose time just looking at these highlands. "Yes, that will suffice for now. Thank you, Buzz."

Buzz left and went out into the courtyard taking in deep breaths of cool air. It should be a crime to look that pretty and be off limits. Her smile could induce armies to do any bidding. It was more than her beauty, he reflected. It was the way she carried herself.

Her manner was similar to that of the laird, he realized. Like she was in control, naturally commanding respect and agreement. One just found himself following their lead, willingly. The only time he had seen his laird lose his composure was last night in the courtyard, shouting at this lady he just left. He now understood what Glynis had been saying all morning. She was indeed the laird's lady.

A big grin formed on Buzz's face as he went to find the soldiers who would help the future Lady McTiernay. He had to pick them with care. Green, easily besotted boys could get themselves killed if they challenged the laird for her hand. No. He needed to find happily married soldiers. He would go speak with Finn and, together, they would hand pick each soldier who would work with her until their laird's return.

Glynis and Brighid gathered several women and a few men to join Laurel in the Great Hall. For some, it was their first time in the large reception area, and all seemed very impressed by its grandeur. It took several moments before Laurel had everyone's attention, and then several more to convince them that she meant every word.

"Milady, are you saying that you want to fix the entire keep?" asked an older man who looked quite spry and active despite his years.

"Well, I don't know if I would put it like that exactly, um . . . uh . . ."

"You can call me Dooly, milady." Dooly had been a farmer for most of his life. Now that his sons had taken over working the land, he was eager to provide a good day's work at the keep, but was unwilling to go against his laird's wishes.

"Dudley, then."

"Umm, Dooly."

"Did you say 'Dooly'?" she questioned, and when he nodded, she continued, "So, where was I?"

"You was explainin' how you were going to fix the keep," said one of the younger boys.

"Oh, yes, thank you. Torrance, correct?"

"Aye, mum. But mostly peoples call me Torrey."

"So many names, but I thank you for your assistance. But, back to Dooly's comment about the keep. I do not want to fix the castle. I believe it is fairly structurally sound."

"Miss? What exactly do you mean by sound? Are you hearin' noises?"

"I mean that it is safe."

"Well, if it is safe, why do we need to fix it?" asked Torrey's friend.

"Excellent question. I am referring to the cleanliness of the keep. Including the maintenance, upkeep and general approach to how people eat, sleep, bathe, etc. All of these functions are terribly lacking."

"Are you sure about this, lass?" asked an older gentleman named Fallon. A burly man, Fallon was built like an ox, but he was not nearly as tall as the highland soldiers she had seen. He had red frizzy hair and a dark red beard just beginning to gray. Despite his appearance, he carried himself with confidence and seemed to comprehend her ideas for change.

"I assure all of you that I discussed and received the laird's blessing to make changes to the keep."

"But, lass, are you sure that he understands exactly what you be changing?" Fallon's voice held an element of command as he challenged her.

Laurel's patience snapped. "I will say this one more time. I *will* be making changes. Laird McTiernay has forbidden me to live elsewhere, and I will *not* live in the filthy heap this place has become since his mother passed. I never met Lady McTiernay, but I can see from some of the rooms she spent time in that she would not be happy about the state of her keep. This place is unacceptable for receiving visitors. If I am to live here, and it seems I must, I will be making changes. This place—at least until spring—will run like a well-organized castle. It will be clean, it will be orderly, and it will be fit for guests!" Just in time, she stopped herself from stamping her foot.

As she glanced around the crowd after her small tirade, she suddenly felt ashamed. Once again, she had lost control of her temper and, once again, it was all Conor's fault. If he had just let her stay in the cottage, she could have faded into the background. Now, here she was, sounding like a shrew in front of his clan.

"Now I understand, milady," remarked Fallon, nodding his head.

"Aye, it is all clear now that you have explained it," added Dooly.

"Oh, aye," said one of the girls in the back. Laurel could not remember her name. "You are now the Lady of the Keep."

"Lady of the . . . ? No, no. I am *not* the lady of the . . . the . . . ," she stammered. "I am just a guest who refuses to live like a . . . a . . . McTiernay . . . man!" Her exasperation with these highlanders did not seem to be limited to their soldiers.

The group now smiled again, giving the impression that they knew some secret she did not. It was if her anger fueled cooperation. She took several deep breaths and tried to regain her composure. But, before she could, the eclectic group of highlanders rendered her speechless once again.

"Well. Now, I'm very sorry about my behavior. It was inexcusable."

"Oh, no, lass. Your temper is fine. We like it."

"I'm sorry, Dooly. Did you say my temper—my horrible tendency to say the most improper things—pleases you?"

"Oh, aye, milady," replied Glynis. "We knew you were a strong lass with courage when you stood up to the laird in the courtyard."

Oh Lord, did everyone know about that? Laurel cringed as Glynis continued, "But now we know that you mean to be honorable. We know that you mean what you say and have the determination to see it is done."

"Well, of course, I mean nothing dishonorable. Did you really think otherwise?" she asked the crowd and received several grins and nods in return. "What in all of Scotland would give you that idea?!"

"You defied the laird."

"Aye, you defied and refused to be repentant."

"Aye, I saw it with my own eyes," said one older lad. It was untrue, of course. His father had witnessed the exchange and relayed the story that either their laird was soon to have an English wife, or that the English grew them stupid, to so disrespect a powerful Scottish laird like McTiernay. His father had suspected the first was true as the laird had demanded that she call him by his proper name.

Just dying of curiosity now, Laurel asked, "So, my contempt for your laird's instructions that I must stay in his keep makes me honorable?"

"Oh, no. That just makes you spirited."

"Aye—that or stupid," said young Torrey under his breath.

His friend immediately defended her. "The laird's lady is not stupid!"

Glynis ignored the squabble and tried to explain. "It is your defense of the laird's mother and her desires that makes you honorable."

Laurel was getting dizzy from all the double talk. These people were certainly friendly, but as a group they could quickly confuse a person. She had to take control of the conversation and now.

"Thank you for the clarification—I think. But now, I would like to discuss my plans for this keep. First the lower hall and the kitchen."

Everyone instantly began to resist the idea. "The kitchen, milady? Are you sure you want to . . ." Laurel cut their questions and doubts off. She hated to do it, but if she let them finish stating all their reservations about every decision, she would get nothing done before Conor returned.

While she had been honest about receiving Conor's permission to make some changes, she was fairly certain that he had not realized the transformation she had in mind. But once it was done, he would be pleased, she told herself. Yes, for who could want to live this way?

"Yes, I am sure that changes are needed in the kitchen," she affirmed. "But first we are to deal with the lower hall. Torrey?"

"Aye, milady?"

"Please go find Finn, and ask if he could meet me later. I need to speak to him about some new rules concerning the courtyard and the lower hall."

Torrey could not hide his shock. "Go now, Torrey," Laurel stated in her most authoritative voice and watched him dash out the doors. She then asked the group to follow her to the lower hall.

Yesterday, she had seen the lower hall and had wondered at its condition. It had been clear that the rushes were old. In the areas where they were gone, she had seen a collection of ale, grease, bones, excrement, spittle, and many other nasty things left to rot, grow or reek.

As they entered the foul-smelling room, Laurel began giving instructions. She had not realized that she had switched to the Gaelic tongue, speaking quickly about how all of the rushes were to be thrown away and replaced with new ones.

She wanted to rearrange a few of the tables so that servers would find it easier to enter and exit the room. The whole room was to be brushed and the windows washed. The fireplaces were to be cleaned and dried logs brought in and placed by the hearths.

"There, well, that should be a good start. I think that returning the lower hall to a decent state will be the most challenging task. So I am assigning most of you to work in this room for the time being. In the following days, I will most likely spread you out to different areas of the keep." Then she smiled.

The hearts Laurel had not secured with her confidence were won by her command of their language. And the last couple of men from the older generation, who were still debating on whether or not to accept her, were immediately ensnared by her smile.

"Fallon. I would like to place you in charge of lower hall if you would be willing."

"Aye, lass, I would be willing. But how are we to clean the hall with the soldiers eating and socializing at the same time?"

"No soldiers are to enter the hall until it is completed."

"But that may take several days," replied Fallon, trying to ensure that he understood her correctly.

"True, and they will just have to find somewhere else to talk and eat. I have eaten, slept, and conversed outdoors and I promise you that it is better than this hall," Laurel asserted as she waved her hand indicating the untidiness of the floor. "Glynis? Brighid? Please lead me to the kitchen. Fallon, that is where we will be if you need me." And then she turned to leave, listening as Fallon began to bark instructions to the remaining group.

Once outside, Laurel turned to Glynis. "Glynis, I want to ask you a question, and I want your complete honesty."

"Of course."

"Would you consider taking on a larger, permanent position here at the castle? Specifically, I am talking about the becoming the McTiernay housekeeper. I realize that those positions are very unusual, but . . ."

"Milady, that is your position."

"But . . . as I am *not* the lady of the keep, the size of the castle definitely requires one regardless. I know this is unexpected, but would you consider it? At least for a little while? Or would your husband . . ."

"Oh no, Dudley would be proud and my girls can take over the work done at home. But it is such a large job. I used to help Lady McTiernay, God rest her soul, with chores, but housekeeper! Only the grandest of places have them and housekeeper, well, it is so important. I do not want to disappoint you, lass."

Laurel could tell Glynis was just a little shaken up at the thought. She had reverted to calling her lass instead of milady. "Do not worry, Glynis. I have experience running large keeps, but I must admit, not one in this condition. What we really need is a castle steward, but I am unsure how to go about finding one." She paused, thinking about how and to whom the work should be assigned. "It will take considerable work to get the castle back into shape and train a staff to maintain it. But, I trust you, and I know that you will be honest with me. I need someone to tell me about highland customs and answer my questions. Will you do it? No, don't answer. Please speak with your husband first and give me your answer in the morning."

Then she turned to Brighid. "If you would please show me the way to the kitchen, Brighid. Glynis, who is the cook?"

"Umm, today it bein' Fiona's turn, so the food should be quite good. She enjoys the kitchen."

"You mean that cooking is shared by many women? And some of them do not like to do it?"

"Oh, most hate the chore, lass. They have family to take care of and the extra burden of cooking for the clan's warriors is difficult for some to manage."

"Why, I assume it would be. And who is the best cook?"

"Definitely Fiona, milady. You should taste her black bun cake. Melts in your mouth it does. Nothing like Melinda's. You had hers last night." Laurel remembered last night's meal. It was one of the reasons that she put the kitchen so high on her list of items that needed immediate attention. The food had been inedible. The bread was hard and stale, and the meat was undercooked and bland. She had been surprised that a clan of this size ate such poor fare.

They reached the kitchen and entered. Built between the great and lower halls, with doorways giving access to each, it was actually a set of smaller kitchens merged into a large room. There were several fireplaces to heat and cook meat plus a large central hearth.

The hearth was striking and surprisingly ornate, being located in the kitchen. It was a square stone structure built so the smoke vented out of the room. Behind the kitchen she could see fragments of the scullery where the utensils were washed and the fowl was prepped for cooking.

Laurel had been in several cookhouses as a child visiting her grandfather and friends of her mother. To her recollection, the McTiernay kitchen was very nice with plenty of room to work and clean.

"Hello, Fiona?" Laurel asked, directing her question to the person thumping and kneading dough on a wooden slab. The gray-haired, stoutly built woman did not even look up but continued with her kneading. "My name is Laurel, and I am to be Laird McTiernay's guest for the winter." Still no response. "In order to get me to stay, he consented to my making some improvements to the keep." Fiona was not making this easier for her. The others in the hall could not wait to talk to her. It seemed Fiona could not wait for her to be quiet and leave. Well, Fiona was going to have to wait until spring to get that wish granted, Laurel thought.

"Fiona, knead away. But listen to me carefully. You are now the cook of this keep. You will no longer be switching duties with other wives and women of the clan. The kitchen and its assistants will be your responsibility. The quality of the food will reflect on you. If it is not suitable for eating, you will be replaced. Do you understand?"

The old woman just kept kneading the dough, except with a little more forcefulness. Laurel knew she was in a test of wills and was not going to be the first to flinch. Suddenly, Fiona's brows bunched together. "Can I choose me own help?" she asked.

"Yes, but you need to tell Glynis who they are. Their duties will include helping you prepare and serve the meals."

"Can I choose the menu?"

"Hmmm. Choosing the menu should be done either with me or the housekeeper. But we will certainly listen to your ideas." As she watched Fiona ponder on the change in her position at the keep, Laurel guessed the true obstacle to Fiona's acceptance.

Fiona loved to cook. She was good at it, and she knew the laird appreciated her contributions. It made her proud. But it was also back-breaking work, especially with the men constantly hollering for fodder at all times of the day and night.

"Fiona, just one more thing. The meals will now be served three times a day. Soldiers who constantly bellow for food are unpleasant and rude, not to mention the havoc it causes in the kitchen. Please coordinate with Finn about when those times are to be. We can be accommodating, but only so far. You think on it, Fiona, and please let me know."

"Did I hear my name?" Finn asked as he loomed large in the kitchen doorframe.

"You did, Finn. Would you walk with me? Glynis, please work with Fiona on today's menu. After Finn and I have talked, I would like a tour of the castle."

"The whole castle? Not just the keep?"

"Yes, the whole castle," Laurel anwered. She turned, smiled at Finn, and then proceeded towards the court-yard with a regal bearing that just commanded compli-ance. Finn wondered if she realized it, or if it just came naturally to her.

"So, milady, I hear that you are making changes to the lower hall and none of my men are to enter," he said gruffly. She was about to defend her orders when she saw him grin. Would she ever understand these highlanders? Most likely not, but she was fond of them. Yes, she liked them quite a lot.

"Finn, I understand that as commander of the guard that you are essentially in charge of the soldiers and their training while Conor is away?"

"Even while he is here, milady."

"Oh, is that so? Well, I would like to ask your assistance with several things."

Finn gave her speculative glance. "If I can be of service."

"Well, first, as you know, I would appreciate it if your men would stay away from the lower hall until it has been cleaned and aired out. I assume that will not be problem or you would have already said something."

His brows rose in appreciation of her astuteness. "You know me well."

"No, I am just beginning to recognize that when high-landers do not like something, they are quick to bellow or quarrel."

Finn laughed out loud, but did not deny the truth of her remark.

Laurel joined his laughter. "It is but a small request, yet the lower hall should be better maintained."

"The men will welcome that," he stated as they strode towards the bake house.

"I agree. But, as the primary cause of the accumulation

of dirt and food on the floor, I expect your soldiers to be the primary solution." Finn understood her point, but did not know what she expected of him and asked for clarification.

"It is your job as their commander to see to their behavior both on and off the field, is it not?"

"Of course."

"Then, Finn, I expect your soldiers to act like the men their mothers raised. I am sure that they were not allowed to be slovenly and without manners while growing up. Please see that they behave properly from now on." Without giving him a chance to argue, she continued. "Next, we need to talk about meal times. The food is going to be much improved in the future but, in order to maintain good help, you have to treat it with respect and appreciation. Fiona is going to be running the kitchen, and you will need to confer with her about when the meals are to be served."

Finn interrupted. "Fiona is going to be doing all the cooking from now on?" When she nodded, he asked, "How did you manage that?"

Laurel gave him a sly smile. "Does it matter?"

"Aye, Fiona is the best cook of the clan. With that single maneuver, I expect you will be able to get away with all your changes now. I was wondering how the laird was going to react to all your changes, but with Fiona cooking—well, I suggest you use it as a lever, and he will cave to all your demands." He grinned mischievously.

"As I said," she tried to sound imposing but failed miserably, "speak with Fiona about the times your men are to be fed. Only three meals, mind you. I suggest you remember your own words when working something out with her. If you want her to feed you, you might want to compromise in her direction."

"Aye, milady. Anything else?"

"Hmmm, just one more thing. The training in the courtyard."

"Now you cannot be asking me to end training. Neither Conor nor I would be having that, even if you did get Fiona to do all the cooking."

"Oh, nonsense. You highlanders love to go off on tangents and assume things that are just preposterous." She sighed, "What I wanted to ask you was about training times. How many hours do your men usually train each day?"

"Several hours, milady."

"I was wondering if we could schedule training times in the courtyard. I noticed this morning that the people of the keep often interfered with your training as they tried to pass and get to other areas of the castle."

It was true. Clan members working inside the castle walls often interrupted training when trying to go about their duties. Several months ago, one man got seriously injured during a sword exercise. It was amazing that he lived.

"What do you suggest, milady?"

"There are several options, Finn. Maybe once an hour they could break so people could pass. Or maybe training could stop for an hour once in the morning and again the afternoon."

Finn didn't seem to like those ideas. "Training is a difficult thing to start and stop, milady. One cannot just call a halt in the middle of practice. It would be counterproductive."

Laurel could see his point. "Perhaps training in the morning could take place in the courtyard, but after lunch they could resume outside the walls."

Finn saw the sense of this suggestion. In the warmer months, training outside the castle would not be a problem. It was only in colder months when unexpected winter storms came upon them that he liked to train closer to—if not inside—the curtain walls. But he was sure that he could find a suitable training area.

Laurel stopped and touched Finn's sleeve to show her appreciation. "I understand that none of the options are ideal for warrior training, but it would help the castle workers to perform their duties while staying away from the soldiers."

"We will all learn and help. I promise you."

Laurel wrung her hands together, embarrassed at her onslaught of requests. "One more thing, Finn. I spoke with Buzz earlier—a very sweet man—about getting some help with some of the more physical tasks. He said that he would meet with you about this?"

Finn laughed quietly at her reference to Buzz the Battler as a "sweet man." "Buzz and I have consulted. We will be sending you at least a half dozen men to help each day. Do they need to be the same men or can I rotate them?"

"Whatever is best for you, Finn. I just appreciate your assistance." Laurel sighed. "Well, I suppose that is all for now. Thank you again. And please see Fiona about food for the men while the hall is closed and come up a permanent schedule for the daily meals."

"Aye, milady," Finn replied and returned to his duties somewhat stunned at their conversation. He had not thought that Laurel could fulfill her promise to the laird about making him "rue the day." But here she was, well on her way to doing just that.

Laurel Cordell certainly did have a way about her, and not just with men, either. He saw the way Fiona had responded to her. Laurel may not have realized it, but Fiona, while the best cook in the clan, was also the crankiest, always was searching for a way to be contrary. Finn guessed that Fiona's uncooperative nature was the real reason the laird had not appointed her cook in the first place. He didn't want to hear backtalk from her. But somehow Laurel had found a way to manage the old, cantankerous clanswoman.

Finn wondered if Laurel realized that with every change she made, with every heart she won over, she was solidifying her future—she was here to stay.

* * *

Laurel was excited about the progress of the day. She and Glynis were assessing the keep and, while there was still much to do, it all seemed possible now. She had been saying aloud to one and all that she was doing this for her own benefit, that she would not live in such a disheveled place. But, in truth, she was thinking about Conor. Making his castle comfortable for him, his family and guests was one of the few gifts she could give him in return for his help.

"May I ask you a question?" Glynis asked as they walked across the courtyard. Laurel jumped, startled. She had been daydreaming again.

Glynis had been wondering if Laurel was aware she often switched to Gaelic when giving instructions or providing suggestions to clansmen. She had wanted to ask her about it all morning.

"Absolutely, Glynis. What is your question?"

"How did you come to be able to speak our tongue so well?"

Oh no, thought Laurel as she bit her bottom lip. How was she to get out of this one? She hated to lie and knew that she did not do it at all well. "I, uh, was taught by my grandfather. He was taught by his grandfather and so forth. All people on my mother's side have known the language for as far back as anyone can remember."

"Was your grandfather a Scot?" Glynis pushed.

Laurel's mind was whirling. How was she going to dodge this inquiry? What if she just refused to answer it? "My home was in Cheviot Hills of Northumberland. It lies right on the border between England and the border clans of Scotland."

Glynis wondered if Lady Laurel was going to sidestep all of her questions. "Do you miss your home, milady?"

"I miss walking along the shores and over the stony fells. There are sandy beaches and pretty fishing harbors to explore and enjoy." Just then they walked by the guard gate and Laurel was able to see through the opening the rolling waves of grass and mountains topped with snow.

She impulsively added, "But now that I have seen your highlands, I will always be able to remember nature's true beauty."

Twice, Lady Laurel avoided answering Glynis's questions, but the new housekeeper was not fooled by her lady's evasions. If anything, Laurel's avoidance of certain subjects just confirmed the housekeeper's conclusion that her ladyship was indeed part Scottish. Glynis pondered on some of Laurel's other odd comments. She referred to her home in the past tense, as if she were never returning. Where was her lady going in the spring, then? Glynis guessed to a Scottish relative. As a lover of any and all gossip, Glynis couldn't wait to pass the word after she finished the castle tour.

"We are now approaching the stables. Neal is the stable master and is responsible for the laird's horses. He has been working in the castle stables since our laird was but a wee lad."

Laurel stopped to see Borrail and say hello to Neal. Neal had not seen her since she had first come into the keep with her dress torn and dirt all over her face. He could tell then that Laurel was a bonnie lass but he was unprepared for what he saw now. Word had spread quickly that the laird's lady was exceptionally bonnie, but he had thought the rumors overstatements in respect to the laird being smitten with her. But those rumors had not been exaggerations. The lady who smiled at him and inquired about Borrail was an ethereal creature sent down from heaven.

"Your horse is happy to see you, lass. He desires to ride and is getting restless in the stalls," he said as he went to stand by her and stroke Borrail's great back. Laurel was nuzzling the horse's neck, caressing his head, and scratching his ears.

"Oh, Borrail, don't worry. I won't forget about you. But I have a lot to do. I promise as soon I can, we will ride. We will ride fast and hard. Will that make you happy?" she murmured quietly.

Neal went over to Glynis and quietly pointed out, "The lass is speaking Gaelic to her horse!"

"Aye, she often speaks her language and then ours. Sometimes even in the same sentence. I don't think she is even aware of it." Glynis then leaned over as if she had a great secret. "She's part Scot, Neal. I put my life on it. She has a dandy of a temper, and no English lass can look that bonnie. That's Scots blood." She paused, pleased to see Neal was receptive to the idea. "And her speech. Her command of our language only further proves my point."

"Aye, the laird has chosen well," Neal confirmed.

"Aye, he has. But you wouldn't believe it to listen to her. She thinks she is leaving in the spring."

Neal shook his head. The lass may believe she was leaving. Even the laird may still believe he would let her go. But Neal knew better.

"You ready to go on, milady?" Glynis asked.

"Yes, but just one more moment. Neal, how many horses are you responsible for?"

"The laird's and his main guards'."

"That is a lot of work. Does someone help you when everyone is home?" Laurel could tell by his stance and the frown on his face that the answer was no. Stable work was hard labor. Neal should be given support so that his knowledge would be passed to the next generation.

"I have no need for help," he replied sternly, not knowing whether or not he should be insulted. Did she think him incapable? Weak?

Seeing his pride had been pricked, Laurel quickly interceded. "There are several young men around the castle who need to learn how to manage horses. It would help Finn during his training if the boys had already mastered the skill of taking care of their mounts. Do you suppose you could do this? Just one or two boys at a time? They need to understand what it means to care of a horse. It is not a simple job that can be done when convenient."

He just stared at her. Ever since the laird banished help from the keep, Neal had watched the knowledge of the elders vanish. Only fighting and battle strategy were passed on now. It seemed that McTiernay Castle was in for some changes, and Neal would do whatever he could to support them.

"Aye, milady. It would be a true pleasure," he answered, his eyes twinkling.

"Onward, Glynis. We need to let this man continue with his work," Laurel grinned and hooked her arm with the woman who was fast becoming a close friend.

The next place Laurel inspected was the chapel. It was a simple, rectangular room covering two stories situated next to the Star Tower. A nave divided the room horizontally separating the laird's sitting area in the upper part from the rest of the clan in the lower half. The majesty of the building came from its large round, arched ceilings, heavily embellished by a traveling artist who had visited the castle several generations ago.

The ornate ceilings were balanced with simple decorations below. The aisles had rows of stone pillars supporting the timber roof and the room was lined with benches that looked sturdy, but dusty. The pews set aside for the laird and his family were padded, but in severe need of repair. The altar looked as though it had been unused for some time.

"Glynis, do you not have a priest?"

"Aye, we do. He just hasn't been here in some time."

"I wonder why," Laurel murmured to herself sarcastically. "Once the men are done with the lower hall have them clean this chapel."

"Aye, milady."

"Do you have material here? The curtains, the padded seats, and the altar coverings all need to be redone."

Glynis artfully guided Laurel out of the chapel and changed the tenor of their discussion. "There are several bolts of material in the North Tower. If I may suggest, you should take some for your gowns."

Laurel's first reaction was to refuse, but then she realized that would be foolish. "I suppose you are right. I cannot wear this same outfit every day, now can I?" She looked down at her gown. Despite her repairs, it was severely worn. "Are you sure that no one is using the cloth? It is serving no purpose?"

"Now would I be telling you about something that is forbidden to use?" After spending a morning with her lady, Glynis was becoming comfortable in speaking her mind. It seemed that her lady responded better to frank talk. Laurel was open to suggestions, but was at ease making decisions. McTiernay Castle was going to bloom again with her in charge of household affairs.

Glynis observed Laurel for a few moments and changed their direction as she declared, "Now, it is time for you to return to your room before dinner. I will have Brighid draw you a bath and bring some fabric to your rooms." It was only then that Laurel grasped she was in the Star Tower at the bottom of the corkscrew staircase. Glynis was ending the day's tour.

"Not yet, I would like to see . . ."

"No, I think you will go now. Laird McTiernay would have my neck if he found out how hard you was working, milady. Remember, I know of your ribs, and I see how hard you are breathing after climbing the stairs in the chapel."

Laurel could not argue about her breathing. It was labored. She felt like such an invalid, but knew that if pushed too far, too fast, she would truly then be bedridden. "Just for tonight," Laurel acquiesced and proceeded up the stairs to her room.

She was sitting in the settee near the far window relaxing looking at the view when someone knocked.

"Come in," she said expecting Brighid to answer. Instead the youngest two McTiernays plunged into the room.

"Why, hello!" Laurel exclaimed. "I thought you had gone with Conor to Laird Schellden's."

"Nah, we weren't allowed to go," said Clyde, climbing up on his mother's bed just like he used to when he was younger. Conan jumped up beside him and fanned out spread eagle staring at the ceiling.

"I love this room. Mother let us play in here all the time," Conan remarked.

"Those must be good memories. When was the last time you were here?" Laurel asked.

"Oh, when Mama died, Conor locked the room and forbade anyone to use it. He only opened it up again when you came," Conan explained.

"Conor must really like you. Are you going to marry him?" Clyde asked innocently. "I hope so. You sure are pretty and nice. Just like Mama."

"Why, thank you, Clyde. I like you, too. But I don't think I am going to marry your brother. He's an important man and needs to marry someone worthy of your clan."

"You're important! What's more, you're smart!" defended Conan, thinking that being intelligent and quick-witted were the most important attributes anyone could have. "Most people think it is wonderful that you are cleaning up the castle. That it was time someone got our brother to agree to changes. Only a few people can't believe you are defying Conor and are scared of what'll happen."

Clyde giggled and fell back on the bed hard. "Wait till they see you throw a knife!"

Laurel ignored the silly laughter erupting from the young boy. "Conan, why would cleaning up the keep be defying Conor?" The idea did not make sense. Conan must have misunderstood his brother's intentions.

"Conor said that we were ... we were ... unappreciated," Clyde said, bunching his forehead trying to remember exactly what Conor had said. The remark had been made several years prior when Clyde was just past six years old.

"Unappreciative," Conan scoffed, flaunting his intellect and vocabulary.

Laurel furrowed her eyebrows. "Hmmm, and was he referring to the clan or to his brothers?"

"Us, I believe. Although not Clyde and me in particular. It was the twins and Cole who were the worst of us. He just got really mad one night and sent everyone home and said that until we could learn to appreciate help, we shouldn't have any." Conan shrugged his shoulders. "I guess we haven't learned it yet."

Laurel smiled in understanding. Poor Conor. He tried so hard to do the right thing, and it just backfired on him. She walked over to sit down on the bed between Clyde and Conor and took hold of their hands.

"Well, the help has returned, along with manners and gratitude. This I can assure you, for your brother is right. If you cannot appreciate the assistance of your clan, you should not have it. However, unlike Conor, I do not intend on depriving everyone from a well-established and clean keep just because of some unruly, *unapprecia-tive* boys."

"Laurel? What do you mean by *unappreciative*?" asked Clyde, still puzzled by its meaning.

A deep voice came from the doorway. "She means that if you are not thankful or do not recognize the work someone is doing for you, you don't deserve their help." Finn startled everyone as he entered the room. "I'm over-seeing getting your bath water."

"Finn! That shouldn't be your responsibility!" exclaimed Laurel.

"Seeing to your welfare is part of my duty while the laird is away." He didn't add Conor's emphatic order it was Finn's responsibility to manage all tasks associated with her. His laird did not want anyone assisting or work-ing with Laurel on personal matters—such as drawing a bath.

"That is ridiculous. I shall go down to the kitchen to bathe. No one is going to be hauling water up and down stairs on my account."

She got up and started towards the door. Finn stepped in front of her. The man was huge. She expected he was near Conor's height, although he lacked his muscular structure. Conor was the perfect balance between height and strength. She wished he was there right now, if only so she could argue with him.

Just then Brighid rounded the corner laden with fabric, ribbon and lace. Her eyes widened at the number of people in her lady's chamber. Conor and Clyde were still on the bed, grinning and watching the commander of the guard and her lady arguing about something.

Brighid's stance turned to one of timidity. "Uh, I'm sorry. Should I come back, milady? Glynis told me that I should bring these up, but if you are in the middle of something . . ." she trailed off, clearly perplexed.

Glad for the interruption, Laurel exclaimed, "Wonderful! Brighid, I assume that is the fabric Glynis told me about?" The young maid nodded. Laurel walked over to the bolts and started shaking her head.

"Oh, no. These will not do at all. I wanted sturdier fabrics for chairs and curtains. Only the plaid looks appropriate, but there is not nearly enough."

Brighid found her tongue. "I was to tell you, milady, that the other fabrics would not be found until at least five new gowns had been made for you." She looked wide-eyed at her lady now. Brighid had been nervous on her way up here to deliver the message. But Glynis had been clear that no matter how much Laurel argued, cajoled or demanded, Brighid was not to give in. The laird's desires outweighed everyone else's, and the new housekeeper was adamant that this was his wish.

Laurel considered arguing, but did not wish to put Brighid in an awkward position of choosing between her and Glynis in front of Finn.

"All right. I am not agreeing, mind you. I just know that I will have to take my arguments up with Glynis on the morrow." Brighid looked relieved.

"Aye, milady. Should I put these bolts over here?" she asked, indicating with her chin towards the settee. Laurel didn't want to give up her favorite sitting spot in the room. She looked around and found an unused ottoman

pushed towards the corner. She went to go drag it out between the chairs in front of the hearth when Conan
jumped up and did the deed for her.

"Thank you, Conan. You have been a great help," she
remarked, remembering her promise to Neal.

"Brighid, please lay those down here. Finn, before you
leave, may I make another request?"

He arched his eyebrows in response, curious to know
what other changes she had in store. "Aye."

"I would like Neal to have one or two revolving appren-
tices to help him. He is getting older and the care of all
the mares is difficult for one his age." She put her hand
up to stop his comment before it was uttered. "No, he did
not complain. Of course he wouldn't. But that doesn't
mean he could not use the help. But mostly, he is a fountain of wisdom from which no one is drinking."

"Whatever are you talking about, lass? Conor is right.
You do talk in circles." Finn stood looming with his hands
on his hips.

Laurel was exasperated. "I do not talk in circles."

"Aye, lass, you do. You could rival my wife in stirring a
man's head into a blur. Aileen speaks just the way you do.
It's either a riddle or some hidden example to get her
point across. And with the baby coming it has only gotten
worse. Never does she just say what's on her mind." He
took a deep breath and let out a sigh. "So, what do you
mean, lass, about Neal being a fountain without water?"

Laurel shook her head, wondering how something so
simple could be so easily misunderstood. "I meant that
Neal knows a great deal about horses. He knows good
stock from bad. He knows what horses need in all types
of weather, can cure them when ill, and can train them
for riding. This knowledge will be lost if there is no one
to teach."

This time Finn consented and promised to procure
two lads to begin their education in the stables. He also
agreed that the job should rotate among the boys,
improving the preparation they would have before they

reached him for training. The only unexpected outcome of the decision was Clyde begging to be the first one trained.

Laurel couldn't sleep. The day had been so satisfying. It was a feeling she had not experienced in a long time. Being appreciated, needed, and, oddly enough, liked were things she hadn't realized she missed.

Her mind kept wandering to Conor. Where was he? What was he doing? Where was he sleeping? She had no idea how many times she told herself to start being sensible. Conor had probably stopped thinking about her the second he had left the castle walls. She wished it were as easy for her to forget about him.

She got up and went to go put on her bliaut and grimaced as she remembered it was wet from washing. She was going to have to add a robe to the list of clothing items she and Brighid had started earlier that evening. She paced the floor a few times and decided that the chemise she was wearing would have to do.

She opened the door and peeked out. She could see no one walking about the tower. Not surprising really. Glynis had told her earlier that the Star Tower only held the chambers of the laird and his lady. The rest of the family slept in the other wing of the castle in the North Tower. All the servants and soldiers slept in either the East or West Towers.

She tiptoed out after putting on a pair of slippers she had found in the room. She felt somewhat guilty about using them, but then everything she had heard about Conor's mother told her that the late Lady McTiernay would have insisted that she use them. Especially for what she was about to do.

Once she was told about how the Star Tower received its name, Laurel knew it was inevitable that she would be making this climb. The tower was seven stories tall.

And one of the rooms she was passing by was Conor's sleeping quarters.

As she reached the top, she exited the door leading to the outside and the battlements. The long climb up the stairs was worth it. She had never seen the stars so clearly. Laurel thought she could see the angels in heaven from up here. She felt carefree, without worries or burdens. Happy. The only thing missing was Conor.

She no longer thought the tree-filled alcove near Stirling Castle was the ideal place to be kissed. No, this soaring tower had to be the most romantic place in the world. She hugged herself against the cool night air and began to twirl along the wall's edge, singing.

Most of the soldiers were sleeping in the tower quarters assigned to the permanent garrison. But not all were. Usually the soldiers assigned as the castle's night guard slept near their assigned posts, many of which were up on the parapets. Their job was to see if anyone approached by looking through the crenels cut out of the castle wall.

"Wake up, Gil," Fergus kicked his friend and comrade. "I think I see the girl of me dreams. Aye, I have to be dreaming."

"Huh?" Gil rolled over and proceeded to snore.

Fergus would not be denied affirmation so easily. He kicked Gil again. "Look, I tell you. An angel is right here in our midst."

Gilroy, tall and thin, but a strong and quick soldier, sat up, about to give his much shorter friend a well-deserved knock in the head. It was then he saw to whom Fergus was referring. The most beautiful of angels was dancing on their Star Tower.

She was dressed in white and her gold hair curled down below her waist beyond what he could see. She was tall and perfect, shimmering in the glow of the moonlight. Just as he was about to suggest they go and see if the vision was real, she disappeared, vanishing into thin air just as she'd arrived. Gilroy vowed to never complain about guard duty at night again.

Chapter Seven

Conor was having another restless night. He had been preoccupied since he left Laurel all alone. He convinced himself that it was simply his oath that kept dragging his thoughts back to her. He was torn between duties, to his clan, to his brothers, and to her. He had sworn to protect her, and then left the task to Finn.

God help Finn if anything happened to her while he was away. Conor had spent almost an hour with his commander detailing what the other men could and could not do regarding Laurel, focusing primarily on the latter.

He trusted his commander to keep her safe from both harm and over-attentive men. Otherwise, Conor would have made Laurel travel with him to Schellden's. Only Finn, with his happy marriage and a baby on the way, seemed to be able to resist Laurel's natural charms. He trusted all his men in terms of battle and loyalty, but he had not claimed Laurel and nor did he have intentions of doing so. And he was not unaware that this decision made her very vulnerable.

He wished he could be like Finn. Admiring, but unaffected. He had never desired a woman like he did Laurel. He wanted her more than he had ever thought it possible to want any woman. Earlier that evening, he was reminded of the way she challenged him, refusing to be

intimidated. The women of Schellden's clan responded
to him like all females did—shrinking away at the merest
glance. Not only were they weak willed, but they could
not compare with his gold-haired mystery with the blue-
green eyes. He closed his eyes remembering the feel of
her soft lips against his. How untutored they were, but so
responsive to his instruction.

He longed to hold her again, mold her flesh against
his as if they were meant only for each other. He was
going to go mad with wanting her. And knowing that he
could make her desire him as well drove him to cold
swims every night in the nearby loch.

He had just under two weeks to figure out a way to
drive her from his mind. If he could not, Conor knew he
would bed her despite all that would come with it when
he did.

"Milady?" Glynis asked from outside the chamber door.

"Come in, Glynis," Laurel answered, throwing on her
new bliaut. Her ribs had improved greatly in the past several days. It no longer hurt to breathe when going up
and down the stairs, and she could now dress herself.

"Oh, milady, you do look fine. I told you Brighid was
an excellent seamstress. The laird will be mighty pleased
when he returns to see you in his plaid." Either that or
mighty unhappy, Glynis thought. The laird had always
been a possessive soul, even as a child. When he saw his
lady looking this bonnie, he might want her to go back to
the disheveled state she arrived in.

Laurel shrugged her shoulders. "Hmmm, maybe. I am
still unsure about the plaid, though. Do you not think it
fairly presumptuous?" She looked down and brushed
imaginary dirt from the shoulder pleats. She loved the
plaid and enjoyed wearing it. "But it is warm and the
nights are already so much cooler than when I first arrived," she said, searching for a rational reason to be
wearing something of Conor's.

"Aye. We were having a brief highland summer. Sometimes it comes this time of year, but not always. Just as it starts to cool, all of a sudden a spot of warm weather will hover for one to several weeks and then will disappear. Many believe it foretells a hard winter." Glynis helped with the pleats. Laurel was picking up the skill, but it was difficult to fold the plaid just right.

They left her chambers and proceeded to the lower hall. The improvements were taking longer than expected, but Laurel hoped to have the room reopened to the soldiers by the setting of the afternoon sun. She had spent so much of her time on the halls and the chapel that she really had not had a chance to finish her tour and visit the other parts of the castle, such as the smithy and the other towers. She was afraid that if she saw the state they were in, she wouldn't be able to stop herself from beginning work immediately on those areas as well. One at a time, she was reminding herself, when Glynis interrupted her thoughts.

"I wanted to speak to you about your request of a castle steward," Glynis broached as they entered into the lower hall.

The hall was now an inviting place for the men to gather, eat, and talk about the day's exploits. The fireplaces had been cleaned out and now would be efficient sources of heat to warm the room. Washed, the windows provided a much brighter, warmer source of light during the day. Dining tables were set on temporary trestles so that they could be easily dismantled between meals. The improvements to this room and the chapel were astounding. And all under Fallon's wonderful leadership, commented Laurel as they discussed the day's agenda.

"That is who I would be wanting to talk to you about," Glynis announced.

"Fallon?"

"Aye. He should be your steward." In many ways Laurel agreed, but she just couldn't see herself asking the difficult man to take the job. She was afraid the farmer would be insulted. For some reason, impressing Fallon was important to her. Gaining his respect was difficult and she was still unsure if she had it.

He seemed willing to impart praise—sparingly—but he was more disposed to point out errors in judgment. He certainly had done so when she started multiple cleaning projects simultaneously resulting in a delayed reopening of the lower hall. Laurel felt especially guilty about that mistake. The days were getting colder, so by the time the men got their food it was not even warm.

"I don't think Fallon wants to be steward, though, and I would hate to insult him after all the help he has given."

"Milady, I do not think you understand. Fallon *is* the steward of McTiernay Castle."

"Did you say *is* the steward?!" exclaimed Laurel, attracting attention from the servants working across the room. She immediately lowered her voice, but could not keep anger from lacing her words.

"Then he is a fairly bad one, is he not? All this work because he couldn't do his job. And to think I thought of Fallon as the hardest and most capable of workers!"

"No, no. You still do not understand. I thought Conan told you about the Conor's command about the castle."

"You don't mean . . . I mean . . . Oh, my. Poor Fallon. It must have crushed him to see his castle come to such a state of disrepair. No wonder he seemed to know just what and how long everything would take." Laurel's anger rose again as she recalled all the times she'd doubted herself, thinking a simple farmer knew more about maintaining a keep than she did. Wily old Fallon. He would be steward again, of course. He was indeed the best person for the job. But she would settle a little score with him first.

She found Fallon in the courtyard speaking with Hamish and Loman. She smiled at them both. This was the first time she had seen either of them since their return and had missed their company. Hopefully with the reopening of the lower hall, they would see each other more often.

Hamish and Loman watched Laurel approach. She seemed annoyed by something at first, but then her expression changed when she saw them. Loman could feel Hamish melt beside him and realized that Finn had been correct to tell Hamish, Seamus, and himself to keep the rest of the guard away from her. Additionally, they were to keep their distance themselves.

Finn had made it easier by increasing the time spent training so that they practically fell into their beds come nightfall. But now, seeing Laurel with her hair cascading in waves past her waist in a new gown that seemed to accentuate the color of her eyes, Finn realized that none of his men would be sleeping tonight no matter how tired they were. The laird better come home and marry her or someone—much sooner than Conor realized—would be asking for her hand.

"Excuse me, gentlemen," Laurel nodded in acknowledgment and turned to Fallon. "Fallon, may I have a word with you, please?" And then proceeded to talk even though she knew the guardsmen were still in earshot.

"You have been a great help over the past few days in restoring areas of the keep. I have been thinking over the position of a castle steward. Do you know what a castle steward is?" she asked as innocently as possible.

"Aye, milady. I am aware of the position and its responsibilities."

"Oh, good. I was hoping you could help me train Scully as the castle steward."

Loman and Hamish looked at each other. Lady Laurel obviously did not know who Fallon was or of his temper. Fallon had sent many kitchen maids fleeing to their homes crying after being reprimanded.

"Scully? You want *me* to train *Scully*?" he asked incredulously, raising his voice.

"Yes. I think he would be an excellent steward." In honesty, he would be awful. He meant well, but he was forgetful and somewhat clumsy, unable to control his large mass in smaller confines. They had to restrict him to just the lower hall, lest he damage some of the items in the chapel and great hall while cleaning.

"He has the biggest heart, and he so wants to please. Do you not think these the two most important characteristics when looking for a castle steward?"

"You are out of your mind, lass, if you think Scully could make even a bad steward let alone a good one!" Fallon shouted, completely shaken. "Intent has nothing to do with being a steward. One has to be organized, capable of giving orders, making decisions, seeing what needs to be done and then doing it. A steward has to anticipate a laird's needs and then see to them before the laird knew he had them. He needs to know the whole castle, how each section is run and by whom so he can coordinate requests or prepare for unexpected guests. Scully has no idea about half the functions of this keep, let alone the ability to coordinate them!"

She sighed, completely unaffected by his short tirade. Loman and Hamish were about to jump to her defense when she raised a hand, warning them not to interfere.

"I suppose you are right. And I also suppose that next time you won't be keeping who you are, and what you are capable of, a secret from me, either, *steward*. While you did not deny you were this castle's steward, you did not disclose it either. You intentionally kept me in the dark. It gave you quite the upper hand when working with me. Of all the skills and traits you mentioned, you forgot honesty. Is it not just as important?"

Fallon was struck dumb. Hamish and Loman could not remember a time that Fallon was caught so securely in his own trap. It was a story that would be recounted many times in the winter and years to come.

Watching him just stand there mute, Laurel took pity on Fallon and decided to give him back some of his pride. "Well, Fallon? You know I need help and only you can provide it competently. I intend to address the bake house issues and the smithy today and would prefer to have your guiding hand by me when I do so."

Her announcement was enough to snap Fallon back to his normal self. "Aye, milady. You would do good to listen to me in these matters."

The guardsmen watched as she and the castle's steward sauntered back to the lower hall discussing next steps, staffing issues, and what not. She had not needed their help after all. She had never needed their help. The mystery about her grew in their minds as they stared at the lady who had stood up to the laird, convinced Fiona to be cook, and then intimidated Fallon.

Later that morning, Laurel, Glynis and Fallon went to investigate the problems with the bake house. Fiona had been very upset the past two evenings with the quality of the bread. The baker insisted that it was the fireplaces. By the time he got the stoneware hot enough to bake the bread, it was too hot, burning the outside of the loaf, making the piece so hard it was inedible.

To Laurel's surprise, the bake house was built into the cliff situated underneath most of the buildings across the northern and western walls. The halls and the kitchen only *seemed* to be on the first floor, when they were actually built atop rooms carved out of the cliff. It was an ingenious way to increase space while maintaining security.

She should have wondered and questioned it when she saw the floor of the great hall was made of timber instead of ground earth. The furthermost bottom floor extended from underneath the lower hall and kitchen, curved under the North Tower and ended at the Warden's Tower.

Mostly, the ground floor seemed to be used to store supplies and materials for the castle. She saw storage rooms containing many of the weapons and others with food. Laurel wondered if the curtain material was down here as well. Glynis and Brighid still refused to find any material for the chapel, claiming that her wardrobe was still not complete. She had argued and pleaded with them then finally gave in, realizing that the only way she would get her curtains was to finish the gowns.

The bake house was much smaller than she'd anticipated, considering most of the rooms and buildings were oversized compared to other keeps. It did have an arched roof and across the room there was a well-built door, strongly secured.

"It leads off to the dungeon," Glynis explained. "Not that we have any prisoners now, but those working down here were wanting to secure themselves against inmates with a solid door."

Laurel continued to look around. There was a drain to the outside, a fireplace, and a communicating drain to the main building. Fallon pointed to the fireplace chute, and Laurel saw that the baker was correct. The fireplaces were in an awful state. "This may take more men," she sighed.

"We will need to rebuild some of the stones around the hearth to help vent the smoke out of the room," Fallon added.

Laurel agreed, stating he should get whatever help he needed and make this the number one priority after the halls were done. The chapel could wait since there was no priest. They needed to eat.

That night, the lower hall opened, and the soldiers tumbled in preparing to eat with the lack of restraint they had been accustomed to in the past. However, by the night's end, the soldiers figured out that if they wanted to eat Fiona's wonderful meal—and they did—they had best learn to stand when a lady entered or left a room, keep their food from dropping onto the new rushes, and refrain from belching in Laurel's presence.

This was the first time many of the soldiers had a chance to meet the Scottish lady from England. The rumors of her demeanor and countenance had now spread throughout most of the clan.

At first, the soldiers were undone by her beauty. Then they fell in love with her spirit. By the time she had left the lower hall so they could finish their meal, every soldier would have done anything short of selling his soul to make her happy. If that meant standing when she left, so be it.

Without raising her voice, she could command a room just like their laird. Her regal bearing ensured respect. She could deny it, but the soldiers all believed she was going to be the next Lady McTiernay. It was largely this belief that prevented any of the men from approaching Laurel or contemplating asking for her hand . . . at least for now. But if Conor continued to refuse the idea of matrimony, there would soon be several battles over her.

Later, after stories about Laurel and Fallon had died, the lower hall buzzed with talk of the white angel that visited the McTiernay castle at night. Some had heard her sing, but most had just seen a waiflike vision in white. Every clear evening, the castle night guard increased in numbers to see the McTiernay angel dancing in the moonlight.

Chapter Eight

Conor was driving his mount hard. He had left Craig and Crevan behind with several of his guard once they had crossed the McTiernay border. He knew that it didn't make sense to ride at such a speed, but it had been two weeks and one day since he had seen Laurel. He wondered how she had fared with him gone. Had she been treated well? Had Finn been able to keep the men away? He urged his horse harder.

Finn would follow his orders, he reassured himself. Most likely, Laurel was going crazy cooped up in the keep with nothing to do. He knew she could act compliant and accepting, but it was not in her real nature to be so.

Highlanders were typically not a tolerant people. He had forgotten that fact when he had suddenly decided to leave with Cole for Schellden's. At the time, all he could think of was removing himself from Laurel's presence before he surrendered to the primal cravings he had been having since they first met.

Now, all he wanted was to return and see to her protection and her well-being for himself. Never again would he hand that responsibility to another. Only he could effectively protect her from his clan's naturally suspicious and hostile nature. As an outsider, especially an English one, Laurel had probably experienced several unkind words since he had left.

He crested another peak and crossed the plateau-like valley at a full gallop. He normally would have stopped at several of his clansmen's cottages to see how they were faring and receive any news. Members of his clan who lived this far out near the McTiernay borders rarely ventured close to the castle—especially during the winter months. But, today Conor did not even pause to say hello. The few who had seen his approach barely saw his wave of greeting before he disappeared.

When Conor rode into the castle courtyard, he jumped off his horse and looked around. He was trying hard to control his impulse to cry out for Laurel. Where was everyone? Usually his soldiers were training here at this hour, but it was unnaturally empty.

He then noticed Neal and some lad he recognized to be the son of Angus the farmer holding out his hand waiting for the reins of his horse. Neal issued instructions. "Take the laird's horse now and walk him a bit before you be brushing him just like I told you. I'll be along in a bit."

Neal turned to address his laird. "Aye, it's good to have you back, laird, although we were not expecting to see you for several more hours. News only just came of your homecoming. Lady Laurel will be most pleased of your return." *As soon as she gets over the shock,* Neal thought.

Conor began to relax. Just hearing that Laurel had thought of him and was waiting for him was enough to ease the tension that had been steadily mounting the past couple of weeks. He had not been aware until now how much he needed to hear that Laurel had missed him.

He wasn't alone, then.

Laurel had thought of him just as he had of her. Enough to pine to Neal about her missing him. Conor smiled to himself. What had he expected? Of course she would miss him. With the exception of his brothers and a couple of his guard, she knew no one. She was probably right now up in her chamber fervently wishing for his return.

"Bring Lady Laurel to me in the great hall," he said, smiling whimsically.

Turning to leave, Conor heard the clattering of hooves on the earth and saw a pleased Finn dismount and advance towards him. "Hope your travel was well, laird. If you are looking for Lady Laurel, you may have a long wait for she is not inside the castle walls."

Finn was not expecting his laird's swift and violent reaction and found himself looking up at the sky and at a furious face from the ground. "Explain . . . now," Conor growled so fiercely that everyone who had been coming to greet their laird and tell him of the keep's improvements immediately disappeared.

"She's fine, Conor. On this I swear." This got Finn a slight reprieve and the ability to sit up. He grabbed his tunic and rubbed his neck and shoulder, which had been the primary targets of Conor's attack. "You know that I would protect her with my life. And so would every other McTiernay man, woman and child."

"Why is she outside the castle walls? You were in charge of her protection while I was away," Conor charged, using anger to conceal the fear he was feeling.

"Good God, man, you told me to protect her, not to imprison her, which—even if you had—would have been highly difficult to achieve. You try detaining or instructing your lady. I do not think even your status of laird would be effective," Finn said, standing up carefully so as not to incur any more of his laird's anger.

"Finn, do not make me ask again, *where is Laurel?*"

"She's out riding Borrail, probably hunting tonight's food." He knew that Conor was not going to respond well to the news and that it was only the first of many shocks yet for him to endure.

"Neal! My horse—now!" Conor bellowed. *Hunting?* Why in the devil was Laurel hunting? He had men for that, or were they refusing to hunt because she was English? If that was the case, several clansmen were going wish otherwise before the hour was through.

"Conor. She is fine. She loves to hunt and is good at it. Despite her arguments, there is always a detail of soldiers riding with her," Finn tried to clarify while getting on his own horse.

"Why aren't the men providing the meat? Are they so weak that they need a woman to hunt for them? Or are they refusing to feed an Englishwoman?"

Finn had never seen Conor so angry and unwilling to listen to explanations. This was most unlike his laird. Lady Laurel was more important to Conor than anyone— including himself—had realized, thought Finn.

Finn needed Conor to slow down and think before he damaged more than just a shoulder. If he continued acting this way, all the plans and preparations Laurel had been making would be ruined. And if Laurel became upset, Aileen would also be unhappy. Finn would do anything to keep his wife happy, including taking the risk he was about to make.

"You are acting most unlike yourself, laird, to get so heated over a woman's welfare."

Those words got an instant reaction. Conor did not believe anyone in his army would challenge him. But the words Finn had just uttered were an insult, and his commander knew it. He stood frozen, glaring at the soon-to-be-ex-leader of his elite guard.

Finn saw his opportunity and quickly took advantage. "Laurel heard of your impending return and has been working with Fiona on a menu for your homecoming feast. Some of the meats are difficult to trap. It may take several hours to stalk and capture the prey. When she first told me of her abilities to hunt for the evening's meal, I also did not believe her. But Conor, she is highly skilled in highlander weaponry. Her accuracy—even when riding—is amazing. You saw what she could do with a dirk. I tell you all your men have fallen in love with her."

As soon as the last few words escaped his lips, Finn realized his folly once again. There would be no escape from Conor's anger now. He had tried, but Lady Laurel was on her own.

As they rode out towards the training field, Conor could see her sitting astride Borrail in between two guards, Loman and Hamish. They were facing away concentrating on some warriors in training, completely unaware of their approach.

Finn advanced to try one last time. "Before you take your anger out on either of your men, I specifically asked both Loman and Hamish to oversee her welfare while I went to meet you. It is the first and only time they have been alone with her without me in attendance."

Conor nudged his mount closer and overheard part of Laurel's conversation. He just sat for a moment, listening and staring at her unnoticed. Her long, pale hair was clean and shimmering in the afternoon sun. She had tied it back, but left it unbraided, giving opportunities for wisps of it to dance along her shoulders in the breeze. Her back was straight, and her bearing—even from this vantage point—showed elegance and quality. He was reminded once again how truly unique she was.

"Aye, lass, a soldier's choice of weapons, clothing, and horses are determined much by the speed he will need in battle," Loman was apparently answering her earlier question.

"But I have never seen any men wear armor while training. Does that not affect your ability to fight in it later?"

"Ah, milady, you're thinking like an English. Armor slows a man down and ruins his speed and accuracy. It is a hindrance and a burden in battle. Now some highlanders like to wear scarves wrapped around their necks for protection. But our laird believes it to be a waste of cloth. No scarf will prevent my broadsword cutting through a man."

Laurel shuddered at the image he drew.

"Besides, if you are trained right, you don't need it," Hamish chimed in. Over the past two weeks, his ardor for the lady had not faded. But the reality that she was not, nor ever would be his, had finally seeped through.

"Armor should be used to protect your horse. It's the soldier's responsibility to protect his own flesh," Loman added.

"Armor for your horse? That makes no sense."

"Depending on the type of battle, Laird McTiernay may order chains to be drawn four or five times around the thighs of the horses to help deflect spear thrusts," explained a grinning Hamish.

"But when do you use swords versus bows?"

"You forgot pikes, spears and daggers."

Loman moved his horse closer to her and directed her attention to a group of men in the distance practicing with long spears ranging from eight, twelve and sixteen feet in length.

"What is that metal staff for?" Laurel asked, pointing at a steel pole about four feet in length.

Conor stepped in and answered. "It is made of old sword blades. The slim edge provides a long cutting edge with a spike at the bottom for piercing. A deadly weapon. But its knowledge and intent should remain with soldiers, not proper ladies," he directed his last comment toward her companions more so than her.

"Conor!" Laurel spun around to see him. "You are back!" The joy on her face was unquestionable. She was a vision to his thirsty soul. His eyes raked her from the top of her golden head to the hem of her burgundy dress.

He wanted her. Badly.

"What are you doing out here, love? Finn told me you were hunting."

"I was. I sent someone ahead with our catches to Fiona. Oh, Conor. I am so glad you are back. We have done so much and I . . ." she paused, her eyes opening large, making her face appear small and fragile.

"What, Laurel? What's wrong? Did something happen?" Conor questioned as he saw her turn white. Obviously she remembered something dreadful.

"What are you doing here!" she shrieked and then turned to Finn. "You said it would be hours, mayhap days before he got here! I am not ready. I wanted to get everything arranged in the hall. There is so much to do!" she whirled her horse around, preparing to ride back to the keep. "Finn, you keep him away until it is time. I mean it, Finn!" she yelled as she prompted Borrail into a light run.

Conor easily caught up to her and pulled back on her reins to slow the pace. She tried to regain control and urge Borrail into a faster lope.

"If you do not halt your struggle for the reins, I will stop us both at once," he warned. She immediately withdrew, and Conor was instantly appeased. It seemed she was finally learning how far she could push him.

"Now, tell me what needs to be ready for my return," Conor began. "You are here, and Finn tells me my younger brothers are well. What could be prompting this foolish ride of yours?"

"Conor McTiernay, if you think to return home and call me foolish after all my hard work, you will have to think again."

"Return home! It's my castle!"

She pivoted slightly towards him while covertly trying to recapture the reins to Borrail. How could a man be so exasperating and so handsome at the same time, she asked herself. He wasn't wearing his tunic, just his kilt, sword, belt, and a shirt dyed with saffron. It was the same type of voluminous shirt all of his men wore when conducting mock battles. Some wore it flowing, but Conor had his heavily pleated to provide himself better protection. Laurel thought the pleats emphasized his strength and size.

She then looked into his silver-flinted eyes. They were sparkling with amusement, a complete contradiction to the rest of him, which was tight and rigid. He wants me to *think* he is angry so I will give in, she thought. She remembered how the man seemed to appreciate her backbone—in moderation. Well, he was in for a surprise.

"Your castle was not fit to live in when you left," she criticized, trying to sound forceful and in command. "You turned over your keep into my capable hands, and the results of your clansmen's efforts should be applauded." She then turned to look at him again so that he would know she was serious. "I wanted to celebrate their results with you, not have you casually walk through the keep acting unaware of their work."

"What makes you think I would not appreciate the work of my clan?"

"Clyde."

He waited for her to explain, but she refused to offer anything more. What had his brother said to convince her he would not appreciate whatever she had done?

They rode on in silence. Just before they crossed the barbican and entered the castle walls, Laurel stopped and beseeched him for several moments with her eyes. Whatever she was about to ask, he was going to say yes. When her eyes turned that smoky sea blue he could think of nothing else. He so very much wanted to make her happy.

"Conor," she began. They approached the keep, her resolve dissipating quickly. "I . . . I just . . ." She tried again. "Please do not get upset. I realize that I may have overstepped my authority, but everyone was so supportive. Your castle is so grand, and it just didn't reflect your status as a powerful laird."

His heart began to stammer. She was wringing her hands, clearly worried about his upcoming reaction to something she did to his home. "Tell me exactly what to expect," he demanded.

Her eyes were very wide as she searched his face. "Oh, I couldn't. I just couldn't spoil the surprise."

He started to question her, but then he noticed her lips—soft, full, and slightly parted. He wanted so badly to kiss her; he couldn't think straight.

Before rational thought took hold, he grabbed her and pulled her onto his horse, not caring how his action would appear to others. He smoothed her hair back and tucked it behind her ears. Her lashes framed her eyes and caught the tears forming in them.

He stroked her cheek to calm her fears. "Laurel, just tell me what you did. I promise not to be angry, love. Did you tear down a building or erect a new one?"

She loved the feeling of being in his arms again. He felt strong and sure, warm and safe. She knew she should respond and answer his question, but at that moment she could think of nothing else but the last time he kissed her. How she wanted him to kiss her again. The craving was almost unbearable. Only the ingrained rules of propriety kept her from throwing her arms around him and drawing his lips down to hers.

Conor, however, did not have such rules restraining him. Her mouth was slightly open, and she was breathing more rapidly. He could feel her heart beating against his chest. Time and distance had done nothing to diminish the attraction he felt for her. It was almost tangible, it felt so strong and powerful. The yearning he had worked so hard to suppress for the past two weeks heated his blood.

He gave into his desires and lowered his head until his lips were against hers. She responded instantly, slanting her head to give him better access. He kissed her gently, exhibiting great restraint. Her lips parted beneath his gently persuasive mouth. His tongue probed her warmth, twirling, darting in and out.

Shy only at first, Laurel started to imitate his movements. Her hands gripped his shoulders drawing him closer and closer. She couldn't get enough. The kiss kindled a fire within her, sparking something primitive and completely feminine deep within her. A groan came rolling up from somewhere, and only after several seconds did Laurel realize it was her. She didn't understand her primal reaction, but only wanted more of what he was doing to her.

Conor was about to explode with need at Laurel's innocent but passionate responses. She melted in his arms. Her
low moans and sighs fueled him further. He wanted
more—needed more. He reached down and cupped her
breast, flicking his thumb across her clothed nipple reveling in its response. He could feel her complete submission to him and was reaching down to discover what was
underneath her skirts when he heard horses approaching.

Conor abruptly ended the kiss and gently shook
Laurel into awareness again. God, she was beautiful. He
looked down at her trying to regain awareness while
bringing her out of a state of heavy passion. He then realized how close he had been to losing all control. He
couldn't do this. Marriage was not for him. Laurel was
not for him. He acknowledged the desire, but not where
it was leading. He would make a commitment to no
woman.

"Ho! Conor! Is Lady Laurel all right?" Craig asked, approaching from behind. He could see his brother shielding Laurel for a moment before placing her back on her
gray steed.

Laurel was once again mortified. Ashamed at her lack
of self control, ashamed at primitive desires, but mostly
she was ashamed at her behavior after all the promises
she had made to herself. The plan was to be polite, but
aloof, to be friendly while remaining at a safe physical distance. How, then, did she end up in his arms again within
an hour of his return?

Still beet-red from her indiscretions, she responded to
Craig over her shoulder while easing Borrail towards the
castle gate. "I am perfectly fine, Craig. It is nice to see you
again, Seamus. You too, Crevan." She waved a hand at
them without actually looking in their direction. She
needed just a few minutes to regain her composure.

Entering the keep, Laurel made an effort towards nor-
malcy. "I was just about to ask your laird a favor," she said
to Craig as she dismounted.

"From his lap, milady?"

"She was falling off her horse," Conor fabricated, trying to divert their assumptions. It was clear that he was also not inclined to advertise what had happened. In fact, he looked like he wished it had not occurred at all. Was she understanding him correctly? Was Conor regretting their kiss?

They were in the courtyard now. She slid off Borrail and led him towards the stables. Clyde ran out to gather her horse and put him up for the night.

"Clyde? What are you doing in the stables?" Conor asked incredulously. He had been trying to get Clyde and his younger brothers to take on some responsibilities with the keep for years.

"It was Laurel's idea. She wanted Neal to have someone to help and . . . and becooth?"

"Bequeath," Laurel said, correcting him.

"Aye, bequeath. For Neal to bequeath his knowledge to the younger generation." Clyde smiled at his ability to restate all the large words he had heard Laurel use when convincing Neal to take Clyde as one of his first charges. "What that really means is that I get to learn all about horses. I get to ride them, brush them, and be with them every day. It's my job! Neal says it is really important and that if I learn it well, I will be a better soldier and guardsman someday."

Conor looked at his younger brother who plainly desired his encouragement and support. "Neal, teach him well. If he shirks his duties, let me know."

"Aye, he's a good lad, laird. Quick and eager to learn, too. He has worked well with your lady's mount. He won't be a-shirking any duties, and if he does, well, Fallon and I will be doing the correcting." Neal was testing the waters now. Would the laird allow them to run the keep as before?

"Clyde?" Conor looked intently at his younger brother.

"Aye, Con . . . I mean, laird?" he corrected himself, catching Neal's disapproving eye. Neal had been instructing him in the ways of respect and loyalty. It was true Conor was

Clyde's brother, but more important—especially when on duty—he was Clyde's laird. That demanded deference and proper recognition.

"I suggest you mind Neal and do what he says. For it appears if you don't, you will have bigger worries than myself. You will have Fallon to explain to and appease." The old stable master smiled and helped lead the horses back into their stalls.

"Neal?" called out Laurel. "You won't be forgetting about tonight?"

"No, milady, I won't be forgetting. And after tonight, I doubt me laird will either," he called over his shoulder trying unsuccessfully to keep his amusement from being too obvious.

This was getting ridiculous, Laurel muttered to herself. Referring to her as if she was Conor's woman and now this. She needed to make it clear to Conor and everyone that she was *not* the laird's lady.

Laurel turned back to Conor, forgetting that Crevan and Craig were standing just behind him with Seamus. She lowered her voice and said, "Conor McTiernay, don't you ever kiss me again like that. Did you tell your men that we were getting married? For they are under the impression that we are, constantly referring to me as the laird's lady everywhere I turn."

Conor was caught by surprise. Was she trying to trap him into a proposal? He had learned this trick several years ago and was on to such schemes.

"No, Laurel. I have told you before that I will never marry," he said loudly through gritted teeth.

She gasped, her mouth hanging open. Her response of indignation just fueled his temper. "I will not be asking you nor anyone else—no matter what games you play!" he bellowed so that all could hear.

Laurel's chin came up angrily, her turquoise eyes sparkling with rage. "I don't think *you* understand, Laird McTiernay," she shouted in return. "It is *I*, not you, who is deciding that there is nothing between us. You may have never asked, but I promise you that if you did, I would say NO! I would never marry you! And furthermore, you big hulking brute of a man, *when* I marry it will be to someone who is chivalrous, polite and thoughtful. Certainly not to a yelling giant who runs his manor in disorganized filth. He will be of a normal height and size and act as a gentleman!"

"Then you will marry a weak, feeble, short, pathetic ENGLISHMAN!" he roared back. It did not matter that he didn't want to marry her. But the idea that she would rather marry some future sap was intolerable.

"I will not marry an Englishman! I'm going to marry a Scot and . . ." She was about to finish her retort, but realized a large crowd had been gathering outside the buildings and on the curtain walls surrounding the courtyard.

Oh Lord, he had done it to her again. Would she never learn to control her conduct around him? These people must think her senseless to be accusing Conor of being less than gentlemanly after he rescued her and gave her shelter. Instantly her composure returned, just as if the last exchange had never taken place.

Sweetly, she said aloud, "I must go now and get ready. But promise me that you will not change a thing until we have discussed it." She paused and whispered so that only he could hear, "And you will not let a single person here know if you are displeased with the results." She was acting so sweet, no one would have guessed she possessed the fiery temper she had just displayed. "Remember, they did all of it for you. They love you, Conor, please remember that."

And then she left, disappearing into the Star Tower, not staying to hear whether he agreed to the promise or not. He was still reeling from their exchange and then her complete change in disposition. One moment she was full of fury and the next, she was pleasant and ingenuous. Only her large eyes could not hide the hurt she was feeling.

He was still unsure about her reference to keep

changes. But he did pick up on the fact that Fallon was back to work, most likely resuming his old duties. He was going to find the old buzzard and ferret out what had been taking place at his keep. Only then would he decide whether or not he would be "changing things."

Conor was sitting in the great hall, observing his soldiers and clansmen recalling the day's events. Laurel still had not arrived, but in the few hours that had passed since she departed he had learned much.

Fallon had deftly maneuvered him into a bath and dressed him for an elaborate evening celebration. While bathing, Conor was able to get his "reinstated" steward to tell him some of the transformations that had been made since he left two weeks ago.

Laurel had accomplished a miracle in direct defiance of his wishes, it seemed. Several years ago he tried to teach appreciation and the value of their clansmen's help to his brothers by removing all support from their daily lives. Unfortunately, that resulted in a keep not fit for living. Rather than admit his error or undo a command, Conor had allowed only work necessary to the maintenance of the structural integrity of the castle to be performed.

When Fallon told him that Laurel had *knowingly* reversed his long-standing command and had re-established order at the keep, he instantly realized why she had been nervous. And she was correct to feel so. Who did she think she was? He wanted to confront her immediately, but his annoyance was so intense he decided to calm down first.

Later, after he had met with Finn, he realized his own folly. Finn reminded him of Laurel's warning. But when Conor began to bellow that she didn't have his permission to make changes and what right did she have to hire staff and clean his manor, Finn could stand no more.

"Now I respect you, laird, more than anyone I know. And I would follow you into battle defending yours and any McTiernay under any circumstances. But I cannot continue to listen to you disavow your own promises."

"Those are not mere words, Finn, and you had best remember that I would kill a man for saying that I don't keep my word." A quiet calm overcame Conor at that moment. His frustration and anger over Laurel and her ministrations had been loud and alarming. But the quiet composure he was demonstrating now was terrifying.

"Then I guess it wasn't you who said she could make the place livable. So all of us misunderstood you the night in the courtyard before you left, when you agreed that the keep was not habitable in its current condition." Finn leaned back against the stone wall, waiting for Conor to understand the trap she had created for him.

Conor fought the realization, insisting she was just being invasive and underhanded to achieve her goal.

"And what goal would that be, laird?" Finn replied, getting a little irritated with Conor's refusal to see what was around him.

"Revenge, pure and simple. She said I would rue the day and I do. But I assure you that my revenge will be doubly as sweet."

"I have never seen you react so recklessly, laird. But I guess there is always that one woman who can make a man act such a way one time or another in their lives."

Conor shot him a look that would have made most men drop to their knees quivering in fear.

"Take a look around you!" Finn insisted. "It is not revenge you see, but love. Aye, love! Do you know how hard she has worked and prepared for your return? Look at her hands, and you will find roughened skin. She was not ordering people blithely about, Conor, but helping. Have you not wondered how and why your people have taken her—an Englishwoman—so quickly and securely under their wing? Every day she went to work helping, organizing, cleaning, and fixing this place she called *your* home. That's right—your home.

"She made decisions that many would shrink away

from. She began repairs on cottages for the winter; she gave jobs to those who wanted them. Your lady took the time to get to know your clansmen and their problems so that she could better balance castle requirements and your people's needs. Not just for safety, but she gave them something that no one seemed to realize they were missing. Their pride.

"I will tell you this, Conor. You can yell, protest, and object to all the changes Laurel has made, but I wouldn't do it in front of anyone besides Fallon and myself. Your clansmen are loyal to you, but they are now very loyal to your lady as well."

Conor sat back, absorbing all that Finn had said. It was only after he recollected how his people had acted toward her that his anger truly dissipated enough to allow him to appreciate the changes that had been made. He had really worried that she would be not accepted. Instead, she was both loved and respected.

"But she's English?" Conor questioned, giving voice to his confusion.

"Aye, she's that. But Glynis, the day after you left, discovered that Laurel is half Scot and has spread the word. Your men and women do not view Laurel as an English-woman, but as one of their own. Her command of our tongue has doubly won them over."

Conor had forgotten about her ability to speak Gaelic. He had meant to ask her where she had learned to speak the Celtic language, but had forgotten to inquire about it. Was she really a Scot?

"Did Laurel say she was a Scot?"

"I do not think so. I believe it was one of Glynis's conclusions that she so likes to conjure up. At the time, it seemed like a good rumor that would serve to help Laurel blend in here so I did nothing to counter the observation. But in this case, I think Glynis may have been right."

The pieces did fit, Conor inwardly concurred. She had admitted that she intended to marry a Scot. And he knew that, while she had spoken the truth about what had happened to her, she had not disclosed the whole story.

Conor continued to mull over the possibilities of her heritage that evening as the celebration began. He saw and mentally approved many of the changes Laurel had made in the halls alone. The changes in the lower hall were astounding. Previously, he refused to enter the foul room so misused by his men and brothers. Now it was clean and with new padding and curtains.

The great hall had also been cleaned, with the furniture rearranged so that people could enter and exit at ease. The room was filled with a nice fragrance from the new rushes lining the floor. The hearths radiated heat without smoking up the room.

An incredible banquet of food was spread out on the tables. There was the typical venison, goose, rabbit, and hare. Yet the kitchen must have been working busily all day, for also available were wild boar and a roasted peacock, served with all its feathers as decoration. Several other birds also adorned the table including doves, larks, thrushes, and blue-tits. Finn pointed out that several of the meats prepared were caught by Laurel earlier that day.

Many times he had met with allied leaders here, wishing that he had more to offer them. Now, he possessed a keep to make any laird proud. The men seemed happier and well-behaved. Even his brothers were having a great time, taking care not to appear slovenly or undisciplined.

Conor noticed that when he ordered the meal to be brought out, it was done so reluctantly. When he asked about it, it was Finn's wife, Aileen, who spoke bluntly.

"What do you expect, laird?" she asked, her tawny-colored hair swaying lightly as she shook her head. She was not a petite woman, but her small feminine facial features made her appear so, despite being large with child. Her light brown eyes usually shined with merriment, but tonight they were full of admonishment. "It was your Lady Laurel who made all this come to pass. It was because of her vision and willingness to see it through that you are even having this wonderful feast. How many people do you know who can persuade Fiona to do anything? But Lady Laurel convinced her to cook for you permanently, she did."

Fallon had not told him about that and Conor wondered what else the crafty steward had left out. Fiona's cooking was legendary. And so was her temper, but Laurel had managed to find a way. His thoughts were interrupted by his youngest brother, Clyde. Sometimes it was the innocent who made things the most clear.

"Aye, everybody would do *anything* for Lady Laurel. She even tricked Fallon, and good. Now she and him are best friends. I even overheard Fallon and several soldiers say that they would protect her from even you." Clyde bit down on a piece of meat and started tearing it off. "Why would they say that, Conor? Don't they know you would never hurt her? That you took her from the bad people and brought her here to be protected?" he asked sincerely.

Conor was saved from responding when a loud toast across the room got his youngest brother's attention. The comprehension of Clyde's words hit him hard. Everyone spoke in awe of her. They defended her and worked hard to ensure that she felt welcome.

This revelation affected him deeply. He wanted his people to like her. He wanted her to feel comfortable and contented at his keep. Then why was he troubled with the amount of love and loyalty she had commanded in his people in such a short amount of time? The question smacked of possessiveness, and he didn't like it, but he also didn't like the idea of another man receiving Laurel's kind words of adoration and gratitude. Those belonged to him.

Several gasps around the room caught his attention. Clyde was overtly staring at something with his jaw wide open. He looked around to see what had captured his younger brother's interest. When he saw her, Conor forced himself to breathe evenly. Heaven had sent down an angel to be in their midst, and her name was Laurel Cordell.

Earlier, Laurel thought about withdrawing from tonight's events. Her chambers were only one floor below Conor's, and she heard much of his bellowing about her betrayal and revenge.

She had hoped that he would not see the changes that way. But then, somewhere deep inside her, she had recognized that with Conor, this would most likely be his first reaction. Hopefully, after some time passed, he would appreciate the improvements and change his mind, she prayed silently.

She thought about his reaction and statements throughout the entire afternoon as she bathed, dressed and did her hair for the evening. Brighid had come in while she tried unsuccessfully to tie the thick waves of hair back with combs.

"Lady Laurel? I think you should just leave your hair down. Leave it long so that it will shine and sparkle. Aye, that would be an excellent way of catching our laird's eye this evening." Brighid winked at her as she plucked the combs from Laurel's fingertips.

Laurel admonished her again for implying that there was more to her relationship with Conor than there was.

"Aye, milady," was all Brighid would reply. But Brighid had seen the interaction between the two earlier that day. She had seen the sparks fly, just like most of the others in the keep. If the laird and his lady wanted to still pretend otherwise, it was none of her business. But she was not fooled.

Laurel did decide to leave her hair down, telling herself that it only helped flatter her dress more. The gown that Brighid had made for this evening was quite stunning. The deep blue bliaut had a crushed dark velvet top that cut straight across her breasts and ended at her waist. It was trimmed in elegant beadwork that Brighid excelled in creating. Matching the trim was a beaded crystal choker that complemented the color of her gown. The necklace was four strands and at the bottom it gracefully draped, making it a very feminine feature.

The long flowing sleeves of the gown were made of a sheer blue-green gossamer that matched the top layer of the skirt. The skirt's under layer was of a lightweight material that caught and reflected firelight. Brighid thought the only thing missing to make the dress perfect was the McTiernay plaid. She tried for some time to change Laurel's mind, but when Brighid left to ready herself for the night's festivities, Laurel was still refusing to put it on.

As Laurel entered into the great hall, she heard the gasps and whispers. Only pride forced her forward into the hall.

Once Conor noticed Laurel at the other end of the room, he could not take his eyes off of her. He felt as if he had just been struck by lightning. For a few seconds, he was too stunned to do anything but stare at her. Her pale gold hair was long and loose, framing her feminine features like a halo. The color of her dress accentuated the blue hue in the turquoise of her eyes, giving them warmth and power.

Her dress revealed her shapely body and hung loosely from her hips, the material swaying pleasingly as she walked. She wore slippers that matched her gown, unlike so many highlander women who opted to go barefoot, even in the cold winter months. The overall effect was incredible causing a rush of desire to grow within him.

He watched as one after another of his people gathered around her to acknowledge her and her accomplishments. He saw and heard how she gracefully refocused the ownership of the improvements back to his people.

After seeing this transfer of love between his clansmen and her, he realized that despite what Finn, Fallon, and even Laurel had said, his people didn't make all these changes for him—they did it for her. They loved her. Just as he did.

He rose and walked over to meet her, joining the rest of her admirers. When she saw him, her heart fluttered for a moment. Gone was the anger she had heard echoing in the halls earlier. All that remained were admiration and affection in his eyes.

He clutched her hand and guided her forward to a chair next to his at the end of the hall. He kept her close to him in case she wavered, fearing that she would decline to eat with him. But she calmly followed him to the table and sat next to Clyde when Conor resumed his seat at the end.

Laurel had tried hard to suppress her feelings when Conor came to meet her. He was dressed magnificently in a long tunic with wide hanging sleeves and a short, elaborately decorated jacket. Unarmed, he was bare-legged and bare-footed. It was funny, she thought, that two months ago, seeing a man in his bare feet would have struck her as inappropriate and offensive. Now all she could think of was how all the more attractive that made him appear.

Laurel secretly observed Conor throughout the evening. She marveled at how the light played against his dark hair and tanned skin. His silver eyes sparkled with merriment as he listened to his brothers relate new and old stories. She could not imagine any man more attractive or sexually appealing.

She smiled and prompted light conversation about his trip to Laird Schellden's. Unsurprisingly, it was Craig who did most of the talking, constantly adding humorous stories about Cole and his first few days as a guardsman. Her laughter was like a beacon of light to all who could hear, making them gravitate towards her like moths to a candle. After a while, she proclaimed it time for dancing and ordered some of the trestles to be dismantled to make room.

Dooly was the first to come and ask her for a reel, to which she heartily agreed. It seemed to Conor that every man in the room was watching Laurel dance and waves of jealousy began to flow through him. He felt extremely possessive, and he knew the feeling wouldn't go away anytime soon. Probably never.

Once that reel ended another began, and someone stepped in to have the next dance. And so it went for the next few hours. Men—young and old, short and tall, thin and wide—kept asking her to dance. She said yes to them all, never turning down a single soul, smiling and laughing, innocently compelling every man to fall in love with her.

While watching the men succumb to her new friend's natural charms, Finn's wife decided to play matchmaker. Finn had tried to dissuade Aileen from coming tonight, thinking a woman due to deliver her first child at any moment had no business coming to a party. But Aileen had refused to listen to him. Finn shook his head at his pretty wife, but she just ignored him and sat down beside Conor, feigning innocence.

"What an absolute triumph of an evening. Is it not?" Aileen was not at all discouraged when Conor did not respond.

"I suspect that you will be quite busy in the next few weeks," Aileen smiled at no one in particular. "I have overheard at least a dozen men wondering how to approach you to ask for her hand. Have you considered how you are going to decide? Among the suitors, I mean." She played with the ribbon on the sleeves of her gown, still looking innocently into the crowd.

"She really is lovely. At first, everyone thought she was destined to be yours. But then when you both so strongly denied the idea—well, I guess that has given hope to several men who have had the chance to make her acquaintance. I know that I fell under her spell when we met. I felt like I had known her all my life. It's no wonder we became fast friends. I hope that I like whomever you choose for her husband. I wonder if she will decide to wait until spring or get married immediately?"

Aileen smiled and clapped her hands. "Well, I must be off. I promised Finn that I would not stay up late tonight." Conor cast her a sidelong glance as she rose and left the hall with Finn talking animatedly to her about something.

He knew what Aileen was doing. He had known Finn's wife for years, and her intentions had become fairly obvious about two sentences into her rehearsed speech. He wondered if Laurel had put her up to it, but then thought that most unlikely. Much of what Aileen had said had actually already occurred to him as he watched men flock to Laurel's side. So far, he had been able to keep his distance and he intended to continue to stay away.

He swallowed a large amount of ale. Behind him were several men by the hearth discussing the servant woman who was responsible for keeping their mugs full.

"She smiled at me!"

"Aye, she smiled, but it was at me," said another.

"I could dance with her all the evening. She smelled like fresh flowers in the spring. Ahh, I could die a happy man if she were near."

Conor continued to listen as they listed the lady's attributes, still believing it was the pretty little serving wench who had their attention. He had seen all three of them dance with the servant several times. It wasn't until he heard them argue about the color of the woman's eyes that he realized the true object of their affection.

All of them were in love with Laurel.

They, too, could not decide whether her eyes were a deep blue with green accents like the colors of the sea, or more green than blue, like their highland lochs.

He moved towards one of the ravine-sided windows to view the night's landscape and tried to restrain the seed of jealousy growing quickly within. Conor knew that he was being unreasonable. Laurel was not flirting or making sexual overtures. But when he overheard another group of soldiers discussing her future, something snapped.

They were arguing about who should ask for her hand in marriage since the laird was clearly not interested in making Laurel his lady. Aileen was right. Soon, a steady stream of men would be approaching him for her hand. How was he going to handle it?

Everyone had noticed that Conor had not once asked Laurel to dance. Some inferred that it meant the rumors were true—he did not want her. Others were still not convinced.

The soldiers were debating which of them Laurel had liked the most. In light of Conor's declarations of non-commitment, they were ready to step into the role of husband and protector. Conor fought to remain calm and unaffected, but when someone mentioned how full and ripe for kissing Laurel's lips were, Conor lost control.

He did not remember what he had roared to clear the room so quickly. Within minutes everyone had vanished, leaving only Laurel staring at him.

"Stop glaring at me, Conor. It was you who so rudely ordered everyone out of the castle walls. What caused you to act out so? And why must I remain behind?"

"We need to talk."

Laurel's mouth tightened. "What about? Your attitude this evening, perchance? You didn't dance with anyone. You just sat all night looking solemn, refusing to speak with a single person besides Finn or your brothers. I saw how you ignored poor Aileen earlier, driving her to leave early."

Conor's mouth twisted humourlessly. "So you noticed me this evening? I thought that near impossible through your crowd of admirers."

Shock, then outrage overcame Laurel. "Crowd of admirers . . . ? Conor McTiernay, if you have a point, make it quickly before I lose my temper."

He walked up right up next to her and grasped her arms to keep her from leaving. "What were you trying to do, Laurel? How many men were you hoping to get to ask for your hand? All of them? You may have to call another event and invite the castle guards to ensure that all have seen and been enchanted by your beauty."

Hot, furious tears burned her eyes. "Well, as long as you are not among them. You are the most insufferable man. I don't know why I even wanted you here."

"Why did you, Laurel? Did you want me to see the loyalty you command? Was it important to you that I know how much and by how many you are loved?"

"Loved? Loyalty? Conor, if they respect me at all it is only because of you!" She choked back a sob. "Why are you so angry? We did all of this for you!" She sniffled and whispered, "I wanted to do this for you." Tears started flowing now.

Conor was undone and wiped the falling droplets of water away with his thumb. "Why would you want to do anything for me, Laurel? I thought you wanted revenge for making you stay at the castle instead of the cottage."

She looked down and her long dark eyelashes rested against her cheeks. "I didn't mean it. I just didn't want to feel any more beholden to you." She looked up. "But then I saw how I could help you. I could give you your back your castle. I could change it into something befitting your status and make it a place where you could proudly entertain your friends and allies."

As he looked into her eyes, all the jealousy and resentment that had filled him so completely just moments ago vanished. Her lips were full and moist from her tears. Her eyes were wide and inquisitive, her emotions accentuating their color. The feel of her skin was smooth and cool. The overall effect was intoxicating.

"You did help. I should have done something about the halls a long time ago."

"Then why were you so angry?"

His voice was deep and affected, husky with desire. "You are mine, Laurel, and it is time I stop pretending otherwise. I do not want other men lusting after you. I found out tonight that the idea of someone else kissing you, touching you, was unacceptable."

Her mouth opened to respond but was stopped by his own. He kissed her slowly, lingeringly, with a deep, tender possessiveness. It was a soft kiss that told of longing and affection. The sheer emotion behind it made Laurel weak, forcing her to rely on his strength to remain standing. A moan escaped her lips followed by a groan of his own.

Her hands stole up his back and entwined themselves in his hair. She unconsciously held his head down to her own, increasing the fervor of their kiss. He flicked his tongue against her lips, and she immediately opened her mouth and welcomed him in. Capturing his tongue and drawing it into her mouth, she longed for something more. Her lower abdomen was tightening with some unknown need.

The inside of her mouth was warm and welcoming, just as before. He gave a low, frustrated groan before releasing her lips. She arched in his arms, and he started a trail of kisses along her cheek and neck. He inhaled deeply. Her elusive, womanly scent tugged at his insides, arousing a powerful need deep within him.

Never had any woman affected him like this. He lost time and self-control when she was in his arms. No other person, responsibility or care was as important. All he wanted was more of her.

Conor effortlessly spun her around and pinned her against the stone wall with his hands on her shoulders, his hips pressed to her abdomen. As his lips came down, almost touching hers, he vowed, "You are mine, Laurel. Now and forever."

Laurel shuddered in response. Conor's mouth closed over hers again while his hands, warm and strong, caressed her breasts. She arched her back, giving him easier access. As he felt her nipples stiffen through her gown, his manhood grew even harder with desire. She groaned his name. He picked her up, went to his chair near the hearth, and placed her stretched out on his lap all the while continuing his assault on her senses.

He removed her slippers, slipped his hand underneath her skirts and started exploring her soft bare legs. "Just let me touch you, love. I need to touch you—need to feel you." And then his lips again covered her own.

His mouth was everywhere—in and around her ear creating pulses of desire between her legs. She was vaguely aware that she was clutching at him now, lifting herself, straining for a more intimate touch. She was in another world of his creation, and she never wanted to leave.

He wanted to explore every morsel of her body, touch every inch of her flesh, and know each sensitive spot. Skin had never felt so smooth and soft. He craved to see her in the throes of ecstasy and know that he was the one who brought her there.

He slowly moved the sleeves of her dress down her shoulder until her breasts were revealed. Somewhere in the back of her mind, she knew that she should stop him. Never in her life had she dreamed that the physical sensations he was building within her existed. Yet, she didn't want to stop him, couldn't stop him.

He had freed both her breasts, but had not moved to touch them. Instead his mouth was ravaging hers, leaving her breathless and wanting more at the same time. Finally, after an eternity, his hands so very lightly touched the silky mounds, slowly caressing their rosy nipples. She gasped at his touch. His hands were rough and hard and felt so very good. Nothing could feel better than this, she thought. And then he increased his intensity.

The need was growing within him, but he held himself back. Her untutored responses were like fuel to a raging fire. He wanted so much to give her pleasure and bring her to passion's end. She needed to know that she was his and no one else's. When tonight was over, the thoughts of leaving him or marrying another would be forever erased.

Laurel thought nothing in the world could increase her pleasure, and then his mouth covered her breast. His tongue flickered over and over the nipple bringing it to a peak. Her hands were now grabbing and grazing his back as waves of pleasure coursed through her. His fingers went back to her leg and stroked her inner thigh, matching the rhythm of his tongue on her breast.

His hand stole up to the juncture of her thighs, and her body went rigid. "Conor, no." But she soon went limp again as he kissed her feverishly, pushing her back into a state of pure sensation. Then his hand began stroking her, artfully easing her legs farther apart.

"You are so soft, so warm, so tight. I have never felt the like. You are truly one of a kind, Laurel, my love."

He inhaled the scent of her, part perfume and part feminine arousal, and he knew she would be moist and welcoming. He brought his hand up her leg until he was inches from the hot, damp core of her. Then, with a low, husky groan, he found her.

When his fingers penetrated her, she caught her breath and froze. Seconds later, her eyes popped open and she went to move his hand.

"Shhh, love." He slowly moved his fingers in and out with his thumb rubbing her sensitive nub. "Trust me. I would never hurt you, you know that. Trust me and let me show you how it will be between us."

"I do trust you, Conor. More than I have ever trusted anyone. But . . . oh . . . Lord . . ." The rest was lost as he continued rubbing and moving his fingers in and out faster and faster.

Tears were flowing again, but this time of pleasure. He was teasing her. She was going mad, but pleading for more.

"Please, please don't stop. Please . . ."

"I won't, love. I promise I will never stop. Just let go and let it take you over. That's it."

Laurel felt the world beginning to spin. His touch, his mouth, were all building to an uncontrollable release. She gasped, arching her neck back, clutching at him, twisting his tunic in her fists. Her muscles clenched and unclenched in small spasms, her entire body trembling. She knew she was going to explode, that she couldn't take any more.

And then suddenly, the heavens opened up and spilled over her body. The sensations rippling through her were like none other. All reason left. The experience was a mysterious, beautiful gift, and it was Conor who had given it to her.

She slowly regained awareness of her surroundings. She was in the great hall sitting in Conor's lap sprawled over him in the most immodest way. Her face was buried in his chest with her arms encircling him, holding him as close as possible. Her breathing was still heavy and her heart pounded so loudly she thought she could hear its echo in the hall. His hand was still under her dress supporting her while she tried to understand what had just happened.

Her scent was intoxicating, he thought, inhaling the mixture of flowers and Laurel's essence. He could feel her heart racing in unison with his. So much of what they just shared he couldn't explain. He had only wanted one thing—for her to receive satisfaction from him. When had he ever placed a woman's pleasure above his? Although he hadn't come to full release, he'd been close. Nonetheless, nothing he had ever experienced, not even with women most skilled in sexual pleasures, had ever been this good.

He had never imagined that giving pleasure to someone as innocent as Laurel would be so much better than receiving it from anyone else. He hugged her close and righted her sleeves. She still held on to him as if he were a safety line in the deepest of blizzards. She needed him, he thought to himself, completely satisfied.

"Conor, what just happened? I couldn't stop myself. I didn't want to stop myself. It is all so strange. I don't know what to do."

Her soft cry for understanding tore at his heart. He raised her head from his chest and kissed her softly, reassuringly.

"You don't have to do anything. You were just loved, by me. And you don't ever have to stop yourself with me, Laurel. We will have plenty of chances to do this again and again." Especially when the winter nights get cold, he mused. His fear of marriage and commitment had totally disappeared, leaving only a desire to possess her every night for the rest of his days.

"We will? I don't understand, Conor. This wasn't proper. We should never do this again. Since we cannot seem to restrain ourselves, we should just stay away from each other."

The words she sputtered were incredibly naïve, he thought, as he picked her up and began to carry her towards the Star Tower. Still in a dreamlike state, she laid her head on his shoulder and asked, "Why is it when you are around me I can no longer think or behave properly? I'm either a raving shrew or some wanton woman unable to keep her hands off of you." Even at that moment her hands were stroking his back as he carried her up the stairs to her chambers.

"It's because you're a Scot, Laurel," he said softly, as he entered her chambers and placed her on the bed.

But no other words could have brought her out of her reverie faster than those. How did he find out? Did he know her grandfather? Had she inadvertently let it slip?

He saw her grow tense, but was puzzled by it.

"I . . . I . . . I am not a Scot, Conor," she said, trying to sound convincing. She got off the bed and stared directly at him.

"Aye, but you are, Laurel. Or at least you will be once Father Lanaghly arrives." He smiled, trying to make her feel more at ease. However, Laurel's thoughts were now focused on what he knew of her grandfather and whether she had placed the MacInnes clan in greater jeopardy.

"Father Lanaghly cannot change the facts," she said, walking over to the window to gaze out into the night's sky. It was clear and cold. Soon winter's snows would be upon them.

Conor watched Laurel as she struggled with some internal battle. "Oh, but he can and will, love. And not a moment too soon."

She whirled around. "But how? I mean, what does a priest have to do with anything?"

His gaze was warm and possessive. "Much, if we are to be married."

"Married!" she exclaimed. "But I cannot marry you! I must leave. I cannot stay. I cannot," she cried out in desperation.

Reacting to the plea in her voice, he advanced and demanded, "Why, Laurel? Why not? Why can't you marry me?" He sensed her reason was related to the missing piece of her story. She was afraid of something, someone. He deeply wanted to be the one she ran to for protection. It was painful watching her mentally retreat—to know that she would turn elsewhere for assistance.

"Is there someone else? Is that it?" She could hear the fear in his voice and had to end his pain. She reached out to grab his arms.

"No, no! Conor, how could you think that? There will never be anyone but you—like that." She was panicking now. She framed his face in her hands. "But please, don't ask me to marry you. I thought you didn't want marriage, commitment, or anyone who tied you down." Her blue-green eyes held his silver ones, urging him to understand and accept.

He pulled her hands down and began to unconsciously massage her fingers. "Laurel, love, I do not know what has you so upset, but I do know this. I will never let anyone hurt you." His words brought momentary relief, and then just as quickly, the hope in her eyes died a quick death.

"If it were just me, Conor, I would trust you completely. But it is not just me, and I cannot let you unintentionally hurt someone I love."

His brow furrowed. His hands clenched hers tightly. "Who would be hurt, Laurel? Another man?"

"I told you. There is no one else nor will there ever be." Her words were like a salve to his long-beaten soul.

Knowing she was his made all the problems of the world seem surmountable. "Is it your brother?"

"No, not him." Laurel turned again and stood near the hearth, trying to soak up the heat. She began to rub her arms for warmth. Conor was going to get to the truth, she realized. One way or another he would find out. Maybe if she would just explain it all to him, he would understand that she had no choice but to leave in the spring and disappear forever. She would change her name, her hair, and anything else that would enable any Douglass to find her.

Conor came up behind her and wrapped his arms around her middle, embracing her so that her back and arms were completely enfolded. He kissed the top of her hair. "Tell me, Laurel. Let me help you. I cannot protect you and whoever you are keeping secret if I do not know. You can trust me."

She took a deep breath and exhaled, realizing that the time had come to trust another, and if she could not trust Conor to help her, then who? Slowly, she began telling him the missing piece from that night of horror. "When Keith Douglass abducted me, I was not on English soil. I was going to visit my grandfather, who lives in Scotland's border country."

So his bride was a Scot. His heart soared. "Tell me about him."

"He was my mother's father. When she was young, she ran away to marry my father who was an English baron. He had been previously married and had a son—my half brother, Ainsley. It is sad to say, but I don't think my father loved Ainsley's mother, at least not like he loved mine."

Laurel took another deep breath, swallowed, and then continued. "Anyway, although my father and mother were very much in love, my grandfather would not accept her choice of husband. After several years, my mother finally had me and with the birth of his first grandchild, the rift between her and my grandfather was mended.

But my father could never forget those first years. He refused to enter Scotland because of Grandfather's early rejection of him. However, he did allow Mother and me to visit Grandfather several times during the year."

"This is how you learned Gaelic so well," Conor said, still holding her, wanting to physically protect her from her memories.

"Yes, my grandfather was a large man, or at least he seemed like one to a child. But I loved him very much. He was so different from my father. He was warm and affectionate. He would swing me around and tell me all kinds of stories. He and I had a special bond. My mother often told me that I took after him. Supposedly, I have his eyes and his color of hair." She paused and turned in Conor's arms to look at him, hoping that he would understand.

"It has been many years since I have seen my grandfather. When my mother died, my father refused to let me travel into Scotland or let Scottish soldiers escort me." She saw the quick flash of resentment in Conor's eyes. "Now, don't look that way. My father did love me, but he had always been a hard man, and he only became harder when my mother died. I think I was a disappointment to him. Between my temper and my looks, he never could forget where I came from.

"So it wasn't until my brother became the baron that I finally saw my chance to return to my home, my Scottish home. My brother, Ainsley, hated the idea of paying a dowry to have someone marry me. His betrothed wanted me gone and out of his keep. So I finally persuaded Ainsley to let me leave for Scotland by promising that I would never return, no matter what the circumstances."

Laurel shuddered slightly at the memory and stepped out of Conor's embrace. He tried to urge her to sit down or let her hold him, but she shook her head, determined to tell this part of her story without support. She gazed into the fire and continued. "We were only a few days into Scotland when Keith Douglass captured me and brought me to his father's keep. Keith was mean and physically cruel, but he was nothing compared to his father. When Laird Douglass offered me to his son, he also spoke of having me himself."

Laurel suddenly felt as if she was transported back in time and place. She could see his dark eyes, small, dull, deep-set, glinting like beetles. The vision of his long tangled black hair framing his pointed face distorted by hate was burned into her mind. She began shivering and rubbed her arms instinctively. Conor was glad her back was to him so that she could not see the fury growing in his eyes.

"I guess Laird Douglass could see my contempt, or perhaps it was rebellion, so he thought to threaten me. Somehow he knew me and knew my grandfather. He swore that if I fought back, didn't obey him, he would attack my mother's people . . . he would kill them. Kill them all."

Silence fell between them for several minutes. Laurel stood like a ghost trying to recover from her fear and the memories. Conor walked over to the window, using the physical motion to regain control over his rage.

"Tell me who they are, and I will protect them."

She turned and looked at him now. His knuckles were white with the pressure he was exerting onto the window ledge.

"I cannot. I cannot tell you. Please do not ask me. I'm so sorry. But do you understand now? Do you understand why I cannot marry you? Why I have to leave? By spring Douglass will have gathered his men and be ready to make good on his word."

He spun around, staring at her incredulously.

"What are you planning to do? What are you planning in spring?"

"I was going to leave and never come back. Change my name, my look, cut my hair. Something so Douglass wouldn't recognize me. And then, I was going to find a way to warn my grandfather about Douglass and his treachery."

Her tears began to spill over and he resisted no longer. Very carefully, fully aware of his tightly leashed anger and his fierce desire to avenge her, he pulled her into his arms.

"I will never let you cut your hair, love," he said gently as he tucked a loose gold strand behind her ear. "Go on. Where would you live? What would you do for coin?"

"I don't know. France, perhaps? I thought maybe I could be a lady's maid or something . . . I really don't know. I hadn't thought that far. This winter, I should be fine. No one travels much, how could they? So as long as I disappear by spring before word travels that I am in the highlands, things should be fine. Douglass would never attack you if I were not here. I cannot stay. No matter how much I love you, I cannot marry you." Her tone was low and mournful.

She just told him that she loved him. There was absolutely no possibility of her leaving and not marrying him now. She was his, both in mind and in spirit. Now he just needed her to lean on that love a little and trust him to deal with all of her concerns.

He lifted her chin and framed her face. "I understand what you have told me. But now you understand something. We are getting married and soon. You trusted me to bring you to safety. Trust me to come up with a way to keep your family safe. Who is your grandfather?"

"Please, Conor, don't ask me that. Please. I don't want to put you or anyone else in danger."

Did she really think so little of him and his ability to keep her safe? He sighed, and decided he would not press the issue.

He was fairly sure he knew who her grandfather was now anyway. He should have realized it as soon as he had seen her in the woods. The hair was a clue, but the eyes— only one clan in Scotland had those eyes. He would send word of her safety and her whereabouts after they were married. Unfortunately, he wouldn't know how the news would be received until spring. Laurel was right; it was difficult to travel great distances during the winter months.

And if he was right about her grandfather's identity, Laird Douglass's threat was as empty as his honor. It was only a means to terrify and control someone he wanted to possess. It was a great mistake on Douglass's part, and one that either he or Laird MacInnes would soon rectify.

"Love?" he held her close. "Marry me. Trust me to solve your problems by spring. If spring comes and the only way to keep your family safe is for you to leave, then you may go. But give us until then. Will you trust me, trust us, enough to do this?" She would never leave him, regardless of what happened in the spring, but he was willing to do anything to buy him the time to convince her.

Laurel wanted so much to believe he could save her grandfather. She also knew that, after tonight, staying away from Conor would be impossible.

"Yes, Conor McTiernay. I will marry you. Even if it only lasts until spring. You are the only man I will ever want, and my heart will always be yours regardless of what happens."

"That is the way it should be. And you, my love, will always be mine. You always have been, and you always will be." *And our marriage will last a hell of a lot longer than spring*, he thought, as he finally succumbed and kissed her.

It was a long kiss full of endless need and love. They explored each other's mouths lingering over each and every taste. She mimicked his movements and tried to deepen the kiss. He forced himself to pull away. He drew her into his arms and kissed her forehead, brushing his lips softly against her skin.

"We should wait until we are married, Laurel. You don't want to stand in front of the priest not a maiden."

She began nuzzling his neck while running her fingers through his hair. He trembled under her tender, compelling kisses.

"I don't think that matters anymore, do you? Or did you forget the great hall . . ." she said, urging his head towards hers so she could nibble his ear. "You taste so good," she said, drawing out the last word.

Conor was on the verge of laying her down and making the intense passionate love to her that he had been fantasizing about since they had first met. And now here she was, making playful, romantic, and undeniably sexual overtures. Even the most tutored of sirens could not have been more intoxicating. With incredible determination he gathered from every fiber of his being, he forced Laurel to halt her advances.

"No, sweet. You are still virtuous, but will not remain that way long if you continue." He had to leave soon. Her passion-filled eyes would quickly cause him to disregard all of his good intentions.

"But I thought we . . . I mean what we did . . . you did . . . Didn't that . . . ?" She could not utter a complete coherent thought.

"No, love. What we shared in the hall was just an appetizer for future delights we will find together. The night we marry, you will become mine—body, mind and soul."

She shivered at his words. She could not imagine anything more wondrous than what he had done earlier. He leaned over and lightly brushed his mouth against hers and went to her chamber door.

"Laurel. Starting tomorrow you are to wear the McTiernay plaid." And then he left, leaving her with her thoughts.

"I'm to be Lady McTiernay," she murmured aloud. She began twirling around the room. "I'm going to be Conor's wife. He wants to marry me!"

And then she threw herself on the bed. For the next several hours, she stared at the ceiling wondering what being married to Laird McTiernay would be like. When Brighid found her the next morning, she was still sleeping in her gown, lying twisted in the coverlet with a smile on her face.

Chapter Nine

Laurel woke up as Brighid tiptoed into the room carrying a dark bundle. "Brighid? Is that you?" she asked in a sleepy voice.

"Aye, milady," Brighid whispered, feeling awkward that she had disturbed the next Lady McTiernay. But rumors had been flying around the castle all morning, and Brighid was eager to know if they were true. "The laird gave this to me for you to wear today."

Laurel quickly jumped out of bed and ran to look at the beautiful plaid cloth Brighid had brought in. "Could you wait and help me with it?" Laurel requested excitedly.

Not being able to refrain from doing so, Laurel hummed as she washed and dressed herself in the McTiernay plaid. She was glad that only the men wore the thick version of the woolen cloth. Highland women wore an arisaid made of a much finer and longer material that reached down to the ground.

"I believe this particular plaid was his mother's," Brighid confided, helping Laurel to fasten it to her bliaut so that the cloth hung properly. The dark plaid of greens and blues was a stark contrast to Laurel's fair features.

"Ah, Brighid, I am sure that I will never learn how to do this. You have somehow turned this bulky ensemble into something feminine and very comfortable." Brighid had pleated the plaid and then fixed it to Laurel's waist, wrapping the spare material around her shoulders before attaching it in the front with a pin. Laurel noticed that an extra swag of material was left to form a hood, which could be pulled up in bad weather.

"Brighid, where did you get the pin?" It was a beautiful brooch made of gold and silver that reminded her of the buttons on Conor's saffron shirts.

"That was also Lady McTiernay's. Normally, fancy plaid brooches as the one you're wearing are passed down from mother to daughter."

"But there were no McTiernay daughters," Laurel said softly as she lightly fingered the heirloom.

"Aye. That is why Lady McTiernay bestowed it to Conor, making him vow to give it to the next Lady Mc-Tiernay. Since the laird specifically told me it was for you, and you're wearing the family heirloom, is it true, then? Are you to be the next Lady McTiernay?"

Laurel's sigh was laced with happiness. Never had she imagined that she would be so delighted at the prospect of marriage, especially to such a large, rugged highlander.

"Yes. Yes, I am. As soon as Father Lanaghly arrives to perform the ceremony."

"I expect you'll be wanting to finish the chapel now." Fallon had made great strides improving the keep, but there was much more to be done. The chapel benches were rotten and needed to be replaced. The seats and the altar coverings had to be remade, and, with so many stained glass parts, the windows would require many hours of labor before they were clean again.

"Umm, yes. Do you know where Fallon and Glynis are now?"

"In the chapel, milady. Word has spread of your upcoming nuptials, and the two of them immediately went there to discuss its restoration."

Laurel frowned. She agreed that the chapel required work, but there were more essential things that needed to be done before the first strong storms of winter struck.

"Please come with me. I need to stop and see them for a moment before we visit the cottages."

"The cottages?" Brighid was baffled. Her lady's first thoughts were not of her upcoming wedding but of the clan's cottages.

"Yes, there are several not ready for the winter. I noticed when I was walking the castle walls the other day that many roofs are in desperate need of repair." Laurel turned and went down the tower stairs.

She found Fallon and Glynis in the chapel exactly as Brighid had said. What Brighid had failed to mention was the tenor of their discussion.

"The windows must be cleaned first," maintained Fallon. "Not nearly enough light is coming in—especially for a sunset wedding. If we are going to have an afternoon ceremony, we must begin with the windows."

"Of course it will be a sunset wedding," affirmed the housekeeper. Everyone knew that all McTiernay weddings were done at sunset. The morning was dedicated to the bride and to the groom, and their individual preparations. After the wedding, there was a great feast and celebration that would continue for hours into the night, long after the happy couple had departed for their chambers. "And I agree the windows must be clean," she conceded. "But you cannot put everyone on that single effort! Lady Laurel specifically wanted the chairs and the coverings to be replaced and repaired. I will need most of the women to complete that task in time."

"Most of the women!" hollered Fallon. It was at that exclamation Laurel interceded. Smiling, she approached them.

"Both of you have identified areas that need attention. But I would like the benches repaired or new ones built first. Fallon, please assign five or six men to do so. The rest of the men I will need elsewhere to prepare for winter." They both squirmed uncomfortably, realizing that their laird's lady had heard them shouting at each other. Glynis was the first to regain her composure.

"Milady, you truly are beautiful in our plaid. You will

do our laird proud. You have given us something back that we had lost a long time ago. For as long as anyone can remember or retell, there was love in the McTiernay castle. It was that love that enabled the McTiernays to rule strongly and wisely for so many years. We had forgotten that until you came."

"Aye, milady. You are truly a blessing sent down to us from heaven." Fallon's words were softly spoken, filled with emotion. Laurel was moved by the kindness given from this man who so loved to be difficult.

"Thank you, Glynis. Thank you, Fallon. I feel blessed to be here myself." Then surprising them all, she leaned over and kissed the old steward on the cheek. He was so stunned afterwards that he forgot to ask about her plans for the day.

Laurel was leaving another home that needed immediate repair before the winter set in. That made three out of the last seven cottages, and there were still several more to inspect.

Normally, Conor oversaw the repairs, but this year, with Colin's marriage and the trip to Laird Schellden's, many winter chores had fallen seriously behind. In England, Laurel had the responsibility for the village upkeep along with the care and nurturing of its inhabitants. Ainsley had felt the chore onerous and beneath him. Continuing the work here, helping where she could, only felt natural.

"They seemed like a lovely family," Laurel commented to Brighid. "It is too bad that my only chance to visit so far has been when so many of the men are hunting or preparing for winter. Did you notice how smart their little girl is? They are going to have an adventurer on their hands, I am afraid."

"Aye, little Maegan does seem to take after her older brothers. Every one of them a mischief maker," Brighid agreed. She was excited to have come on this latest excursion with her lady. Most women would never have interfered with the laird's responsibilities, even if he wasn't able to do them. But not Lady Laurel. She just forged ahead, making decisions and daring to go where all other women would have been afraid.

Several of the clanswomen were reluctant to talk about cottage repairs and what was needed to maintain their home's upkeep. But after Laurel had spent just a few minutes discussing needs, families, and whatnot, she somehow gained their trust.

Laurel had gained entrance into their homes by being genuinely interested in their families. She'd gained acceptance after suggesting that the women of the cottage spent the most time there and were just as knowledgeable about what needed to be done as the men. Respect came after discussing the order of the repairs, who would do them, and their timing.

At first, Brighid did not think that Laurel could remember all that had been said, but later, when talking to another family, she discovered that she had been mistaken. It was clear that Laurel had handled such matters before and had an excellent memory for details. Laurel was also very clever about how to frame statements and questions so that everyone would understand and support the order in which the cottages would be repaired. When the laird issued an order, it was obeyed without question or comment. The concept of getting group input and acceptance about such matters was novel to Brighid.

As they were deciding which cottage to visit next, a young boy no more than four or five years old came running up to them, speaking fast Gaelic. Finn's wife, Aileen, was in labor and needed help. They followed him, dashing quickly around carts, animals, and cottages for what seemed a long time before arriving at Aileen's home.

Laurel started knocking repeatedly on the door. "Aileen? Are you here?"

"Lady Laurel, please help me," a panic-filled voice cried out.

Laurel entered and saw Aileen pale and in pain, tightly gripping the coverlet on the bed. "Where on earth is Finn?" Laurel gasped.

"He left with Conor. They wanted to visit some of the outlying villages the laird had missed upon his return from Laird Schellden's." Then she grimaced and bent over again in pain.

"Aileen, how long have you been having your pains?" Laurel walked over to provide what support she could to her friend.

"Not long," Aileen grunted and then eased into a chair by the hearth after the sharp twinge had passed. "But they are quick. So much closer than those I have seen in others. Everyone said the first baby takes a long time to arrive, but I don't think that's true for me."

Laurel could detect the concern in her voice. "Don't worry now. Have you fetched the midwife?" When Aileen shook her head, Laurel turned to Brighid. "Go get her. And if she isn't home, find her. Don't come back without her."

Laurel did not want to do this without the midwife. She had never delivered a baby and didn't know exactly what to do. She didn't want Aileen to know, but she was terrified about the whole process. Her mother had died giving birth to her brother Daniel, who entered the world stillborn.

As she watched Brighid depart for the midwife, Laurel made a quick prayer for guidance and patience. She began fanning her face. The room was unbelievably warm.

"Aileen, does the heat help you?"

"To be honest, I find it nearly intolerable. But I don't want my baby to be cold."

Laurel went over and removed several of the logs, significantly reducing the heat coming out of the hearth. "There, it will still be warm without suffocating you in the process."

She turned in time to see another pain hit Aileen. Her face became contorted, and her hands were white-knuckled as she held onto the chair. Time seemed frozen until the pain had passed.

Laurel reached over and got a cloth, wet it and began mopping Aileen's face. She whispered to her, "I don't know, Aileen. Maybe I should go get help. Another one of the women, perhaps. Someone. Anyone. Of all the people to be here to help you, it should not be me."

Aileen grabbed her hand and squeezed hard. "No. I told little Alec to find *you*. The midwife and I argued yesterday, and she left for her home in the northern country. If Brighid finds her in time and convinces her to return, it will be a miracle. Besides, I want you. Please."

"Me? But Aileen, I don't know anything about helping you birth a baby!"

"You are a healer, Laurel. I have seen it. So has Finn." Aileen rose and went to stand by the stove to pour Laurel something to drink.

Laurel just stood staring in astonishment. No one would have known that the woman pouring water was in absolute agony two minutes ago.

Aileen continued, "Finn and I both watched how you stitched, bound and cleaned the wounds of the men during training."

Laurel suddenly recovered. "Stop that at once!" She darted over and snatched the flagon away from her. "Aileen, those were men. Their injuries were just shallow cuts. I couldn't do them any more harm. But you, your baby," she choked up, not finishing the terrible thought.

"No, you listen to me now," Aileen said with even more force. "You were not just cleaning their wounds. You knew the ointments to apply, the herbs to drink. You knew what needed to be bound and what should be left open. You can do this, Laurel. I know you can." Just then another pain hit and Aileen reached out to grab something for support. It just so happened to be Laurel's arm. "Please, don't leave me," she groaned through the agony.

Laurel made up her mind at once. The little she did know about herbs and healing, she remembered from what her mother had taught her as a little girl. She would just have to rely on that.

"You're going to lose some of your linens," Laurel remarked as she headed for the chest that housed such items. Aileen just nodded, thankful that her new friend was going to stay and help. The past few weeks, Aileen and Laurel had become as close as sisters. Each had lost a beloved parent at an early age. Both had siblings, but neither had a close relationship with them. After many years, each had finally found a female companion to lean on, listen to, and confide in.

"Do you feel better standing, sitting, or lying down?" Laurel inquired.

"I think sitting. But then I get antsy and feel like pacing."

"Hmm. Then pace. I will place chairs sporadically around the room so when a pain hits, you just find one and sit down." Then Laurel began stripping linens and tying them to the corners of the bed. Next, she used boiling water to cleanse the items she would need, just like she did when sewing up wounds.

Over the next several hours, she continued to bathe and help Aileen as much as possible. For someone who seemed so close to having a baby, it was taking a long time.

As the pains came in rapid succession, Laurel gave Aileen the linen loops on the bed posts to pull and hang on to. "That's what these things are for!" Aileen exclaimed as the brief interlude from pain disappeared. "Where is Finn! Why isn't he here?" she yelled. "Why did he do this to me!"

Laurel retrieved the shears. The way Aileen was bending over and bearing down, it could be any time now. How was she going to do this? Where was the midwife? She suppressed her fear and thought of Conor's strength. When this was all over, she was going to collapse in his arms, she promised herself.

Conor, meanwhile, was tearing up the keep. No one knew where Laurel was. The last time they had seen her, she was venturing outside the keep on some mission with Brighid. Neither of them could be found. Where did she go? Why?

He had just returned from riding up and down the river bank looking for her. Fallon and Glynis had disappeared on separate searches, trying to appease their guilt. All they could remember was that Laurel had said something about needing men for a more important and immediate task than fixing the chapel.

Finn rode in. He had gone to see if Laurel was around or near the soldiers' practice field. "No word."

Conor grew cold with fear. If anything had happened to her, he would never recover. He needed her. He had just discovered what it was like to be truly and fully loved. Finally, he had someone that yearned for what he did from a marriage—a union built on support, desire and trust.

His muscles were tense with fear, his abdomen tight. He was going to find her, he resolved. And she was going to be unharmed. Once safe, he was never going to let her go out unprotected again. Never again would he experience the terror growing inside him.

He shouted at Neal, "Bring me my mount!" A few minutes later, Borrail was brought to him by his brother Clyde.

"It's the only fresh mount, Conor. All the others are out or needing a rest." He looked up, worried. "Is she going to be all right? Laurel is so nice and everyone loves her. If she were in trouble, someone would have helped her, wouldn't they?"

"Aye, they would." He tried to sound convincing.

"But what if those men that had hurt her came and snatched her? What if she's in trouble?"

He listened to his younger brother echo all of his deepest fears and vowed again to never let her out of sight once she was found. If Douglass had dared to cross into his land, there would be hell to pay.

He looked at Finn. "I'm going to look in the woods again in case she was hunting and got lost. Go home to your wife." Both Clyde and Finn watched their troubled laird ride off into the night.

As Finn approached his cottage, he noticed that there were several clansmen standing around. Someone opened the door and said something to one of the men and then went back in. Fear struck his heart. Had something happened to Aileen or the baby?

He started running and didn't stop until he broke through the front door. Inside he saw his wife lying on the bed and Laurel cradling an infant in her plaid arisaid.

"Finn," Laurel said, looking up. "Come meet your son." He stood stunned, unable to move.

"Aileen?" His voice wavered with fear as he glanced at his motionless wife.

"She's fine. She was wonderful, actually. She was strong and came through quite fit. She's just tired. Your son is healthy and large." She looked down and spoke softly at the infant in her arms. "You just wore your mother out. Now, we are going to be quiet and let her rest, aren't we? Finn, would you like to hold him?"

Laurel outstretched her arms and helped the stunned commander adjust his hold to support the baby's head. Tears were forming in his eyes.

From the bed, Aileen awoke. "Isn't he beautiful?"

Finn walked over and sat next to his wife, cradling their son. "Aye, that he is, sweetheart."

"And you should have seen Laurel. She stayed with me all day and delivered him. I think at times she was more frightened than I was." She reached out for her friend's hand. "Thank you. Thank you for coming and staying with me."

It was then that Finn remembered Conor. He handed his son to his wife.

"Conor!" he yelled. The result was two disgruntled women and a wailing baby. He whirled, grabbed Laurel, and said aloud, "We must get you back to the keep immediately. Conor is going mad looking for you. We have searched the keep, the river, everywhere! He is riding in the woods to search for you even now."

"Oh, no! I must leave. I wasn't thinking. He must be furious."

"No, but as soon as he sees you he will be," Finn warned.

That immediately got Laurel's attention. "Why?"

"A man's fear will turn to anger once the fear's cause is removed. I warn you, the larger the fear, the greater the anger," Finn counseled.

"Thank you. I will leave right now." She hugged her friend, kissed the baby, and left running into the night, not waiting for an escort.

Returning from his search, Conor spotted her running. He rode up beside her and picked her up in one swoop. He realized immediately that she was unharmed. The icy fear that had enveloped his heart dissolved quickly into an inferno of anger.

Oblivious to his dark fury, Laurel hugged him. "Conor! I'm so glad I found you! You won't believe what happened!"

He didn't return the embrace, and Laurel sat back to look at him. His expression was dark and stone-hard. "Be quiet, Laurel. Do not say one more word."

Laurel cringed at the coldness in his voice. She decided to take her friend's advice and not let his anger spark her own. She rode in silence, feeling the tension radiate from his body.

Conor rode hard, straight into the keep. He got off Borrail, lifted Laurel down and threw the reins to Neal, who ran out upon their return. Neal almost said something about how happy he was to see her safe, but one look at his laird and he changed his mind. Laird McTiernay was furious. Really furious.

Neal grabbed the reins and brought Borrail into the stables, yelling at one of the stable lads to take care of him. He then went to search for Fallon.

"Fallon, I'm worried about Lady Laurel." Neal was pacing back and forth in the empty lower hall.

"He would never hurt her." Fallon appeared calm, but his pulse was pounding, and he was apprehensive for his lady. The laird's temper could be cold and leave a lasting impression.

"Not physically, no," Neal returned. "But he could break her spirit. She is like a wild filly, a thing of beauty. Spirits like hers, once broken, never recover. What are we going to do?"

"We? Nothing. I will go and see if interference is required."

"Hmmph. I'll be going with you," Neal responded.

"Me, too!" Clyde and the other stable hand yelled out, emerging from a hiding place behind some dismantled tables.

"I think maybe I should go as well, in case milady needs some female assistance," added Glynis, rounding the timber partition that screened the hall from the service area.

Conor held her hand firmly and walked straight towards the Star Tower. He marched her brusquely up the stairs and made her follow him into his chamber. Once inside, he closed the door in a very controlled manner. That act alone told Laurel just how angry he was.

He went to stand by the hearth. Grabbing the mantel, he stared into the flames for several moments.

"You are to never leave the keep again unless I am with you," he stated evenly without turning around.

Laurel had been standing there unsure of how to react or what to say.

"Don't you want to know what happened?" she whispered.

"No, I don't."

"But Conor, if you would just let me explain, I think you would understand why it took so long for me to return."

"I don't want to hear it, Laurel," his knuckles were now white against the mantel's dark stone. "All I want to hear is how you will never leave without an escort again."

"Never leave without an escort?" She couldn't help it. Her temper took over. "So, I am a prisoner, then? You don't want a wife, Conor, you want some pet to follow you around, come and go at your bidding, and pine away in your chambers until you return."

"Don't challenge me, Laurel. Not after what you put me through this evening!"

She moved closer. "What *you've* been through! How about what *I've* been through? Has it even occurred to you to be curious?"

His eyes narrowed. "Aye, and I thought it be best if I did not know. I cannot imagine anything you could say that wouldn't make things worse right now."

"Oh, and what were you thinking then? That I was off with a man?"

Until she said the words, the thought had never entered his head. But the idea of her with another man tore his soul wide open.

He moved so quickly Laurel never even saw it coming. Conor clamped a hand around her wrist and pulled her to him. His eyes glinted. "God help you if you were, Laurel. I would kill you both."

She freed her arm and struggled for composure. Adrenaline pumped through her, causing her to tremble violently. "I don't take well to threats, Conor."

"And I don't take well to hearing that my soon-to-be wife was with another man!"

"You are insufferable!" She backed up a couple of steps.

"So you've told me before!"

"I will not stay here with you. I will not! And no number of soldiers can keep me here! I will find a way to escape this keep. I promise you."

"I will throw you in the dungeon if I must, but you will be staying!"

She turned around and tried to leave, but he was too fast. His hand thudded loudly against the door. He leaned forward. "Were you with another man, Laurel? Did you spend your day in another's arms?" The soft deadly whisper in her ear gave her chills.

"Would it matter to you if I did?"

"Aye, it would matter. No one takes what is mine. Ever."

"Then, calm yourself, laird. I was with no man today, only Aileen while she was birthing her babe." Her contempt for him and his assumptions was unmistakable.

Conor felt the wind knocked out of him by her words. "The baby? Finn's wife?" he asked, releasing the pressure on the door to keep it shut.

"Both fine," came the brittle reply.

She barely had time to say the words before he took her face in his hands and began kissing her. All the anger that had begun as fear exploded as irrepressible primal need, resulting in a torrent of harsh, unyielding kisses.

He needed to know that she still wanted him. He needed her to know that he desired her so much it was akin to pain. That, regardless of arguments and words, fury and fear, he would always be hers and she would always be his.

Conor felt her initial resistance begin to melt. As Laurel began to respond to his touch, her fingers clenched around his shoulders. He groaned aloud. No matter what he did, no matter how angry she became, she still reacted with passion when he took her into his arms.

With the pressure on the door gone, it swung open and several people poured in ready to defend their lady if need be. But what they saw was a man loving his woman. Both were oblivious to their entry. Fallon shooed the group out onto the staircase and closed the door behind them.

Relief flooded their faces. Clyde was the only one who spoke. "I knew that Laurel could do it." He grinned. "From now on, when Conor gets mad, we should send her to him to make him change his mind."

Fallon gave the lad a loving shove and indicated for the others to return to their homes and beds. All was well here.

In the chamber, Conor cradled her face in his hands, and he drank her in. Her smile was soft and inviting, telling him in every way that she was his.

Conor touched her cheek so tenderly Laurel could barely find her breath. She tipped her head back and let her hair tumble over her shoulders. He closed his hand around the back of her head and brought her mouth to his. He kissed her slowly, taking his time, letting her feel the endless need and love inside him.

With that kiss, everything that had taken place between them was forgotten. Gone was the anger that had arisen between them. All that remained was his touch, his kiss, and the way he made her feel when she was in his arms. Laurel never wanted the feeling to disappear again. She shivered with unfamiliar need.

Sensing her reaction, Conor was suddenly swamped with desire. He closed in for a deeper kiss, silently urging her to comply.

"Conor . . ." His name was a soft moan causing his already mounting desire to rage out of control.

Her hands roamed his body, pulling his shirt free of his belt so that she could feel the skin underneath. She loved the feel of him. He was driving her wild. Some deep craving inside her was growing, and she didn't know how to fulfill it.

Her nails grazed his back and sent him over the edge of reason. His need consumed him. Not daring to interrupt their kiss even temporarily, he started to undress her.

He unpinned his mother's brooch, glowing inside that she had worn it for him. Next, he deftly removed her bliaut and began to move her chemise down her shoulders.

Laurel was floating. Conor was kissing her with such tenderness, such passion, that it took her breath away. She moaned his name over and over again. Only when he took her breast in his mouth did she realize that her gown had been completely removed, and her chemise was off her shoulders hanging from her waist.

Conor lifted Laurel in his arms and carried her to his bed. His lips never left hers as he crushed her into the soft bedding, his mouth hot and feverish on her skin. Instantly, she responded to the heavy, but delightful weight of him.

He resumed his exploration of her breasts, grazing each nipple, capturing and teasing it with his mouth until she cried out for more. She gasped, trembled, and closed her eyes. Conor thought he would go out of his mind with the craving he felt.

Laurel wanted to explore his body as he was exploring hers. She twined her fingers in his hair, reveling in the sensations Conor was evoking. As he lay on top of her, she could feel him grow tight and hard with arousal.

Something profound and mysterious inside Laurel swelled under the impact of Conor's primitive gaze. The urge to touch him there was overwhelming.

His hands were caressing her inner thighs, driving her wild with need. Laurel moved restlessly beneath the caress wanting more, wanting to give more. Conor felt her untutored hands caressing his stomach, but when they moved under his kilt and stroked his manhood, he froze. Never had he imagined Laurel would try to give him pleasure in that way. He was undone.

He clutched her hand, preventing further torture. His eyes never left hers. Her hair spilled around her head like a golden halo, her turquoise eyes suddenly confused.

"Conor, have I done wrong?" She immediately pulled her hand away and began to retreat.

"No, love." He kissed her brow, then the tip of her nose. "Nothing we do here is wrong. You can touch me anywhere you would like." Then he clasped each of her hands in his, raised them above her head, and resumed his onslaught on her senses. He ravaged her mouth, re-stirring the flames of passion, then yanked impatiently at his clothing.

Once free, he lowered himself until he covered her body with his own. He had never felt this way before. The rightness of being with her, the intensified pleasure of his naked body touching hers. She was soft, sweet and vul-nerable.

He cupped her breasts, grazing his thumbs across the rosy peaks. He bent his head and kissed each one, captur-ing and tantalizing each nub with his lips.

Laurel's very breath was stolen away. She moaned and trembled with need.

When Conor felt her hips move against his thighs, his already aroused body tightened even more and he could only think of one thing—making Laurel his.

Conor lowered his mouth from her breasts to her stom-ach, his tongue swirling around her navel causing her back to arch in response. Every kiss was executed with exquisite passion and each touch gentle but insistent.

He removed the chemise completely and shifted to kiss the fragrant heat between her legs.

Laurel instantly responded, trying to sit up. "Conor, no!" She grabbed his shoulders trying to make him stop. But Conor didn't even raise his head. Suddenly, she felt his tongue slowly tasting her most intimate place. He found her female flesh and sucked gently. She fell back against the mattress and into oblivion.

She was spinning faster and faster, going deeper into something she could not name. He cupped her hips and his tongue started flicking in and out, driving her to mad-ness. She was writhing underneath him on the brink of igniting into flames. He lifted her higher and tighter against his mouth, refusing to let her climax fade despite her cries and weak struggles.

Then, suddenly, she exploded.

Watching Laurel experience sexual fulfillment was the most intense encounter Conor ever had. She was his soul mate. Just being with her was enough to make him whole.

He was drinking in her large turquoise eyes when his own raging hunger broke free from the last of his defenses. A great shudder of need wracked him, and he no longer possessed the will to resist.

He parted her legs even wider, lowering himself until he covered her body with his own.

As Conor pressed his hips closer, Laurel could feel the long, hard length of his erection. She gasped and instinctively lifted herself against him. She bit his shoulder with her teeth, silently urging him to continue. She knew there was something more, and she wanted it—needed it.

Ever so slowly, Conor lightly touched Laurel until his fingers closed around her precious mound. When his fingers slid into her heat and began rubbing her nubbin, her breath caught in her throat. Laurel writhed against his hand. She felt him teasing her with fingers and thought she would go mad.

"Conor! Please! . . . Oh . . . please!" she pleaded, quivering at his touch.

Conor knew she was ready. He was so hard he hurt. He kissed her and then reached down and carefully opened her to his first thrust. He felt the initial resistance that proved he was her first and only lover, and then, in one bold stroke, he felt her close around him.

She cried out again, but this time in pain.

Conor halted deep inside of her and trapped her face between his hands. She was so tight and hot. It was near impossible to hold his need at bay.

"Shhh, love. It will pass," he murmured while stroking her cheek. Her tears tore at his heart like nothing ever had. He kissed them away.

The pain had shocked her at first, but his voice and

touch soon calmed her and the pain receded. She moved so that she could caress his back, slightly disappointed that it was over.

Conor found each move she made exquisitely painful. She was wonderfully tight and fit snugly against him. Never had anything felt so amazing and perfect. This woman who had just stumbled into his life was his, now and forever.

"The pain is gone?" he choked.

"Yes, mostly. Are we done?" Her smile was innocent and yet so intoxicating.

"Oh no, love. We have only just begun."

As soon as he spoke the words, Conor started to move within her and suddenly, Laurel understood what he meant.

He was so big. At first she thought he was too big, that it would never work. But as he eased himself out and slowly back in, opening her, stretching her, he found a place for himself in the very heart of her.

The rhythm intensified. The sensations that coursed through her with each stroke carried her to another world.

Conor then began to massage her breasts with his tongue, matching the rhythm of his thrusts. The sensations were almost painful. She arched her back and cried out again and again. Laurel's soft cries of sensual fulfillment were the most incredibly stirring sounds Conor had ever heard.

"Conor," Laurel cried with building need.

"I know, love, I know." His voice strained with his own exploding release.

Laurel trembled as she clung to him as if he were the only solid thing in her life.

She felt him retreat and then plunge back into her with deeper, quickening movements. "Oh Lord . . . Conor, I don't . . . I can't . . . oh . . . Conor!"

Her turquoise eyes popped open, and they were the most intense blue he had ever seen.

She felt the delicious twisting sensation building once again swiftly inside her, but this time even stronger than before. He reached down and found the point their bodies were joined, and touched the sensitive female flesh. She cried out and then felt herself shatter into a million pieces.

Conor shuddered and surged forward into her one last time. She was finally his, he thought possessively. Now and forever, she belonged to him just as he belonged to her.

As they slowly returned to earth, savoring what they had just shared, Laurel's hands roamed aimlessly over Conor's chest, and she sighed in wonder. Never in her life had she felt so alive, so protected, or so loved.

Conor was momentarily too stunned to do anything. Nothing in his life had ever felt this right, this perfect. He would have no other woman for as long he lived. He only wanted her. He wanted her in his bed, by his side, as his wife, and as the mother of his children.

He stirred and turned to his side, stroking her arm. His gaze was possessive, still blazing with sexual desire. He had wanted to wait until they were married before her first experience, but that had become impossible after she returned his kiss.

He looked forward to ending more arguments in the same way.

"Love?" he asked.

"Hmm?" Laurel nuzzled her chin against his chest, perfectly relaxed and happy.

"I'm sorry if I hurt you."

She turned toward him, her smile glowing with love. "I love you."

She said she loved him. This time not in fear, not out of passion, but because she just did.

"And I love you, more than I thought possible."

"Oh Conor, let us never fight again."

"I would agree, but I think that a little unrealistic with your temper."

She playfully jabbed him. "My temper? How about yours? I realize that I shouldn't have reacted to your fear, Conor. I should have known that you would be anxious, and I should not have responded with anger."

Conor rose up on his elbow, looking down at her, gaining a physical advantage. "I don't think you understand. I was not *anxious*. I was angry."

She twirled her finger in his chest hair, completely unfazed by his dominant position. "Mmm-hmmm. You were afraid when you couldn't find me and then all those emotions turned into anger once you realized I was fine," she said lightly as if the idea of him being afraid of something was an everyday event. He rolled completely on top of her and looked directly into her eyes so he had her full attention.

"Now you listen to me. I am a chieftain of a large clan. I am a highlander, and I am a McTiernay. I am never afraid, Laurel."

Not recognizing the seriousness of his tone, she teasingly replied, "Are you telling me that because you are a laird you are incapable of feeling fear?"

"Aye."

Laurel then detected the change in his demeanor. His eyes were distant and serious. Gone were the desire and the passion they had just shared.

She pushed against him and sat up, swinging her legs over the side of the bed clutching the coverlet to her chest.

The concept of never admitting fear seemed ludicrous to her. Conor was a man full of great passions, including fear, anger, and love. He was also a very complex man, sensitive to appearing in the least bit needy or weak.

Laurel took a deep breath and turned back to face him. "Oh, well, thank you for explaining it to me. Please relax, Conor. I don't want to argue. Not now. Not after what we just shared."

Her expression was full of hope and contentment. Her eyes were large, sea-green pools of longing. Conor didn't want to fight with this woman, he wanted to love her. He reached up, pulled her head down and gave her a long, deep satisfying kiss that conveyed all he felt for her.

When finished, he turned on his back and cradled her next to him. Once again content, he thought about the day's events, playing with her hair and stroking her cheek. Something that she had said a moment ago reminded him of a comment that Fallon had made earlier that day.

"I understand that you are now working on repairing the chapel for our wedding."

"Mmm-hmm. Fallon and Glynis were arguing earlier today about the order of what should be done. Highlanders like to argue, I think."

"Is it going to be ready? Father Lanaghly should be here within a few days."

Laurel sighed. "Most likely it will not be with all the work on the cottages still to do. There are just not enough men to spare to complete work on the chapel."

His hand stilled. "What work on the cottages?"

"Oh, the repairs on the clansmen's roofs, doors, windows, and hearths. Typical repairs for winter."

"What would you know of winter repairs? Laurel, don't tell me that you have been talking with my men about such matters."

Laurel felt Conor's body still and become rigid. "Now, don't get all prickly, Conor. Mostly I spoke with women. It has been my experience that they know more about what needs to be done anyway. Besides I had only started my rounds this morning when . . ."

Without warning, Conor sat up and Laurel found herself abruptly thrown aside. "This morning!" Conor bellowed, "I thought you said you were with Aileen."

Conor's eyes penetrated into hers. Laurel was shaken.

"I did. But I didn't say I was there all day. In fact, you did not give me much of a chance to explain anything," she said, finding her nerve.

"Well, I'm giving it to you now."

Laurel did not like the tone of his voice at all and sat up, donning her chemise before she continued. The action helped her regain control of her temper. She reminded herself that he was still somewhat sensitive due to their earlier argument.

"You have been very busy with many clan duties, and I just wanted to help. I have assisted with village upkeep before when I lived with my brother and knew I could do the same here. Brighid and I went out to meet with your clansmen to see who needed assistance in preparing for the winter storms. We had only time to meet a handful before we were called to assist Aileen."

"You had no right, Laurel." His voice had taken that low ominous sound again, telling of his growing ire.

"No right? Whatever do you mean? I'm to be lady of this clan. Granted I am not yet, but I will certainly be performing these duties after our vows."

"You are a woman, and no wife of mine is going to do the work of a man."

Her jaw became temporarily slack. "You mean *Finn* or *Fallon* could do such duties, but not I?"

"Aye. They're men."

She was off the bed now, fuming. "So what am I to you? What is the lady of this castle supposed to do? Weave?"

"You are to do what all ladies do. Sew, clean, and prepare the meals. You are to see me go and receive me when I return. When guests arrive, you should see to their comforts. You know what a lady does and does not do, Laurel. Do not pretend otherwise."

"I have *never* pretended who I am, Conor. And I am not likely to start *pretending* that I like to be confined to only domestic responsibilities. I like to ride, to hunt, and to help manage the village or the clan estates. I'm good at it, and you know it!" She was yelling now. Somewhere deep inside her she knew that he would never see her point of view so long as she employed this tactic.

"Not any more!" he roared back.

She threw a pillow at him. "I will not be married to a

toll-toine of a man who will not see the wisdom of having help where warranted and needed."

"Your help is not warranted nor is it needed."

"Just because I'm a woman."

"My woman."

"Oh, no, I am not. Not yet. And, after this conversation, I am thinking not ever!" She grabbed the rest of her clothes and proceeded towards the door. He made no effort to stop her.

"You will be married to me, Laurel Cordell. And it will be as soon as the priest arrives. Do you not realize what happened tonight? You have been bedded. By me. You are mine by all rights except God's, and I will have his approval before this week's out."

She stared at him, cold anger flaring to life. The arrogant man. He really thought she would marry him now. She opened the door and paused just before leaving. "Hear me now, Conor McTiernay. I never plan on changing, *ever*. Not for you or any man. If you want *all* the clan responsibilities, you can have them. I love you, but if you cannot accept me and what little I bring in the areas of experience, skill, and order, then I will not marry you. Regardless of whether or not I have lost my virginity, *I will not marry you*." And she left.

Chapter Ten

The next day, Laurel woke up early and went to go bathe in the river but was stopped at the guard gate.

"I'm sorry, milady. The laird requested that you remain inside the keep." The guard felt very guilty about repeating the order, especially when he saw her eyes change to a cloudy blue-green. He hoped that he never had to be the bearer of bad news to her again.

Not wanting to punish the young man for simply being an unlucky messenger, Laurel bade him good-bye and walked towards the Star Tower as if she were returning to her room. Instead, she snuck into the stables and quietly led Borrail out of the stall past the sleeping stable boy. She jumped on him bareback, and then flew by the guard towers before they had a chance to realize her intention and react.

Ha! Keep me prisoner! I will show you, Conor McTiernay. If you think that you can control me—think again, she thought, as she made her way to the river. It was quite chilly for what she was about to do. The weather was getting colder each day, and soon it would snow. The river would ice over in many areas before too long. She peeled off her leggings, exposing her toes to the biting cold of the rocks.

Laurel knew she was insane, but also knew that she

needed time away from people and the castle. And she
needed a bath. Just thinking about Conor's high-handed
command that she remain within the keep's walls fueled her
anger anew. She quickly stripped the rest of her clothes and
ran into the freezing water, hoping that it would diminish
her vexation with Conor. She scrubbed her hair and her
body with the lilac soap she had brought, and was rising to
return to shore when Conor appeared.

He didn't stop at the river's edge but rode straight into
the icy water and hauled her up on his lap. Returning to
shore, he wrapped a plaid around her and told her to get
dressed.

Laurel knew he was angry with her. By leaving in such
an obvious and defiant way, she had expected to get his
attention. Just not so soon. But what Conor didn't understand yet was that she was just as furious with his auto-
cratic decisions made earlier that day.

After the morning meal, Conor had been sitting by
the fire mentally reviewing the previous night. Once
again, he grew hard just thinking about it. It had been an
incredible experience—unlike anything he had ever
known. She had made him feel so alive.

Conor swore under his breath. She had made him feel
needed, important, loved in a way he never had before.
Until she dropped her bombshell. After they exchanged
those harsh parting words, she had been on his mind all
night—hovering, taunting. And, at the edge of every
dream, he lost her to a dark and dangerous void. Each
time he awoke, he was alone and full of fear that she was
gone. After one of those many dreams, he arose and ordered the entry guards to prevent her from leaving the
keep without him.

When he was first told of her escapade, he was shocked.
No one had ever disobeyed a direct order of his before. He
was still working out why she would defy him so publicly
when he discovered her bathing by herself in the freezing
river water.

"What in the hell did you think you were doing?" he

demanded as he watched her dress. His body was rigid and tense with a mixture of fury and primal desire at seeing her wet and naked.

She pulled on her bliaut and looked up at him defiantly. She couldn't believe that he could stand there scowling at her with patronizing masculine outrage. "Be more specific, laird. Do you want me to explain the phases of a bath or were you referring to my ride outside the keep on Borrail?" Despite trying not to, she began shivering, making it difficult to argue and, at the same time, put on her leggings with numb fingers.

Conor saw Borrail tethered to tree branch a few feet away and moved to stand between her and her horse. "Did you ride that huge animal bareback? Are you trying to get yourself killed?"

"Oh, good grief. You and your superior attitude. It's not only men who can ride bareback." She was dressed now and feeling a little more confident. She lifted her chin, her eyes glittering with anger, and continued, "I'll have you know that I have seen your men ride and hunt, and I can outperform most of them. So, stuff your ridiculous ideas and let me pass." She straightened her shoulders and picked up her dress to go around him.

As Laurel tried to walk by, he caught her by the arm and whirled her around to face him. "You will not bathe in the river, Laurel. It is too cold for your blood. You have yet to become accustomed to highland weather."

"I was just fine until you barged in riding like a madman." She tried to shrug off his hands. They remained firm.

"I was protecting you."

She brought her hands up the middle and forced them out, breaking Conor's hold. "Bah! You were furious that I left the keep. It has nothing to do with where I chose to bathe. Only that I chose to do it despite your wishes."

Conor ran his fingers through his hair, trying to get his temper under control. He really had not intended to

start the day like this with her. Last night had been exquisite pleasure followed by the acute pain of her departure.
He had convinced himself that her refusal to marry him
was just bluster to save her pride. But, still, he wished they
had not ended last night with so much anger between
them.

They stood glowering at each other for several moments before he decided he could no longer stand there
and watch her shiver. Her wet hair was dripping and had
caused her gown to become saturated along the shoulders. Without warning, he lifted her in his arms and
mounted his horse. Her teeth chattering too much to
argue, she let Conor wring out her wet strands and
bundle her in his plaid. He then grabbed Borrail's reins
and walked the horses back up the hill to the dirt road
leading into the castle walls.

"Despite what you believe, I don't want you hurt. These
rivers are deceptive this time of year. It's only their strong
currents that keep them from freezing over. Many a
person has entered and became too cold to return to the
shore. That is why you should bathe in the keep."

The answer was logical, which didn't help. "But I like to
bathe in the river sometimes. It helps free my thoughts," *and
cool me down,* she added to herself.

"Then, when you want to bathe in the river, I will join
you," he said, thinking it an excellent compromise. He
could conjure up many ways to keep them warm despite
the frigid water temperatures.

"No, thank you. If it is just the idea of my bathing by
myself, perhaps one of the other women could join me."
Warmer now, she could feel her spirited nature return.

"They could not pull you out should you need assistance. And no other man would dare to accompany you."

She didn't want another man, but she certainly was not
going to admit as much to him. "Am I a prisoner, laird?"

He didn't like the way she was referring to him as
"laird" all of a sudden. It was as if she was intentionally
trying to imply that there was nothing between them with

that single word. "No. Why would you think such a thing? Who told you that you were a prisoner?"

"A guard told me that I was not *allowed* to leave the curtain walls. Is that true? Am I not *allowed* outside the castle? Am I a prisoner or a child to you?"

Conor swore underneath his breath. "Stop it, Laurel. You are neither, and you know that. I just cannot escort you all the time, and I need to know that you are safe." Again, the nightmares of her disappearing into a nameless void flitted through his memory, causing him to tighten his grip.

Feeling the restriction, Laurel assumed the worst. "You mean that you need to control every movement I make. I won't live like this, and if you force me, I will find a way to leave."

"And I will drag you back," he growled, not liking the direction of their exchange.

"I will just try again and again until I succeed. You may be laird and can control the activities of the clan, but you do not control me."

Conor felt his temper start to slip again. "I don't want to control you! I want to keep you safe! Not knowing where you were last night shut down the entire castle. We are vulnerable when that happens, Laurel. Do you understand? I had all my men scouring the countryside for your body when we couldn't find you! The castle was open to attack. I cannot have that, and if that means you have to stay behind the castle walls, then I will see that it happens."

Laurel had not realized that so much effort had gone into looking for her. So many men and women—searching for her. Conor must truly have been afraid for her welfare, and that was what was driving him now. She was instantly mollified and remorseful.

"I had not realized but, even so, you cannot expect me to never to leave! Please do not ask that of me. What if I promise always to let someone know where I am at all times?"

"If you wish to go somewhere, I will take you," he said, believing this to be an adequate solution.

Laurel did not think so at all. She did not want to be near him. His unbending stance on her contribution in clan affairs was intolerable. There was no way she could marry him if he expected her to be a meek, uninvolved wife. The thought of being near him and not having him for her own would tear her apart.

"But, what about when I want to stay all day at Aileen's to help with the baby?"

Conor had not considered that. He certainly did not want to spend large amounts of time with two jabbering women and a baby. "You may have another for an escort. But you must inform someone of where you are going at all times."

No one knowing Conor well would believe him capable of compromise. But ever since he had met this woman, he had found himself adjusting, even changing some of his long lived-by principles. But when he was the source of her engaging smile and the sparkle in her dazzling blue-green eyes, it made it all worth while.

"Thank you, Conor, and I promise to always have an escort and notify someone of where I am going."

Her voice was cheerful. She was again happy. She called him "Conor." Finally, he thought, things will return to normal.

If Conor thought that the truce about her comings and goings around the castle had resolved other issues, he was mistaken. Him yielding to the idea of an escort had not at all addressed the issue of her role—or lack thereof—in clan affairs, as he discovered with Fallon later that afternoon.

"What do you mean, she told you to see me?!" he bellowed at Fallon in the chapel hall.

"Precisely what I said, laird. Lady Laurel said that, from

now on, all clan issues were to be discussed and overseen only by you."

"Exactly! But what does that have to do about whether windows should be cleaned or which material should be used on some benches?" He was totally perplexed as to why he had been called in on such domestic matters. These were exactly the type of affairs he had outlined as her responsibility.

"When I asked for an explanation, she told me that you had directed all labor to be determined and conducted under your discretion. Since additional men will be required to . . ."

"She what? If she expects me to submit to her demands this way, she will have to think again!" he yelled, stomping out of the chapel.

"But, laird? Windows or benches?" Fallon cried out.

"Hell, I don't know. Windows!" He would be damned if he gave in to her again. She was not going to manipulate him as if he were an inexperienced chieftain new to the role. He was in charge and, by God, she was going to accept that!

"Glynis!" he shouted across the courtyard as he saw her leaving the kitchen and heading toward the Star Tower. She immediately changed her direction and came scurrying towards him.

"Aye, laird?"

"Tell Laurel that she is to dine with me this evening in the great hall." *Tonight, my love, we will have this out,* he said to himself. He started to leave.

"Laird? My lady told me to tell you, in case you inquired, that she would be dining at the commander's house, visiting with their new babe." Damn, Conor thought. But if she thought to avoid him forever she was mistaken.

Actually, it was he who was wrong. Laurel was able to successfully steer clear of him for the next several days. She was always visiting some ill person or dining with Finn and his wife in the evenings. But she kept her promise. She always had Brighid with her, and someone at the keep was always informed of her whereabouts.

Unfortunately, she had also made good on her threat to abandon all keep responsibilities to him. Added to that, he could never confront her because he could never find her inside the castle walls. Now that the castle was up and running again, there were several things that needed to be dealt with every day. He didn't want the keep to return to its previous state, but the time required to see to its maintenance was more than aggravating. He knew Laurel was testing him, driving him to surrender. But, he, too, could hold firm. And, unlike her threat to never marry him, when he said never, he meant never. And he would never yield when it came to her role in clan affairs.

Every night, he waited until she returned from Finn's to confront her. But, each time, she somehow got past him and was in her chambers asleep when he finally retired for the evening.

"You cannot keep this up, Laurel," Aileen said the fifth night Laurel had come over. Brighid was cradling the sleeping baby by the hearth.

"I know. But I just cannot face him."

"What are you going to do when the priest arrives? Finn says that the laird is still convinced that you and he are going to be married." Aileen retrieved her bairn from Brighid. He was a wee boy and very sweet natured.

Laurel inhaled deeply and let out a forlorn sigh. "Well, he will have to be unconvinced, won't he? I will not be married to a man who is going to try to change me into something I am not."

Aileen laid her sleeping little boy in the middle of the bed and rejoined her friend by the hearth. "I agree that he should not change you, but I think you are going to have to marry him." Aileen leaned over to whisper, "You're living with him, Laurel. You have no choice."

"Normally, I would agree. I really would. But where Conor and I sleep shouldn't have anything to do with us getting married. He refuses to let me do the things that make me happy. He wants me to become some boring, dull version of myself. If he loved me, he wouldn't ask this. He would be glad of my assistance and what I can do. Not ashamed."

Aileen listened again to her friend's criticism of her laird and heard the torment in her voice. "He is not ashamed, and I think it unfair for you to say so. And he loves you a great deal, from what I have seen," she said, reaching out trying to comfort her friend. "It takes a long time for people, especially men, to change their minds. Be patient."

"She's right, milady," Brighid added from across the room. "Men are most stubborn about such things as traditions and what they consider their responsibilities." The misery in her voice was unmistakable.

"Why, Brighid, you sound as though you are having troubles with a man yourself!" Both Aileen and Laurel turned towards the young woman, who was on the brink of tears.

"Aye. My man, Donald, feels that he is of a lower station than myself since I have become your maid and escort. He says I should find someone nearer to my status. It matters little to him that I don't care, that I want to be a soldier's wife. Still, he refuses to listen."

"Oh, Brighid. I had no idea. What a ridiculous notion! Whatever are we to do with such men as ours?" Laurel threw up her hands in exasperation.

"I don't know, Lady Laurel, but I hope you discover the answer soon," Brighid said despairingly.

Hands on hips, Laurel started to denounce whoever was denying her friend happiness. "Who is this man, Brighid? He should realize how fortunate he is to have your love and quickly seize it while he has the chance. Your status versus his is so unimportant in the bigger scheme of things."

Aileen shifted uncomfortably in her seat. She was healing well, but had torn a little during the birth. It was still dif-

ficult for her to move around. "The same could be said to
you," she chided Laurel. "You should take the love that is
handed to you. While your problems seem large, they will
shrink with time. You will see. Marry Conor and be happy."

Laurel thought on those words the rest of the evening.
When it was time to leave, Laurel and Brighid returned
to the castle the same way as they had the previous nights.
They used the east side castle door that led straight into
the Warden's Tower. From there, Laurel had access to
the walkway on top of the curtain walls. She went directly
to the Star Tower, climbing up to the battlements. Then
she descended the tower's stairs to her chambers.

She knew that Conor waited for her return every
night. Before he would retire, he would always open the
door to her chambers and watch her feigning sleep. After
a while, he would leave, closing the door behind him.
Once he had gone, she would cry herself to sleep.

Tonight was no different. He stared at her for the
longest while and then said, "Good night, love. Tomorrow, Father Lanaghly arrives. Our games will be over and
you and I will be married." After he left, her tears started
falling. Aileen was wrong, she cried to herself. They loved
each other, but it didn't change anything at all.

Early the next morning, Laurel rose and went down to
the kitchen to find Brighid.

"Hello, Fiona. Has Brighid arrived?"

"Aye. She's in the back cleaning a pot I need. One of
me girls isn't feeling well. You can't be expecting me to
feed an army with no help." Fiona was as surly as ever in
her domain, but she was still an excellent cook.

"I am sorry to hear about that. Please see Glynis for
someone to assist you today. I realize that cooking for so
many is difficult without the proper help."

"Brighid?" Laurel called aloud.

"Coming, milady! Here, Fiona," Brighid said, handing
the cook the clean pot.

"Fiona, please tell whoever should ask that we will gone until late. I am riding out to visit the midwife and see if she has a treatment for Aileen. She is not healing as quickly as I had hoped, and I am praying that the midwife has something to ease the pain."

Fiona nodded in acknowledgment, keeping her attention on the potatoes she was peeling. "You be sure to get me the help you promised."

After sending Glynis to her favorite cook, Laurel and Brighid headed towards the stables. As Clyde was getting their mounts, Laurel grabbed her bow and dagger, repeating her plans to Neal about visiting the midwife.

They rode for several hours into higher country. It was much colder and rockier, making it slower for the horses to climb. Brighid was fair on a horse, but not nearly as skilled as Laurel, and the trip took longer than Laurel had anticipated.

"There it is," Brighid waved at a stone house surrounded by tall pines on top of a crest.

As they rode up, a large robust woman opened the door and strode out. She had wild red hair that refused to stay in its pins. She wore a crimson chemise. Over that was a McTiernay plaid arisaid reaching from her neck to her ankles. It was plaited all around, secured at the waist with a large leather belt similar to the one Conor wore.

"Who are you?" she directed towards Laurel in a harsh tone.

"I'm Laurel Cordell," she said, sliding off the horse. "Are you the McTiernay midwife?"

"Aye," the surly woman responded, refusing to offer anything more.

The midwife's hostility gave Laurel the feeling that not only did she not like visitors, she especially disliked non-highlander visitors.

"I guess you have heard of me," replied Laurel, who, after a long cold ride, was not in the mood for sniping women.

"I know you are English and are marrying the laird."

"Umm. Well, that is yet to be seen," Laurel replied, tying Borrail to the nearest tree.

"You aren't marrying him?" The red eyebrows creased noticeably.

Ahh, it seemed the midwife who knew everything did not know about her and Conor's latest feud. "I do not wish to do so, no."

"You too good for our laird?" asked the midwife, trying to assess the proud, regal beauty she had heard so much about.

"Not at all. I just won't change for him, or any man. I love your laird, but I refuse to pretend I am unskilled in things he thinks I shouldn't be. And I will apply my knowledge when I can. Until he accepts this, we will not be wed."

The older woman nodded as if approving. It seemed that she had passed some test. "Come on in, then. You, too, Brighid. I see you hovering back there. Get yourself in where it is warm." The large woman turned and entered her cottage, leaving the visitors to fend for themselves.

Brighid and Laurel entered the stone cottage and went and stood by the fire to warm. Laurel could feel the midwife's eyes on her, studying her. Mayhap she had only passed the first of many tests.

"So, I understand that you helped deliver Aileen's babe."

It wasn't a question. It was a statement of fact. The churlish redhead may live far away, but her knowledge of clan activities was apparently fairly current.

"Yes, I had hoped that you would arrive in time to help. I had no idea what I was doing." She rubbed her hands bringing them back to life and took a look around. The cottage was essentially one very large room with the hearth situated in the middle.

"You did fine."

"You weren't there," countered Laurel. "I am afraid it was sheer luck that all went well. I am much better with scrapes and cuts. Much simpler."

"I was there. You did fine." The news surprised her. She

had sent Brighid to get the midwife, but when she didn't arrive Laurel had assumed Brighid had been unsuccessful. Why had the midwife not come in to help?

"I'm sorry, milady. Hagatha promised me to silence," pleaded Brighid, looking like she wanted to dissolve into nothingness.

"You were there?" Laurel asked, still not comprehending.

"Aye. Wanted to see what you were made of. I thought Aileen a fool to trust an English, but seems she understood more than I."

"Well, umm, Hagatha, Aileen needs your help again."

"Midwife," corrected the redhead.

"Excuse me?"

"Call me midwife, English." The nickname she called Laurel wasn't exactly said derogatively, but it certainly was not a compliment, either. It was more like a statement of fact, not leaning one way or the other.

But loyal Brighid was not so easygoing. "Hagatha, you know you should refer to her as my lady, Lady Laurel or soon as Lady McTiernay."

"Over me dead body will I call her by another term other than English."

Laurel tried to defuse the situation. "It's all right, Brighid. It is actually refreshing to hear someone call me something without a title."

Brighid knew that her lady did not care much for titles and the respect they conveyed. But Brighid honored and loved Laurel, and proper deference was required. "But, Lady Laurel, you are just as much a Scot as you are English."

"Is that right now?" said a surprised Hagatha. "Well, in that case I can't be callin' you English. Would insult the Scottish half of ye. Depending on me mood, I might call you Laurel." Laurel was beginning to really like Hagatha. She was a character who kept her own code of ethics.

"So, midwife, I came here for Aileen," she reminded Hagatha. "She tore while delivering, and she is still in quite a bit of pain."

"Must have torn quite a bit then."

"Yes. I thought to stitch her, but she was not open to the suggestion."

"Hmm. Probably should have. Next time do. Tearing isn't uncommon with bigger babes. Well, it's too late to stitch now." She went over to a cabinet and opened the doors. The shelves were filled with various ointments and herbs.

"You have an excellent collection," Laurel spoke her thoughts aloud as she came closer to take a look.

"You know some of these, do you?"

"Only the ones used for fever and for wounds. I sometimes was allowed to help my mother tend to the soldiers, but I was very young." She looked at the shelves, pointing to the pots with alder, centaury, common rue, and ground ivy.

"I hear you have been doing the same for the warriors after practice."

"For a while, but the herbs are now all gone. In the spring, I was going to collect more and dry them."

Hagatha reached up and grabbed a jar of ointment.

"Here. Have her use this twice a day and make a tea out of these," she said, handing over a bag of dried herbs.

"What are these?"

"That," she said, pointing at the jar, "will help with the healing. Those cloves will help with the pain. It's safe for the baby too." Hagatha started walking to the door, indicating the visit was over.

"Hagatha? Do you live here alone?"

"Ever since me man died. Don't like company none nor socializing in the castle. The laird's all right, though. A lot like his father."

As they got on their horses to return, Hagatha reached up and grabbed a hold of Laurel's hand. "I'm glad you came, Laurel. The laird's a lucky man, or will be once he realizes what he'll lose if he don't let you be. Me man tried to change me once. Didn't work out so well. Tried to change him, too. Finally, we struck a bargain to let each other be. Was happy ever since. You try it with the laird. You'll see. You'll be happy, too. It's the only way, I tell you. Let the other be." She turned and disappeared back inside in the cottage. Laurel looked forward to the next time she would get to visit with this special, shrewd woman.

The ride back to the castle took even longer with Brighid who was unused to riding far distances. Although they had left early and did not stay at Hagatha's for any length of time, darkness overcame them long before they were near the castle walls.

Laurel could see fairly well in the moonlight and tried to lead Brighid along, keeping an eye out for danger. Thankfully, none came as they reached the plateau of rolling hills and cottages. In the distance, the castle walls could be seen. Silhouetted against the night were dozens of guards lining the walls, obviously searching for someone.

Me, Laurel thought. *Oh, Lord, he really is going to lock me up forever.* She stopped their horses before entering the soldiers' view. Reaching into her sporran, she handed Brighid the ointment and herbs. "Give them to Aileen in the morning with Hagatha's instructions."

Brighid tried to persuade Laurel to let her come and help explain the reason for their delay, but Laurel could not be swayed.

"Look up there, Brighid. Those men are looking for us right now. I have no idea how Laird McTiernay is going to respond to this, but I am pretty sure he is in a quarrelsome mood right now. I don't want you to get caught in the middle of an argument. So I want you to ride directly home. I will see myself the rest of the way. It will be best if I face his fury alone."

"But you told him where you were going. Everyone knows the distance to the midwife's," Brighid said naively.

"Yes, well, I don't think that is going to matter, and, if you think on it, neither do you."

"What will happen to you?"

Laurel tried to give a nonchalant hug. "He won't hurt me, if that is your concern. I just doubt I will be let to leave the keep any time soon, even to visit Aileen and the baby."

"Oh, milady! But you were doing it to help. Surely, that will make all the difference."

"Unfortunately, the idea of me helping will only make things worse."

She nudged Borrail forward and started to ride towards the castle gates. Just as she had guessed, she was immediately spotted by several of the guards lining the walls. She was surprised when she entered the keep and Conor did not come to greet her. She handed her reins to a stable boy and headed for her chambers.

"You must be Lady Laurel," came a voice from the chapel doors. Laurel pivoted to see the most kind-looking priest she had ever seen. He had a white beard that matched his hair. His eyes were a deep brown and surrounded with wrinkles from years of smiling.

"I am . . . Father Lanaghly?"

"You surmise correctly. Conor will be glad you have returned safely."

"Ummm, yes, I'm sure he will be. Is he here?"

"No. I believe that you have arrived before he and his men have returned."

"Returned? But didn't Neal or Fiona tell him where I went?"

"I believe so. He seemed to think you wouldn't survive a trip that far out without guardsmen to assist you. Seems he was wrong."

"Oh, Lord, he is going to be furious. I had absolutely no idea it would take so long. And, God as my witness, Brighid is the *slowest* rider," she said absently, her eyes suddenly growing large as she realized what she had just uttered in front of the priest.

Father Lanaghly was enchanted. When he saw her ride in with a proud back and golden hair flying all around her, he thought he knew why the laird had finally broken his vows of eternal bachelorhood. But now, seeing her eyes and her lovely expression, he was certain he understood.

"Hush, now. I suspect you are right about our laird. But

like all tempers, his will subside. I think it's time you go to bed now. I suspect you will see the laird as soon as he arrives."

"Thank you, Father." She climbed the stairs to the keep, unable to stop the tears from forming. It had not been her intention to have the men search for her again. She just wanted to help her friend.

She prepared herself for bed, stripping down to her shift, and began combing her hair in the chair by the fire. When would she and Conor be able to work *with* each other? It seemed that unless she was in his arms, they were arguing about something—everything.

Conor was told of her safe return by soldiers sent to intercept him and his guard. Relief flooded through him. Snow was just coming down and the ground would be covered in white before daylight. And, just like last time, his fear was quickly replaced by matching levels of fury. Asleep or not, she was going to have to explain herself.

He strode into her room, searching her empty bed. When he didn't see her, he hollered her name so loud that the windows shook. "Laurel!"

She had been asleep when he entered, curled up on the chair near the fire, awaiting his return. His yelling made her jump out of her skin.

Suddenly, Laurel appeared out from behind the hearth chair. "I'm here, Conor."

So much of him wanted to cross the room and pull her into his arms. Instead, he exploded. "What did you think you were doing going to Hagatha's? It's snowing outside! Didn't you notice the weather? Do you constantly roam the world without a care for anyone but yourself? You once again forced my men to hunt you down. Never again, Laurel! Never again! Do you hear me!"

She was tired and cold and wanted to cry. Only pride enabled her to keep the tears from falling. "I was thinking of Aileen when I went to Hagatha's. I didn't know it would take so long. I'm sorry that you felt you had to send your men after me, but I assure you that I can take care of myself."

"Well, you had better be able to! Another stunt like this one, and you'll be someone else's concern. In the past week, I have twice had to run out after you. I have never seen anyone more self-centered. You have used your charm and beauty to get me to back down and give in to your desires, but no more. Do you hear me! No more. So take those blue eyes that make men do your bidding and point them elsewhere."

All of Laurel's fury, temper, and pride vanished at his words. Never had anyone cut her more deeply than he. She had thought he loved her, but no one could say such things to someone he cared about. She lowered her eyes and looked at the wood seams in the floor. "I understand. The next time I leave, it will be for good."

"There won't be a next time."

Yes, there would be. Come spring, she would leave and never return. Maybe she would have a chance in Ireland if she hid her ancestry, she thought to herself. She turned around so that her back faced him and wiped the tears from her cheeks.

Conor knew he was being unfair. He just felt so damn powerless around her and so worthless when she was in harm's way. In the past, women had used many different ploys to entice him to do their bidding. When he was young, it had worked. But then he caught on to their selfish, conniving ways. He'd thought he was immune to the ploys of such women. But today, he came back to find out that Laurel had abused his goodwill. Oh, she had left word of where she was going. And she had an escort, but she knew, *she knew,* that he wasn't going to approve of her trip to Hagatha's. Her blatant deceit was inexcusable.

"Do not leave this tower, Laurel. Do not try me again," he stated in a flat voice. She heard him close the chamber door. His footsteps retreated down the stairs.

She collapsed onto her knees and wept for several minutes. How could he think so little of her? When would he ask for an explanation before attacking her motives? She wiped her tears and hugged herself. She needed to think.

So, she started the climb up to the tower battlements. It was cold, but she didn't care. She was already numb.

"Hey, look!" cried Fergus. Gilroy looked up to see what his friend was yelling about. "It's her! It's our angel sent down to warm us on this cold night."

Gilroy and Fergus looked out through the night's snowy sky and saw a white vision walking along the Star Tower battlements. At first, several of the men had scoffed at them when they mentioned the angel who appeared and disappeared as a spirit in the moonlight. Then, when several others also saw her, their post became quite crowded for a while. It had been several days since their angel had last appeared, so—once again—it was just them doing night guard duty.

Gilroy and Fergus sat and watched their angel move about the battlements for several minutes in silence. There was very little light as a snow storm had settled in, and it was hard to make her out. Her arms were moving more animatedly than normal.

"She dancing?" asked Gilroy.

"Don't know. Kind of hard to tell," Fergus replied, squinting.

They continued to watch her for a long while before sleep snuck up on them both.

Down in the great hall, Father Lanaghly was doing an excellent job of making the great McTiernay chieftain feel about two inches tall.

"Whatever got into you? Why do you McTiernays let your tempers run away with you when it comes to your loved ones? First, you practically destroy your keep in teaching a lesson to your brothers. Now, you accuse a woman loved by all, including you, of being conniving, selfish, and spiteful. She is a beautiful miracle. Look all around you! Do you hear the laughter? Look at yourself! Is it going to take another miracle to admit you were wrong?"

Father Lanaghly had expected Conor to be angry with Laurel. Everyone had anticipated that. But no one imagined the laird would be so harsh. Many had overhead his comments. Everyone near the Star Tower certainly had and had passed the word. When Brighid arrived, she tried to defend her lady with explanations of their trip, claiming that they would have been back sooner if she were a better rider. Already the clan was beginning to splinter off into groups backing either the lady or their laird.

Conor felt miserable. He had come down from Laurel's chamber and started drinking ale from the buttery. When Father Lanaghly had first approached him, he still felt himself rightfully angry at Laurel's deceit. Only after the priest forced him to listen did he realize how completely cruel he had been.

He remembered her last words. "The next time I leave, it will be for good."

He dropped his head into his hands. The dark void of his nightmares had come, but now he knew what it was. He was not going to lose Laurel, but her love. What had he done? A new fear flooded him.

Conor knew that he had abused Laurel's trust and her love, but he had all winter to make up for it. He would convince her to stay and forgive him, just as he had persuaded her to marry him. If need be, he would use the ruse of protecting her grandfather to force her hand. Anything, he promised himself, anything to get her to give him time to make it up to her.

Loman trudged up the guard tower stairs to the curtain wall leading out to the night guardsmen. It had been a stressful night and, the way things were looking, it was only going to be worse in the morning. He knew his laird had never been this emotionally raw before. And because of that, Loman realized that everything his laird had said, had been said out of fear. Conor's fear for her, fear of her—that she was like the others—and fear of himself. Loman shook his head as he saw the two sleeping guards.

He kicked Gilroy and Fergus awake. "What are you two idiots doing? You'll freeze to death. I'm switching the guard every hour until the snow storm is over."

"Hey!" yelled Gilroy, nudging Fergus. "Our angel is still with us!"

"What are you two blubbering about?" Loman asked.

"Our angel," smiled Fergus. "She comes and visits us at night. Usually she only comes when the stars are shining, but tonight she came in with the snow."

"You two are daft. Come on, let's go."

"Look for yourself." Fergus pointed towards the Star Tower.

Loman gave a sideways glance towards the tower, expecting to see nothing but snow. However, he could see movement up there. It looked like someone trying to bang something. It was very difficult to see. Who would be up there in this weather? Then he saw the long golden hair and instantly realized who that was.

"That isn't an angel, you fools!" And he started running.

Chapter Eleven

Loman didn't stop when he glimpsed Father Lanaghly and Conor emerging from the hall. He pushed them both violently out of his way and began climbing the tower steps two, three at a time. He reached the battlement doors. The weather had made the wood expand, and they were frozen shut. After several hard blows, they swung open.

Laurel was on the stone floor, frozen in a ball. Her hair felt like icicles on his skin. He picked her up and was heading down the stairs to her chambers when he collided into Conor.

Conor looked at the frozen girl in Loman's arms. His greatest fear was being realized. He was going to lose her. Loman handed Laurel over to his laird, panicked that she wasn't moving. Conor ran, carrying her the rest of the way down the stairs to his solar and placed her on his bed. From behind, he could hear Loman and others running and shouting.

Soon, there were buckets of warm water and blankets being flown around. People were surrounding Laurel, trying to rub life back into her limbs, but she was not responding. Conor just stood there holding her head, mentally pleading with her not to leave him. He could not find his voice.

After what seemed to be an eternity, she blinked her eyes. Her lips were still a scary shade of blue, and her eyes looked hollow. "Love, you are all right now. Loman found you." He kissed her cheeks, her lips, her hands. All were much too cold.

"I know you didn't mean it." Her voice was a hoarse whisper barely loud enough to hear.

"Shh, love. Don't talk now." Tears were streaming down his cheeks. He felt like she was leaving him. Her words reminded him too much of those who had spoken similar phrases on their deathbeds.

He grabbed her face in his hands. "Don't leave me, Laurel. Please don't leave me. I will hunt you down no matter where you go and bring you back. Do you hear me? You are mine, and without you, I am incomplete." He held her close, swaying gently back and forth, murmuring words of love into her ear.

The men and women rubbing Laurel's limbs, trying to bring circulation back into her arms, legs and feet, were all silently praying. When Conor saw Father Lanaghly, he immediately assumed the worst. No one was giving last rites to his heart and soul. She was not going to die.

"Get out of here, Father. Your services won't be needed tonight. Leave us alone."

"I'm not here for her, son, but for you. I'm praying just as hard as the rest that this generous soul remains with us."

Conor spent the next several hours overseeing Laurel's care. Her limbs started regaining color, but she remained very cold. Her body often would shake uncontrollably no matter how many layers of bedding were placed upon her. Eventually, he sent everyone away, stripped them both down, and held her as close he could. Finally, she seemed to respond. Her lips now looked pale, not blue. Her fingers and toes all had some color within them.

But, just when he thought the horror had passed and that she would survive, a fever took hold. Never in his life did he feel more lost and out of control.

For the next several days, she wandered in and out of

lucidity as she raved about his inability to trust her or lean on her. Throughout it all, he never left her side.

One time, she woke and sat straight up, demanding that he explain why she was conniving. After he explained how wrong he was, how he didn't mean it, she contradicted him, going into a lengthy discourse on her childhood. In it, she described several events that proved he was right. When she was five, she intentionally charmed the cook into letting her have extra desserts every night. She had cajoled the stable master into teaching her to ride and hunt on bareback. She had even convinced her brother that he would be better off if she left England.

"So you see, you are right in your assessment of me, Conor. You will be much better off without me." And with those words, she went back into a fretful sleep, her fever rising to terrifying levels.

"She can't go on this way," he moaned to Hagatha, who had arrived down the day before.

"Aye, she can and will. You can and will." She bathed Laurel's brow trying to keep her cool. "You best be eating something, laird. Once she recovers you will need all your strength to convince her you won't be changing her ways."

The next day, her fever broke. Her throat was parched, and she was extremely weak, but she was no longer burning to the touch. Conor's spirits lifted.

Laurel felt as if a herd of horses had trampled her. When she reached up to massage her temples, she moaned aloud. Every muscle in her body ached, and every joint screamed in pain. Her head was pounding. Immediately, Conor was by her side.

"Don't move, love. Just tell me what you need."

"Water." As she watched him move to bring her a cup of water, she noticed how haggard and withdrawn he was. Her giant had lost a lot of weight. "Conor, what happened to you?"

He smiled at her and sat down. "He hasn't been eating is what's wrong," Hagatha said from across the room.

"You've been feverin' for five days. This one," she rotated her thumb towards Conor, "refused to leave. Practically had no sleep, and what little food he ate was forced."

Laurel squinted, trying to focus. "Hagatha? What are you doing here? You hate leaving your cottage," she murmured, closing her eyes.

"Glad you appreciate me sacrifice."

"I need a bath." Laurel felt grimy and unclean but completely powerless to do anything about it.

"Aye, you do," replied the old midwife. "But not for a couple of days, and no arguments. Now, I've got to go see the cook about some broth."

Moments later, Conor and Laurel were alone.

Laurel turned her head and gazed at the man who had so deftly stolen and then shredded her heart. He was standing by the window sill just staring at her. His hair was matted, and his clothes were wrinkled and unkempt.

"What happened? I feel as bad as you look," she commented.

He smiled, walked over, and stroked her hair, tucking it behind her ear as he was so fond of doing. She was going to be all right, he said to himself. She was still Laurel. She was still the same woman who had unexpectedly stumbled into his camp that fateful day. Relief spread like a summer day's warmth all over him.

"You were stuck outside in the snow on top of the tower."

"I remember. I wanted to think, and that is where I go when I need to clear my head. I was so cold, and the door would not open. I tried and tried, but it was jammed, trapping me outside. I called out, but no one heard me. I thought I was going to die."

"Shhh." He closed his eyes and cradled her in his arms. "You are never going to leave me. I won't let you. I would follow you anywhere to bring you back to my side. Don't you know that by now?"

She fell asleep in his arms. Conor held her until Hagatha made him go eat and rest himself. Over the next couple of days, Hagatha oversaw their recuperations. On the third day, she declared that she was going home.

"Thank you, Hagatha."

"I told you to call me midwife."

"I know, but you are so much more than that. You are the McTiernays' precious own Hagatha." And she reached up to give the redheaded woman a hug.

"Now, you stay in bed until your strength returns. You can get up for a bath, but only limited activity. This kind of weather brings on sickness that fills the lungs to those that are weak."

"I promise."

"Don't worry. She's not going to do anything to risk her health," Conor promised as he came up and put his hands on Laurel's shoulders. She craned her head to look at him.

"You're worse than she is," Laurel said, shrugging his hands off, unconsciously rising to challenge him.

"Aye. I will be."

"Will be! You already are."

Hagatha left while they were still squabbling over Laurel's recovery. She chuckled to herself as she descended the tower stairs. Those two will be fine, she thought. They will be just as she was with her man. Always debating something, but always making up, too. Aye, the McTiernays have finally gotten a lady again to help lead the clan.

Upstairs, Conor and Laurel had not even noticed Hagatha's departure.

"I think you should rest now, Laurel." Conor buried his hands in her hair, twisting his fingers in the silken tresses, hugging her to him.

"I'm going to take a bath."

"Maybe tomorrow. You have already exerted yourself too much today."

"Conor, I'm going to exert myself a hell of a lot more by throwing you out that window if you keep this up." She tried to shove him out of her way, but he refused to be budged. The effort exhausted her.

He picked her up and carried her back to the bed. "See? I told you, you are too tired."

"I wasn't until you manhandled me," she grumbled back. "Conor, I don't think you understand. I feel awful, but mostly because I feel unclean. If I could just have a bath and wash my hair, I would feel so much better."

"Will you behave and stay in bed for the rest of the day?"

She hated convalescence. She was rarely sick and always recovered quickly the few times she had succumbed to illness. But, knowing she should take any opportunity where Conor appeared to be the least bit compromising, she caved. "I promise."

"Fine. I'll have the bath drawn up for you this afternoon. Meanwhile, sleep."

She squinted her eyes at him. He was so arrogant. "You are insufferable."

"So you have said many times before."

"Not that it has done any good."

"Aye. I doubt that it will make a difference to my habits, but if it makes you feel better to say it, then do so." He was tucking her in now. She was tired, but didn't want to give in so easily without receiving something in return.

"If I am going to sleep, you are going to eat."

He smiled at her stratagem. All the times before when she had argued with him, he thought of it as defiance— something she intentionally did to force his anger. It suddenly occurred to him that it wasn't defiance at all, but pride that spurred such a reaction from her. She was bold, and like him, did not want to appear weak. He smiled to himself, satisfied that he finally had figured out one of his bride's many little mysteries.

"Aye. Because you have requested it."

His apparent acquiescence made her feel better, and she closed her eyes and slept for several hours.

"Absolutely not, Conor McTiernay."

"Do you want a bath or not?"

"You know I do. But not with you giving it to me."

"It's either a bath with me, love, or no bath at all."

"What about Brighid?"

"What about her?"

She was getting more than just a little frustrated with his intentional dim-wittedness. "It isn't appropriate! Men don't bathe women."

"This man does if the woman is you."

"But you are a laird."

"And you are my woman."

"First of all, no, I am not. Second, I am unmarried. There! What would everyone say if they found out their laird bathed an unmarried woman?"

"I'm sure they would be glad that I had personally overseen the health and safety of their future Lady."

She was not winning this argument at all. He was leaning against the mantel, totally calm and relaxed. There was no yelling, no anger and certainly no flexibility. She was desperate.

"Conor, it just simply isn't done. You cannot demand this of me," she pleaded intensely.

He walked over to her and drew her up to his side. He held her there for several minutes, just loving the feel of this woman in his arms. Whether it was proper or not, only he was going to oversee her activities until she was completely recovered.

"I almost lost you," he said and then kissed her hair. "I thought I had when you went to Hagatha's, and then when Loman found you . . . my whole reason for living disappeared until you came back to me." He framed her face with his hands and lifted her head so that he could look into her eyes. "Until I am completely assured of your recovery, I'm going to act a little unorthodox, and very possessive, love. I ask you to indulge me." The kiss that followed confirmed the words he had just uttered.

It was deep and long, conveying the need and passion he felt for her. Laurel responded in kind. Her arms stole around his back, and her hands began to massage his neck muscles. No matter what arguments they may have had or would have in the future, she would always love this man with all of her heart and soul.

"Now," he said smiling, raising his head and ending the kiss. "About your bath." He swung her into his arms and walked over to the hearth, which was now blazing.

Slowly, he undressed her, stopping every once in a while to take a taste of exposed skin. She loved the way he touched her with gentle, feather-light caresses that filled her veins with liquid fire.

Once she was naked, he quickly put her in the warm tub and began to rub her body down with her lilac soap. Suddenly, Laurel's list of reasons why he shouldn't do this vanished. Sensation took over. It wasn't exactly a sexual stirring, although passion and attraction were definitely there. It was love. Conor touched her and bathed her as if she was the most precious thing in the entire world.

When he began to wash her hair, Laurel decided she wanted to do the same for him. She turned around and reached up, grabbing his shirt and lifting it over his head.

As she rose slightly out of the water, Conor was momentarily stunned at the sight of water glistening on her skin in the firelight. She was perfection to him. Seconds later, he realized that she had also removed his belt as his kilt fell to the floor, free of its strap.

"It's my turn to wash you." Her voice was husky with desire.

Tight and hard with arousal, he allowed her to pull him in, falling with a splash. She grinned at him. "I think that you, too, are in need of a bath." Somewhere in his mind, he realized as she started lathering him that he was going to smell like flowers, but didn't care.

"Ah, love. You will be the death of me yet." He bent his head, aiming to capture her lips with his own.

She dodged him. She nibbled on his earlobe instead. "Hmmm. How's that?"

"Well, if I don't die tonight from the wanting of you,

I'm sure my men will humble me into nonexistence when they get a whiff of me in the morning," he said as he moved to return the favor by nuzzling her neck.

For the next half hour, they played and kissed and nibbled. He often had to dissuade Laurel from escalating their passion, claiming that he was already allowing her too much excitement.

When the water started to cool, he lifted her out of the tub and onto a plaid placed in front of the warmth of the fire. He briskly dried her and helped her don her shift. Next, he started combing her long hair to help it dry. She fell asleep to the soft soothing rhythm of his strokes. Her last thoughts before she drifted off were about Conor needing to give her another bath before she fully recovered.

Three days later, Laurel was finished with placating Conor and staying in bed. He had gone too far when he put a guard at the door and hid all of her dressing gowns. By the time he returned with food, she was fully prepared for all-out war.

"What are you doing out of bed?" he asked, swinging his leg to close the door.

"Attempting to leave."

"Empty threat," he said, indicating her state of undress. He was right, of course. Dueling issues of pride, Laurel had decided that she would rather cave in to his demands—for the moment—than humiliate herself by walking about semi-dressed in front of his people.

"You are being completely unreasonable."

"Probably some, but not completely." Conor shrugged his shoulders.

"Hagatha said . . ." she started, but he interrupted, finishing the sentence for her.

"Hagatha said that you were to remain in bed until your strength returned. I am unconvinced that it has," he said, calmly removing the food items from the tray and placing them on the make-shift table they had been using for the past few days.

"Conor, you are pushing me to become inventive in finding a way to defy you. I warn you—I will."

He didn't seem impressed as he reached out for a buttered roll and began to eat.

"You come and go at your leisure. You spend most of your time out of the keep while I am kept like a prisoner in here going crazy from boredom." She was pacing now.

"You could make your wedding dress," he suggested, watching her go back and forth. "I understand from Glynis that you have yet to sew one."

"One only needs a wedding dress if one is to be married," she said sweetly, but through tight lips.

"Aye. And you fall into that category."

"I do not."

"You do, and you will."

"Hmm. That may be very difficult as the next time you come to see me, I will be gone. Not just from my room, but from you, you insufferable tyrant."

Conor was starting to become a little concerned with the promise held in her voice. Time for a different tactic. When calm redirection didn't work, what would? And then he remembered the wise words of Hagatha: ". . . you will need all your strength to convince her you won't be changing her ways."

He put down the bread and rested his elbows on his knees, looking directly at her. "I'm not going to change, Laurel. Not now, not ever. I'm chieftain of a clan, and it is my responsibility to see to all who belong to it. You belong to me, so my responsibility and determination are even stronger where you are concerned."

"But you don't want me! You said so yourself. I'm conniving and self-centered."

"Aye, I said those words, and I was wrong. I just couldn't understand why you would deliberately set out to make me go mad with worry."

He pointed to the chair across from him and motioned

for her to sit and eat. Laurel hesitated, but then sat like some regal queen who had decided, not been told, to do so.

"But it wasn't deliberate. I had no idea that I would be gone so long. Besides, I could have made the trip in a fraction of the time if you had not made me promise to take an escort." Laurel reached out for the remaining roll and tore off a piece.

"Aye. Another cause for my anger." Conor leaned back in the chair. "When I realized it was Brighid who was with you, I became doubly concerned, knowing that it was more likely you were escorting her than the other way around. If you wanted to see Hagatha so badly, why didn't you say so? I would have sent one of the guards to see to your safety. You would have also been able to ride at the speed you desired."

Laurel shook her head, causing gold strands of hair to become free from its ties. "Don't rewrite history with me, laird."

His eyebrows rose visibly. "Conor."

"*Laird.* You know as well as I that you would not have let me go to Hagatha's, and certainly not with an escort other than yourself." She munched on some new dish of Fiona's that, while looking revolting, was surprisingly good.

Seeing her doubtful look change to one of enjoyment, he offered, "It's called haggis."

"It looks awful, but it tastes wonderful. What's in it?"

"It's tricky to make well. Fiona is an excellent cook. You were right to hire her on full time and get rid of the rotating schedule. Haggis is a mixture of minced heart, lungs, and liver of a sheep or calf, depending upon what's available. You then mix it with suet, onions, oatmeal, and seasonings and boil it in an animal's stomach."

Laurel thought she was going to become ill all over again. That information just ended the meal for her. From now on, she was only going to eat items she knew. She sat back in her chair and clasped her hands in her lap. From a distance, anyone would think she was a demure, proper lady, but Conor knew otherwise. Her blue-green eyes were as dark as a storm on the North Sea.

Getting her stomach under control again, Laurel tried to correct his visions of their future. "I don't want to fight any more, Conor. I just don't think we can be happy together. It seems all we do is battle and argue about everything. I understand your need to protect what is yours, but it seems that you want me to be someone I'm not. I'm a lady, but I also break the rules of society. I have to be free to ride and make decisions about helping those who need it. If I cannot do so, the essence that makes up me will be gone."

"Then we will just have to figure out how to achieve both our needs without changing each other," he said with complete confidence. He leaned over and grabbed her hand, gently massaging the soft skin.

"It's possible, Laurel. My parents were both stubborn, but they figured out a way to be both strong-willed and married."

"And what exactly do you want to achieve? Me?"

"No, you are already mine. I just have to find a way to let you experience the freedom you desire without risking your safety."

"That's unreasonable. I could slip on the stairs and fall," she said, getting up from her chair and moving towards the window. It was snowing again, and world was covered in white. "You cannot protect me from everything. Has it not occurred to you that I worry about you? You are a chieftain of a powerful clan. I'm sure you have enemies who are actively seeking opportunities to hurt you. Do I beg and plead for you not to go out? Not to see other lairds when you need to?" She turned and caught his eye. He was still seated. "It is not protection you give, Conor, but confinement. I don't want to be your captive—I want to be your wife."

He shook his head. "You want more than that, Laurel. You want to lead this clan in areas that are ultimately my responsibility. You make arbitrary decisions that impact my ability to lead my people without asking me."

She had not thought of it like that before. "That is not my intention. But there are some things with which I can help, especially those concerning the care and maintenance of the clan. I do not claim to know how to train warriors, but I do know when a roof needs to be repaired—and I know how to repair it!"

"You cannot be ordering my men around outside of the keep. That is my responsibility. To allow you to do so only creates confusion and division of loyalties."

"What's the difference between me asking men to clean the hall versus repair a thatched roof?"

Conor sighed, rising to join her by the window. "The lady of the keep has always undertaken the maintenance and cleaning of the castle. You know this, Laurel."

"I know that traditional philosophy, yes. But if you are the laird, why can you not say that I can also fix things outside of the castle walls?"

He reached out with his thumb, raising her chin so that their eyes locked. "I will not share my responsibilities with you or anyone. There is only one laird."

"I don't want you to share your responsibilities. I just want to help. I want the ability to make changes and improve things where and when I see them. I don't believe I am doing anything that you wouldn't do and say if you were there."

"But that is just the point. You cannot make decisions that should be mine."

Decisions that should be mine, he said. Laurel finally saw the true issue behind the problem. She threw her arms around him with a huge smile on her face like she had discovered a precious stone of great value. "So it isn't the decisions *themselves* that is the problem. It is my attempt to make changes that you have not approved."

"Something like that," he murmured. The soft feel of her breasts through her chemise was distracting, but the sudden change in her disposition from antagonistic to energetic made him guard his response.

"What if I promise to go through you from now on?"

Laurel asked, barely able to contain the excitement beginning to bubble within her. What she cared most about was being useful. If Conor could empower her with the authority of such work on a case-by-case basis, that would be enough.

"Meaning?" he tried to ask evenly. He realized that she was quite unaware of what she was doing by hugging him so closely, but it did not change the fact it was excruciatingly painful. He had promised himself that the next time they lay together, it would be as man and wife. But there was no way he was going to pull away now, not when she seemed so positive about them and their future.

Laurel's hope soared again. He didn't immediately cut short the opportunity to compromise, she thought to herself. "For example, the issue of the cottage roofs. What if I inspected them and then came to you to let you know my assessment and suggestions about improvements? If you approved, *then* could I assign work?"

He thought about the suggestion. It had merit. His decision-making authority would be preserved, yet she would be able fulfill this need of hers to help.

"I would prefer to be notified in advance of the inspection."

She let go of him and twirled around the room before falling onto the bed. There *was* a solution, she mentally shouted with joy. He was going to let her assist with more than just the weaving and cleaning of the keep!

"And I will want to assign the work," he added roughly, noting that the physical need built up by their closeness was not dying even though she had pulled away. He moved to sit down and hide the evidence of his desire. "But I am sure something could be managed just as long as my men know it is my decision."

She couldn't help herself, but jumped up and ran over to him throwing herself into his lap. She stunned him further by kissing him long and hard. She searched his eyes. When they had first met, the silvery depths were cold and distant. Now, his eyes were like liquid pools of moonlight. "I will tell you in advance of anything that I am planning."

"You will *ask* me, not tell me."

She wrinkled her nose. "Fine, I will ask you, but if you say no, I reserve the right to argue you into a yes."

He ignored this somewhat uncompromising deal and decided to clarify the rules. "And you are still to be escorted when outside of the castle walls."

I can establish new compromises too, she thought. "But I can ride Borrail."

"Aye, you can ride your horse."

"Fast."

"Aye, you can ride fast—but your escort has to have similar riding capabilities."

"I want one more promise, Conor."

"I, as well."

"I won't go through another argument like we had last time. You said some horrible things. Things that were not true and if you had taken the time to hear me out, you would have felt differently."

"Fine. Then I will give you my word that when angered by something you did or did not do, I will give you the opportunity to explain."

Her smile could have lit up northern Scotland.

"Now, I want a promise from you," he said. She looked at him cautiously. "I don't ever want you to call me laird as if you were just another member of my clan. You are more than that, even when you are annoyed, and I want you to remember it."

She stroked the hair around his temple. It was such a little promise, but it obviously meant a great deal to him. "I promise, Conor." Last week, Laurel had not thought it possible that she and Conor could find a way to agree on so much. He was right, there was a way for two stubborn people to come together and live happily. They just had to learn how to give.

She looked at him, her adoring eyes sparkling like the crystal waters of the highland lochs. "Thank you, Conor."

At that moment, he realized that she would almost always win any future arguments just so that he could see the look of joy and appreciation on her face again.

Neither of them thought all future arguments had been averted by agreements made that evening. But neither did they realize how quickly their next differences of opinion would come.

First was the argument of when she would be allowed to resume her duties. They finally came to a compromise after a heated discussion. She could leave her room starting on the morrow, but limitedly. The resumption of any other activity could be done with the start of the new week, depending on how she was faring.

The second argument happened in the great hall after dinner and dealt with their sleeping arrangements. Conor refused to sleep anywhere else besides the solar, and he rejected any suggestion about Laurel being moved to other chambers now that she was well.

"Father Lanaghly is here!" she stressed.

"What has that have to do with anything?" he asked, taking a long drink of ale.

"But we are unmarried, it isn't proper."

"I can rectify that in just a few minutes, Laurel. It is your wish that we wait until Cole can be here."

"I would like Colin to be here as well, but it would be dangerous for him to travel to and from the border country this time of year."

"Choose. Do you want to sleep together married? Or do you want to wait for Cole?"

"Conor, you are not being reasonable."

"I am probably being insufferable, too," he added knowing how much she liked to use that word to describe him. He stood, walked over and lifted her to a standing embrace. "But I am going to be there if something happens to you at night, if you relapse, or get ill." He kissed the top of her head.

Instinctively, she returned the embrace and rested her head on his shoulders. "I am fine, and you know it. You are just trying to get your way even though you have nothing to support your side of the argument."

"One of the better things about being a laird," he said, leaning back and looking at her as his lips broke into a wide grin.

"Ahh-hem," interrupted the priest from the doorway. "Excuse me for overhearing." In truth, when these two were at it, it was difficult not to overhear, he thought to himself, advancing into the room.

"One of the better things about being a priest is my authority over who gets married." That got both their attentions.

"My Lady Laurel, you are correct to move back into your own chambers until after the ceremony. I have turned a blind eye to your current sleeping arrangements for too long." He raised his finger to stop Conor's impending eruption. "If you do not, I am afraid that I will not feel comfortable ordaining your union." He felt somewhat guilty about deceiving his laird, but one did what one must with what one had, he told himself.

Laurel knew that only the priest's intervention had allowed her to win this one. But she tried not to gloat as she moved back into her chambers.

Despite knowing that Laurel had recovered and seemed to be in full health, Conor still woke up several times each night and visited her room to check on her.

The two weeks flew by in a blur. With preparing for the winter, overseeing his clan, and training the warriors, Conor had much to do. It seemed someone always needed something or some decision from him. Laurel didn't know how he could be so tolerant with his clansmen. It was no wonder that he lost his temper with her so much; he had no patience left by the end of the day!

Meanwhile, the making of her dress and preparations for the wedding celebration were keeping her busier than she anticipated. As she had promised, she limited her activities, often taking breaks in the afternoon. She hoped that her full strength and stamina would return soon.

On the first day she was allowed to leave the keep, she visited Aileen and her baby, whom they finally named Gideon. He had already grown so much in the few weeks since he was born.

"When is Cole due to arrive from Laird Schellden's?" asked Aileen, eager for the wedding to take place. She knew that Conor and Laurel would eventually get married, but she knew an ill-timed argument could halt the wedding plans.

"Either tomorrow or the day after," answered Laurel, helping Aileen prepare the afternoon meal.

"Is the chapel ready?"

"Enough. The benches are all now safe to use. Some were in deplorable condition with rot. The seats have been reupholstered in the McTiernay plaid. The altar coverings should be done tonight. Fallon is upset that the windows will most likely not be cleaned in time, but Conor will not delay the ceremony any longer. Even if Cole is not here the day after tomorrow, the ceremony will take place."

"Are you not also eager to have the wedding?" Aileen asked, shifting Gideon to the other hip while she stirred the broth cooking on the hearth.

"Here, let me take him," Laurel said, reaching for the little bairn. "Oh, I want to be married to Conor. I guess I am just a little nervous about the ceremony. So many people will be there, and I want everything to be just right."

"From the gossip that I hear from Glynis and Brighid, it will be wonderful. Everybody is going to be there, and those who aren't will wish they could be."

"That is exactly my point. What was I thinking agreeing to such a large event? Conor and I should have just met with Father Lanaghly and said our vows quickly and privately."

"Perhaps you were just unconsciously delaying your wedding night," Aileen cagily prodded. Many knew that the laird had stayed with his intended during the time she was unwell. Some speculated whether or not the wedding was just a formality as their chamber rooms were just a few floors apart.

"I suppose so," Laurel answered. She understood what Aileen was suggesting. She did not regret what she and Conor had shared, but she did not feel the need to explain or excuse their actions. She had noticed that Conor had also deftly evaded answering such queries coming from Father Lanaghly.

Chapter Twelve

The next two days went by faster than any Laurel had ever known. Cole had arrived and was having a merry time with his brothers, who were constantly teasing Conor—the eternal bachelor—about getting married.

Laurel had remained so busy preparing for the wedding that—with organizing the feast, arranging rooms in the keep, and making her dress—she could hardly believe it was now *the* day. The early morning light was brightly streaming through the window curtains as she lay on her bed staring at the ceiling, grinning like a child on Christmas morning. Today, she was going to marry Conor McTiernay.

She rose and was putting on a robe when the door to her chamber flew open and a half a dozen highland women entered. Fluttering around for the next several hours, they bathed, washed, and pampered her. Someone would put her hair up, and then another would take it down. Arguments arose over flowers, the numbers of herbs to be carried, whether or not she should eat, and a multitude of other things.

After a while, Laurel felt overwhelmed and asked everyone except Aileen to leave while she caught her breath. It was her wedding day, and a bad case of nerves was setting in.

A few months ago, Laurel never dreamed she would
ever get married, especially to a man like Conor. Her
only focus had been to find a safe harbor with her grandfather. Since then so much had happened and, in the
past two weeks, even more had transpired. The new-
found ability to seek and grant compromises that she and
Conor had achieved was creating a life of happiness and
hope. Sometimes she was afraid she would wake up and
realize it was all a dream.

Aileen was standing near the bed, looking at Laurel's
wedding garments and accessories. She reached out and fingered the fragile cloth. "This is the most beautiful wedding
dress I have ever seen. You have created a masterpiece."

Laurel smiled but did not move, attempting to focus
on the view from her window. "Not I. Brighid." Aileen decided not to contradict Laurel although she knew the
truth. Brighid was very skilled with a needle and her embroidery was superb, but it was Laurel's hard work and
design that made the ensemble so exquisite.

"I suppose it is time to get ready," Laurel sighed nervously, not moving from her single point of solace. The
idea of marrying Conor brought her joy and peace. But
the thought of becoming Lady McTiernay was quite
daunting.

Conor was the chieftain of a powerful highland clan.
She had only realized how large and powerful it was
these past several days. All week, there had been a con-
tinual stream of men coming to pay Conor respect in
regard to his upcoming nuptials. Hundreds of warriors,
dozens of lairds from smaller nearby allied clans, and
countless highland men and women had come to wish
them both well. Laurel's growing apprehension spiked
when Finn explained that Conor could easily call over
twice that many to battle. His personal army was over a
thousand warriors strong.

What made her think she could be the next Lady Mc-
Tiernay? What was Conor thinking when he asked—no,
demanded—that she become his wife?

She had become uncharacteristically nervous the past few days, repeatedly seeking Conor's affirmation that he wanted to marry her. And, each time, he had been able to convince Laurel that he was absolutely, positively sure.

As Laurel stared out the window, her hand crushed the velvet gold curtains she had pushed aside. She longed for just one more of his assurances.

She let out a barely noticeable groan.

"Laurel?"

"Hmm?" she responded absentmindedly.

"Come here and sit down with me."

Still deep in thought, Laurel replied, "What?"

"I said, come and join me. I know a nervous bride when I see one, and there is no doubt that is what you are. So come, sit, and let's talk."

Laurel let go of her grip on the gold cloth and sat down in the other chair facing the hearth. She bent her knees and tucked her feet underneath her.

"Tell me about England," Aileen casually requested.

Laurel blinked and cocked her head. "England?"

"Aye. I've never been there. You once mentioned it, and I would like to hear more."

Laurel raised her brows, shrugged, and began talking about her childhood home. Laurel spoke about Cheviot Hills in Northumberland, and how it was recognized as the main barrier between England and Scotland.

"Much of it is treeless, and there is a lonely eternal breeze that blows over the ridges of its rough grass. I used to sit for hours, comforted by the sound. Hadrian's wall—built by the Romans—was supposed to keep the Scots and English apart, but it never did. Both sides are always climbing over it or ignoring it."

Laurel found herself relaxing. "England is beautiful but, just as these picturesque highlands are hard and rocky, the Hills are also difficult. Much of Northumberland is made up of salt marshes, peat bogs, and broad rivers. But there is also beauty to be found in the green wooded valleys and deserted beaches."

For the next few hours, Laurel continued answering Aileen's questions and forgot her fears and need for reassurance.

Just as Aileen was going to suggest it was time to dress, Laurel's helpers arrived, saying that everyone but her was ready.

Laurel smiled, realizing that with Aileen's help, she, too, was now ready for the day's main event. She stood and walked over to the bed, lifting her garments, taking in their beauty and meaning.

Glynis rushed over. "Ho, now. We are going to help you with that."

"Glynis is right, milady. You just stand there and let us help you do everything," Brighid added, removing Laurel's robe.

Laurel, now calm, was able to withstand the eagerness surrounding her. Moments later, the diaphanous undergarments were placed on her, followed by her gown.

The outer portion of her wedding dress was made of a luxurious ivory silk damask that showed off Brighid's intricate embroidery. The gown's inset was a simple light gold satin and was lavishly embroidered around the hem. The needlework on the waist, cuffs, arm, and neck line was beautifully enhanced with crystals. Most of Brighid's embroidery was about an inch or more in diameter and contained a mixture of blue for purity and gold to match Laurel's hair.

The front of the gown was cut in the shape of a *V*, which rounded and closed in the back between her shoulder blades. The back ties that stitched the fabric together were made of the same material as the gold inset. The detailed belt hung high on her waist in the back, delicately draping and tying in the front to match the V-cut of her gown.

The gown's short, puffed sleeves were bound in the same embroidered pattern. The inner, tightly fitting sleeve was made of a light satin and silk mix, while the outer sleeve was made of thin chiffon, lined with a smaller width of embroidery.

Laurel decided to leave her hair long and loose, displaying its natural curls and waves. She wore a six-point gold tiara that had belonged in the McTiernay family for decades. On the front, it had a Celtic design embellished with blue crystals, pearls, and silver. Attached to the back of tiara, five strands of pearls made of blue and gold beads draped elegantly over her hair, accenting the blue needlework in the gown.

Last to be donned was a necklace that had been in Laurel's family for generations. It was one of the few items that she had sewn into her undergarments for safekeeping when she left England. It was a fairly simple, but striking necklace, made of white pearls, accented with a gold-tone star and a floral motif in a center pendant.

A knock echoed, and a clanswoman dressed in her very best opened the door.

"It's time?" Laurel asked, feeling nervous all over again.

"Aye, milady," whispered the woman.

"Milady," said a tearing Glynis, "you do us McTiernays proud today. Aye, you do, lass."

Everyone then surrounded Laurel, lifting her gown so that it would not drag upon the floor or stairs as she descended. When she arrived at the bottom of the tower and walked outside, she noticed that the courtyard, battlements, walls—everywhere a man could stand—were filled with highlanders. The chapel could not accommodate anything close to the number of men who had arrived on this cold day. The snow had melted away, but the frigid air remained.

She stood just past the tower doors, staring at the crowd, overwhelmed that these men had risked leaving their homes, their keeps, their families during the winter months to partake in this event.

Suddenly, Finn was by her side to escort her to the chapel. The huge man was fighting tears. "You are pure beauty, milady. I fail to understand, looking at you now, how I didn't recognize it that first night you stumbled onto our camp. But I am glad that my laird was not so remiss."

Laurel smiled at the memory and wiped her friend's tears away. "That is because you have the stunning Aileen to keep you company."

He nodded and grinned at his wife who was standing just behind Laurel, helping the others keep her gown from falling on the melted snow. As always, his heart fluttered a little when he captured his love's eyes.

It was true that Finn had found his own highland beauty, and that he would want no other. But he was not blind, and neither were any of the men in the courtyard. Each looked like he had been struck by lightning as they gazed at the vision before them.

As Laurel began walking towards the chapel, every soldier moved his sword upwards in salute. There they remained, motionless, except for those making a path for her, until she vanished from view. The gesture of respect initially stunned and then deeply moved her.

As she approached the chapel doorway, Laurel mentally reminded herself to stop twisting the herbs and flowers she carried. The women had put much effort into selecting the ones that symbolized fidelity and spiritual protection.

Conor was laughing with his brothers about something when Laurel entered the chapel. Both instantly became aware of each other. Nothing could have prepared Conor for the breathtaking vision that was venturing towards him.

This morning he had risen from bed and gone to the stables, thinking a long ride in the cold air would help him focus and stay composed. It was just a wedding—his wedding—but a wedding nonetheless, and he had been to plenty of those. But the private ride only caused his mind to race. He decided to seek companionship.

It had been a long while since Conor had spent any time in the lower hall. Mostly, the stench had driven him away. But today the idea of camaraderie and a drink were appealing. Both Fallon and Finn had found their laird drinking with the younger soldiers, telling them of glorious battles. Each taking an arm, they marched the groom to the North Tower.

At the base of the stairs, Conor pulled his arms free. "Where do you think you are taking me?"

Finn walked up to try again. "Now, laird, it would be better if you would just . . . laird?" Finn took a couple of steps back and eyed Conor, who now stood quite composed with his arms folded across his chest. "You aren't drunk?"

Conor eyed them both and asked again, "Where the devil did you think you were going to drag me?"

Fallon immediately took charge. "*We* are going to the tower's solar, of course."

"I'd prefer my own chambers, thank you." Conor replied sarcastically, his stance firm.

Standing just as resolutely, Finn replied, "Well, you may prefer them, but you aren't going near them. So you might as well give in now and follow Fallon."

Seeing the large furrow form on Conor's brow, Finn quickly added, "Now you may be laird, but your bride is getting ready in that tower, and Aileen made it absolutely clear that if even a toe of yours enters that part of the castle, I am going to die . . . painfully. So, unless you want to take on my wife, and Glynis, and Brighid, and a half a dozen other women other who are there right now, I would just give in. We gathered your clothes, and they are upstairs now along with a hot bath."

They both stood staring at each other for what seemed several minutes before Conor silently turned and ascended the staircase to the North Tower's solar. The tension radiating from him was palpable.

After his bath, he dismissed everyone from the room and lay down to think. Why was he so on edge? He and Laurel had gotten along so well the past few weeks.

He raked his fingers through his hair and stood to get dressed. The door opened, and Finn entered.

"Laird?"

"Aye."

"Seamus is outside. You requested him?"

"Aye."

"Is there something I need to know about, laird?"

"No. Send him in. Then check and make sure that all is ready."

Finn wondered at his laird's strange behavior, but did as Conor requested.

After speaking with Seamus and gaining his pledge, Conor felt somewhat relieved. His promise would soon be fulfilled but, until then, he would not feel completely at peace until he saw Laurel again.

Now, watching his bride coming towards him, Conor felt all his worry, frustration, and responsibilities fall away. His heart began to pound in his chest. Part of him felt intense pride at the vision that was coming towards him to be bound to him forever. The other part desired only to banish every last person, especially the men, from the chapel and his keep. There were no other women to compare. She was an angel sent down from heaven to save him from a life of solitude and loneliness. His only goal was to make her happy.

Laurel looked at the man who was about to become her husband. All of a sudden, her fear dissipated. She did not see the great Laird McTiernay, only Conor, her friend and protector. With him, she could finally allow herself to trust completely and totally. Never would she have to rely solely on her skills and abilities to survive. She could focus on loving her highlander.

By the time Conor and she left the large reception party for their solar, Laurel was quite anxious. She had been nervous all night, and with every dance, every toast, and every kiss from a well wisher, her anxiety grew.

Laurel had inwardly laughed when Aileen had suggested that she would be apprehensive about her wedding night. She thought the idea naive since she and Conor had already been intimate. But, in reality, knowing exactly what to expect did not alleviate her nerves. Instead, it excited them. She wondered if their lovemaking would be as intense, powerful and all-consuming again. After all, last time was a product of passion resulting from a fight.

The whole night she had been thinking about what was to come. Even now, in Conor's arms watching him latch the solar door, she could only remember bits and pieces of the ceremony and the festivities afterwards.

She remembered Conor in his white crisp leine and outer mantle with the McTiernay colors. The shirt was drawn up to his knees with a leather belt that also held his plaid.

Laurel had never seen a finer-looking man.

His brothers and honor guard wore the same attire. All of them carried swords—even Clyde—and used them to create an arch Conor and she walked under at the beginning and end of the ceremony.

The only two parts of the service Laurel could clearly recall was the quaich ceremony and the rings. The quaich or unity cup ceremony symbolized the union of the bride and the groom's two families, as well as the bride and groom themselves. Cole poured water into two silver toasting goblets with the McTiernay crest on them. Then she and Conor simultaneously poured the water from the goblets into a beautiful quaich. Drinking from the cup, they drank to past, present, and future happiness with each other.

She had not recognized the cup they used. There were several in the great hall kept aside for offering whisky or brandy to guests, although most traveled with their own. Like most quaiches, this one was wide and shallow and made of wood with a pair of small silver lug handles projecting horizontally from opposite sides of the rim. The lugs, though functional, had intricate carvings that gave the quaich much of its special character. This one, unlike the others made of commonly available wood products, was built with light and dark wood staves and bound with withies or metal bands. Masking and sealing the centre of the bowl where the points of the staves met was an engraved coin of the McTiernay crest.

The only other thing she could recall of the ceremony was the giving of the rings. Scots, including her grandfather, believed that a vein in the third finger of the left hand ran directly to the heart. As Conor slipped the simple gold band onto her finger, he spoke of their strong connection and heartfelt love for and commitment to each another.

The rest of the ceremony, including the vows, was a blur. When they left the chapel, a thin loaf of bread was unexpectedly broken over her head. She stared dumbfounded, watching women scurry about eagerly picking up the crumbs. She was told later that the bread symbolized fertility, and the crumbs were considered good luck charms. *If all these charms and traditions work, Conor and I will have an untold number of children,* she thought.

The reception must have been a great success. She remembered dancing with many guests and laughing at the antics of her new brothers.

Fiona had outdone herself. The food was superb and relished by everyone. It seemed that every other minute someone was toasting her, or Conor, or them both. Suddenly, as she was pressured into another reel, Conor came over, picked her up and headed out of the great hall indicating that, for them, the party—at least the one in the hall—was over.

"Aren't you going to put me down?" Laurel asked as Conor carried her up the stairs to his solar in the Star Tower.

He didn't answer, continuing his march towards his room. He had not been able to breathe properly since the second he saw her in the chapel looking amazingly exquisite. The woman of his dreams had married him today. Several times, he felt himself growing overcome with emotion. In such a short time, she had become the most important thing in his life. These past few weeks had proven that they could depend on, listen to, and support each other for the rest of their lives.

He locked the door behind them before he put her down. Standing so close, it was impossible not to touch her face and stroke her hair. He thought her to be the most beautiful creature in Scotland and, from the expressions he kept seeing again and again, so did every other highlander who saw her. He had tried not react to the jealousy that pulled at him all evening, but when the last soldier—from Laird Schellden's guard—had physically lifted Laurel and whirled her around in a supposed dance, he could stand no more.

It was tempting to declare a new rule that no one other than himself could go within five feet of her.

Conor drew Laurel close, holding her near to his heart. He inhaled. The smell of her hair was driving him wild with a need that had been plaguing him since they had first made love. And now, his one thought, his one focus, his one overpowering desire, was to make Laurel his wife in every way.

"I love you, Lady McTiernay," he told her, his voice raspy with emotion.

"And I love you, Conor," she replied, her face radiant with joy. And, with those words, all of her nervousness and questions disappeared. She reached up and put her hand behind his neck as he bent down to give her the night's first kiss.

As their lips met, Conor lost all thought as he tasted and drank from her soft and supple mouth. She yielded all, even in the simple kiss they were sharing.

Conor framed her face with his hands and continued the slow, seductive, mind-numbing kiss, suffusing her body with an aching need for more.

He felt her shiver in his arms, but she did not pull away. He was already fully aroused. Kissing her long and soft and deep, playing with her willing and open lips, he captured her tongue and drew it into his own mouth.

Moaning, Laurel tried to deepen the embrace and increase their pace. Refusing to rush anything they were going to share tonight, Conor moved along her cheeks and temples, continuing the light, soft, tender onslaught with his mouth. He reached her ear and began nibbling her earlobe.

Her throat constricted with desire.

"I thought I'd never get you alone," he muttered as he covered her mouth with his own.

He nipped playfully at her lower lip, then caught and held her close for a deeper kiss. Conor let his tongue probe the warmth of Laurel's mouth as he slid his hands slowly up her spine.

She was melting in his arms, remaining upright only due to his strength. Shivers ran through her as he kissed her neck and shoulders once again. His caresses were so soft, so completely different than the last time. Different, but just as powerful.

"Hold me," she pleaded. "Never let me go. Promise me, you will never let me go."

He looked up and stroked her cheek with his knuckles. "Never, my love. Never." His liquid silver eyes were luminous with love, possession and desire. "You are forever mine. And I will forever be yours."

His fingers tightened tenderly on the nape of her neck and then slipped beneath the back of her dress. Conor returned his lips to hers. Their lips embraced, moving hungrily against each other. Their tongues teased, tasted, tantalized.

His hands moved toward her hair. He briefly interrupted his gentle, yet persistent foray over her skin to remove her headpiece, and then her necklace, placing them on the table next to the window. Next, he bent down and slowly removed her slippers caressing her calves. Every time he made contact with her skin, he craved her more.

Laurel never dreamed that she could need to touch a man as much as she wanted to touch the highland chieftain who now stood before her. When he reached out to continue his unhurried removal of her gown, she stopped him by clasping his hands in her own. She kissed them and then moved them down to his sides. She smiled when his silver eyes sparkled with curiosity.

She couldn't believe her boldness and started biting her bottom lip. She reached out and took off his tunic and then his plaid, leaving only his saffron shirt cinched by his leather belt. She reached down and with timid fingers began to loosen the leather. They were standing so close now, but still only touching through her finger tips. He radiated primitive masculine vitality, and she started to hesitate.

The light touches, her breath on his skin, the view of her heaving chest caused him exquisite pain. And he wanted more.

"Ahh, don't stop there, love," he pleaded, seeing her freeze with apprehension.

She refused to look up, knowing that she would not be able to continue if she did. Only her pride refused to let her stop.

Her fingers were like butterfly kisses against his skin despite the leine he still wore. Conor watched her try to avoid touching him as she untied his belt from his waist. Once she succeeded, he felt her exhale. Unable to stand any more, he held her face in his hands, bent his head and kissed her, this time revealing all the desire and need that had erupted when she began to undress him.

Laurel's response was unbelievable. She opened her mouth and welcomed him in, swirling her tongue against his own. He thrust into her mouth, then withdrew, then thrust again, stroking her boldly, forcefully.

Laurel clung to him, trembling. Her arms came up, and both her hands dove into his dark locks. When they first met, she was ignorant of kissing, of passion, and of sexual longing. Now, she was a raging inferno of desire, ready to burst into flames. It was staggering.

Her breasts were suddenly pressed against his chest as she moved closer demanding more. His hands went from her hair to untie the back of her gown, freeing the restraints of the sleeves. His lips left her mouth and started a trail of sweltering kisses along her cheek.

As he worked his way down, she felt her gown release and slip away, leaving only the thin gossamer shift she wore beneath.

When his mouth encircled her breasts through the filmy material, she gasped and shuddered in response. "You are so beautiful," he muttered, completely awed.

Laurel sucked in her breath, her fingers biting into Conor's shoulders. How could something so simple as a kiss through her shift make her feel like she was about to dissolve into nothing?

His tongue swirled around her nipple over and over again, teasing the taut nubs. The stimulus was almost too much, and Laurel thought she could stand no more. Then she felt his hands on her legs slowly stroking her as they lifted the sheer garment over her head.

Suddenly, she was naked in front of him, but so fueled with desire that thoughts of shyness were abandoned as he continued his attack on her senses.

"God, you taste so good."

His hands could not seem to stop moving, wanting to feel and caress every piece of her body. Not one feature would go left untouched by him tonight, he vowed silently.

Laurel was now quivering so violently she could no longer stand. He smiled hungrily, his eyes full of love and unfulfilled need, and scooped her up in his arms.

She closed her eyes, loving Conor's strength as he carried her across the room and placed her in the center of his bed. Quickly, he removed the final piece of clothing that separated them and moved to lie beside her.

"Your eyes are the deepest shade of blue right now," he whispered.

"I thought they were green," she answered, softly fingering his dark hair. Just a few nights ago over dinner, he had been telling her they were the purest of sea greens he had ever seen.

"Aye, they are. But they are ever changing with your

moods. Right now I am drowning in the colors of the ocean. You are truly are beautiful, Laurel. But your beauty is not only of the body, but of the spirit as well. I had come to believe that I was alone in this world. I no longer thought that there could be someone like you out there. Someone who cares for others as you do, but with the fire and determination it takes to survive in these lands. But here you are, and you are mine," he said, looking deep into her eyes. "I will never let you go."

She felt tears form at his words and they began to fall along her cheeks. "I love you, Conor. With all of my heart. Forever."

He leaned over and caressed her lips with his own, positioning himself over her, still bearing the burden of his bulk on his side. He began stroking her breasts, rubbing his palms over the rosy nipples until they were hard with desire. His heart pounded.

Continuing to caress her bosom, Conor started a trail of kisses from her neck to the valley between her breasts. Then slowly, he lowered his mouth and encompassed a pink bud. Flicking his tongue over the sensitive flesh, he lightly squeezed and suckled the taut nub between his lips.

Her body began to writhe with ferocious need. "Conor! It's too much," she cried, clutching at the blankets on the bed.

Conor responded by using his leg to nudge Laurel's knees apart so that his hands could stroke her soft skin. His fingers caressed her inner thigh, sending shockwaves throughout her body. Her lower region was tightening in response and the warmth between her legs was growing hot, very hot.

Slowly stroking her thighs, his hands reached closer and closer to her apex. She remembered what sensations his fingers had produced last time and lifted herself, wanting more. But each time as he approached the core of her desire, he would move away. Then, instead of touching her there, loving her with her fingers as he had before, he moved to massage her breasts. He stroked and then massaged until she was out of her mind calling his name over and over.

His control was on the verge of snapping. Only his need to see her come to fulfillment kept him sane. His lips broke away from hers, and he positioned himself on top of her moving down until his mouth roamed the valley between her breasts. He tasted the salt of the glistening film of perspiration forming there. His teeth were light and tantalizing on her taut nipples. Repeatedly, he flicked his tongue over the sensitive flesh, and then he began to suckle.

The added stimulus was almost too much, and Laurel arched beneath him. Still, he continued to suckle and lick each nipple, causing torrents of shudders to run through her body.

The pleasure she felt was so akin to pain, it was overwhelming. She could not stand the pressure any more. She would explode if he did not touch her there soon. "Please, Conor. Please!" she cried.

Suddenly his hand gently closed around her, and he dampened his fingers in her liquid heat. Testing her with one, then two fingers, Conor stroked her slowly, parting her, opening her. Laurel buried her head in his shoulder, trembling violently with need.

Gradually, he increased his pace, deliberately teasing her female flesh. His fingers twisted, moving in and out of her, stroking the flames. He did it again. And again.

Her back arched and the vortex of need grew exponentially until the world burst into flames as spasms took over her body.

As she climaxed, Conor plunged deep, sinking victoriously in her snug, tight channel. He nearly emptied himself upon his entry. She was tight, and wet, and so hot.

When he entered her, she was suddenly brought back to earth and was very aware of him inside her. He waited briefly for her body to become accustomed to him. He then gripped her hips and urged her into a passionate rhythm. As with the first time, her body molded to his, accepting, stretching, accommodating, as if she were made only for him. Except that this time he was able to penetrate deeper and harder.

As Conor moved inside her, Laurel arched her back, clinging to him, drawing him in even further. Straining to meet each thrust, she lifted herself against him, silently demanding that he move more quickly.

Suddenly the heavens exploded. Conor froze and then collapsed in intense pleasure, feeling Laurel climax simultaneously beneath him.

Conor had known that each and every joining he and Laurel were to share over their lifetime would be incredible, but he had been unprepared for this. He felt as if he left his body and his soul had met with hers on another plane. Only much later did he feel himself drift back to his castle, solar, and bed.

He was on his back, and she was cradled against him with her head on his shoulder, her hair splayed against the pillows and linens. A deep, tender, ineffable feeling of affection rose in him.

Laurel sighed as he kissed her again, more softly this time, with so much tenderness it felt like her heart was swelling in her chest, nearly choking her. The love Conor felt for her was never more clear, and she knew it would last forever.

With her, he had experienced a sense of underlying oneness that could only be shared with a soul mate. Neither spoke, but each kept giving small tokens of love through undemanding kisses and feather-light caresses.

Throughout the night, they shared their hearts and souls, bringing each other pleasure again and again before finally collapsing from exhaustion, wrapped in each other's arms.

The next morning Laurel awoke with Conor still by her side. She was somewhat surprised, knowing that he was a early riser. She had half-expected him to have been gone before she awoke.

He had been awake for some time when he finally felt
her stir. While he knew his men were waiting for him to
begin the tournament, he just could not force himself to
leave her side. He had never felt so complete in his life.
It was the fact that she was now married to him, not just
by the Church, but by her heart. He had claimed her
Scottish heart for his own.

"Good morning." Conor smiled, rolled over and gave
her a kiss that made her toes curl.

"Good morning to you," she said sleepily, stretching
her muscles, finding herself somewhat sore from the
night's activities.

"How are you, wife?"

"Hmmm, blissful. I got married yesterday."

"Aye, that you did."

She grinned playfully and pointed a finger at his chest.
"I told you I was not going to marry an Englishman, but
a Scotsman."

"Aye, you did. But you promised to marry more than
just a Scotsman."

"You mean when I vowed my husband would be chivalrous and thoughtful. You are indeed those."

He nibbled her ear. "And polite, I believe you said."

"Well . . . ," she said, drawing out the word. "You are
polite—sometimes. When I fell in love with you, I realized
that I was going to have to compromise on some things."

He rose and looked at her. "Such as?"

"You are a giant."

"No, I am a normal-sized gentleman."

"But you yell."

"Aye, but my keep is no longer disorganized or unclean."

"See? A compromise. I get a thoughtful man with a
clean keep. All I have to do is learn to live with a yelling
giant who . . ."

He cut off her words with another kiss, rolling her on
top of him. Just before it grew into something more that
neither of them could stop, he pulled away.

"I have to go to my men," he said, not moving.

"Mmmm-hmm. I, too, have much to do," she added, without even adjusting the lock of hair tickling her nose.

"And what are you planning to do today, wife?"

"Mmmm, watching you win, I think, is on my list," she said, looked down mischievously at him.

"Think I will win, do you?"

Feeling quite the imp, she responded, "Perhaps. But Finn is quite skilled, and there seem to be several other soldiers that look very large and extremely strong."

Suddenly she was on her back, and he was above her. Her eyes reflected joy, and his own silver ones were filled with the endless love he felt for her. Without words, they both realized that their plans for the day were going to be slightly delayed. Only when all their needs were satiated again was he able to leave her side and dress.

As Laurel was dressing, Conor opened a large chest and rummaged through it for several minutes. When he emerged, he held something in his hand. He walked over and helped her fix her plaid so that it would remain pleated when secured. He reached down to get the silver and gold pin she had been using.

"This belonged to my mother," he said, fingering the gorgeous brooch. "Before her, it was my grandmother's and so forth. This luckenbooth has always been given to the new Lady McTiernay in the days before she was married. I'm sorry it was Brighid and not my mother who gave it to you."

Laurel looked down at the heart-shaped brooch in his hand. He turned it over. Because Brighid had always helped to pin her plaid, she had never seen the engraving on the back.

My heart is thine and thine I crave

Reading the words, she could not hold back her tears. The McTiernay men had always married for love, Glynis

had said. Love had always filled these castle walls, and
now it would again.

"Thank you, Conor. I will treasure this until I pass it
down to our son's betrothed."

The highlander games began once Conor reached the
tilting yard he had established for the tournament. Although usually played in early fall, today's games, having
vowed to be no different despite the cold conditions.
Robert the Bruce was a friend of Conor's and a keen pro-
ponent of the games, having vowed to establish them as
regular events in the future.

Because so many different highland clans had ridden
a fair distance to congratulate Conor on his marriage, an
impromptu game session was convened. All day, there
would be contests trying to determine the best warrior
clans and finally the best soldier. Some events honored
brute strength, others rewarded sharp cunning.

Several of the women gathered on the higher side of
the fields, sitting on their plaids to watch. Laurel sat with
Aileen, Brighid, and Glynis.

"Look, there's Cole!" a girl cried out from behind.
Other shouts about Craig and Crevan soon followed. Although not quite the focus of too many girls yet, Laurel
watched how Conan and Clyde handled the McTiernay
soldiers' horses and brought out event items with pride.
After all, these were her brothers, too, she thought, as she
smiled and waved.

One contest consisted of throwing a heavy rock
fetched from the bed of the nearby river. Another event
involved using a huge club with an iron head. Laurel
watched as Conor and Finn led the McTiernays through
a series of games that included stone throwing, pole
vaulting, high jumping, the *geal-ruith,* which consisted
of three jumps, the *gaelbolga,* which compared the accuracy of a soldier's dart-throwing ability, and the *roth-cleas.*
This last event was extremely exciting as the participant

had to spin around and throw an entire cart axle with an attached wheel. To do so well not only required strength, but coordination, balance, and a sense of steadiness that one only gained through experience.

When the day was done, the McTiernays were the clear winner with Conor the mightiest of them all. Later that night, in the great hall, Laurel laughed as one by one the other lairds came up and told Conor to revel in his winnings for next fall, he would sing a different tune. That Conor only won today was because they had brought just a small number of guardsmen and had to leave their most talented and strongest to protect their land. To allow them to save face, Conor quickly agreed that it *might* have been different if all their men had been able to attend and participate.

Laurel leaned over and whispered, "Well, I think he could have brought every living man from his clan and you will still have bested them, and probably by just as large of a margin." Conor grinned and, in front of everyone present, kissed her so possessively that none were in doubt about how this laird loved his lady.

Later, when the festivities were dying down, Laurel stood to leave. "Go ahead, love," Conor encouraged. "I'll follow in just a moment." After he knew that she had left, he went over to Loman and Finn, who were standing near one of the hearths drinking ale. "Laird!" they both exclaimed together.

"Has Seamus departed?" he asked. That morning he had pulled Finn and Loman aside and informed them of his plan. They whole-heartedly agreed that it was a wise and necessary step toward securing Laurel's future.

"Aye. Just as you requested. He left this morning. He was mighty upset when he found out he wouldn't be participating in the tourney."

"He'll have other games."

"Aye, but none like today. Our men showed that the training practices have been quite successful."

"When did Seamus leave?"

"I believe some time before the noon meal. With MacInnes's land so far south, I doubt he will be able to return until spring after the thaw of the winter snow."

"He'll be all right. MacInnes will take him in."

"Most likely 'tis so. But the message you asked him to deliver was a little short. And ordering him not to speak further about the subject is going to make it somewhat hard on our Seamus."

"Seamus is a warrior, not a woman, Finn."

"Aye. But he is fiercely loyal to Lady Laurel, and if he hears a negative word about her, he will be hard-pressed not to speak up."

They discussed a few other details and then Conor left for the solar to join Laurel. On his way, he hoped that he had done the right thing, sending Seamus to MacInnes's with such a cryptic communication. But it seemed to be the most straightforward way to ensure MacInnes's arrival. Finn was right about how the old highlander was going to react. He was going to be very furious, especially since Conor had taken so long to send him word.

Nevertheless, if he had to do it all over, Conor knew that he would again delay sending any information on Laurel's whereabouts. Only now, after he had Laurel bound to him forever with commitments made in front of God, a priest, and most of his clan, was it safe to go to MacInnes and let him know that his granddaughter was alive.

Chapter Thirteen

The next few months passed by in a blissful fog for Laurel. Conor and she developed a routine in which the days passed by smoothly and without event. They were learning to trust and depend upon each other for the everyday things in life.

More and more, Conor found himself relying on Laurel to let him know about the needs and wants of his people. She was able to differentiate between what his clansmen truly needed and what they merely wanted. In just a few weeks, she had helped him prioritize the villagers' needs, soldier requirements, and castle repairs.

Then, one morning, it all fell apart. It started as the best day in her life. Laurel learned she was pregnant. She had been irregular most of her life and so missing her monthly had not been a surprise or a sign that she had physically changed. Her breasts were the true indicator. They were getting larger and much more tender and sensitive.

She thought it might be the result of their frequent lovemaking. It was only when Hagatha visited did she learn that she truth.

"You thought it was . . ." Hagatha couldn't continue, she was now laughing so hard. They were sitting in the great hall, which was currently separated by a temporary wall that split the large room into two sections. Divided, the room seemed cozy and comfortable as they sat in enormous chairs in front of the large hearth. It was warm and inviting, enticing all who entered to sit, relax, and put their feet up.

"You be quiet," Laurel responded with laughter. "How was I supposed to know?"

"You know, English, you have to be the most unaware child I ever met." Laurel was too excited over the news to pretend to be offended.

"A baby," she said again with a smile. "When?"

"Ahh, from your statements, could be April or May. I'll be able to tell as you get larger and closer to your time."

"You will be here, Hagatha, won't you?"

"For Laird McTiernay's first bairn? Absolutely. Wolves could not keep me away."

Laurel reached over and squeezed the older woman's hand in her own. "Thank you. Thank you so much. I am the luckiest woman in the world."

"Told you that you and the laird could find a way."

"And you were right."

"Well, just you remember those words later when you be wanting to get rid of me like Aileen did."

Hagatha's words affected Laurel like of a bucket of ice water poured on her head. She instantly became nervous and jumpy. She couldn't help it, the memories came flooding back, suppressing all the joy.

She physically resembled her mother. Same height, coloring, and the same body structure. Her mother barely had the strength to deliver her. She hadn't enough for her brother. If her mother could not do it, most likely she would be unable to as well. Laurel knew there was a high probability she was going to die.

She turned to Hagatha, her eyes boring into those of the midwife. "Promise me that, no matter what, you will not leave me. Promise me, Hagatha. I need to know that regardless of what transpires, you will be here to make sure that my baby lives."

Hagatha recognized the worry on Laurel's face and

spoke the words the lass, for some reason, needed to hear. "Aye, child. No matter what, I will be here for ye and the bairn."

Laurel visibly relaxed. "Thank you. You have no idea how much that means to me."

The older redhead eyed her carefully. "What happened, lass?"

Laurel's head snapped up. "What do you mean?"

"I mean, you are afraid of very little, yet the idea of going through labor without me seems to be terrifying to ye. I know when a women is scared of labor. Most are, but ye? No, there's something more to it. Spit it out now. I's got to know if I am going to be able to prepare and help ye."

Laurel couldn't stop her tears. "My mother died in childbirth with my brother. When she had me, it was a difficult labor. She should never have tried again." She paused, remembering her childhood memories. "She went into labor early, and there was no time to get help. By the time the midwife arrived, they had both died. My father never recovered."

Hagatha nodded. She had seen and heard similar stories in her years as a midwife. They were the tragedies, the other side of having a baby that people never discussed.

"Lass?" she prompted, trying to pull Laurel out of her memories and into the present. "You will not die. I won't allow anything to happen to you or the laird's son. Do you hear me? Laird McTiernay will not lose you," she said emphatically, realizing she was trying to convince herself as much as Laurel at that moment.

They hugged then and got up to leave the hall and see if Fiona had some of the herbs that Hagatha came to collect. As they entered the courtyard, Hamish came charging in. Seeing Laurel, he immediately went to her.

"Hamish! It's so good to see you! I haven't seen you for such a long time! What has . . ." All of a sudden Laurel recognized the fear in his expression. "Hamish! Hamish—what's wrong!" Somehow Laurel knew it had to do with Conor.

"No!" she screamed, fear seizing her.

Hagatha instinctively grabbed Laurel and kept her from falling. "What is it, Hamish? What's going on?"

"My lady! You need to come. Hurry! It's Conor!"

Laurel started running when she heard a formidable shout from behind her. "NO!" Hagatha emerged beside Laurel again, turning her so that she had Laurel's attention. "You cannot do this. You cannot run or ride a horse as you could before. It is too dangerous. I will go."

Hagatha could see the battle raging in Laurel's stormy eyes. She grabbed her friend by the shoulders. "He will be all right. I promise you—he will be all right. But I will not have him live to hear that you and the bairn are not just as well. Do you hear me?" She gave her a little shake, until Laurel nodded yes. "Now, go and prepare his room. Most likely he got hurt from a sword or something similar. Prepare for such an injury. Now, go!" And then Hagatha was gone.

It turned out that Hagatha was right, and Conor had only received a mean, but non-lethal, flesh wound. A novice soldier had lost control of his sword in a challenge near where Conor was standing talking to Finn. It was deep and serious but, under Hagatha's and Laurel's ministrations, he recovered.

Laurel spent the first several nights tending his wound and checking him often for fever. Thankfully, it never came.

Hagatha approached her, "Lass, you are wearing yourself out. You need sleep."

"I know, and I will," she said stroking Conor's brow as he slept. She still had not told Conor the news of the baby. She wanted to find the exact right time, when they both could enjoy the moment and each other. But when she finally did tell him, it was far from the romantic interlude she had hoped for.

At first, he was too weak to argue with her rules and restrictions. But, after two weeks of being what he considered coddled and overprotected, he had enough of the smothering.

"Conor! You get right back into bed!" she yelled at him as she saw him don his leine and then his belt. She ran and grabbed his plaid.

"I will not let you leave before you are ready. Do you hear me? Hagatha said three weeks minimum before you return to your duties and, even then, you should only do so limitedly."

"I heard what she said, and I have decided that I am well," he said, holding his hand out for his plaid.

"You are not well! The stitches are barely closed now. They could rupture easily at the littlest strain. Please believe me, I have seen it happen."

"Not to me, you haven't," he replied, yanking his plaid from her grasp and beginning to wrap it around himself.

She ran over and tried to stand between him and the doorway. But he easily sidestepped her intentions.

"I'm not going to lose you, Conor McTiernay." Tears were forming, but she made no move to brush them away.

Feigning patience, Conor replied, "And I'm not going to lose you either, Laurel, but I am laird and I have much work to do. Finn has filled me in on all the squabbles that have arisen since you imprisoned me in my own chambers. Now," he paused as he bent down to firmly, but quickly, kiss her, "I have to go. I promise not to overdo and keep it short."

She watched him leave the solar, knowing it was fruitless to make any more efforts to entice him to stay. Even if she did make the effort and it worked, he would have only stayed for the day. She sat down in the hearth chair and massaged her temples.

She had been feeling poorly since she awoke that morning, with a headache the size of the highlands banging in her head. Her argument with Conor had only intensified the pounding. She rose to go get something to eat, and then the world dissolved into white nothingness.

"Milady?" Someone from a distance was tapping her cheek. "Milady, please wake up." She recognized the voice, but it sounded far away. She wanted to open her eyes, but they seemed impossibly heavy. She kept hearing distant voices calling to her as if from inside a tunnel, but she could not understand what they were saying. They wanted something from her, but she couldn't figure out exactly what that was.

Suddenly, she was floating as if she'd been lifted high in the air and placed on a soft cloud. The next voice she heard was much more compelling. She wanted so much to help the person, but she didn't know how.

"Laurel, wake up, love. Please wake up for me." Conor was cradling her in his arms, just as frightened as everyone else. He had sent for Hagatha, who mercifully was visiting one of the women just outside the castle walls.

It seemed forever before she arrived.

"What happened?" Hagatha's question was direct and full of authority.

Conor looked up, his voice was rough with concern. "We don't know. One of the maids came in and found her unconscious on the floor. She's moved a little and moaned some, but otherwise she's been unresponsive." Panic then invaded him and emerged as the demanding laird. "Do something, Hagatha. What's wrong? Why would she be fine one moment arguing with me about staying in bed and moments later be . . . be . . ." and then he lost it. Tears started falling. The universe had suddenly opened up and snatched his heart and soul right from underneath him.

Hagatha was looking at her now and asked for a glass of water. When she started pouring some down Laurel's parched throat, Laurel woke up and joined the conscious world.

"What . . . what happened?" she sputtered. Her brows bunched together in puzzlement as she became aware of where she was and the people around her. Conor was holding her on his lap sitting on the same hearth chair she got up from moments ago.

"You passed out, English," said Hagatha, using the endearment to hide her fear, but as she continued it became apparent.

"I told you to be sleeping and eating more. What did ye think? That me only orders that should be listened to were for the laird? You have to take care of you and baby. When was the last time you ate, a real meal mind you, not just pieces of bread and ale?" she asked, fully focused on Laurel, unaware of the shocked expression on Conor's face.

Snapping her fingers, Hagatha ordered, "Bring her food—some broth at first, I think. Maybe tonight we will work up to some food. But you must not miss a meal again. Do I have yer word? Promise me, Laurel," she demanded, using the same tactics Laurel had extracted from her a few weeks ago.

"I promise," came the soft reply.

"Fine, then. I was in the middle of delivering a bairn when I was dragged away. Most likely the little chit has not arrived, but I best go now. Conor, you keep that one from missing another meal. And don't be pampering her overmuch, that will drive a woman just as insane. Come now. All of ye, it's time to leave them be for a moment." And then she left, followed by the crowd of shocked clansmen.

Conor just continued to sit there for several more moments holding Laurel in his arms. "You gave me quite a scare there, love."

"I'm truly sorry. It wasn't intentional. I just forgot to eat."

"Aye, and it is my job to see that you do not forget again," he said as he picked her up and placed her on the bed, ignoring her protests.

"Wait here until I return." He bent down and lightly brushed his mouth across hers. Then he stood and left.

When he did return, it was with a large bowl of meaty broth and several slices of bread. Only until she had finished a significant portion did he continue their conversation.

It had taken that long for the news to sink in. He was going to be a father.

"Did I understand that correctly? Are you with child?"

Conor was acting strange. She knew he had heard Hagatha and that the news of the baby had come somewhat of a shock. She'd expected questions, but she'd also expected excitement. Instead, she detected none. His deadpan tone as he asked the question filled her with foreboding.

"Yes."

"When is the babe due to arrive?"

Laurel spoke in unusually hushed tones. "Some time in April or May. Hagatha should be more specific in a few months time."

Conor stilled as he assimilated that bit of information. He raked his fingers through his hair and groped to keep the cold anger from flaring to life. It was truly the first time his promise to wait for explanations before exploding was put to the test. She was practically halfway through her pregnancy. She must have kept it from him for months.

He spoke through clenched teeth, struggling to keep his voice from rising. "Why am I only discovering this now? I am the father, am I not? Did you think I would not find out? Why would you keep this from me?" He couldn't help it. The more he talked, the louder his voice grew.

Indignation set in. "Whatever are you talking about? Of course I was going to tell you. I had only discovered the fact the morning you were injured. I was waiting until you healed to tell you, since I did not want you to turn the tables on me, making *me* the invalid before you were completely well!"

"I thought you said the baby is due in April."

"Yes, that or May."

"But how could you not know . . ." That did it. For Hagatha to laugh at her ignorance was one thing, but Conor! She was not going to be humiliated by him as well.

"I didn't know! Do you hear me? I didn't know. I am

not stupid, and I am not withholding anything from you. I am just plain ignorant about babies and the whole subject. It took Hagatha to explain to me why I was suddenly hungry more often, becoming tender and getting fatter."

She was thoroughly disgruntled now, with her arms crossing her chest and her North Sea eyes lashing out at him, daring him to continue. Instead, he picked her up and swirled her around the room, looking at her with so much glittering emotion in his eyes that Laurel wanted to weep and laugh and cry out with joy.

Then he kissed her long, hard, and deep.

It was a kiss that was meant to show her how much he loved her and how happy he was over the baby, but it quickly grew into much more. Suddenly, they both were consumed with sexual desire. Simple kisses and touches were not enough. It had been so long since they had been with each other. Gone was her fainting spell; gone was his injury.

The rush to fulfillment was felt on both sides as they tore at each other's clothes. Only when he entered her in a quick deep stroke did the frantic feeling begin to dissipate only to be replaced by a different, powerful sensation.

Laurel felt as if she were about to explode. She dug her nails into Conor's back. She kissed him frantically, her lips moving everywhere—his mouth, his throat, his chest. He eased himself partway out of her channel and then surged forward again. The intense, impossibly good sensation was incredible.

Together they exploded with shuddering sensual release, collapsing, sagging against each other, still tingling with what they had just shared.

"Conor, that was unbelievable."

Conor put his arms protectively around her, and stroked her arms. "It only gets better, love."

"Aye," she responded, trying to imitate his burr. "I wouldn't have believed it could, but you amaze me every time, husband."

He rolled over and looked into her passion-filled eyes. "Promise me you will take of yourself, not overdo and *eat*?"

"I promise," she said, smiling in reply. "And you promise me that you won't be doing any activity that will strain or pull at your wound until it is completely healed."

He bent down and kissed her forehead. "Done." If only she knew the power she had over him, he reflected. *I would promise her the world right now.*

That Christmas was the merriest holiday that Conor and Laurel had ever experienced. The festivities lasted from Christmas Eve to the feast of the Epiphany on the sixth of January—twelve days after Christmas Day. Every night the clan gathered to enjoy food, drink, and music within the curtain walls. On the three main days of the Epiphany—Christmas, New Year's Day and the Twelfth Night—there were grand celebrations with dancing around big bonfires both in the courtyard and outside the keep walls.

The halls, chapel, and cottages were decorated with green plants, particularly mistletoe, ivy and holly, as symbols of the fertility and rebirth the new season would bring. Laurel convinced Fallon to bring in some evergreen trees for added decoration. She invited several of the women of the keep to help decorate the trees and halls with candles and bows made of the McTiernay plaid.

Every day, music filled the keep, reflecting the gentler moods of Christmas. There were traditional Scottish carols, wassail tunes, and at night, there was an array of dance music played associated with the celebration of Christ to bring out the merry spirits of the season.

Each night there were festivities being held in both halls. While Laurel refrained from dancing jigs and reels, Conor made sure that her favorite songs were performed each night on the *clarsach*, a Celtic harp, before she retired.

But what most enthused the highlanders were the banquets. Because of the amount and variety of foods prepared, there were scores of women "helping" Fiona. Fiona agreed she needed the assistance, but several times Laurel had to come down to the kitchens and remind everyone who was in charge. Aileen questioned her tactic one day after they left.

"I noticed you never told them who it is."

"Who what is?" Laurel responded, trying to act innocent.

"Who is in charge."

"Hmm. You're right. I don't think I did." Laurel smiled at her friend as they emerged into the courtyard.

"So, are you going to tell me?"

Laurel laughed. "Why, they all are! When I put forth the question without answering it, each answers it as she sees it. Fiona thinks she is in charge, so of course she thinks I am referring to her. Glynis believes the same. Most of the others think I am referring to Conor. You should see Fallon if he is around when I ask. He always puffs out his chest, smiles secretively, and leaves in silence."

"What a devious woman you are! I should take lessons."

Laurel elbowed her friend. "Ha! Everything I know I have learned from watching you handle Finn." They continued to the bake house to cope with the latest squabbles erupting there.

There was a constant battle between the kitchens and the bake house about who had the majority of the work and contributed the most to their splendid feasts. Every meal had Scottish shortbread, a Christmas biscuit-type treat made of oatmeal, so the bake house was always busy. But the rest of menu varied greatly, each seemingly more sumptuous than the last. The clan reaped the benefit of the kitchen and bake house efforts to outdo each other.

There were soups and stews, birds and fish, breads and puddings. Then, on the three days of the Epiphany, there was also boar, venison, goose, and swan served with buttered mashed potatoes and mashed turnips. The days after the grand feasts, the kitchen would bake the most splendid mince pies filled with all sorts of leftover shredded meat along with spices and fruit.

On New Year's, Fiona made her special New Year's Black Bun cake. But, most wonderful of all, the crusty old woman, who had become so dear to Laurel's heart, made her childhood treat—English pudding. The thick porridge was blended with currants and fruit as well as the precious spices of cinnamon and nutmeg.

Conor had teased Laurel kindheartedly as she greedily consumed the dish, stating that it was a good thing she was eating for two. He was right. She seemed to be ravenous all the time and, though only halfway through her term, she was already getting large.

The festivities did much to lift people's moods and strengthen their spirits for the long cold months ahead. Although it was winter, there was much to do before spring planting began.

Conor was always either training his men in the tilting yard or assisting his farmers in mending and making tools, and repairing fences. Laurel thought it was an excellent idea when he ordered the twins, Crevan and Craig, to help cart and spread manure and marl on the ground for fertilization in between snows.

The rest of the winter passed uneventfully. Laurel was growing very large, but Conor saw only beauty.

"I'm growing fatter by the minute!" she grumbled to herself one evening as she prepared for bed. She went to bed early these days and took breaks often. Every morning and night, Conor insisted that he escort her going up and down the stairs to and from their chamber.

"In truth, you are large, but only around your middle, and even there—you still look perfect."

Laurel looked at him from the corners of her eyes. He was definitely delusional. Her ankles were swollen, and she no longer could walk with dignity, always waddling about.

"Hmmm. You must admit, you are a bit biased."

"Aye, but I am sure I can find several to support my claim," Conor said, coming behind Laurel to nuzzle her neck lovingly.

"They are loyal to you. I doubt they would give me their impartial judgment," she said, taking off her plaid. She walked over and dropped onto the bed. She fell backwards, letting her legs dangle off the edge.

Conor watched her, hiding his concern. She was very tired, and she was quite large, much larger than any pregnant woman he had seen. He lifted her feet and removed her slippers. "Do you want me to fetch Hagatha again?"

She shook her head. "No. She will only tell me that I am well and healthy and not to overexert myself."

Conor remembered Hagatha's comments as well. The last time the midwife had checked Laurel, she had cornered him about his wife's condition. Laurel was unexpectedly large, so large that Hagatha thought the babe may be here sooner than originally anticipated.

Conor sat down and rubbed Laurel's feet. "What's wrong, love? Is it the baby? Are you not feeling well?"

She raised herself up on her elbows. "No, that's not it at all." In truth, she felt fine, tired, but very good. "I think I am bored."

Conor nodded. He stretched out beside her. His wife was passionate about many things, most of which she had not been able to do for some time.

"I want to ride Borrail."

"Laurel . . ." he said in a cautioning voice. He didn't want to argue with her, but he would.

"No, no. I know that I cannot. I promise I won't. I just *want* to ride him. I want it to be spring and to ride up and down the hills feeling the wind in my hair."

He leaned over and kissed her passionately, full of love and longing. "Soon, my love. You will get to do all those crazy things that make you smile again very soon," he whispered.

At first, her pregnancy had not altered their lovemaking even a little. Their passion for each other was so new, it was inexhaustible. When Laurel's girth increased, they had adapted, finding new ways to give each other pleasure. It had just been during the last month that their activity had been reduced to playful fondling and kissing.

But now, she fell asleep as soon as she settled down on the bed. There had been more than one night when Conor found himself undressing his pregnant wife who collapsed into unconsciousness after she was "just going to sit down for a moment."

Laurel leaned back against him and stared at the ceiling. "I'm scared, Conor," she said after a while.

His fingers caressed her blonde locks as he considered her remark. "Scared of what?"

"I need you to promise me something."

"Anything."

"That you will take care of my grandfather and ensure his safety if I don't live through the birth."

Hagatha had told him about Laurel's mother. He refused to believe that would happen to her.

"You are not going to die."

It was time to be honest, she thought to herself. Unable to look at him while giving voice to the truth she feared, Laurel continued to look at the solar's ceiling. "My mother died in childbirth. And you know that I am too large. I know it, you know it, and even Hagatha knows it."

She felt him grip her hand as if to change the facts of her size by mere will. "You are *not* going to die."

"I love you, Conor." As she spoke the words, words she had said hundreds of times, a tear escaped and rolled down her cheek.

He turned her around and framed her face so that she had no choice but to look at him. "Listen to me. You are not going to die. I will not allow it. Nothing is going to take you or my son away from me. Do you understand?"

She nodded, blinking the now streaming tears away. "Yes, I understand."

"Good," then he held her close to his chest, molding her body to his.

Hagatha had warned him of the dangers. He didn't want to hear it then, and he certainly did not like hearing Laurel speak about life without her. Not now. They were supposed to have decades to raise their children and to grow old together. Last year, he fully expected to die a young chieftain on the battlefield, but now, he wanted so much more. And it was all because of his wife, who had breathed new life into him, his brothers, his castle, and his clan. The concept of that going away was just not acceptable to him.

Laurel could feel Conor trembling. Her face was buried in his chest, but she guessed he was crying. She had not wanted this. Never had she wanted to scare him as well. She hadn't realized how much he leaned on her strength and belief that all would be well.

"Conor. I think I will be all right. You just have a some-what large son already growing into a highland laird. Hagatha has been here several times, and every time has pronounced me fit and healthy. All will be well, just like you said." From now on, she would keep her fears to herself.

He knew she was putting on a good face for his sake. He decided to do the same.

"Aye, love. All will be well, and we will have a strapping bairn to prove it in no time," he said as he kissed her hair.

Chapter Fourteen

Brighid was getting married. Donald, the man to whom she had lost her heart last fall, had finally conceded and asked for Brighid's hand. Her acceptance was instant. They were to be married in the spring.

As Laurel was busy helping Brighid prepare for her upcoming vows of marriage one bright and clear morning, the castle was unexpectedly brought to high alert. Soldiers were running in and out of the tower house. The house was three stories high and was one of the structures on the curtain wall used to fight battles. The ground floor was where supplies and weapons were stored. Laurel had never seen the tower house so active before.

Suddenly Conor appeared before her, along with Loman. "Come with me," he ordered, indicating for her and Brighid to follow.

"Conor?" Laurel asked, trying to find out what was going on. She had stayed in the great hall when the battle cry was heard, realizing that she needed to be easily found, but out of the way.

She was sure that, while it sounded like a call to arms, it must be something different. No lairds were expected, and it was still winter. Although spring was imminent and the snows were melting, the chill in the air was ever present, and the night's frost still blanketed the earth. It was too cold for travel and unexpected blizzards were still possible.

Conor didn't say a word until they reached the warden tower opposite the tower house. He opened the tower's doors, then carried Laurel down to the lowest room that had a latrine, but no windows. Essentially, it was a prison. She had seen Conor use it on occasion during the winter months when an unruly or mean drunk needed some time to sober.

"Conor, you are scaring me. Why are we here? What is going on?"

Brighid walked to Laurel's side and clasped her friend's hand both to give and receive support.

"You are to stay here until I or Loman comes for you. If Loman comes, follow him next door to the postern. I am sorry about the conditions, but this is the safest place closest to the rear gate."

Now Laurel understood. She nodded so that he knew she wouldn't argue. Something dangerous was happening, and he had to prepare for battle. Early that winter, Conor had shown her around the castle from a fortification point of view. It was an extremely well-protected fortress. But even the strongest of castles could be overcome with enough men and time. That is when he showed her the passage that led to a cistern chamber outside the curtain walls and a means of escape hidden beside the stream. However, one must leave through the rear gate to access the passage.

"Conor, I know you must go. But, please be careful and come back to me."

"I will. Trust me. It should not come to blows, but I had not anticipated this laird's reaction to a message I sent to him right before winter."

"The one Seamus sent?"

"How did you know . . . ?"

"Conor! Did you think I would not see that Seamus was gone?" Laurel straightened her shoulders and masked her fear with a light-hearted attempt at a wifely command.

"Now hurry and settle this matter and retrieve Brighid and me from this cold dank room."

"Aye, love." And then after a brief kiss he was gone.

After he left, Laurel walked back and forth nervously, waiting and wondering what had spawned such a precaution. "If I just knew what was happening, I would be able to relax a little. It is the not knowing that is driving me to pace, Brighid," she told her friend, who was encouraging Laurel to sit by her on the makeshift bed in the corner.

"The laird will come and get us soon, milady. He will be rather upset if he finds you tired out and distraught." *And yell at me as if I could control his lady any better than he,* Brighid grunted to herself while trying to convince her stubborn friend to concede and take the weight off her feet.

Laurel was not interested in being pacified. "He said something about a laird not taking well to a message that he sent this fall. Why would a laird get so riled about a message? What could Conor possibly have done or said to evoke such ire?"

"There is no way of knowing, milady. A man will act like a man, despite what a woman wants. At least that's what Donald is always saying. Especially any time he knows that he is doing something I wouldn't like." This statement brought Laurel to a complete stop.

Donald was an affable man and always eager to please. Finn told her that he was a skilled soldier when she inquired whether or not he was good enough for Brighid. Since their engagement, she had watched Donald from afar. He was always trying to emulate Conor in all that he did.

"You know, I think you are onto something, Brighid. Conor did not *forget* to tell me anything. He *intentionally* didn't inform me."

Brighid instantly recognized that Laurel's ire had sparked to life. "I am sure that he just didn't want to upset you."

Laurel began tapping her foot. "Hmmm. Yes, I am sure that he didn't want an argument. I am also sure he is

going to get one as soon as I find out what is going on."
She resumed her pacing again, but this time she walked
around the edges of the room taking brisk, long strides.
She was getting angrier with each step.

Brighid stood up wringing her hands. "Milady, please
stop! You are making me dizzy. If not me or yourself,
would you please rest for the baby's sake?" Laurel slowed
her pacing, but refused to stop or to be seated.

"Seamus left right after our wedding. I'm sure of it. He
is part of the honor guard, but I don't remember him
partaking in the games afterwards. Conor must have sent
him on his mission that very day. What could have been
so important that it prevented Seamus from participating
in the celebration?" she asked aloud, but to no one. It
was like trying to work out a puzzle with only a portion of
the pieces.

"More important . . ." She stopped and looked at her
friend, not because Brighid would have the answer, but
because she was the only live body in the room. "Nothing
of interest happened that week prior to the wedding.
Why then, if it was so important, did he wait until *after*
the wedding? It doesn't make sense. The message was important enough to keep Seamus from the games, but not
important enough to send Seamus prior to our vows. It is
as if Conor had to wait until we were wed. But that
doesn't make any sense. But what else could it be?"

Then, unexpectedly, Brighid did have the answer. "I
don't know, milady," she sighed, deciding to sit down
again on the small bed. "I wonder, though, if it is related
to what Donald told me the day after you were married
to the laird."

Laurel was immediately attentive. She finally stopped
her pacing and sat down with Brighid. "What did Donald
tell you?" she implored without trying to sound too as-
sertive. Brighid was, after all, a somewhat timid girl. Eventually, she would get her bearings but, until then, Donald
would be able to dictate their household as he saw fit.

Fleetingly Laurel wondered if Conor wished she was more like Brighid, always willing to defer to his orders.

"Nothing important. Nothing bad," she tried to assure her mistress. "He just couldn't wait until he was selected to run an errand for the laird."

"What errand? Did he tell you what the errand was?" Laurel intuitively knew these were the pieces to the puzzle. She also knew that the picture they created could affect her and Conor's future. "It's really important. Can you remember if he said *anything* about the errand?"

Brighid was startled by the intensity radiating off of Laurel and started to shrink away. "But it's trivial, milady. He just wanted the chance to run an errand to the laird's godfather. I never met him, but Donald did once when he was a lad."

"Conor's godfather?" Laurel inquired. "Seamus was sent to see Conor's godfather?" she repeated, stunned. This didn't make sense at all. "Why would Conor's godfather be causing such a stir and fear? Are you sure it wasn't someone else?"

"Oh no, it was definitely him. The laird's grandfather and his godfather were best friends, and he used to visit quite often. Now do you understand why this couldn't be related to what is going on today? Laird MacInnes would never attack our laird. Their alliance is unbreakable."

Laurel felt like a bucket of stones had come crashing down on her. Her *grandfather* was here. Conor had known exactly who her grandfather was. She didn't know how he knew, but she was sure that Conor was well aware of her Scottish heritage when they married. That was why he was so sure he could resolve her family's safety.

Tight-lipped, straining to remain calm, Laurel continued. "Tell me, Brighid, what do you know of Laird MacInnes?"

"Only that he was a highlander before he met his Scottish bride from the lowlands. He became laird of her clan when her father died and has done much to unite the border clans. He is now one of the larger chieftains, I believe, in Dumfriesshire. At least, that is what Donald has said. I know it isn't much, but that is all I can remember. But how does that change anything?"

Because I am Laird MacInnes's heir, Laurel screamed to herself. And Conor knew it. He knew all this time and intentionally didn't tell me. And now her grandfather was here and obviously not for filial pleasantries.

All of a sudden, Laurel knew why her grandfather was here—and prepared for battle. She had to get out of here now.

Laurel stood up a little too quickly and almost blacked out. She was larger than any pregnant woman she had ever seen and there were still a couple more weeks before the baby was due. Sometimes, she thought she would explode before the day ever arrived.

"Brighid, come. I would normally not involve you in my escapades, but I am too big and need your help."

"Milady, you cannot be thinking of leaving. The laird! He told you to stay right here until he came. You cannot be thinking of challenging him this way!"

She grabbed Brighid's shoulders. "Listen to me. I am walking out that door right now. I admit I need your help, but I will understand if you don't go with me. But, either way I am leaving. I know what is happening, and only I can stop it."

"Only you?" Brighid shouted to her mistress as Laurel opened the door and walked out of the tower's lower room. "How can you stop it? Stop what?" she whispered as Laurel motioned for her to lower her voice. They reached the rear gate and went down the passage to the cistern chamber. They went into the chamber and stood by a large wooden chest.

"Brighid, help me move the trunk. It just needs to be moved out slightly." Once moved, Laurel slid open a small hidden door concealed within the wall.

"Milady! You cannot be thinking of crawling through that!"

"I am not thinking. I am doing," Laurel stated evenly and proceeded to crawl through.

Brighid followed, far from sure of the wisdom of their actions. The tunnel was slightly muddy but, thankfully, very short. Laurel stood up immediately once they were out and started walking towards the tilting yard.

They had emerged from the tunnel by the river, completely hidden from anyone near or around the castle. But Brighid soon realized that Laurel did not intend to remain unseen for very long. She raced towards Laurel to help her up the hill. Brighid was afraid of what was about to happen, but there was no way she was going to leave her mistress to face the wrath of two chieftains without some support.

By the time Laurel could see Conor and a man she assumed was her grandfather, she was seriously winded. She would be glad when the babe was born and her stamina returned.

Both lairds were on horses on facing each other, holding swords in their hands. Laurel had not seen her grandfather in several years. His hair had grown white, but he was still the large, strong man she remembered as a child. Except, in her memories he was a laughing, welcoming giant, warm and generous, not the furious, enraged individual ahead of her. And he was not the only angry one.

Even at this distance, she could see that Conor, too, was incensed. She would have to get closer to hear their words or to get their attention. Behind each man were dozens of warriors on horseback from each clan. Behind them and to their sides were even more soldiers on foot. War was brewing.

"We have to hurry, Brighid," she said with such urgency in her voice that it propelled her friend to quicken her pace.

"Lean on me, milady. We'll get there in time. I don't know what you intend to do, but you do have a way of both quickening and calming a man's anger."

"Well, let us hope that I can do the latter."

Suddenly, Finn was blocking Laurel's way. She had not even seen him approach.

There was no compromise in his voice when he issued his orders. "Go back now, milady. This is not for you."

"Get out of my way right now, Finn," Laurel said fiercely, leaving no doubt that she was not about to turn around with his simple command.

"I cannot let you pass."

"Finn, let me explain this to you so that we are very clear as to what is about to happen. If you don't let me pass, and I mean now, I will begin to scream so loud that those two hardheads," she pointed to Conor and her grandfather, "will hear me and come running. I doubt that in their angered states they will wait for explanations as to why you caused me to scream. I, of course, will give Aileen my condolences and see that your son is taken care of."

Never had a woman so threatened him. But this was no threat. Finn had spent enough time with Lady McTiernay over the months to see the change in her eyes. The more she was agitated, the darker and cloudier her eyes became. He had heard Conor mention that when angered they looked like a storm brewing on the North Sea. As he looked her now, Laurel's eyes were near black.

"Stay here," he ordered Brighid, who was only too willing to comply. He then picked up Laurel and carried her the rest of way. She tried to get him to put her down, but soon realized that it was fruitless. At least Finn was no longer commanding her to retreat.

As they neared, she could hear the heated exchange. And, just as she feared, she was the cause of the whole situation.

"If you do not bring my granddaughter to me right now, we will have war!"

"Laurel is mine! Mine by law and by God. She has sworn and given herself to me."

"Not by choice she didn't! She was abducted on her way to MacInnes lands."

"And it was I, not you, who saw her to safety."

"Safety! You dare to mention her protection! I have heard from many a man that she swore to renounce you and come to my clan by spring."

"Over my dead body will she be leaving McTiernay land. Not in the spring, not ever. And if war is what you want, so be it. My men have sworn to protect her. They consider her their own and will lay down their lives before she is forced to leave against her will."

"But is it her will to stay? Why is it that I cannot address her myself?"

Finally, Finn brought Laurel close enough, and he put her down. However, both chieftains were so engrossed in their clash of wills, neither noticed her appearance.

Laurel squared her shoulders.

"He's right, grandfather. I have no intention of leaving McTiernay lands," she said without compromise, craning her head to look at the two men she loved the most. "But, Conor, I would love to hear the answer to what my grandfather asked. Why did you hide me away rather than give me the chance to meet with my family?" she demanded, looking directly at her husband, her eyes blazing.

Both men were shocked into absolute silence at her appearance. Conor couldn't believe that his very pregnant wife had done the unthinkable. She had plainly disobeyed him and his orders. Then, she proceeded to walk into the most dangerous ten feet of Scotland.

The only thing that did penetrate his stunned mind was her furious glare. That was fine by him. He was mad as hell, too.

"Well?" she demanded, refraining from crossing her arms and tapping her foot so as not to appear too shrewish.

Conor's eyes narrowed. "If your grandfather was just interested in talking with you, you would have been speaking with him already," he replied directly and without inflection, redirecting some of his anger towards her.

"But he just said . . ."

"He would have abducted you and brought you to his keep before he took the time to talk. He would not have taken the chance that you might want to stay. He believes you feel obligated or guilty."

"But that is ridiculous. I'm pregnant! I could not have made that journey . . ." She turned to her grandfather. "You would not have made me . . ." But, the look on her grandfather's face convinced her that Conor spoke the truth.

At first, Laird MacInnes drank in the sight of his only grandchild. She had grown from a freckled, skinny towhead to a beautiful, stunning woman. A very pregnant woman who was standing out on a battlefield. That was all the evidence he needed that his godson, who had sworn off marriage for all time, was not the one to oversee her protection.

"This is all the proof I need, Conor," he said, pointing to Laurel without looking in her direction, maintaining eye contact with her husband. "What is my granddaughter doing in her condition *out here on this battlefield!*" he roared, finally showing all of his raw emotion. His worry and concern for his granddaughter had nearly been unbearable. Ever since he received the message from Seamus he had been vacillating between fury and relief. The message had been infuriatingly short. "I have Laurel. She is well. Laird McTiernay." No explanations, nothing.

When MacInnes first learned that his granddaughter was in Scotland on her way to live with him, he was euphoric. He sent out two dozen of his top warriors to escort her onto his lands. But they had been too late. His men had brought the two soldiers who had lived after the ambush back to their laird, but the Englishmen were of little help. They didn't know who had his granddaughter, only that another Scottish laird had taken her unwillingly and had beaten her into submission. His fury knew no bounds.

He went to clan after clan, inspecting and questioning, trying to discover Laurel's whereabouts, but it was not until Seamus arrived with Conor's message that relief and then anger flooded through him. He knew that his godson was an honorable man and could not be responsible for the cold murder of her escort. But he was also sure that Laurel had not chosen to be taken into highland country and wed so soon to an unknown man. In his mind, Laurel had been abducted twice. Once by an unknown evil fiend, and second by his godson, who—instead of returning his granddaughter to MacInnes—had stolen her for himself.

Winter immediately followed, and it was not until now that the conditions had improved enough to make the dangerous trip north and retrieve his granddaughter. Now that he was here, nothing was going to stop him, even if he had to war with his own godson.

Conor, goaded by the older man's bellows about Laurel being on the battlefield, shouted with equal force. "You obviously do not know how mulish she is. She is by far the most frustrating, infuriating, disobedient woman I have ever met! I put her away in the safest spot in the castle. But where is she? Here! So why don't you ask her why she is here! It's the stubborn MacInnes in her that causes her to be so difficult."

Laurel's temper flew. "I may be infuriating, Conor McTiernay, but only you can surpass me!" Then she turned on her grandfather. "And you can just forget all that nonsense about me going back. As you can see, I am quite well, and when not angered by some illogical dictate or *hidden secret* I have just discovered," she said, emphasizing to Conor that there would more on this subject later, "I am quite a happy wife. I love this pigheaded man, and I am about to have his son. Now, I am tired and am going to return to my chambers for a rest. You may continue to argue and fuss out here for the next week if you so desire. But, hear me now, I will not have one man get hurt or one drop of blood spilled."

"Feisty," was all that Laird MacInnes could think to say as he watched the proud straight back of his granddaughter waddle away from the crowd.

"You have no idea," said Conor, urging his horse forward. "Come up to the keep. Finn, see that Laird Mac-Innes's men have a place to be settled and food to eat. There will be training tomorrow with their clan so tell the men to get ready." With those departing words, a resounding cry erupted from both sides of the field.

Conor rode up to his wife and, just as easily and swiftly as he did when she was not burdened with child, lifted her onto his lap. He rode slowly to reduce any jarring movements. Both of them meant to continue arguing their positions—he about obedience and she about secrets—but Laurel fell asleep almost as soon as she leaned back against his hard, strong frame.

He rode in and dismounted careful not to wake her. Carrying her upstairs to the solar, he placed her on the bed. He took off her slippers and then undressed her down to her shift without her stirring. He then settled down beside her and just drank in the sight of her.

Despite being heavy with his child, she was still the most beautiful woman he had ever seen. Her outward beauty was striking, but it was her inner beauty that had truly captured his heart. Today, she had renounced her grandfather and declared to all that she was staying.

"I love you, Laurel McTiernay," he vowed to his sleeping bride, "and I will never let you go." She unconsciously responded to his voice by turning over and wiggling closer to his body so that her back was against his chest. He was completely content.

His hand rested on her belly and he felt the non-stop movement and kicking. He wondered how she was able to get any sleep at all with the activity that was constantly going on within her. The slight pressure he was exerting must have been evident within the womb because he received several sharp kicks that persuaded him to move his hand so that she wouldn't awake due to the internal thumping.

Conor remained by her side for some time, enjoying the feel of his wife, before rising and seeing to their guests' needs. He had never before been at odds with his godfather. He realized that it had been a difficult day for both of them as he entered the great hall and saw the older man in one of the padded chairs by the hearth.

"MacInnes."

The old man turned briefly and then resumed his stare into the fire. "McTiernay."

Conor took a seat and grabbed the quaich of ale that was on the table.

"How is she?" MacInnes asked.

"Tired. It was hard on her to make the trip."

"She shouldn't have made it. Why did you not take steps to prevent it?"

"You try telling a MacInnes not to do something she intends to do." Conor took a swig. "Damn near impossible, I've learned. Never compromised a day in my life until I met that woman, and now I find it commonplace in our discussions. She may have called me pigheaded, but I can promise you that it is she," he pointed in the direction of their chambers, "who is the most stubborn one of all."

Conor swallowed a large amount of ale. "She's right, you know. You should stay. It is the only way for you to truly appreciate the joy and frustration I live with. At first, she will play the dutiful hostess—gracious, social, and affable in all ways. But, then something will happen that will bring the feisty, she-cat into the open. God only knows why, but I love all aspects of her." And then he finished his drink.

MacInnes just sat and listened to his godson talk about Laurel. He had seen the sparks flying between the two. Not sparks of brutal anger, but the kind that can only be caused by two kindred spirits. Listening to Conor talk about his love for his wife's strong will and passionate nature convinced MacInnes that his godson's union was a happy one.

When MacInnes first learned of Conor's marriage to his sweet Laurel, he had been stunned. Conor had sworn never to marry. He had said many times women were only necessary for breeding and alliances, and he required neither. MacInnes never thought that Conor would physically harm Laurel, but he was afraid that her spirit would die with someone who kept himself emotionally distant.

When Conor's father died and he became laird of a large and powerful clan, he had changed. He became more reserved, less willing to engage in filial activities, and less inclined to show any type of emotion. Today on the battlefield, Conor had been stone cold in their discussions. It was only when Laurel appeared that his resolve and control broke.

"When is the bairn due to arrive?" MacInnes asked.

"Hagatha, the midwife, says that it will still be a few more weeks."

"Son, the woman looks like she is about to pop. Is your midwife knowledgeable about such things?"

"Laurel trusts her completely, so please do not doubt her in front of Laurel. Despite what you saw today, I don't want her getting agitated at all. She tires easily and I think the weight of the babe is quite a strain, but she'll never voice a complaint. As to your question, yes, Hagatha is more than knowledgeable, and we both have been worried about her size. She is so small to be that large."

"I have never seen a woman so round in my life."

Conor swallowed and verbalized his greatest fear to the only person who would understand. "Laurel is afraid she is going to die."

Immediately, MacInnes was alert. "What haven't you told me?"

"Told you? You've been here, what? Half a day? And less than an hour of that has been on speaking terms. Besides, there is nothing to tell. Her mother died in childbirth, and she is afraid that she will, also. In truth, I am scared. So is Hagatha. So is everyone. But not one word must reach her about our fears. It's important for her to believe that all will be well."

The old man saw the strain on his godson's face. It was obvious Conor was deeply in love with his granddaughter, and the thought of losing her was a constant torment.

"You won't lose her, son. In a few weeks, she will be fine, and you will have a brand new heir to liven this household. You won't lose her."

Conor nodded, needing to hear the pledge from someone else's voice besides his own. His grip on the quaich increased, and a tear fell.

"I cannot. If I do, I will surely perish as well. I know that I cannot think of living in these walls without her loving me, encouraging me, pestering me, and trying to order me about. Aye, she does that," he responded when the old man lifted his eyebrows at the mention of a woman ordering a laird. "Most of the time I ignore it, but then, alas, those eyes of hers can sometimes bend even the strongest of metals and my heart has no chance."

Laurel woke up somewhat disoriented at first. She remembered stopping the war, at least she thought she had stopped it. She remembered Conor's strong arms lifting her effortlessly onto his horse. She had wanted to talk to him regarding his silence about knowing who she was, but she could not remember that discussion or anything afterwards. Conor must have brought her to the room and undressed her. It was the only explanation.

She got up and went to the window that overlooked the northern country. She loved this view. The highlands had never been lovelier than now, as the mountains reluctantly let go of their winter snows to let the spring through in its brilliance of green and color. The sun was beginning to set, showering the fields with its rays of promising warmth.

Turning from the window, Laurel found one of her two bliauts that she was still able to wear. It was made of a dark teal material trimmed in gold. Contrasting with her fair hair and skin, the ensemble made her look feminine and glowing. Her eyes picked up the color of the velvet tunic and the gold ribbon braid accented her pale wavy locks. She could no longer wear the McTiernay plaid, since she could not cinch a belt to anchor the pleats.

Conor had argued that he had more than enough material for her to have a variety of tunics, but she refused to allow more to be made, thinking it a complete waste of material and effort. On this, Laurel never wavered and would not be persuaded. "I promise to use your wonderful goods once my figure returns," she had pledged, moving over to his side of the bed to give him a deep kiss that promised that nights of passion would also return.

As Laurel went down the tower stairs, she decided to avoid the two men who had caused her so much worry that morning. Instead, she headed towards Aileen's cottage. She needed some perspective on what Conor had done, or had not done. As she was walking across the courtyard, she saw a soldier and waved him over to escort her.

He practically fell over his feet, running towards her until he reached her side. Brion was a member of MacInnes's elite guard, and the privilege of escorting Lady Laurel was an honor. He had been stunned by her beauty that morning. She was a golden vision, somehow managing to look regal and graceful despite carrying what appeared to be a very large bairn. It was easy to see the MacInnes resemblance. The golden hair, the fierce blue eyes, the rigidity in her mannerisms when mad—each characteristic was clear proof of her MacInnes blood.

As Brion approached her, they strode out of the gate at a much quicker rate than he would have expected from someone carrying such a large load.

She smiled at him and continued walking. "Hello. My name is Laurel, and I assume from your plaid that you arrived with my grandfather."

The soldier's eyes rounded in surprise. "Aye, milady."

"Would you mind escorting me to a cottage just out-

side the curtain walls? It is not far, I assure you, but my
husband feels that I need to have an escort wherever I go,
and you appeared to be the most available."

"It is an honor, milady."

Laurel was bemused. "Not an honor. A duty, perhaps."

The soldier shook his head deliberately. "You are
wrong, milady. I have long looked forward to meet the
granddaughter of my laird."

"How so? You cannot tell me that you are old enough
to have known me as a child?" she asked.

He smiled. "No. Unfortunately, I did not join your
grandfather's guard until several years after your last visit.
But, let's just say stories of your days at the MacInnes
castle still echo the walls."

Laurel rolled her eyes. "Oh Lord, please tell me you
are not serious. All my adventures, I believe, were quite
innocent."

Chuckling aloud, he said, "Aye, milady. But the stories
bring laughter and smiles back into our great laird's
eyes."

The idea that her grandfather had been anything but
happy during these past years was quite upsetting and silencing. When they arrived to Aileen's cottage, she could
hear Finn's son bellowing about something. He was getting quite mobile and causing much chaos.

Brion waited outside when she quickly entered to see
if she could lend a hand. "Here, let me do that," she said
as she freed Aileen's hands of potatoes so she could chase
down her ever-a-handful son. Aileen watched Laurel absentmindedly work on the potatoes, taking a much
longer time with the task than was warranted. After a few
moments, she decided to prod Laurel into the conversation her friend so desperately needed to have.

"Are you here to discuss Brighid's nuptials?" Aileen
asked calculatingly. She had heard the story of what
Laurel had done from an irate Finn.

Slowly, Laurel confided her emotional battle. "No. I
am hoping that you can provide me some perspective on

THE HIGHLANDER'S BRIDE   291

a problem I have. I am afraid that if I see my husband right now, I will explode, and then he will explode. I feel like I have all the facts, but they just do not agree with what I know to be true of Conor." She felt like she were about to cry.

"So, does this morning have anything to do with your problem?" Aileen tried to sound casual, as if marching nine months pregnant into a war zone were an everyday occurrence.

Laurel let go of a large sigh. "No, not exactly, but it is related," she responded absently. Seconds later, Laurel realized that Aileen was aware of what had happened. "How did you . . . You know what happened?" she whispered in a squeaky voice, grasping the answer before she saw a smiling Aileen nod her head.

"Aye." Aileen chuckled. "I have never seen Finn as angry as he was today when he returned for noon supper. I was glad all that energy was directed at you. He actually said that he wondered how Conor had the patience to remain married to you." The growing grin that enveloped Aileen's face told Laurel that Aileen thought her friend's confrontation wonderful, even if her husband did not.

Laurel felt a wave of embarrassed warmth go through her. "He didn't! How could he? Didn't he realize what was going on?"

"Aye, and that is the reason why he was so upset about your stubbornness. He was afraid you would get hurt."

Laurel waved her hand, dismissing the idea. "Nonsense, I was never in any danger. Neither Conor nor my grandfather would have let me be injured."

"Only if they saw you. The way Finn describes the scene, they had no idea of your presence until you started shouting."

"Oh my," Laurel sighed, never having seen it from that point of view before. Perhaps she had been in more danger than she had thought. "Finn must think me stupid."

"No, but mayhap a little foolish. Do not feel bad. I

think what happened today is absolutely fantastic!" she said with such enthusiasm and happiness that it sparked curiosity in Laurel.

"Why, Aileen? Why did putting myself in a wee bit of danger make you so happy?"

"Why, Finn, of course. I think for a long time he has placed a high value on your consistent displays of what he used to call 'courage' with Conor. Finn has always been besotted with me—and I with him—but I think now, he is even more glad to be married to me. He told me after he ate today's meal that I have just the right amount of feisty in me, without being so much that it causes him to worry." She grinned back at her friend. "Yes, you can do me those kinds of favors any time."

Laurel just stared at her friend, not knowing whether to join in laughing and grinning or be horrified that Conor's guard thought so little of her. "I didn't mean to be so obnoxiously 'feisty.' I was just trying to avert a war. The least he could do is try to understand."

"Don't worry. Finn is still one of your greatest admirers, but I hope that you two don't have to go head to head again for a while. Hurts his ego when he loses."

"Aye, but it seems to do wonders for yours," Laurel pointed out.

Aileen just beamed with mischievous joy. "It certainly does." Then both women started giggling. It felt good to release some pent-up tension.

Once they settled back down, Aileen finally got her son down for a long nap. She turned back towards her friend and tried again to find the source of stress in Laurel's eyes. "So, if it wasn't this morning's activities that caused the pain I'm seeing in your eyes, what is it, then?" she asked directly and then sat back, waiting for Laurel to respond.

"Conor lied to me," Laurel said sadly.

Aileen sat straight up and looked her friend in disbelief.

"Well, not lied exactly," Laurel corrected, "but he definitely misled me. I don't understand why he would hurt me like this."

"Are you sure he misled you on purpose?" prompted Aileen, trying to pull out more facts before she said any more.

"Very sure. Of that, there is no doubt. He knew I was a MacInnes, Aileen. And he knew that I was worried about my grandfather. He deliberately led me to believe otherwise."

"You are right, that doesn't conform to what I know of our laird's character." Aileen sat still for a moment and asked, "Do you think that the laird expected Laird MacInnes's arrival?"

Laurel tried to recall what Conor had said when he left her in that awful lower room in the warden's tower. "Yes, I think he was expecting him. Just not so soon, and not so angry." She looked up. "In fact, I am sure that he was fairly surprised at my grandfather's hostile arrival."

"So, maybe Conor was reserving it for a surprise?"

"Believe me, I wish that were true, but it just doesn't explain why he let me believe that my grandfather was in danger."

"But your grandfather *isn't* in danger."

"But I didn't know that until this morning! I had no idea that he was chieftain of a large and powerful lowland clan. I believed him to be vulnerable and unable to defend himself against attacks. Conor knew otherwise. He knew how worried I was, but instead of correcting those apprehensions, he continued with the masquerade."

Aileen sighed in understanding. "Ah, I now see."

"You do?" Laurel asked with hope.

"Mmm-hmm. It makes perfect sense. You were right to come to me. I actually think I may have the perspective you were hoping for."

"Then speak! How could Conor deceive me so?"

"You are forgetting highlander pride. What is the one thing that Conor desires to do for you above all else?"

"I assume 'make me happy' is not what you are aiming for." Laurel looked at her friend, who was sitting so pleased with herself that if Aileen had feathers, they would be colorful and quite beautifully displayed along her peacock backside. Laurel rolled her eyes. "He wants to keep me safe."

"Exactly. Highlanders protect their own. What's more, they take great pride in it."

Laurel nodded. It was true. They did. "So?"

"First, now be honest, were you truly anxious and worried about your grandfather throughout the winter?"

Laurel thought on the question and realized that, while she was sensitive to her grandfather's vulnerability and perhaps curious as to how Conor was going to protect him, she was not truly worried about him.

"I suppose I was at first. Then, Conor promised that my grandfather would be safe and that I no longer needed to worry. After that, I was no longer troubled, now that I think about it."

"Now I ask you. From a *male highlander's* point of view, what man is going to intentionally remove himself from being a hero to his love's eyes by correcting her and saying, 'But save your gratitude and admiration, because it will not be necessary for me to protect your grandfather.' Ha! Every man I know, especially the chieftain of a powerful clan who is married to one of the most desirable women . . ." Laurel opened her mouth to protest, but Aileen cut her off and continued, "Yes—you are. Every man would bask in the idea that his woman believed in his ability to save her family from harm. No highlander would ever say anything to change that, especially if he knew that he had succeeded in making you feel confident of your grandfather's safety." Aileen sat back in her chair and crossed her arms and legs, completely smug, knowing that she had made the right assessment of the situation.

Laurel knew Aileen was right, too. She had never thought of it from Conor's point of view, only from her own. Why, this way, yes, he *was* being slightly devious, but there was no malevolence involved. Only pride that he could make his wife feel safe and happy, with the possibility of arranging a surprise for her in the spring. It wasn't Conor's fault that her grandfather had reacted so much more quickly and strongly than anticipated.

"Of course, it isn't," Aileen interjected, as she listened to Laurel murmur her thoughts out loud. Aileen was about to add something more when a commotion was heard outside. She was going to kick some young men around if they woke up her son. She strode over and opened the door just in time before Conor knocked it down.

When Fallon had entered the great hall to ask who was the MacInnes escorting Lady McTiernay outside the curtain walls, Conor's heart had stopped. His first thought was that they had taken her, just as MacInnes had sworn to do that morning.

The old man had seen the blood disappear and then rise again in his godson's face. He could imagine exactly what was going through the lad's mind.

"My man didn't take her."

"Who was it?" Conor growled, trying to keep this fury from exploding.

MacInnes held Conor's gaze. "I do not know, but my men are as loyal to me as your men are to you. No one would move without my explicit command."

"And is that command forthcoming?" Conor asked directly. For hours they had skirted around the issue of Laurel's removal from the McTiernay lands and from him.

"No, it is not. Laurel made it clear that she wants to be here with you. Unless that is . . . wrong?"

Conor's mouth tightened. "No. It did not matter your answer, but I am glad I will not have to fight you. She's mine."

"So you said earlier."

"Earlier, your men had not taken my wife somewhere."

MacInnes spread his hands out. "Maybe it was the other way around. Maybe it was your wife who took my man somewhere."

Conor winced. "Unfortunately, you may be correct.

She does have the MacInnes obstinacy and bullheadedness. You saw an example of what I live with every day this morning. Here's another."

The older laird smiled at the young man's frustration. It was clear that he had a love-hate relationship with Laurel's independent personality. "I am glad that time has done little to diminish that trait. She was always a self-governing child. Impossible to tell her what to do. Tell me, do you have to run after her every day?"

"In truth, I do not. But about every four months, there is a bad week or two where it seems that I do nothing but. I have a feeling you have arrived on such a week."

The old man laughed and then again harder when Conor tried to intimidate him with one of his daunting glares. "Then I guess you only have a about two years worth of bad weeks to look forward to in your lifetime with my granddaughter. If you are lucky. Come," said MacInnes, clapping Conor on the back. "Let us find my granddaughter and ensure her health."

However, it was not nearly as easy at it had first appeared. Conor had surmised that she had asked a MacInnes to escort her to their camp to see that they were cared for. But no one there had seen the Lady since that morning. It also seemed that Brion had disappeared. MacInnes recalled that he had been most anxious to meet and bring Lady Laurel home.

By the time it occurred to Conor that she may have gone to visit Aileen, he was extremely tense. He did not like having to search for his wife, especially his very pregnant wife. By the time, he, MacInnes, and now Finn had arrived at the cottage, he was very close to panicking with thoughts of her going into labor without any help. When he saw her well and in good spirits, all the apprehension turned into anger.

Seeing the tension boiling underneath the surface, Laurel immediately knew that she was the source. "Don't scowl so, husband. I took an escort," she said defensively, pointing to the warrior outside the cottage.

"He's a MacInnes," Conor bellowed.

Stubbornly and knowing that it would irritate him, she shrugged. "And he is an escort. I do not recall you specifying that the only escorts I may have are McTiernay soldiers. In fact, the argument—which I won by the way—ended with the compromise that any able-bodied person could escort me as long as I did not venture any farther than the immediate cottages from the curtain walls." Laurel quoted. "I saw no one else, and Brion was gracious enough to join me."

Before Conor had the chance to retort with the laundry list of items that he was annoyed with her about, Brion stood up to her defense. Conor remembered him as the warrior who rode as part of the guard for MacInnes. He was thinking that, if she had to pick a MacInnes escort, she had picked the right one, when the MacInnes soldier opened his mouth.

"I am glad you have arrived, Laird MacInnes," he said authoritatively to his own chieftain. "It seems that we were correct in our original assertions. Lady Laurel is being mistreated here."

"What?!" shouted all three—Conor, Laurel and MacInnes—so loudly that the doors rattled on the cottages nearby. The noise woke baby Gideon. All three ignored the child's howling and Aileen's glower.

Laurel was the first to regain her voice. "Brion. Please explain yourself. You make no sense." Her words were brusque and to the point.

"Aye, I do," he replied steadily, holding her gaze, refusing to capitulate under the evil glares he was receiving from the McTiernay highlanders. It was as if he were unaware how close to death he was. But Laurel knew, and she quickly stepped in for the second time that day to avert blood being spilled.

"Brion. What on earth gave you the idea that I was mistreated?" she asked in hushed tones.

The soldier gave her a quizzical look. "You did, milady, while speaking with your woman friend," he answered, nodding towards Aileen. Laurel instinctively pushed back

Finn's arm to remind him not to do anything rash. Finn was very sensitive about his family, as all highlanders were. Brion was walking a paper-thin line right now and appeared disinclined to retreat. If a fight did break out, it would be to the death and then both clans would be at war.

"Brion," she said, slightly shaking his arm to get his full attention, "tell me exactly what led you to this conclusion."

"You said that you were lied to and deceived. Laird Mc-Tiernay intentionally led you to believe that your grandfather was in danger and did not tell you that he knew we would come upon receipt of his message. Why would you want to stay here under such conditions? Come home with us where you will be respected and loved, not lied to and deceived."

The entire time he was speaking, he looked unswervingly at Laurel, captured by her sea blue eyes, which were growing larger by the moment. Then he saw their crystal clear depths turn murky, like the change in the sky just before it opened up and drenched those below.

Conor saw the change, too. Her back went rigid, her chin jutted out, and her eyes blazed with fury. Suddenly, Conor felt his world become a little brighter. Finn was right. While it was not a pleasurable experience being the focal point of Laurel's anger, it was amusing to watch it happen to someone else.

Laurel's voice became dangerously sweet as her stormy eyes engulfed the soldier. "Brion, let me make a suggestion for your future. Take it to heart, or I believe that you will live a very short life, especially if you ever marry a woman of any gumption."

Brion was stunned by his lady's reaction to his words. He thought she would be comforted by his defense, not offended. Before he could right his wrong, however, Laurel continued, just beginning her verbal flaying of his skin.

"If you are going to eavesdrop on a person's conversation, make it an accident. If then you ever *accidentally* eavesdrop, don't ever let the person know you overheard them talking. And, finally, if you are going to be so dense as to not only eavesdrop *and* announce it, at least repeat the conversation correctly and in full."

Brion felt like disappearing into a deep hole in the earth as Laurel went on with her tirade.

"While I felt *misled*, it was a temporary feeling that was replaced with relief when I realized that my husband *had only my best interests in his decisions*, which I may add, he always does." And seeing the grin erupt on Conor's face, she added, "*Although* we seem to disagree on exactly how he likes to protect my interests."

Brion choked out, "My apologies, milady."

Suddenly Brion's world changed again as she favored him with a blindingly bright smile. "Forgiven and forgotten." Turning to the two clan leaders, she eyed them both with a warning before asking, "Right?"

"Aye, lass, you have the right of it," her grandfather chuckled as he gave her a big bear hug that looked much stronger than it was.

He so enjoyed the spirit his granddaughter possessed. Even as a little girl, she could outtalk and outwit most of his men. Her clever schemes to avoid punishment or constraint had caused many of them to plea to their laird for help. She could exasperate, infuriate, and then captivate a man within minutes. He had missed her greatly when her father had kept them apart. Never again would he be away from her for long.

Conor picked up his wife for the second time that day and proceeded to carry her back to their chambers. But this time she was awake and not going quietly or compliantly. He assumed she would submit eventually, realizing that he was not going to put her down. But pride would never let either one of them admit defeat, especially in front of others.

In their chambers, Conor put Laurel down and then gave her a long, deep kiss, completely drugging her senses. It was supposed to keep her from renewing her quarrel with him. Instead, the kiss took away his ability to think about anything except the woman he held in his arms. She was so soft and her scent affected his ability to think. The sight of her intoxicated him even after all this time. He believed it always would.

The next few days were full of revelry and mock competitions between the two clans. Training sessions—or so her grandfather and Conor liked to refer to them—were held in the tilting yard outside the castle walls with more difficult tasks and objectives being set each day. The men thought the idea splendid; Laurel and Brighid thought the idea ludicrous. Brighid wondered if she was going to make it to the altar despite her lady's reassurances that the laird would not allow any jeopardy to fall on Brighid's husband-to-be.

Laurel spent most of her time either in the great hall or in her chambers sleeping. She felt large, uncomfortable, and exceedingly irritable most of the time. She did not like her grandfather seeing her this way and tried every day to send him home, promising to visit once the baby was born, and she had recovered. Every time, he would just calmly reply that he was going to stay until his great-grandson entered this world.

What aggravated her the most, though, was Conor's and her grandfather's indifference to her anger or mood swings. She knew she was often being demanding or impolite, but their casual reaction when she did so only added fuel to her frustration. She just wished that someone somewhere would do *something* either to force this baby to arrive, or redirect her anger. Unfortunately, her wish was granted in the worst way possible.

Chapter Fifteen

Keith Douglass rode next to his father and a dozen of their guard right up to the McTiernay castle gates. They had been surrounded by McTiernay men since their entrance onto Conor's lands. Warning of Laird Douglass's approach preceded them by only a couple of days. The message that had arrived stated only that Laird Douglass had important news for the McTiernay chieftain and that he would arrive along with minimal guards to deliver it personally.

It was only as they approached the castle gates that Conor learned that Keith Douglass had come as well. Upon word of Laird Douglass's imminent arrival, Conor had told Laird MacInnes what he had learned of Laurel's experience at Douglass's hands. As Conor feared, MacInnes's explosion had brought half of his men running with their swords drawn. Conor had delayed relating the story knowing that MacInnes would fight him for the right to confront his enemy. After a lengthy discussion, both Conor and MacInnes decided to let the Douglasses enter the highlands and deliver their news. Only after that would they decide who executed the fate of the dishonest, treacherous clan leader and son.

Now Conor stood on the castle wall, refusing to go down to meet the vermin that approached. MacInnes watched from the shadows. They both agreed it might be better for Douglass to not know of MacInnes's presence until they heard his message.

The sight of an alive Keith Douglass enraged both lairds. Conor knew that Laurel thought the Douglass heir was dead. His presence meant danger. Killing him outright without clear cause would spark a war. Robert the Bruce had set down the law about such internal feuding, stating that wars were to be fought with the King of England, not each other. He had received Conor's, MacInnes's, and even Douglass's pledges on the matter.

But, knowing what Laurel did to the man, and the way Keith had retaliated against others who had slighted him even a little, Conor knew the man had come for revenge. It was just unclear what form his revenge would take.

"Line the battlements and secure the gates!" Conor yelled as additional McTiernay soldiers surrounded the fourteen Douglasses. "Not one Douglass is to enter these walls," he said coldly while looking at the group of evil men who stood outside his fortress, "or eat the food of our land."

"We brought our own, McTiernay," snarled the older Douglass.

"State your message and then get off my lands," McTiernay retorted.

Keith rode forward and ignored his father, who obviously wanted him to remain silent.

"I came for my wife!" he shouted at the top of his lungs, unable to conceal the hideous glee from his voice.

Laurel had been asleep when Conor and MacInnes learned of the group advancing towards them. They had decided to not inform her, hoping they would be able to handle the situation before she was aware of its existence. They realized the futility of their intent the second they heard her scream.

Conor raced down to the courtyard to his wife who was unconscious on the ground near the north wall. When she came to, she was still dazed from hearing Keith Douglass's voice. Panic immediately followed.

"It's not true, Conor. It's not true." She grabbed his tunic and pleaded with him to believe her.

"Hush, love. I trust you unconditionally and absolutely." He looked into her beseeching eyes and tried to reassure her of his certainty that she was his, and only his, wife. "You told me what happened. Remember? I believed you then, and I believe you now." She began to calm with his words and his strong arms encircling her.

Conor wanted more than anything to protect his wife from hurt and pain. But, as he sat there holding her and glancing at MacInnes, they both knew that in order to buy the time he needed, Conor was going to be forced to cause both—enormous hurt and unexpected pain.

Conor first looked at MacInnes, giving him a nod followed by two words. "Go now."

The older Scot looked at the most precious thing in the world to him and gave her a quick terse order before he left. "Stay strong. You can do this. Whatever happens, do not tell a soul I was here." And with one solid kiss on her brow, her grandfather conveyed all the affection he felt for her and then he vanished quickly, heading toward the passage hidden in the cistern chamber.

Conor took hold of his wife's hands, realizing that he had never been this afraid of anything in his life. "Love, listen to me now. I need you to trust me and believe in what we share. Can you do that? Douglass and his son are coming in and . . ."

"You are letting those monsters into my home!" Fury filled her voice and eyes but, before he could answer, Laird Douglass had entered the doorway.

"Aye, daughter," he growled menacingly. Even from twenty feet away she could smell his stench.

"Get out of here!" she yelled, hating to see the vile man in her home.

"Well? Did she admit her folly? I admit my son is lacking in several qualities, but she chose her lot when she said her 'I do's.'" The pompous man sneered as he spoke, showing his rotting teeth.

Laurel looked dumbfounded for an instant. Then outrage lit her eyes. "You are despicable. I cannot imagine why my husband let you in here."

"Perhaps," Douglass drawled out, "because he is not your husband."

"Not my husband? You malicious, evil snake. The only one more foul than yourself is your odious son." Conor's grip on her arm was no longer just there for appearances; he actually caused her physical pain when she tried to lunge forward.

"You stay here," Conor ordered forcefully. Then he turned around, not able to look her in the eyes as he drove a stake directly through her heart. "And God help you if those men outside back Keith Douglass's account of your wedding night." The enmity ringing in his words stunned her into silence as she watched him retreat into the courtyard to confront the Douglass guards.

She could not prove her account of what happened, and there was no doubt what lies those guards were going to spew. Would Conor really believe them over her? But, he said he believed her. She was still grappling with the shift in his demeanor towards her when he returned, looking very cold and distant. Both Douglasses were on his heels, eagerly anticipating the next round.

Keith, especially, looked pleased with events. After Laurel attacked him and left him for dead, he swore his revenge upon her head. He would have Laurel back and see to it that the rest of her life was spent begging for his mercy. He would have the wench as often as he wanted and treat her as he pleased.

At first, his father was disinclined to agree to his idea. It was no secret that the wench had made her way into McTiernay good graces. Then the marriage plans he had for Keith were suddenly called off, followed by the reason why. The moment Douglass learned that it was McTiernay who ended his hopes for an alliance, he quickly became eager to help with his son's revenge and seek personal retribution for his loss.

Douglass knew there was no way he would win a war against McTiernay, but to take away the wench? That would hurt a man's pride a great deal. Despite the blood and dirt on her face that day, he remembered her being something of a beauty, a prize to be had. McTiernay had robbed him of that as well.

Conor needed to buy time. With enough time, he could avert a war and kill Douglass and his son without raising Robert's ire. But if it all worked according to plan, there would still be an unintended casualty—his beloved Laurel's love. He prayed she had the strength to stay strong for him, for their future, and for their son. He listened to the lies of the Douglass men, then returned to Laurel, his expression stony.

"Get someone to move your things from the solar into the North Tower. I don't want to see you ever again." The coldness of his words drove deep into her soul. Time froze still for a few moments. The next person who spoke sounded as if he were far away, when in reality he was just a few feet away from her.

"Move into the North Tower! She's mine!" shrieked Keith, who began to move towards her with an evil look of possession on his face. It was the same look of crazed rage he wore the night she refused to marry him in front of the priest.

Conor moved with lightning speed, blocking his path, preventing him from getting anywhere near her. "Stay away from her." There was no doubt in anyone's mind what would happen if Keith challenged this command. "The babe she carries is mine. Once it is born, then you can have her. But, until then, she remains alone."

He then drilled his eyes on Keith's father. "I will not yield on this." He grabbed Laurel's arm forcefully and walked her to her new room in the North Tower.

He had prayed that he would at least get a few minutes to explain, but Laird Douglass followed. "Here is where you will stay until my bairn is born. You will eat here and sleep here. The midwife may visit you daily to ensure that the bairn is well. Other than that, you are to remain out of sight." He paused, then looking directly at her, pleading with his eyes for her to understand, and added, "I can't abide liars." Then the door was shut, and she was alone in the room.

Laurel stood for a long time looking at the door that had just closed, wondering at the cruel twist of fate that had kept Keith alive and let him have his revenge.

She shed no tears. Only when a servant opened the door and brought in her brush, some of her personal belongings, and her only other tunic, did true despair settle in. The young girl had tried to tell her all would be well, but Laurel could tell by her shaky voice that even she doubted what she was saying. As soon as the servant left, Laurel's tears started to flow.

Later, the same servant brought her food, but Laurel did not feel like eating, and left the bread and stew to grow cold and stale. When Conor heard of her refusal to eat, he realized she had not understood the deception in his performance, but had taken his words as truth. After they survived this, he vowed never to let anyone threaten to take her away again. He would beg her forgiveness and pledge never to hurt her for the rest of their lives. He would promise to always acquiesce when they argued if it would just get her to understand why he had to protect her this way.

Laurel didn't go to sleep that night, but sat by the window looking out at her precious highlands. The moon was bright and, while the night air was cool, it was not too chilly. It would have been an ideal night to visit the stars on top of the Star Tower. At least she had a room fairly high up, and it provided her with a view to think by.

Morning came, and with it another meal she decided to pass on. She knew she should eat for the baby's sake, but she was not hungry. After a while, she crawled into the bed and fell asleep from sheer exhaustion.

When she awoke, it was dark, and moonlight filled the room. But with the darkness came enlightenment. She was surprised she had not recognized the truth earlier. In her dream, she went to see her wise friend Aileen, who, as always, enabled her to see the other side of her world.

Removing the emotion from behind the events, Laurel was able to better understand what had happened the day before. First, Conor had told her that he trusted her unconditionally and absolutely. He said he believed her. Then her grandfather had said to remain strong and not to tell anyone that he came to visit. Finally, Conor had asked her to trust him.

Awake and watching the moonlight ripple on the river below with its strong current engorged by the melting of the winter snows, Laurel tossed the words over and over in her mind. She then reluctantly replayed what happened afterwards. Conor had acted as if he hated her. But then, when Keith made a move to attack her, Conor had immediately reacted and protected her.

All at once, Laurel understood. Conor needed to buy time. Time and protection. All of it, the anger, the words, even the grip on her arm, was all a ruse to deceive both Douglass and his son. He was using her pregnancy to buy him and her grandfather some time as well as protect her and his son from having to be with the Douglasses. At the realization, her heart went out to Conor, who was having to endure the Douglasses—their words, their stench, their presence in his home—by himself. The sympathy poured out of her and into the night sky. If there was only some way that she could tell him that she was fine, that she understood, and that she would keep their son safe until he found a way to solve this disaster. She then ate all of the dinner left on the table.

Conor got the message. She was eating, sleeping, and receiving Hagatha. She wouldn't have given in this quickly unless she had understood or at least trusted him.

308 Michele Sinclair

Four days passed. If Laurel had not regained her confidence and faith in him, he never would have made it so long. He had been able to keep the Douglasses outside the curtain walls, but only after agreeing to allow four Douglass guards to stand watch at the North Tower doors. Hagatha was escorted to Laurel's room on the third day, but not allowed to leave again. One guard escorted the servants as they came and went to ensure no messages were being exchanged.

Conor allowed it all. He kept Brighid and Aileen away and even detained his brothers in the Star Tower. Conor hated to do it, but he knew their loyalty to Laurel could jeopardize his abhorrent plan.

Conor was fortunate that his brothers had cornered him in his solar and not in one of the halls. Their frustration over the idea that Douglass and his men were allowed on McTiernay land was understandable. They had not even heard of Laurel's imprisonment. Their youth and inability to control their emotions forced Conor into his decision. Everyone he loved was living in forced confinement but him. He was living in a hell of his own making.

Laurel woke up to a sharp pain. She looked over at her old friend snoring next to her. Early dawn light was coming around the curtains that now hung in the window. Hagatha had complained that she was sensitive to light when sleeping and required complete darkness to sleep well. Laurel had happily acquiesced to her friend's request.

Hagatha was her one companion and, consequently, her one confidante. While agreeing immediately with Laurel's assessment of the situation, Hagatha could not figure out what Conor's plan was, either. Both of them just prayed and hoped he would be able to end this before her baby was born.

Unfortunately, it did not look like that was going to happen. Laurel was going to have a baby today and, remembering Aileen, there was no way she was going to be able to keep silent through the pain towards the end. Regardless, Laurel knew Conor would never give her to anyone, let alone the Douglasses. She just wished she could give him some warning so that he could think of another plan.

Her pains were consistent, but still fairly far apart when Hagatha awoke and stretched. "Laurel? Looks like they brought food while we were sleeping. It's cold, but edible," she said while sampling a couple of the dishes. "Your Fiona sure knows how to cook."

Laurel had been awake when the guard had brought in the trays but had feigned sleep. While Aileen had felt compelled to walk between her pains, Laurel felt like just resting, building up strength before the next one came. She watched Hagatha prepare a plate.

"What are you waiting for? Usually you are the first to dig in and the last one to devour the remaining scraps."

"Not hungry, I guess." She was trying to delay the inevitable, but it was pointless to do so around the experienced midwife.

"How long now?"

"Just since I awoke earlier."

"Probably will be a while then." They looked at each other, knowing Conor's plan was in jeopardy. By that afternoon or evening, the whole keep would know Laurel was in labor.

"Don't worry, lass. You will be all right."

Laurel clutched the midwife's sleeve. "Make me a promise, Hagatha."

"Another one? I already fulfilled the first one. I'm here."

"Please," she said through gritted teeth as a pain ripped through her stomach to her lower back. It then slowly dissipated.

"Promise me that if it's between me and the baby, the baby will live."

Hagatha looked at her friend for a moment before answering. "I won't make that promise, Laurel."

Laurel's eyes pleaded with Hagatha. "You and I both know that this baby is too big. If you have to, cut me open and get him. I will not have us both die like my mother and brother."

Throughout the morning, Laurel tried again and again to get Hagatha to swear she would put her baby first, but the old woman refused to entertain the idea of losing either the laird's wife or his bairn. Nothing would sway her.

The first indication that something was going on in the keep was when the noon meal didn't arrive. Laurel's pains were coming closer together now, so she wasn't as aware of time as Hagatha was. To Laurel, it seemed like she had been in labor for days, not hours. The second sign was all the shouting later that afternoon. Even Laurel thought she heard the clashing of swords in the courtyard.

By early evening, Laurel was pacing the room trying to remain calm, but the pain was excruciating and, based on Aileen's birth, she knew it was only going to become worse. She tried to focus on anything besides how her body was being ripped apart.

Laurel swallowed heavily. "Hagatha. What do you think is going on?"

The sun was setting, and still no food or water had been delivered to the room since that morning. Additionally, no sounds had been heard from the keep for some time. Hagatha had not said anything, but she, too, was concerned about the silence that followed the earlier call to arms. She had been nervous to leave Laurel alone in case she wouldn't be allowed to return. But, very soon, the keep would realize that Laurel was in labor. So far, Laurel had been able to keep her cries of pain down, but Hagatha knew that they were getting worse and Laurel's strength was fading. She needed Laurel to save her strength and not waste it unnecessarily on keeping silent.

Hagatha grimaced. "I don't know. But I'm going to ask the guard for at least more water. I cannot believe Conor would allow them to starve ye like this."

Laurel lay down and gripped the sheets, struggling through another wave of pain. "You and I both know that he is at war."

Hagatha shook her head in denial. "I know no such thing."

"If he were here, we would have food and drink. You cannot deny this."

Refusing to answer, Hagatha made a decision. "I'm going to get you something to drink. We are almost out of water, and I may not have a chance later."

Laurel nodded.

Hagatha opened the door and noticed immediately there were no guards at the bottom of the tower. She quickly descended the staircase and scanned the court-yard. There was not a single soul in sight. The silence was terrifying. Where was everyone?

Hagatha went directly to the kitchen. Food had been left semi-prepared and the fire in the hearth had been doused. Now Hagatha was sure that something serious had happened. Events may empty the courtyard, but there was always someone in the kitchens for the hearth was rarely not lit. She grabbed some things to eat, a flagon of water, and returned to Laurel, who was no longer able to hold back her cries of pain.

"Let it out, lass. The guards have been called off."

"Called off? We are free to leave?" Laurel asked haltingly.

"Aye, but first you need to drink something," Hagatha replied, placing the food and flagon on the little table.

"Isn't help on the way?"

"They will be here soon." Hagatha felt terrible about lying, but she decided that in Laurel's condition it would be better to not fully disclose what she had—or had not—found.

"Go get them," Laurel pleaded.

Just as the words escaped, another pain hit, and Laurel screamed.

"I won't be leavin' you."

The next hour passed, and Laurel could no longer

hold inside what was happening. With still no help arriving, Hagatha wondered if anyone ever would come.

The midwife was cleaning Laurel up and getting her settled again when the door flew open and Brighid and Aileen flew in.

"My god!" Aileen choked, looking round-eyed at Laurel and then at Hagatha. Laurel was white as a sheet. "How much longer?"

Hagatha gave Aileen a silencing look and said, "As long as it takes."

Brighid, who was standing behind Aileen, turned and ran down the stairs to get Conor.

Aileen closed the distance between her and the midwife, staring at Laurel who appeared to be sleeping between pains. "Please," she whispered, "please say she is going to live."

Hagatha gave her another silencing look with her eyes. "Help me now."

Aileen went to sit by Laurel and held her hand. Laurel opened her eyes. "Is it over?"

"Aye," Aileen replied, trying not to cry at seeing her friend in so much pain.

"Conor?" Laurel asked, her voice barely a whisper.

"Fine. We are all here to help you. It won't be much longer now."

Laurel shook her head. "Something is wrong. I just know it."

Conor's composure broke as soon as he found out Laurel had been in labor since early that morning. When he came to the tower to see her, Hagatha and Aileen refused to allow him in. He had to retreat, hearing her cries of torture from the other side of the door.

With his agonized heart in his eyes, Conor said, "Tell her it is over."

"She knows," Aileen said, returning to the room with a bucket of fresh water.

Conor watched her vanish into the room. He wondered if he would ever again feel the confidence and assurance he had known before he met Laurel. Laurel would call it arrogance, he chided himself, as he descended the stairs and walked toward the chapel.

MacInnes found Conor the next morning in the chapel. "Please tell me it is over," Conor begged his godfather.

The older man only shook his head and joined him on the bench. MacInnes had left late the night before to escape the bloodcurdling sounds of his beloved granddaughter. He had not been able to save his precious daughter, and now he feared he was going to lose the last of his family. He felt incredibly weary. He wanted to help Conor, but knew of nothing to alleviate the young man's pain.

Conor rested his elbows on his thighs and buried his face in his hands. "I thought this past week was difficult. I never should have kept her locked up. The stress I caused . . ."

"No," came a firm command. "You did what was best. You kept her safe and away from them. You made sure she had Hagatha, and most of all, *she knew the truth.*"

"Nothing I have ever been through could surpass this torture." For the first time in his life, Conor was frightened. Genuinely, thoroughly, deep-down scared.

His godfather said nothing, as he, too, was afraid.

The previous morning had started out so differently. Conor was on the verge of reclaiming his perfect life.

The day the Douglasses arrived and announced their lie, Laird MacInnes had ridden out with Father Lanaghly to find the priest who had presided over Laurel's supposed nuptials. Father Lanaghly had often met Father Uron on his travels among the clans during the winter months and knew where the priest usually stayed. They only hoped he was still there.

It had been a long ride, but they had been able to find the priest, who supported Laurel's story and agreed to accompany them. Since he was the only priest in the vicinity at the time, he could easily refute Keith Douglass's claim. MacInnes had no problem convincing two impartial lairds to join them on their return journey. When they arrived back at the castle late yesterday morning, Conor had ordered all the Douglasses to be rounded up and brought into the tilting yard. He then freed his brothers to testify on Laurel's behavior and physical condition on the night they had saved her.

The whole keep stopped work to witness the event. The anger and resentment about tolerating the Douglasses' presence was well known. The Douglasses had attacked Lady Laurel's honor. Everyone wanted them dead. But Conor wanted one more thing before he took their lives; he wanted Laurel to be vindicated.

The tilting yard was surrounded with McTiernays and MacInneses. Soldiers stood by farmers standing by servants who had locked arms with clanswomen. All had come to witness.

For the first time, the story of how Laurel came to join Conor and his men was told. Hamish told of her courage. Seamus told of her skills. Each brother recounted her physical state and her regal bearing during their journey home. Glynis told of her generosity. Aileen spoke of her healing skills. Finally, Father Uron was brought forward and he denounced Keith Douglass's claim.

When Douglass and his son tried to argue with the priest, the two lairds who had accompanied MacInnes cut their words short. Throughout it all, Conor stood stone-faced, seemingly emotionless, and terrifyingly silent. Watching the pathetic, evil, twisted men who had dared to hurt Laurel made his blood boil.

Slowly Conor turned to the two impartial lairds. "You will inform Robert?"

"Aye," they replied. Both knew what was about to happen, and both supported the decision. Robert the Bruce would as well, once he learned the truth.

Conor eyed the men he was about to slay. "One of my men for each of yours."

Douglass could not hide his surprise. He had assumed it would just be a slaughter. "And if we win?"

"You leave."

Douglass took several deep breaths. He had heard that

McTiernay was a talented, strategic leader of men. But how clever was he one-on-one? Did he teach underhanded tricks to his men? Before he got an answer, MacInnes walked forward.

"Half are mine," he said resolutely. Conor nodded in agreement.

"Pick your men." Conor looked at Finn and nodded. Instantly, six McTiernay men, including Finn, came forward, swords drawn. Seconds later they were joined by MacInnes and six of his men.

The battle was quick. Douglass had made the mistake of underestimating the loyalty and love Conor's men had for Laurel and should have found a way to retreat. That mistake in judgment ended that line of Douglasses without a single injury to either a McTiernay or a MacInnes.

By the time the battle was over and the bodies had been removed off of McTiernay land, Laurel had been in labor for almost twelve hours. Conor had gone to the river to bathe before greeting his wife, but when he arrived, it was too late. She was too far into labor for visitors, including him.

At first, he was the typical panicky, soon-to-be father. But, as the cries of pain lasted throughout the night and into the morning, the fear that he and Laurel had tried to ignore surfaced with an almighty vengeance.

"You did it, Laurel! You really did it!" beamed Aileen as she helped her friend don a clean shift. The babies had taken their sweet time in arriving, but arrive they had. One boy and one girl. Laurel had stayed awake long enough to kiss and briefly hold each one before succumbing to the blissful state of painless oblivion.

Hagatha finished her midwife duties, all the while smiling and wiping away her tears. She had been afraid for a while. The boy had been born breech, which explained the pain and why the birth had taken so much longer than normal. His sister was much more cooperative and arrived minutes after her brother, head first.

Some time around dawn, something had come over Laurel, and she was suddenly determined to see her child born. When, finally, her son popped out to see the world, Hagatha realized her folly.

The little boy was far too small to account for Laurel's wide girth. Immediately, Hagatha gave the boy to Aileen and prepared for the second child. Soon the head crested, and Hagatha was holding a little girl.

Laurel had said that multiples had never ran in her family—just large children and with them, the associated risks to the mothers. And so both had assumed the baby was just large. In truth, Laurel's babies were still large for twins. Most twin bairns barely were bigger than Hagatha's hands. When Conor's mother had Craig and Crevan, she had been only slightly more round and both had been incredibly tiny. The McTiernay twins, however, were each practically as large as regular babies.

Brighid ran down with the news as soon as the babies were pronounced pink and healthy. "Laird! Laird! Laird McTiernay! Laird MacInnes!" she called through the halls.

Both men ran out of the chapel afraid to ask. "Laird," Brighid started again, unable to get the words out she was so happy. Conor's heart froze in his chest at the sight of the tears running down Brighid's face.

"You are the father of a son *and* a daughter!" she finally exclaimed to both men, who seemed to not understand her announcement.

Visibly shaken, Conor asked, "Laurel?"

"She's fine. Very, very tired and sleeping even now, but well, I assure you. It was hard, but she is so strong and stubborn that she outlasted the two bairns' refusal to visit us in person."

Conor closed his eyes and leaned back against the outer stone wall of the chapel. His family was safe, Laurel had given him twins, and—for the first time in months—he was reassured about the future. He had been so afraid for his wife for so long he was unaccustomed to feeling true happiness and hope.

MacInnes was not faring much better. He had sunk to his knees upon the news. He had lost his beloved daughter to childbirth and had been so afraid for Laurel, yet had been unable to give voice to his fear, knowing that Conor was leaning on him for faith, strength, and support.

Brighid did not know what to do. She had never seen her laird act so emotional. This man had nerves of steel and a will of iron. It was disconcerting to see his weaknesses unveiled. But, after watching his reaction to the happy news, she secretly hoped that her strong, undemonstrative Donald would be the same upon the birth of their first child. She smiled and ran back to the chambers to help with the babies.

Laurel had finally convinced Conor to let her leave her chambers and go into the great hall. The only requirement was that he carry her both down and back up the stairs. It was a small concession, especially since it had been less than three days since her two precious loves had entered into the world. But, as she explained to Conor, because of her necessary confinement to chambers the previous week, she would go mad if restricted to a single room any longer.

Conan and Clyde were the first ones to greet her when she arrived cradled in Conor's strong, capable arms. When Conor brought her to her chair by the hearth, he seemed reluctant to let her go.

Finally settled in, Laurel held her beautiful black-haired boy as Conor embraced his daughter, whose head was graced with tufts of white gold. Conan was the first to start talking.

"Are you going to continue with *C* names? I know I tease Clyde, but there are still a lot of great *C* names left. How about Calum and Colleen?" offered the excited fourteen-year-old.

His brothers were no better. Craig and Crevan kept offering advice and only backed off when Conor threatened them with cleaning duty. Both babies slept through the entire lively debate.

That afternoon, when they were finally alone, Laurel smiled and asked again what Conor thought their names should be. Since the babies' birth, both Laurel and Conor kept passing the responsibility back and forth.

"That is for you to decide, love. I give you full discretion to name our children. It is the least I can give you for all that you have given me." It was his favorite defense for not giving her an answer. He stroked her cheek and then bent over and gave her a soft, lingering kiss on the lips.

"I love you, Conor McTiernay."

"And I love you, Laurel McTiernay."

She looked back down at her two miracles. "I like the idea your mother had of using the same letter to name all of her children. And I would love to honor her by continuing the tradition. However, I also want to honor my mother. She would be very proud and happy this day. But her name was Brenna."

"Then why not use *B* names instead?" Conor offered as a compromise.

Laurel's dazzling blue eyes danced and her smile broadened. Watching her, contentment and a sense of peace deeper than he had ever known filled him.

"Conor, I would like you to meet Braeden Conor and his sister, Brenna Gillian."

As they cradled their children and each other, Conor and Laurel realized that they now had what they had always wanted. They had found, fought for, and produced their very own Scottish hearts.

Discover the Romances of
Hannah Howell

My Valiant Knight	0-8217-5186-7	**$5.50**US/**$7.00**CAN
Only for You	0-8217-5943-4	**$5.99**US/**$7.50**CAN
A Taste of Fire	0-8217-7133-7	**$5.99**US/**$7.50**CAN
A Stockingful of Joy	0-8217-6754-2	**$5.99**US/**$7.50**CAN
Highland Destiny	0-8217-5921-3	**$5.99**US/**$7.50**CAN
Highland Honor	0-8217-6095-5	**$5.99**US/**$7.50**CAN
Highland Promise	0-8217-6254-0	**$5.99**US/**$7.50**CAN
Highland Vow	0-8217-6614-7	**$5.99**US/**$7.50**CAN
Highland Knight	0-8217-6817-4	**$5.99**US/**$7.50**CAN
Highland Hearts	0-8217-6925-1	**$5.99**US/**$7.50**CAN
Highland Bride	0-8217-7397-6	**$6.50**US/**$8.99**CAN
Highland Angel	0-8217-7426-3	**$6.50**US/**$8.99**CAN
Highland Groom	0-8217-7427-1	**$6.50**US/**$8.99**CAN
Highland Warrior	0-8217-7428-X	**$6.50**US/**$8.99**CAN
Reckless	0-8217-6917-0	**$6.50**US/**$8.99**CAN

Available Wherever Books Are Sold!

Visit our website at **www.kensingtonbooks.com**